Bernard Taylor was born in Swindon, Wiltshire. He studied Fine Arts at both Chelsea School of Art and at Birmingham, and worked as a book illustrator and teacher before going to live in the U.S.A. Whilst there he took up acting and writing, with which he continued on his return to the U.K. He has been resident playwright at the Queen's Theatre, Hornchurch, and now lives in Greenwich.

SINCE RUBY

It had all begun in the most ordinary way: eight friends getting together for drinks and a companionable evening. It was not to last. Long before the evening was over there occurred the dreadful happening that was to shatter the remnants of their peace and breed deep and lasting suspicions. But that was years ago. Much of the horror has receded and the remaining seven old friends are getting on with their lives. Or are they? Now, eleven years later, new horrors are taking place. Inexplicably, one by one, those old friends are dying . . .

Books by Bernard Taylor
Published by The House of Ulverscroft:

MADELEINE
EVIL INTENT

BERNARD TAYLOR

◆

SINCE RUBY

Complete and Unabridged

ULVERSCROFT
Leicester

First published in Great Britain in 1999 by
Robert Hale Limited
London

First Large Print Edition
published 2000
by arrangement with
Robert Hale Limited
London

British Library CIP Data

Taylor, Bernard, *1934 –*
    Since Ruby.—Large print ed.—
    Ulverscroft large print series: mystery
    1. Suspense fiction
    2. Large type books
    I. Title
    823.9'14 [F]

    ISBN 0–7089–4248–2

Published by
F. A. Thorpe (Publishing)
Anstey, Leicestershire
Set by Words & Graphics Ltd.
Anstey, Leicestershire
Printed and bound in Great Britain by
T. J. International Ltd., Padstow, Cornwall

This book is printed on acid-free paper

This is for Victor, and for Jenny
and Douglas.
And with special thanks to Mary Danby

Prologue

In searching for a beginning, Addie would acknowledge that in reality stories had no beginnings or endings. So it was with hers and that of Ambrose and Christie and the others. A relating of the events surrounding the first death might have used any moment of that evening as a starting point. But it would as well begin when the seven of them, after an hour of coming and going, finally got together — starting with Ambrose returning with the takeaway.

Setting the bags on the coffee-table, he glanced around at the untidy room with its ugly, mismatched furniture, winced at the over-loud music from Christie's tinny, portable stereo, and asked, 'Where is everybody?'

'Harry and Matt are off getting the wine,' Addie said, looking up at him — he fairly towered above her — 'and Kieron's getting the videos.'

He groaned. '*Kieron*? Does that mean something worthy with subtitles?'

'No, he's under strict instructions.'

1

'Good.' As he took off his cap his dark, curly hair sprang to reclaim its shape. 'Where are the others?'

'Dolores is in the kitchen, and I think Christie's still in the bathroom. Ruby was here a while ago. I don't know where she is now.'

'Shame — I miss her already.'

'*Ambrose*.' She frowned, smiling. 'What brought that on?'

'Nothing. Forget it.' He looked again towards the source of the music. 'Must we? I've got nothing against Bob Dylan, but at *those* decibels . . .'

He crossed to the stereo and turned down the volume. As he did so a door opened and Christie appeared, looking striking in a lilac silk dress that she had designed and made herself. 'Ah,' she said to Ambrose, 'you're back.' With a pink-nailed hand she pushed back her long, red Pre-Raphaelite hair, and slowed outside the open kitchen door. 'Come on, Dolores,' she called. 'Ambrose is back. Move your arse.' She flicked a conspiratorial smile at Addie and Ambrose and added chuckling, 'There's certainly enough of it to move.'

'*Cruel*,' Addie said; then: 'I've been doing her hair. She's been changing.'

'*Changing*?' Christie's tone was Lady

2

Bracknell out of Edith Evans. 'I don't know why she bothers. She never looks any different at the end of it.'

A moment later Dolores emerged. 'I heard that,' she said. 'All of it.'

'And all of it in fun,' Christie replied.

'So you tell me.' Dolores gestured back. 'I put the plates to get warm.'

Bearing out Addie's words, Dolores had indeed changed. She had replaced one shapeless sweater and pair of jeans for another set. Christie might dress for effect, but Dolores thought first of comfort. Her hair, though, was different today. It had been fashioned into a French plait, and with it drawn back from her face showed that she might have some possible potential. For the moment, though, she was concerned with more important matters. 'Great,' she said, looking at the carrier bags that Ambrose had brought, 'I'm hungry as hell.'

As Dolores stepped to the food, Christie turned up the volume on the stereo and Bob Dylan's 'Slow Train' swelled. Ambrose frowned. 'Have we got to?'

'The trouble with you, Ambrose,' Christie said pityingly, 'is that you don't like any music written after 1960. How can you listen to all that old-fashioned crap? Those big bands — and Doris Day and all those other naff singers.' She shrugged. 'But to each his own. And we still like you.'

Dolores had begun to take the cartons of food from the bag and set them on the coffee table, its surface long since ruined by cigarette burns, and rings from hot cups and wet glasses; anything was good enough for students. 'Good,' she said, pulling the lid from one of the cartons, 'you remembered my prawns.'

When the doorbell rang a moment later, Christie yelled, 'It's not locked,' and the door swung open and Kieron entered, holding two video tapes.

'What did you get?' Dolores asked him.

He put the tapes on the TV set. 'Well, for a start, I couldn't get the Mel Gibson, so I got a thriller they recommended.'

Christie picked up the cassette box and groaned. 'Never heard of it. What's the other one?' Then she added, moving towards the small kitchen, 'No, surprise us. Knowing you, it'll be something really accessible — like *Wild Strawberries* or *Battleship Po*-fucking-*tempkin*, I shouldn't wonder.'

'Aw,' Kieron said, 'you peeped.' He was a young man of middle height, and everything about him had a rather solid, blunt appearance, from his chunky build and short nose and solid jaw, to his hands

4

with their square-cut fingers — fingers that were capable of the most delicate work in wood carving or sculpture, not to mention taking apart and repairing the oldest of old cameras. Addie had perforce to view him a little differently from the others, by reason of the fact that a couple of months earlier she had introduced him to her cousin Camilla, and the two had hit it off and had been in contact ever since.

As Kieron hung up his jacket, Christie set down a collection of cutlery.

'I fetched the crystal,' Addie said, indicating some cheap wine glasses on the battered sideboard. Christie nodded, 'Fine,' and looked around her with a sigh of impatience. 'Where are the others? This'll get cold. Did Harry go off for the booze?'

'Yes,' Addie said, ' — with Matt.'

'Oh, Matt agreed to join us after all, did he? There's kind for you.'

Following Christie's words the door opened again and two more young men entered, holding bags. 'Right,' Dolores said, 'now the only one we need is Ruby.'

The newcomers, Harry and Matt, put the bags on the table and began to take out cans of lager and bottles of wine. The men were of average height, but that was where any similarity ended. Behind Harry's glasses, his good-natured face was unremarkable, its plainness not aided by his thinning hair. Matthew, however, would have been striking in anyone's book, his movie-star features made even more distinguished by his thick, black hair — which already, however, at twenty-three, was showing the finest flecks of grey above his ears. The only flaw was a small scar high on his left cheek, the result of a childhood accident.

'Didn't Ruby go with you?' Dolores said.

'No — why should she?' This from Harry, at the same time flicking the briefest of glances at Matt. 'She was here when we left — sitting out on the terrace.' He gestured over to the closed French windows, beyond which was a tiny balcony on which a small, weathered garden chair could be seen.

Christie hooted. 'Terrace, he calls it. That's really sweet.'

'The price you girls pay for this place,' Harry said, 'I wouldn't dare knock it.'

'This food,' Dolores said, 'is going to get cold.'

'Oh dear,' said Christie, 'it must be at least half an hour since she last ate.'

'I'm merely asking,' Dolores said, 'where Ruby's got to.'

'Well, I don't know,' said Christie, ' — I've been in the bath.'

6

Ambrose, draping his body over the sofa, in one move diminishing its size, said, 'She ordered food, so she wouldn't have just left, would she?'

'Wouldn't she?' Christie tossed her hair in an over-the-top gesture that smacked of contempt. 'I wouldn't be surprised at anything she does.' She began to pull the lids off the cartons and slap them down on the table. 'Anyway, to hell with her.'

Addie glanced around, taking in the faces of her companions. How things had changed. They had come together some nine months before, the eight of them, and almost at once a warm, bright fellowship had been established. For the most part eschewing the company of other students on the course, they'd formed their clan and done everything, gone everywhere, together. In some ways, maybe they'd been too happy, and when that happened there'd been nowhere to go but down. Perhaps it was as well that in a few weeks they'd be going their separate ways. Familiarity had bred contempt, and the cracks were beginning to show. The strain was apparent in so many different ways, not with all of them, but between some it had become increasingly discernible and the differences threatened to be irreconcilable. This evening, Addie was sure, would be the last time they all got together for anything like a social gathering. As it was, it hadn't been easy to get everyone to agree to come; excuses of prior engagements had been made by two or three, and only after some persuasion from Dolores and Kieron had everyone eventually consented.

Harry's voice interrupting her thoughts, Addie heard him say, 'Ruby was a bit quiet earlier this evening, I noticed.'

'Not only this evening,' said Dolores. 'For the past two or three days.' She turned to Ambrose where he lounged on the sofa. 'Did you notice it?'

With a shake of his head, he said, 'I can't say I've noticed anything different about her,' but his eyes only briefly met her questioning glance.

'For Christ's sake,' Christie said, laughing, 'you men are so fucking unobservant. Something's got to be right under your nose before you see it.'

'Well, *I* noticed it,' Dolores said. 'I could see it in tutorial this afternoon.'

The Bob Dylan tape had come to an end, and in the little silence that followed Dolores's words, glances flicked briefly, surreptitiously to Matt. Catching the looks, he said defensively, 'What're you looking at me for? She's no concern of mine.'

'Any more,' said Christie — who clearly didn't believe in oil on troubled waters and added with a sneering little laugh, 'I'll bet you wish she were.'

He bridled. 'What does that mean, exactly?'

'Oh, come on,' she said, 'don't lose your sense of humour. You'll go on to other things. And as long as you keep to that maxim of yours you'll be all right. What is it? Never make a promise while you've got an erection? Yes, that's the one.'

He gave an exclamation of realization, long and drawn out: 'Ohhh,' the cadence rising and falling. 'What's this, then? Hell hath no fury?' Although he smiled as he spoke, his mouth was tight with ill-hidden anger, and his face was pale. Seeing him squirm, Addie felt no regret.

Straight-faced, Christie said evenly, 'Fuck you.'

'No, fuck you,' he said.

'In your dreams.' And sensing the whip-hand, Christie added, 'But that's what you've got to be content with now, isn't it? Dreams?' She nodded towards the balcony. 'Where our Rubes is concerned anyway.'

'You think you're so funny, don't you?' Matt said. The scar on his cheek was as red as a bite, 'A laugh a fucking minute, you are.'

Christie's laugh was hollow, not taking anybody in. 'I'm joking, for Christ's sake. Lighten up, will you?'

'Hey, come on, you two,' said Dolores, making an effort to save the situation. 'Let's eat, shall we? I've warmed the plates.'

'But Ruby's not here,' Kieron said.

'Too bad,' said Christie. 'If she gets a bug up her arse and chooses to go off in a snit that's her affair.' She flicked a glance around her. 'I don't know about the rest of you, but I'm hungry, and I'm not waiting for Miss Privileged to do us a favour and grace us with her presence. She'll come back when it suits her. And when she does, maybe there'll be some food left, and maybe there won't. We can — ' She saw that Matt had started back across the room towards the door, and her words came to a halt.

'Matt,' Kieron called, 'we're about to eat. Where are you going?'

'I'm not sure,' Matt replied. 'But away from here.' He turned in the doorway. 'I didn't think this was going to work in the first place, and now I know it's not going to. And I for one don't have to put up with this shit.'

10

'Oh, come on, Matt,' Ambrose said. 'You've paid for your food.'

'*You* have it,' Matt said. 'I'm not hungry any more.'

A moment later he was gone, the door closing sharply behind him, leaving the room in silence. Then Christie, giving a little laugh, as if knowing she had gone too far, said, 'Oh — what happened there? Did somebody say something?' Nobody spoke. 'Anyway,' she added, 'let's eat, before it all gets cold.'

* * *

When they had eaten, and the first of the videos had been viewed and condemned, Kieron took from his bag an envelope containing photographs taken several weeks earlier at a happier time, when they had gone off into the country one Sunday for a picnic. He handed out the photographs to the other five sitting around. Those for Ruby and Matt he put on one side.

Later, Dolores and Ambrose gathered up the empty cartons and carried them out to the kitchen. At the same time, Addie took the few remaining crusts of bread and opened the windows onto the terrace. Standing at the rail, she tossed them out into the twilight and watched them fall the three storeys to the ground. Most of them fell onto the strip of red-brick paving beside the yard. Others fell closer, dropping onto the body of Ruby as it lay impaled on the spikes of the railings directly below.

1

As they drove, they spoke of Ruby's death — or rather one of the men spoke of it while the other listened in something less than comfort — when the speaker broke from the subject to say, 'Hey, we could pull in down there and cut along by the river. What do you think? You fancy a little stroll?'

'Fine,' said the younger man. His companion had invited him for dinner with friends, and it was immaterial to him how they travelled the last few yards.

At the foot of the hill, straggling woodland grew up to the verge. Here, the driver parked the car in a spot where it was almost completely screened by the summer foliage. 'It'll be OK here,' he said, then added with a chuckle, 'And it might do us good to get a breath of fresh air when we walk back.'

The passenger got out and stood to the side while the driver took from the boot a large hold-all. 'A little house-warming present,' he said. The way he lifted it out indicated a considerable weight. 'Doesn't look so little,' said the younger man, and stepped forward, adding, 'Here, let me have it.' Before the other could protest he was taking the bag into his own hand. The weight was far greater than he had anticipated and just for a split-second it pulled him off-balance. 'Jesus Christ,' he said, chuckling, 'what are you giving them — cement?' The other laughed along with him. 'No,' — he slammed the boot shut, 'but you're close.'

With the older man leading, they stepped in among the trees and soon came upon a footpath that led towards the riverbank. The light was starting to fade; there was no one else about.

'Yes — Ruby Burnham,' the older man said, continuing the conversation that he had started earlier, 'that was a sad, strange business.'

'It was,' said the other, shifting the bag from his right hand to his left. They were walking close beside the river now, the path meandering through the straggling trees. Up above them the branches were dark against the sky.

'Did you see it happen?' asked the first man.

'What? No.' A pause, frowning. 'It isn't something I like to dwell on.'

'No, I suppose not.'

14

'It was eleven years ago. It's over and done with.'

'Right. Some things belong in the past.'

With his words, the first man came to a halt. The piece of lead pipe was so heavy that he was keeping his hand in his trousers pocket in order to support it, afraid it would go through the fabric. The younger man came to a halt beside him, wondering why they'd stopped. The trees on the waterside had thinned to nothing and the two men had an unimpeded view of the river as it flowed by at the foot of the precipitous bank. On the other side of the water, the colours of the valley were beginning to lose their intensity and merge into one, thrown into shadow by the light of the dying sun.

'There,' said the older man, 'there's a view for you.' He knew this spot well; he had chosen it with care. 'And look at that sky,' he added. 'It's lavender.'

'So it is,' the younger man said. 'I've never seen a sky like it before.' He never would again, this sky or any other, but he, of course, was not to know this.

'Excuse me,' said the older man, 'I've got to pee. I can't wait.' As he moved as if to unzip his fly, the other turned away to give him a measure of privacy. It was what the first man had waited for. In one single move

15

he whipped the lead pipe from his pocket, raised it high and brought it down. Although he struck with all his power, however, he was not accurate, the weapon catching the other's head a low, glancing blow. Even so, it was enough to make him stagger. As the bag fell from his hand he gave a moan, spun, and reached out, snatching at his attacker's sleeve. But the strength in his grip was only momentary, and when the second blow came, he went down, pitching forward onto his face.

In a second the other was at his side, feeling for a heartbeat, a pulse. Then, after a minute spent pinching the felled man's nostrils and covering his mouth, he was satisfied. The next step was to search his pockets — a search that yielded a wallet, keys, a handkerchief and some loose change, all of which was taken and stored away.

The hold-all, when opened, revealed five large bricks with ornamental holes in them, the kind of brick used in the making of suburban garden walls. It also contained a length of thin, strong wire. It was all prepared, with the wire secured to the bricks; all that had to be done now was to attach the bricks to the man's body. It took some effort to wind the wire around the dead man's waist — binding too his arms with their clenched hands — but it was soon accomplished. Then, with a last look to left and right to check that he was not being observed, the man pulled the body to the edge of the bank, hoisted it up into his arms, and, using all his strength, pitched it forward, out into the river. The splash as it hit the water seemed deafening in the still evening air, the sound seeming to reverberate long after its actual echo had died.

Picking up the hold-all, empty now and light — like his spirits — the man turned and set off back the way he had come.

2

They stood side by side, Addie and Milla, silent. Although first cousins — their mothers had been sisters — they were not physically alike. They were much of a height and age, but other than that there were no similarities; Milla's fair hair and narrow face were quite unlike Addie's straight, dark-brown hair and squarer-set features.

Helen, Milla's five-year-old daughter, gave an impatient tug at her mother's skirt, sighed, then sat down in the cropped grass. Milla

17

kept her face lowered to Kieron's grave. In the two weeks since the funeral, the wreaths and sprays had died, and all that now lay on the soil, arranged in two pots, were Milla's yellow roses and the pink carnations that Addie had brought with her today.

Addie turned to Milla. 'Are you all right?'

Although Milla nodded, Addie knew that tears were not far below the surface; and her own experience had taught her how quickly they could rise, and with what force. Addie wanted to hold her, but she hesitated, knowing how one could be strong until touched by sympathy, and how all control might then be swept away — one soft word like a crack in a dam. Almost casually she laid her hand on Milla's shoulder, and they stood like that, while in the warmth of the summer afternoon the bees hummed in the clover, and a thrush sang in the branches of a nearby yew.

After a while the three set off to the gate and beyond to where Milla's old Vauxhall waited.

Later, in the little suburban semi-detached house, Milla poured Helen some milk and then made tea, which she carried into the sitting-room. Addie was sitting on the sofa. 'I'm so glad you came,' Milla said as she sat beside her.

'You know you've only got to pick up the phone.'

Milla gave a little nod and began to pour the tea. 'How is Charlie?'

'Fine. He's just been off to Dubai for a few days for a toy fair.'

'Doesn't he get tired of it — all the travelling around?'

'He loves it. He complains — but that's mostly about the lack of time available. He's never happier than when he's making some sale that he's worked at.'

'You used to go with him sometimes at the start, I remember — New York, Nuremberg — all those places.'

'That was before Robbie.' Addie's face was shadowed for a moment then, 'Anyway,' she added, 'it was never my scene. I got to hate going to the fairs with him, or killing time while he visited the manufacturers. And the only alternative was stay in the hotel or go sightseeing. No — he's better going on his own. He asked me to go to Hong Kong with him in a few weeks, but I said no.'

'It might do you good — occasionally to get away.'

'No, thanks. It's never a holiday. He's in his element; I'm not.'

'He keeps occupied,' Milla said carefully, 'that's what he does. And maybe that's the important thing. We all have our own ways of coping.' She looked towards Helen where she played with a doll on the rug nearby, then added, keeping her voice low, but her words coming out in a little burst, as if they had been waiting, under pressure, to be released, 'Wasn't it enough to lose Kieron, for God's sake? Did there have to be all that terrible suspicion as well?'

Addie had heard similar words before, but some wounds refused to heal quickly. 'Oh, Milla,' she said, 'surely it — it wasn't genuine.'

'Not genuine? The suspicion? With all those questions?'

'From the doctors, you mean?'

'Yes. They made it perfectly clear — they couldn't account for his death. God, there were so many questions. And then the police getting involved, and asking all their questions as well.'

'Milla — don't.'

'You should have heard them — talking to me as if I had something to hide.'

'But — they've *got* to ask questions in such a situation. A sudden, unexplained death. It's standard procedure. They have to make certain.'

As if Addie had not spoken, Milla said, 'How could they think that — that he might

20

have taken something? Either voluntarily or — or not.'

'Milla, they have to explore every avenue. It's their job. They've no choice.'

Milla sighed. 'Yes. You're right, of course. And it's what I tell myself, but — oh, when I think of all the questions — and then the post-mortem — and the wait for the death certificate. It was a nightmare.'

A little silence, then when Milla spoke again her voice was heavy with irony. 'And after all that it turns out to be something as mundane as blood-poisoning. But even then they couldn't say how he contracted it. Which is something I'll never understand — not today, with all the advances in medicine.'

Addie could think of nothing to say that she had not said before. Milla would go on tormenting herself, it wasn't the first time and it wouldn't be the last.

'They couldn't even say what strain it was,' Milla went on. ' 'Of unknown origin' — those were the words they used.'

Addie looked at Milla as she gazed through the window to the untended garden beyond. Untended because there had always been more pressing calls on Kieron's creativity, whether it had been his passion for photography or his wood-carving or other delicate

21

work. The dolls' house in Helen's nursery had been made by Kieron, every tile on its roof, every stick of furniture within its carefully papered walls, walls on which he had hung miniatures of famous masterpieces — all executed by himself. And so it was that the tiny dolls were laid to sleep, or ate, or played, in rooms in which the walls were hung with Leonardo's *Mona Lisa*, Gainsborough's *Blue Boy* and Van Gogh's *Sunflowers*.

Unable to leave the wounds alone, Milla said, 'Why would he go and take something, anyway? That's the last thing he'd have done. He had no reason to.'

'Of course he didn't. Anyone who knew him would know that.'

Milla sighed. 'We had all kinds of plans. We were talking about moving — and maybe taking a holiday in the autumn. And only a couple of days earlier he'd accepted an invitation to some photographic exhibition. He was looking forward to that. Oh, Addie, his life was so full; he had so much to live for.'

★ ★ ★

Later, Milla drove Addie to the station for her train to Reading. Coming to a halt in the car-park, Milla turned in her seat and, after studying Addie for a moment, said, 'Listen, I don't want to build up your hopes, but I've been talking about you and Charlie to this woman I know.'

Addie knew what would have been the subject of the conversation, but she was afraid of having it denied. 'Go on,' she said after a moment.

'I mean it,' Milla said, 'don't go getting your hopes up, *please*.'

'Milla . . .'

'Well, there's an acquaintance — a friend of a friend — who lives in London. And she knows a young woman, a student — Susan, her name is — who's pregnant.'

'Go on.'

'Well, I gather that the girl doesn't want to keep the baby. Motherhood isn't part of her plans. So, I told her about you and Charlie.'

Addie briefly closed her eyes in a little gesture of happiness. 'Oh, Milla, thank you. Thank you so much.'

★ ★ ★

Addie had left her Citroën at Reading Station and was back home in plenty of time to prepare dinner. She heard the sound of

23

Charlie's car just on 6.45, and minutes later he was coming through the door and bending to kiss her on the cheek.

When he had showered and changed he came into the sitting-room where he poured drinks — Scotch and soda for himself, gin and tonic for Addie. Then, sitting in his favourite chair and stretching out his long legs, he asked after her visit to Milla. 'I suppose you drove to Reading, then took the train.'

'Yes.' He knew she wouldn't go on the motorway.

'And how is she?'

'Bearing up — as they say.'

'Poor woman.' He gave a sigh. 'But at least Kieron's buried now. So perhaps she can try to get on with her life. Though I wouldn't know where she's to start.'

'Nor I.' A pause. 'She keeps on about the investigation. The grilling she got.'

'She's still on about that?'

'It's on her mind. Hardly surprising.'

'God,' Charlie groaned. 'As if she hadn't enough to deal with.'

As he turned his gaze from her she noticed not for the first time the little lines radiating from the corners of his eyes, and the deeper ones running down beside his mouth. He was looking all of his thirty-eight years.

Not that he wasn't still very good looking. He was. But his youth had gone — as had her own. But that was what time did to a person — little by little, adding a millimetre of grey here, the deepening of a line there. A constant chipping away, breaking down. Yet the deepening lines in Charlie's face were not due only to maturity. The thought occurred to Addie that in demanding so much of him for herself she had perhaps not allowed him time and space for his own grief. And the loss had been as much his as hers. But knowledge of another person's grief could never lessen one's own. It was like watching the TV news with scenes of suffering in some other country; you could tell yourself that in comparison your own suffering was small and that you should count your blessings, but it never worked other than as an intellectual exercise. Thoughts of another person's agony could not even diminish the pain of one's own toothache. Awareness of the depths of Charlie's grief had done nothing to ease her own.

She looked out at the lawn, bright in the late sunshine, the dark, dappled shadows lengthening. Her glance moved on over the herbaceous borders, the wide flower garden, the kitchen garden and orchard beyond, and the paddock, unused, over to the left. Set in three acres on the outskirts of Liddiston, a small village near Pangbourne, the two-storey Edwardian house was large and roomy. Beyond the distant trees of the orchard lay farmland, stretching almost to the horizon. For Addie it was space to which she had yet to become fully accustomed. How different it all was from their previous home, the unattractive semi in the nearby town of Newbury, and how much a sign of Charlie's success and hard work.

She sipped at her drink, then adjusted the gold watch on her wrist; since she had lost weight the watch kept slipping round. Still, her weight had steadied now, and with a little more effort she would begin to put on a few pounds. Progress.

'Is there anything you'd like to do tomorrow?' Charlie said. 'The forecast's good, so if you wanted to drive out somewhere . . .'

She shrugged. 'Well, nothing in particular — though there are one or two things we need from the shops.'

'Fine. We'll go into Hungerford or Pangbourne. We can have lunch out. Are you going to the cemetery in the morning?'

'Yes.' He didn't need to ask; she went every Saturday morning.

'Right, we'll leave as soon as I get back from the office.'

'Do you have to go in tomorrow morning?' He looked tired, she thought. 'Can't you ever take it easy?'

'Addie,' he said, 'there's so much to be done. Apart from the work here, there's the trip to Hong Kong. We can't be stuck with a balls-up like last year, getting landed with thousands of components we can't use.'

'I know,' she said, 'I know.' His dedication still surprised her at times. Since he had joined Adanco, her father's company, to assist with the marketing, his enthusiasm had never waned. She thought back to those days of their beginnings together. Her father had not wanted her to marry him, but she and Charlie had won him over eventually. And since her father's death, Charlie had transformed the business and made it the success that it now was. And how bitterly ironic, she thought, that its more recent successes had been due in part to Robbie's death. Whereas the loss had made her almost incapable of action, it had been for Charlie a spur. He had thrown himself into his work, searching out new inventors, branching out, never missing an opportunity. Were her father still alive, he would be amazed at the dynamic enterprise that Adanco had become, and delighted at his son-in-law's commitment.

On the coffee-table was a small vase holding some roses of the palest cream. Carole had put them there that morning. Looking at them, Addie had a sudden vision of herself holding a white rose, hand outstretched over Robbie's coffin, her fingers opening, letting the flower go. And to her saturating sorrow had been added a vague disappointment in the action. It was as if she had expected the flower to float, gently, slowly, down onto the white coffin lid. Instead, the flower had simply dropped, taking no more than a fraction of a second for its fall, catching the edge of the coffin and slipping off into the space between it and the dark, moist earth of the grave.

'Charlie — ' She hesitated, then went on, the words coming in a rush. 'Milla told me something today. There's somebody she knows — who knows somebody — ' She sighed, frowning. 'What I'm saying, is that there's a young woman, a student, who's expecting a baby, and she's got no intention of keeping it.'

'I see.' He nodded.

She would not be deterred by his lack of enthusiasm. 'Milla's friend is going to talk to her about us,' she said. 'Put in a recommendation, so to speak, so that when the time comes we could be among the first to be considered. Wouldn't that be wonderful?'

'And who is this young woman?' he said.

'Milla didn't say — apart from referring to her as Susan. But nearer the time they'll get in touch with us. And then — '

'And then,' he cut in, 'we'll be off on another wild goose chase.'

'Oh, Charlie, don't.' The disappointment came like a wave. 'Something will work out.' She set down her drink and moved to him. Crouching between his knees, she put her hands on his chest. 'They won't all be disappointments. Our time will come.'

'Our time is *passing*,' he said. 'We'll be considered too old if we have to wait much longer. If we aren't already.'

'Don't say that.' She put a finger to his lips. 'It'll happen — if you want it to.'

'I want what you want, Ads.' His free hand came up to rest upon her hair — a gentle caress. 'I just want you to be happy.'

★ ★ ★

Carole didn't come in on Saturdays, and after Charlie had left the next morning Addie cleared away the breakfast things and packed the dishwasher. That done, she drove off in the Citroën, a small bunch of pink roses lying on the seat beside her. When she reached the cemetery she parked beside the verge, entered through the gates and made her way between old weathered tombs, stones and carved statuary to the area where lay the newer graves.

Robbie's grave lay towards the southern side. She came to a halt at its foot, and stood looking down at it. The thought came to her that one day, when she and Charlie were lying beside their son, there would be no one to lay fresh flowers, no one to contemplate what might have been, no one to read the inscription on the stone with anything but a passing curiosity; no one to mourn Robbie's passing.

A movement caught her eye, and she saw that a robin had alighted on the adjacent stone to the right. Perched on the grey marble, its dark button of an eye seemed to regard her for a moment, and then it was off again, skimming away over the stones and the green of the paths.

The stone on which it had briefly rested marked the grave of a young man, beneath whose name was inscribed YOU WERE THE WIND BENEATH MY WINGS. Addie had recognized the words as coming from a popular song of the eighties; she could recall Dolores playing the tape. Robbie's stone bore no poetic legend of grief. She and Charlie had chosen to add nothing to the information that it now held. Although she had sought for some phrase, some brief verse, nothing had been right, nothing was enough. No words could express or sum up what he had meant to them, or give an indication of the emptiness that he had left behind. And what did it matter, anyway? — the stone was not there to inform others; it was there for him, and for herself and Charlie. And all that was to be known they already knew.

On the stone, above the dates of his birth and his death was written:

OUR SON
ROBERT CHARLES CARMICHAEL
AGED FOUR YEARS AND THREE MONTHS

From the terracotta pot she removed some dying roses, and then placed inside it the fresh ones. With a battered watering-can filled at a nearby tap she added water to the pot and then arranged the flowers, their scent drifting up, unbearably sweet. Then, after brushing some non-existent dust from the carving of Robbie's name, she rose and made her way back to the car.

31

When Charlie returned just before twelve she was ready to leave, and they set off soon afterwards for Hungerford. Following lunch at a small Italian restaurant they did some shopping and then wandered around the antiques arcade, looking at the display of artefacts that ranged from genuine antiques to over-priced junk. At one stall Addie's eye was caught by a little porcelain bust. As she bent to look at it more closely, Charlie, standing beside her, said, 'Tchaikovsky, yes?'

'It looks like him.'

The elderly proprietor smiled, saying, 'A nice little piece, don't you think?'

Addie said, 'It's Parian, isn't it?' Memories were flooding back.

'Yes, it is.' As the man placed the piece in her hand, Charlie said to her, 'You like it?' His tone intimated that he would be glad to get it for her if she chose.

'Oh, yes,' she said, 'but it's not that. Just that someone I knew had one like it.'

'Fond of Tchaikovsky, was he?'

'It wasn't that it was Tchaikovsky; it was this kind of porcelain that he loved.'

Charlie held out his hand, and she put the bust into it. 'Who was that?' he said.

'Oh — just a friend.'

'From your Birmingham days? It has to be, judging by your reluctance to speak about him. It's only your pals from that time that you don't talk about. It would have to be one of the magnificent seven.'

Eight, she almost said, *there were eight of us,* but she kept silent. In his face she searched for some sign of irony, but saw only his warm, uncertain smile.

'So which one was it?' he asked.

'Harry.'

He nodded. 'Not that I'm much the wiser.' He looked back at the bust, at the price ticket, and gave a little nod and murmured an aside, 'Not cheap, is it?'

'Parian rarely is,' she said. 'I remember Harry buying a piece and spending half his month's allowance on it.'

Charlie held it up. 'Are you sure you wouldn't like it? It's really nice.'

'No.' She shook her head. She didn't want to be surrounded by constant reminders. 'Thank you, but no, really.'

★ ★ ★

She was quiet in the car on the way back, and Charlie asked her whether there was anything wrong. She assured him that she was fine.

The little bust of Tchaikovsky had brought

33

back memories of Harry, and from him her thoughts had gone on to take in the others in the group. She thought of them at the beginning when they'd gone about in their tight-knit little bunch, congregating in each other's rooms and flats, and then, as time had passed, how the intrusive emotions of one kind or another had crept in. And then, of course, Ruby had died, and for the little that was left of their time together, nothing had been the same.

Soon afterwards, before they had separated at the end of the term, they had exchanged addresses, Addie, however, had not kept up contact with anyone other than Kieron. Apart from him, whose story she knew well, she had limited or no knowledge about the progress of the others since that dark time. Christie had made something of a name for herself in the field of fashion design, and for a time had enjoyed some fame and celebrity. But her success had proved transitory, and Addie had read nothing about her for some while. Harry, however, was occasionally in the news. He had gained a reputation as an illustrator of children's books — even winning awards for his work — and had become very much in demand. Of Matt and Ambrose, Addie had learned nothing at all, but Dolores she had once chanced to meet. That had been some two-and-a-half years back. Addie and Charlie had been about to enter a shop in Earl's Court when Dolores had emerged. After Charlie had been introduced, the two women had chatted for three or four minutes. They would have stayed longer, but Charlie had been impatient to get going. The women had parted with one another's address and promises to keep in touch, but then, just two months later, Robbie had been killed, and when Dolores had written, Addie had not responded.

Only yesterday Addie had stood at Kieron's graveside, and today Harry had come into her thoughts. And now here they all were, in her mind's eye, taking her back, reminding her of Ruby's death and what had happened afterwards. But it was over now, she told herself, it was finished. Ruby was long gone. And now Kieron was gone too. As for the others, they no longer had any part in her life.

And besides, why should she let Ruby's death bother her still? It was in the nature of things that there were mysteries. Only in detective novels could one expect to have loose ends tied up, the last piece of the jigsaw put in place. She accepted that the mystery surrounding Ruby's death would always remain. And she must be content with that; she *would* be; she had no wish to resurrect it all and go looking for answers.

3

'So,' — Charlie was regarding her over his glass — 'what have you been up to today? Not very much, I'd guess — as usual.' It was Friday again. He had not long got in from work, and they sat with their drinks in the living-room. 'Have you been out?'

When she did not answer he sighed. 'It's not good for you, staying around here all the time.'

'What d'you mean? Only last week I went to see Milla.'

'Addie, you don't need to be defensive. I just want to see you your old self again.' He paused, considering his words. 'I think part of your trouble is that you haven't got enough to occupy your time.'

She gave a little laugh. 'With so much to do around here? A home this size?'

'You're talking about household chores. And what do we have Carole for?'

'Actually,' she said — and the notion had indeed touched her — 'I've been thinking I might get back to doing some painting.'

'Really? That would be great. Are you serious?'

'Yes.' Before Robbie's death she had painted regularly. But Robbie had died, and since that time her brushes, paints and canvases had lain untouched in her workroom.

'I'm really pleased to hear this,' Charlie said. 'I was beginning to think you'd given it up for good.'

'Well, maybe it's time I got back to it.' She had no real enthusiasm, but she would like to give evidence of progress. Charlie had been so understanding; he deserved some sign that it was all working. And perhaps it was true that she didn't have enough to occupy her time. Others who were bereaved got by without going to pieces. If she'd had other children, other responsibilities she'd have had to get on with things; there'd have been no choice; but for her, time had hung so heavy.

'Trouble is' — and now she was already backtracking — 'there's the problem of getting started again. I mean, certain things I need.'

'Fine, we'll go to the art supplies shop.'

'I don't just mean the materials.'

'Well, what else?'

She gave a little shrug, a small laugh. 'I just — don't know what to paint.'

'You mean you need inspiration?'

'I need *something*.'

'Well, if it's inspiration you need, then do what you used to do. Go to the galleries. Isn't that what you did in the past? It always did the trick, you said, looking at the work of other painters.'

'Yes, it did.'

'Then what's to stop you this time?'

'Nothing, I guess.'

'Good, then get up to London and take in a couple of exhibitions.'

'London?' Was he serious? He knew that nowadays she only ever drove on local roads. She would never drive on the motor-way again for any distance, and as for driving around London's West End, she couldn't even contemplate such an action.

'I wasn't thinking of you going alone,' Charlie said. 'Of course not. I'm going up next Tuesday, so I could let you off and meet you later on. What do you think?' He smiled encouragement. 'Come on, now, Adelaide, it'll do you good. Get a change of scene too. We could get tickets for the theatre if you like.'

38

She gave a slow nod. 'Well, yes. I suppose I could.' She nodded again, decisive this time. 'Yes, if the weather's good, why not?'

★ ★ ★

Tuesday dawned bright and clear, and when Addie arose that morning she knew she had no excuse not to make the trip.

At breakfast Charlie regarded her over his newspaper, a little curiously, as if he might be expecting her to back out of the jaunt. 'I'll understand if you'd rather not go, Ads,' he said. 'You *are* allowed to change your mind. Don't do it just to please me.'

'No, I'm fine, Charlie,' she said, then added the lie, 'I'm looking forward to it.'

'Good.' He looked at his watch. 'I'll finish getting my things together and we'll go.' Setting down his paper, he got up and started out of the room.

Addie began to collect up the breakfast things and take them out to the kitchen. The thought of the trip caused her heart to flutter, and she tried to thrust the fear away. For God's sake, they were just going to London. What was there to be afraid of? And in any case, it was too late now. She'd been given the chance to back out and she'd let it pass. She had no option now but to go through with it.

Absently she picked up the newspaper and straightened it, turning the leaves. And suddenly she was halted in her movement, her eyes riveted to the photograph before her.

It showed Christie as she had been at the height of her fame some five or six years earlier — matured a little from the Birmingham days, but looking more striking for the maturity. All the knowledge of her that Addie had gained over the years had come from the media, generally from articles reporting on her growing success as a designer in the fashion industry. And while the journalists had been loud in their praise of her on her way up, those same ones had later taken delight in reporting her subsequent failures, both in her professional life and her private affairs.

The text below the photograph was headed INQUEST VERDICT ON DESIGNER. Below the headline was written:

The inquest that opened last week into the death of fashion designer Christie Harding was resumed and concluded yesterday in Hampstead, north-west London. Miss Harding, thirty-six, died at the New

Hampstead Royal Hospital on 11 July. Dr Sajit Mukerjee, resident pathologist of the hospital, who performed an autopsy on Miss Harding's body, gave it as his opinion that she had died as the result of ricin poisoning. Police testified that no evidence of foul play had been found, and although the coroner heard testimony to the effect that she had lately been suffering from depression there was no evidence of suicidal intentions. An open verdict was returned.

Addie read the piece again. Beyond the words she could see Christie as she had been in those past days — so much vitality and zest for life. It was hard to believe that it was all gone. Christie, dead, and in such a strange and terrible way.

'Well, I'm just about set.' Charlie's voice came as he entered the room. 'So if you've — ' He came to a halt. 'What's up?'

She gazed at him for a moment then looked back at the page. Frowning, he came to stand at her shoulder. 'Christie Harding,' he read, and gave a little nod. 'Oh, yes she was a friend of yours, wasn't she? From Birmingham? I don't remember.'

'Birmingham, yes.'

He held out a hand and Addie released the paper into it. When he had read the article he shook his head. 'Christ,' he groaned, 'that's sad. And what in God's name is ricin?' He put the paper down. 'Are you all right?'

'Yes. It's a bit of a shock, that's all.'

'I'm sure.'

'She died on the 11th. That's two weeks ago. There might well have been something in the paper about her death.' She had got out of the habit of reading the daily papers, at best giving them no more than a cursory glance.

'The 11th,' Charlie said. 'I was in Dubai then, wasn't I? I wouldn't even have seen an English paper.'

'She had so much going for her once,' Addie said. 'And now it ends like this.'

'Yes.' He sighed. 'But — try not to think about it.'

'For God's sake, Charlie,' she said. 'How can I not? We were friends. I can't just — pass it off as if she were some stranger.'

'No, of course not. It's just that — with this coming so soon after Kieron's death and — well, I just hate to see you upset.' He wrapped his arms around her. 'Addie, I was thinking of you.'

'I know you were. I'm sorry. I over-reacted.'

'It's a very sad business.' He released her. 'Anyway, I think we should leave. The traffic's bound to be heavy, and I can't be late.' He paused, studying her. 'You still want to come? You don't have to.'

'Yes.' She had to. She couldn't let something like this influence her. Besides, it was necessary. If there was to be the chance of a child, a baby, then she had to prove herself a suitable potential adoptive mother. In order to do so all her difficulties must be consigned to the past. 'Yes,' she said again, 'I want to.' She turned, stepping away. 'Just give me a minute.'

In the utility room she went to the side table where Carole stacked the discarded newspapers before taking them to the recycling unit, and quickly began to go through them. The article she sought was in the edition of the 12th; in one small paragraph, the item merely reported Christie's death in the north London hospital with the added information that an inquest was to be held.

Addie put the paper back on the pile, then turned and left the room.

★ ★ ★

43

The roads that wound through the Berkshire countryside were fairly open, but the M4 was congested. Charlie wasn't fazed — he had long since learned to take it as it came — but for Addie it was a different matter; she sat tense, and they had travelled some distance before she began, by degrees, to relax And then, just past the exit for London Heathrow Airport, they came upon the aftermath of an accident.

The delay that forced them to a crawl had signalled an obstruction, but she had given it no thought. Then with the traffic funelled into a single lane, they eventually drove past two cars, smashed and mangled, straddling the verge and the inner lane. Nearby, lights flashing, stood an ambulance and two police cars. Addie just had time to register shattered windscreens and blood, and then they were past. As they speeded up again, Charlie gave her knee a gentle squeeze. Hardly aware of his touch she sat rigid, staring ahead, hands clasped so tightly that her knuckles were white.

★ ★ ★

It was 11.45 when they reached London's West End. Charlie pulled up in St Martin's Lane, where Addie would be handy for the

44

National Gallery, and turned to her. He knew she had been affected by the scene on the highway. 'You going to be all right?'

'Yes, of course. I'll be fine.'

'Are you sure?'

'Yes, really.'

'Good. Then I'll see you in the teashop about half-past four.'

'I'll be there.'

Moments later, having watched the car rejoin the traffic, she herself set off. It was years since she had been in the West End, and while relieved to be out of the car she was dismayed at the crowds and the activity. She had forgotten what it was like. She looked around her. She seemed to be surrounded by fast food outlets, arcades selling cheap souvenirs, and windows stacked with computer materials. With all this, the appalling sound of the traffic, and the babble of tourists' foreign tongues, it was like being in an alien city.

At the corner of Trafalgar Square she turned to her right. She hadn't visited the National Gallery in ages, and whereas in times past she had approached it with an unmistakable *frisson*, she now went up the steps — skirting a group of oriental students who lounged there — and through the entrance feeling nothing more than desperation to find a refuge.

Whether the interior of the gallery had undergone changes, or she had forgotten what it was like, she found that she no longer knew her way around as she wandered from room to room. Eventually, in one of the rooms dedicated to the English school, she sat down facing a portrait of Gainsborough's two young daughters. Gainsborough had been the subject of her special study in her final year at art school, and the familiar picture filled her with nostalgia. There they were, little Mary and Margaret, one in yellow, the other in white, hand in hand, one of them reaching out for a butterfly that danced by. A scene of happiness and contentment, it was ultimately sorrowful. Two beautiful, pink-cheeked young children, captured as it were by a camera lens, in a moment of childhood joy. Neither, of course, knowing of the unhappiness that lay ahead, neither giving any sign of the madness that would affect them in later life. Turning from the sunlit scene, heels staccato on the floor, she made her way from the room and out of the building.

Back on the pavement she saw the wide space of Trafalgar Square laid before her with people moving around the fountains and crowding about the foot of Nelson's Column.

Fed by the milling tourists, pigeons swarmed and fluttered. She turned and set off once more, hurrying along until she found herself at the opening of a wide street with a tall monument at its entrance, and realized that she was at the foot of Haymarket. Moving up past the theatres she came to the chaos of Piccadilly Circus. There she stood at the kerb, looking over the surging traffic till the pedestrian light turned green and she let herself be swept forward with the crush. On the other side she stopped while the tide moved past her. What was she doing there? she asked herself, the whole idea had been crazy. But while she wanted only to get back to the peace and safety of home, she had to face the day ahead. It was only just after 12.30; there were four hours to go before she was due to meet Charlie again.

A little way up Regent Street she took a turning off to the left, intent on getting out of the way of the hordes of pedestrians who thronged the pavement. Her steps took her into a narrow and relatively quiet sidestreet, in which, twenty yards along, she came upon a small café. It was not a place that, with options, she would have chosen, but it was away from the rush, and she went in. From the Spanish waiter she ordered coffee and a ham sandwich, and sat looking out at the street. The sandwich was adequate but she had no appetite, and after a bite she set it down on her plate and sat sipping the coffee and willing the time to pass. She had given up any idea of visiting more galleries, and the very thought of fighting her way through crowded department stores only filled her with dread.

She remained for a further twenty minutes then paid her bill and set off again, after a while finding herself in Oxford Street where the pavements were so crowded that at times it seemed difficult to make any but the slowest headway. Eventually she got to Marble Arch and stood on the corner while the traffic rushed past into Park Lane. It was not far from here that she and Charlie had arranged to meet. But that was not for ages yet. On the far side of the busy intersection the green of Hyde Park beckoned like an oasis, and after a moment's hesitation she sought out the entrance to the subway and made her way across. Soon she was in the park, and minutes later, at the edge of one of the gently winding paths, she sank down upon a bench.

She was shaking and her palms were damp. It had been the accident on the M4, she told herself; but for that she could have managed, done as she had planned. From her bag she took out her handkerchief and dabbed at her brow. Over to her left the cars and buses roared by on Bayswater Road, while on the grass before her two children, a boy and a girl, played ball with their mother, a homely-looking woman whose good-natured features were alight with happiness. The girl called out to her, 'Mummy, look!' and she replied, 'Oh, very good. *Very* good.' The girl was aged about eight, Addie guessed — the boy about five — a little older than Robbie had been when he died.

Robbie. Addie found herself mouthing his name. Had things been different he would be alive still. He would be alive, and she would not now be fighting panic in this awful city.

Feeding her despair, she reached into her bag again, took out her wallet and looked at the little photograph behind its plastic window: Robbie in his last summer, on the patio, his face tight with concentration as he bent over his little wooden truck. Moments after she had taken the picture a flock of starlings had alighted on the lawn and he had run amongst them, whooping, yelling, sending them rushing up into the sky. And the pain of the memory tightened her throat, and the tears sprang to her eyes and ran down her cheeks. Bending forward, still holding the wallet, she put her hands to her face and sat rocking in her misery.

Eventually she straightened and sat looking ahead through dull, dry eyes. She realized that the children and their mother were no longer there. When had they gone? An elderly man and woman walked by with a small dog on a lead. A youth flashed past on roller blades. The wallet was still in her hand, its leather damp under her clammy fingers. She replaced it in her bag. Looking at her watch she saw that it would soon be time to meet Charlie. With relief sweeping over her she got to her feet and started off along the path.

The teashop was situated in a narrow street not far from Selfridges. She and Charlie had visited it on occasion in years past when it had proved a handy and useful meeting place. Reaching it now, she was relieved to find it unchanged, and she went into its cool interior and sat down at a small table. From the waitress she ordered a tuna salad sandwich and a cup of tea. They were brought to her almost at once. The sandwich was good, and when it was finished she sat sipping her tea. After a while a woman approached the next table and sat down. Addie did not glance at her but, becoming aware of her gaze, self-consciously put up a hand to touch at

her hair; she must, she was sure, look a
fright.

'Addie . . . ?' The woman was speaking
to her.

Addie turned at the sound of her name.
And, after a second, recognition came.

'Dolores,' she said. 'My God, Dolores!'

4

'Addie, it *is* you! I was willing you to turn
so that I could be sure.'

'Dolores!' Addie was almost stammering.
'I can't believe it.'

The waitress came over at that moment
and Dolores ordered a cup of coffee, adding
with a gesture, 'I'll have it with my friend.'
Then, as the waitress went away, she gathered
up her bags and moved to the chair opposite
Addie's.

'Oh, Dolores,' Addie said, 'it's so good to
see you.'

The sight of Dolores now was surprising
in more ways than one. She had altered
so much, was so different from that girl
with pudgy hands, heavy thighs and no
dress sense. She had changed drastically

even since their last, brief meeting in Earl's Court. The Dolores who now sat before her wore a flattering, well-cut linen outfit that revealed a straight, slender figure. This, with her clear skin, and heavy, dark-honey hair, simply and stylishly cut, presented a woman more physically attractive than Addie had ever imagined she could be.

'*You* are looking *well*,' Addie said. 'You really are.'

Dolores pulled a face. 'Getting older. But that's life.' The laugh she gave was her same old laugh. 'And you look good, too, Addie.'

Addie shrugged, said, 'Oh — well,' and gave forgiveness for the white lie.

'So,' Dolores said, 'are you still living in Berkshire?'

'Oh, yes. Are you still in London?'

'Yes. But I'm in Hammersmith now. What are you doing here today?'

'Just visiting. Charlie has some business to attend to — a couple of meetings — so I thought I'd come along for the outing.'

'A little shopping and stuff, huh?'

Addie's answering laugh was short, faintly tinged with the desperation that had so recently driven her. 'Well, that was part of the idea. But I didn't get round to it.'

'I don't come into the West End that

often, but I had no choice today. So I decided to get a few things while I'm here.' Dolores glanced around. 'I came into this place to get off my feet for ten minutes. You did the same, I suppose?'

'I'm supposed to be meeting Charlie.' Addie glanced at her watch. 'He should be here by now.'

Dolores said in a laughing whisper, 'You *chose* this as a meeting place?'

Addie protested, chuckling, 'Oh, it's not so bad. It's convenient, and it's away from all the rush.'

The waitress appeared at Dolores's elbow, placed a cup of coffee before her and went away again. Dolores sipped from the cup, pulled a face and murmured, 'I hope your tea is better than my coffee.' As she set the cup down, she added, 'So if you haven't been shopping, what have you been doing?'

'Oh, just killing time. I spent a while at the National Gallery. But not long. Somehow I just — ran out of energy.'

'Tell me about it. All that standing around, moving from foot to foot. Ten minutes in an art gallery and I start discovering muscles I never knew I had.'

Addie laughed. Looking at her watch again, she said, 'I think I'd better give Charlie a ring. He said I should call him

53

if he's not here by four forty-five.'

'There's a phone over there.' Dolores pointed through the window to a phone kiosk on the far side of the street.

Leaving the café, Addie dodged the traffic to the phone box on the opposite pavement and dialled Charlie's mobile. If he was keeping to his schedule he would be with Philip Green, a games inventor who lived in Old Compton Street, Soho. He was, and he answered her call at once. Unfortunately, he said apologetically, he wouldn't be through till nearer six. 'Can you meet me here at that time?' he asked. Yes, Addie said, she'd get a taxi. When she had written down the address she said goodbye and returned to the teashop where she told Dolores of the change of plan.

'Does that mean you're free for a while?' Dolores said.

'It looks like it. For an hour or so.'

'That's great! Listen, let's get away from here. I don't like being surrounded by all these cream cakes. It's dangerous. Let's go find a nice little pub nearby.'

'Yes, that'd be nice,' Addie said. 'Just give me five minutes to tidy myself up.'

In the ladies room she did what she could to remedy the day's wear and tear, and then together they left. It took only a couple of minutes before they came upon a little pub in another of the backstreets. Moving ahead, Dolores pushed open the door and poked her head inside, then turned back to Addie with a nod. 'Looks OK. No blaring jukebox either — for the moment anyway. Let's give it a try, shall we?'

Addie followed Dolores into the cool interior, which for some moments appeared dim after the brightness of the sunlight. In the gloom they saw three or four customers perched on stools along the bar, while others sat singly or in pairs at small tables. The two women found a vacant table beneath a patterned window, and Dolores dumped her bags on the padded bench and asked Addie what she'd have to drink. Addie said she'd have a gin and tonic. As Dolores went to the bar, Addie sat and looked around, taking in the smoke-darkened walls hung with engravings of prize-fighters. The only sounds were the murmur of conversations and the clink of glasses. As her eyes returned to Dolores where she stood at the bar, she silently remarked that there was a difference about her that was something apart from her physical appearance. There was a certain self-assurance that had not been there before. And however it had come, the old Dolores — eager to please, dull and drab and so often the butt of the odd little jibe — seemed now to have quite gone.

Returning to the table, Dolores handed Addie her drink, sat down and hoisted her glass. 'So — cheers.'

'Cheers.' Addie sipped from her glass. Looking around, Dolores said, 'I could have found a place like this in the first place, instead of that bloody awful teashop, but if you go into a pub on your own you can bet there'll be some creep trying to put the make on.' She grinned. 'Still, we're safe enough, right? Two respectable ladies just wanting to rest their feet.'

Addie chuckled, and as she did so there came the sound of music rising from the far end of the room. 'Uh oh,' she said, 'I'm afraid you spoke too soon.' Dolores cocked her head, listening, while the melody and words of *You Don't Know Me* fell into recognizable form. 'I can stand that,' Dolores said. 'And it's not loud, thank God.' Opening her bag, she took out a pack of cigarettes. 'D'you smoke? I seem to remember that you did.'

'Not now. Not for ages.'

Dolores lit her cigarette and blew out smoke in a stream above their heads. 'That's another thing — it's a relief to be able to smoke a cigarette without getting the fish eye.

There's no fun in eating out any more and hoping to enjoy a nice after-dinner cigarette. You light up nowadays in public and people look at you like you're on the same level as a child molester.'

Listening to Dolores's chatter, Addie was aware of a great sense of relief. It was what she needed, a touch of reality after the insanity that had been the day. 'Oh, Dolores,' she said impulsively, 'it really is so good to see you again.'

'It's good to see *you*, Addie.' Dolores drank from her glass. 'So, you say your husband — Charlie — is in town for meetings?'

'Yes. You remember him, don't you? From when we met that time? You were just coming out of a shop in Earl's Court.'

'A meeting that lasted all of three seconds flat, right?'

Addie nodded. 'Well, yes, it was a bit rushed.'

Dolores gave a wry smile. 'A bit! I remember how he stood there chafing at the bit while we were talking.'

'Oh, *don't*,' Addie protested with a groan. 'It wasn't really like that, was it?'

'It was,' Dolores chuckled. 'Not that it matters. But he didn't take to me. That came over very clearly.'

'Oh, that's not so,' Addie said. 'He was

just in a hurry, as I recall.' Which wasn't strictly true, for she could well remember that following the brief meeting Charlie had commented on Dolores in less than positive terms.

'In fact,' Dolores said, 'I thought that was part of the reason you didn't keep in touch afterwards.'

A moment of silence, then Addie said, 'I'm sorry. Things — got in the way.'

Dolores nodded. 'They have a habit of doing that. But in any case, I had my own things to deal with — like coping with my husband. Listen, I know how it is — you leave the letters and the phone calls too long and in the end you've left them too late.'

She drew on her cigarette. 'So, what's Charlie's business here in town?'

'He's calling on some games inventors.'

'Games? Wasn't that your father's business? Manufacturing board games and all that stuff?'

'Yes. I met Charlie when he joined Dad's company. Then, after Dad died, Charlie took it over.' She smiled. 'He'd have needed to. I couldn't run it, that's for sure. I didn't have any interest in it, I'm ashamed to say.'

'I should have thought it would have been fascinating.'

'To some people. I tried it for a while after Birmingham, but it wasn't for me. So I gave it up and went into teaching. It was just Charlie's cup of tea, though. He took to it like a duck to water.'

'And it's doing well, is it?'

'Well, we've got no complaints.' Where she herself was concerned she wasn't anxious to have the conversation go any deeper. 'How about you?' she said. 'Are you still married?' She had noticed that Dolores's hand bore no wedding ring.

'Not any longer.' Her voice heavy with irony, Dolores went on, 'You're lucky with your Charlie — someone who gives a damn about earning a crust. I'm afraid my husband, Geoff, turned out to be one of the most shiftless, feckless bastards imaginable. Trouble is, he hid it so well — at the start.' She gave a little chuckle that smacked more of bitterness than humour. 'The man was just so charming, that was the trouble. It wears off, though — the charm — especially when the wolf comes hammering on the door.' She waved a hand, brushing away the subject. 'But I don't want to get onto him. I've been divorced now for two years, and that's it. What he's doing now I don't know and I don't care.' She stubbed out her cigarette.

'I'd be very wary of taking a similar step again.'

'Like marriage, you mean?'

'Like marriage, I mean, yes.' Dolores sighed. 'Anyway, at least there was just *me* to get hurt. We didn't have any children to get caught in the crossfire.' She looked at Addie with a slightly enquiring light in her eye, and Addie knew with dread that she was about to ask about Robbie. But thankfully, the question did not come.

Covering her relief and putting space between herself and the moment, Addie said, 'I thought about you the other day. And again just this morning.'

Dolores returned her gaze. 'And I thought about you. And the others.'

'You — you read about Christie, right?' Addie said.

'Yes.'

'I read about the inquest just this morning. I hadn't even known she'd died.'

'Bit of a shock, eh? I got it from her family. The news of her death.'

'You're in touch with her family?'

'Her sister. Christie and I had made contact again a while back, and after that I met her sister Janice. Then, when Christie died, Janice phoned and told me. Christie'd been ill for three or four days before she

60

died, I understand.'

'In the paper this morning,' Addie said, 'the report on the inquest said she'd died of poisoning. I was so shocked by that. I've forgotten the poison they named.'

'It wasn't one I'd ever heard of before. Oh, poor Christie. It's so sad. And doubly so in that they more or less hinted that she might have killed herself.'

'You don't think that's likely, do you?'

'No, I don't.' Dolores's tone was emphatic. 'I can't for one moment imagine her doing such a thing, in spite of the change in her circumstances — her career going on the skids like that. It must be very hard to have had everything, and then find it's all just — slipped away from you. But Christie would have stuck it out. I'm sure she would — the Christie that I remember. She always seemed to be such a survivor.'

A little silence fell between them, then Addie took a deep breath and said, 'Dolores, Kieron is dead too. Did you know that?'

Dolores looked at her, mouth slightly open. 'Kieron? Kieron Walderson?'

Addie nodded. 'Just a few weeks ago. In June.'

Dolores gave a groan. 'Addie, how terrible. That dear, sweet man.' A pause. 'Was he married?'

'Yes, he married my cousin, Camilla. They had a little girl — Helen.'

'Oh, dear. I don't know what to say. What happened to him?'

'He died of blood-poisoning.'

'God, that's awful. How did he get it?'

'Nobody knows. They couldn't say what caused it.'

'I don't understand. How can they not know what it was caused by?'

'Don't ask me.' Addie took a drink from her glass. She would say nothing of the deep suspicions that had followed Kieron's shocking death. 'Poor Milla, she still hasn't grasped what's hit her.'

Dolores sighed, 'Apart from it being so sad, it's just the weirdest coincidence. Both Kieron and Christie dying within a few weeks of each other.'

The two sat in silence for a few moments while the general buzz of the place went on about them.

'So you kept in touch with Christie,' Addie said. 'After we all split up.'

'Oh, it was much later that we met again. Just a couple of years back. Probably soon after you and I ran into one another. I saw, locally, a poster saying that she'd been invited to speak at a meeting of some feminist group. It wasn't really my cup of tea, but I went along. And — oh, it was great to meet up with her again. We went for a drink afterwards, she and I and a couple of other people with her. We didn't get much opportunity to talk, but at least we'd made contact. She looked just the same — all that marvellous red hair, that great face.' She paused for a moment, remembering. 'She was just — so alive, wasn't she? That's how she always struck me.'

'I know what you mean,' Addie nodded. Christie had been like a flame, and seemingly unquenchable.

'We kept in touch after a fashion,' Dolores went on, 'and met once or twice. And of course there'd be bits about her in the media. She'd been doing well in the past, but times had started to get hard. She never talked about it. In fact once things really began to fall apart we didn't meet. I think she didn't want to see anybody. She kind of — drew into herself. Fortunately or unfortunately, I've never been that ambitious.'

Looking back, that was the impression Addie got from her memories. Whereas Christie had been constantly keeping an eye out for the main chance, Dolores had seemed content to take life as it came and accept what it had to offer.

'Which is why I went into teaching,' Dolores went on. 'I suppose I thought it would be easy. Easy! My God, that was a misjudgement and no mistake.' She gave a wry shake of her head. 'You said you went into teaching too, didn't you?'

'For a while. But then, fortunately, Charlie came to work for the company.'

'Lucky you. But you know what it's like, though — teaching. God, I'd love to get out of it. Nowadays I just do supply work. At least it relieves you of a few of the responsibilities. And you can choose when and if you want to work. As for doing it full time, no, thank you. I didn't study all those years in order to be a fucking zoo-keeper — and to kids whose parents don't give a shit about their offsprings' anti-social behaviour when they're out of their sight.'

'True,' Addie said, remembering how it had been. 'Still, at least you've got the summer holidays now.'

'From school, yes. But I spend them working as a temp. General office work. Bit of this, bit of that. It helps out. Can't afford to be idle.'

Their glasses were empty, and Addie got up and went to the bar to buy fresh drinks. Back at the table she set the glasses down.

As she sat on the bench again, Dolores said, 'You know about Harry, I suppose?'

'Harry? What about him?'

'Well, his work as a children's illustrator.'

'Oh, yes! I've seen some of the books he's done. Beautiful. But his work always was. He deserves his success.' A pause. 'You know anything about the others?'

'I ran into Matt about a year ago, here in London. He was on the platform at Oxford Circus tube station.'

'Did you get a chance to speak?'

'Just briefly. He was rushing one way, and I the other. A hello-how-are-you-goodbye kind of thing. He looked pretty much the same, except that he'd gone quite grey. Beginning to look a bit seedy too. We didn't get a chance to exchange any news.' The slightest pause. 'Even if there'd been the inclination.'

Addie looked at her a little more keenly, trying to read behind her words. Were they some oblique reference to what had happened to Ruby, and the fear and suspicion that had followed?

And the silence was there again, and then Dolores spoke once more, her words and tone sounding uncertain.

'Do you — ever think about *then*? — that time?'

5

Two or three seconds passed, then Addie said, 'Yes.' She barely mouthed the word.

Dolores nodded. 'I, too. Though not often. When Christie and I met up again we talked about everything but that. D'you think that's strange?'

'No,' Addie said quickly. 'I've told Charlie hardly anything. And nothing at all about the letters. I think now he's given up expecting to learn anything more.'

'I still find myself wondering about it all — what really happened that day. And if she *did* do it intentionally, then *why* did she?'

The same questions had so often come into Addie's mind. She could see them — images in little flashes, like in some film of stop-frame photography. At any time, the images bidden or unbidden, there they would be, crowding the rail, looking over. Ambrose is next to her, eyes wide, his usually ruddy complexion chalk-white. Christie, hugging her body, is screaming, while Dolores stands with hands pressed to the sides of her face. Kieron, like Harry, stands open-mouthed.

And once again she hears the sound of their feet on the stairs as they rush down. Of her own actions she can remember little, only that in the garden she comes to a sudden stop, unable to move any nearer to the dreadful, blood-soaked object that drapes the spiked railing. Ruby's head hangs down, the blood coming from her mouth, her nose, her ears. She wears only one ear-ring, a little pear drop, and a single drop of blood, a bead like a small red fruit, is attached to it — a ruby, like her name. Later — how much later? — it couldn't have been long — there had come the sound of the ambulance, and then the paramedics and police swarming around, the latter with their endless questions.

Afterwards had come the inquest, adjourned for further inquiries, and when resumed, the verdict: misadventure. And then, so she had thought, it was over. But soon afterwards, only days before the course ended, there had come the letters.

Now, as if reading Addie's mind, Dolores, looking down as one fingertip touched at the rim of her glass, said, 'And then — then the letters.'

Addie nodded.

'And who wrote them?' Dolores said. Looking Addie directly in the eye, she added,

'There's only one thing I know: it wasn't me.'

'Well, I know that.'

'No, Addie, you don't know that. But it happens to be the truth.'

'I never thought for a moment that it was you.'

Dolores gave a wry smile. 'No? Well, I have to confess that I did wonder at one time whether it might be you.' While Addie tried not to show the surprise and dismay she felt at this, Dolores added, 'Not that I thought it was, you understand, but I had to consider everybody.'

Addie said, mollified, 'I guess you'd have to.' Then, returning Dolores's gaze with a directness of her own, she said, 'Anyway, for the record, it *wasn't* me.'

'I believe you. But you all went through my thoughts at different times. As I suppose I must have gone through others' minds — been considered by *them*.'

They'd had a similar conversation at the time of the happening, Addie recalled. Amongst all of them, the same desperate need to be believed. 'And?' she said.

'You mean, did I end up suspecting anyone in particular?' Dolores shook her head. 'No. But *somebody* wrote them.'

'But why?'

'You tell me. Either it was the sickest joke ever — or somebody really did know something.'

'That — that Ruby's death wasn't an accident? But is it possible that somebody really could have — have killed her?'

'I don't know. But what did we really know about her? Very little as far as I was concerned — apart from the fact that no girl's man was safe with her. She certainly put a few people's backs up, I know that. But she could also charm the bloody birds out of the trees. Yes, and at the same time be an absolute bitch.' She gazed off past Addie's shoulder, as if thinking back. 'She was the only one of our group, I thought, who was never really a part of it. She never *quite* fitted in, did she? But come to that, I thought the same about Matt at times. Didn't you?'

Addie gave a little laugh, awkward, unable to find words for a reply.

'There was an aloofness about him,' Dolores added. 'A certain distance.'

Addie drank from her glass, set it down precisely in the centre of the coaster, then said, 'Why d'you think it might have been one of us seven who wrote the notes? After all, we each one of us received one — and they all had the same wording.'

'I'm not saying it was. Just that it could have been. And so what if we each got an identical letter? What does that prove? The writer would obviously have sent one to himself — or herself — in order to appear innocent. It'd be the obvious thing to do.'

'Yes, of course.' Addie sighed; what was the point of going over it all, picking away at it like a child with a scabbed knee? What had happened had caused wounds, but the wounds had more or less healed. It was senseless going over it all again.

'So,' — into her thoughts came Dolores's voice once more — 'if the games business is going well, I don't suppose you need to work now. You can be a full-time housewife and mother.' She smiled. 'How is your little boy? You told me his name when we met briefly that time, but I'm afraid I've forgotten it.'

And there, just when Addie had been least expecting it, the question had come.

'Robbie,' Addie said, addressing her answer to the patterned glass of the window. 'He — he died.' She was determined that she wouldn't let go, but all of a sudden her throat was painfully tight and she was struggling to keep her voice on an even note. Pressing her lips together she lowered her gaze, hiding the tears that filled her eyes.

70

'Oh, God, Addie,' Dolores said. 'Oh, my dear, I'm so sorry.' Her hand came out and touched Addie's cheek. 'Blurting it out like that. I had no idea.'

'Of course you didn't.' The smile that Addie forced to her mouth felt like some dreadful rictus. 'It's all right.' Silence for some moments, and then, keeping her voice low and controlled, she said, 'Robert — our son — he died two and a half years ago. Only a few weeks after you and I met again, as a matter of fact. Which was why I never got in touch. I just let everything go.' She would say nothing of the way he had died, nor of the days, the weeks, the months that had followed; the depression so deep that at one time their GP had suggested that a spell in a psychiatric clinic might be beneficial. Of course, she had resisted the suggestion. Then, slowly, had come the process of her rehabilitation. But with what success? She was still unable to move far from the security of her home territory with equanimity. 'I'm all right,' she said. 'I'll be OK.' A pause. 'As a matter of fact we — we're trying to adopt — if we can.'

'You want to *adopt* a baby?' More than one question came with Dolores's words.

Avoiding her eyes, Addie said, 'Well, we can't have any more.'

'Oh, *no*. Addie, how sad.'

'Yes. Unfortunately, after Robbie was born Charlie contracted mumps. It can be very serious in an adult male, as you may know.'

Dolores nodded. 'Yes, I've heard. How terrible. How on earth did that happen?'

'It — it was me.' The admission was torture. 'I caught it first — got it from a friend's child — and passed it on to Charlie. And, well, it affected him very badly, and afterwards . . . ' She shook her head; there was no way she could diminish the gravity of the situation. 'Well, his sperm count turned out to be so low as to be almost non-existent.'

A moment of silence. 'Addie, I don't know what to say.'

'There is nothing to say.'

Seconds ticked by. Addie looked at her watch. It was just after half-past five. 'I shall have to be going,' she said.

'Yes, I too.' Dolores dipped into her bag, wrote on a piece of paper and slid it across the table. 'Here's my address and phone number. I'd love to hear from you. I'll leave it to you, OK? But I really would like to see you.'

'Oh, I'd like that too. Though I hardly ever come to London.'

Dolores smiled. 'I can't say I blame you.

But who knows — if you do, and you have time to spare . . . '

'Of course.' Looking at Dolores's scrawl, Addie observed, 'You're still McCaffrey, I see. You went back to your own name after your divorce, did you?'

'Oh, you bet.' Dolores gave a slow shake of her head, her breath coming out in a little groan. 'The fewer reminders I have of that bastard the better.'

'You make it sound pretty bad.'

'It was. He was.' A sigh and a brisk, dismissing wave. 'Anyway, that's all in the past. Now I'm getting on with my life again.'

'And with a change.'

'A change? Oh, yes, indeed. 'Good old Dolores, whatever you want she'll do; she'll put up with anything'. Well, I decided in the end I wouldn't.'

Smiling, Addie said, 'I was referring to the way you look.'

'Oh — right — well, there too I decided that enough was enough. I'd had my fill of the jokes: 'I can see you're a girl who eats all her dinners'. 'Give it to Dolores, she'll finish it up'. Very funny. I don't think. So, I did something about it.'

Addie nodded. 'You did the right thing.' Taking one of her cards from her bag she placed it before Dolores. 'Maybe you'll be visiting the country some time.'

'Well, I suppose anything's possible.' Dolores smiled. 'And if Charlie promises not to set the dogs on me.' Looking again at the card, she added, 'Oh, yes, you're Adelaide *Carmichael*. I'd forgotten your married name.' She dropped the card into her bag. 'Listen, whatever happens, let's keep in touch this time.'

Out in the sunlight they walked to the corner and there came to a stop.

'Just — take it easy, Addie,' Dolores said.

'Yes, you too.'

For a moment they looked at one another, and then Dolores stepped forward and gave Addie a hug. 'It was so good to see you again,'

Addie returned the embrace. 'And you. Truly.'

As they stepped apart, Dolores said, 'Something's just occurred to me. Christie's funeral is a week Thursday. Her sister Janice has invited me. Why don't you come?'

Addie hesitated. A part of her wanted to say yes, she would like to pay her last respects to her old friend; while another part shrank from the idea of the journey. 'I hardly ever drive,' she said. 'Only locally, anyway.'

Dolores looked slightly puzzled at this, then said, 'Well, if you could get the train up here to London I could meet you and we could go in my car.' She reached out and pressed Addie's hand. 'Come on. I don't want to go on my own, and it would be good for you to be there.'

Another moment of hesitation, and Addie nodded. 'Yes. Yes, I will,' and was instantly glad of her decision.

'Good. I'll phone you and we'll make arrangements, all right?'

'Fine.'

They said their goodbyes, and then Dolores was turning, stepping away. A taxi pulled into the kerb. Addie waited until its passengers had left, then gave the driver the address that Charlie had given her, and got inside.

The flat in Soho was situated above a shop selling sex aids, the window displaying an assortment of videos and varied kinds of supposedly-erotic apparel. Addie rang the doorbell marked *Green*.

Philip Green himself, a short man in his thirties, opened the door after a minute and announced that Charlie was just about ready to leave. As he spoke, Charlie came down the stairs, and after brief introductions and goodbyes he and Addie set off for the car-park. A short while later they were in the car and heading through the busy London streets towards the M4.

'So,' Addie said, 'did you get everything done that you wanted?'

'Yes, pretty much so,' Charlie replied. 'Philip's come up with a couple of interesting ideas. One of them looks like it might have potential.' Unlike many other games manufacturers, it had always been Charlie's policy and preference to keep a hands-on approach where his inventors' work was concerned. He had always believed in the personal touch, the close involvement.

'So will Adanco be offering a licence?'

'Well, we'll wait and see how the ideas develop. It's too early to say. Certainly I don't recall seeing anything similar at the last toy fairs.'

The games inventors and the manufacturing companies who licensed and made real their inventions were now in the process of perfecting their products for the series of toy fairs that would be held across the world in the early months of the coming year. In the meantime there was much to be done.

Keeping on the subject of the company's business, Charlie said, 'Oh, by the way, I talked to Lydia this morning.'

'In London? She was in London?'

'No, we spoke on the phone. She's come

up with a new game and is keen to show it to me.'

Lydia Newmar was an inventor who had created a number of concepts for games which Adanco had marketed over the years, some of which had been very successful. Unfortunately her more recent efforts had proved less so.

Charlie went on, 'She's suggested lunch, a week on Sunday. She wants to demonstrate the game.' He shrugged. 'Who knows — it might be a winner. We'll see how it goes. You'll get to meet her new partner too. Peter Lavell. You'll like him.'

'You want me to go too?' Addie said. 'You don't really need me there, do you?'

'You don't have to go if you don't want to.' Charlie's tone was cool. 'But I'd prefer it if you went along.'

She felt guilty at her display of reluctance. 'Oh, Charlie, of course I will.'

'Just for a little moral support, if nothing else.' He smiled now. 'Then once we've given her project the once-over, we can relax.'

'Relax? With Lydia?' Addie smiled. 'Isn't that a contradiction in terms?'

He groaned. 'Don't remind me. She's such a fucking ball-breaker. I don't know how Adam puts up with it. But look on the bright side: it'll do you good to get out.

Besides, your input is valuable.'

'Input? What input is that?'

'I value your opinion, Ads.' He reached over and briefly touched her knee. 'Listen, we won't stay any longer than we have to. But we've got to put up with her.'

'Of course.' Whatever her feelings, business was business, and there was no place in it for sleeping partners — especially those who were counter-productive. She smiled. 'Who knows, it might even be fun.'

'Fun?' He shot her a jaundiced glance. 'We're not talking quality time here, Adelaide, we're talking Lydia.'

★ ★ ★

The traffic heading out of London was heavy. As they approached the exit for Heathrow Airport, Addie realized that they were nearing the scene of the accident whose aftermath they had witnessed on their way out. Unable to prevent herself, she looked over to the east-bound highway as they passed. The wrecked cars had long gone, and now there was nothing she could see that indicated the precise spot where it had happened.

'So,' he said, 'how was *your* day? Did you get to some exhibitions?'

'No, I'm afraid I didn't.'

'Oh? How come?'

'I — I don't know. I did go to the National Gallery, though.'

'Well, that's something,'

'And I met somebody. An old friend.'

'Really? Who was that?'

'Dolores McCaffrey.'

'Dolores . . . ?'

'You met her yourself, a few years back, in Earls Court.'

After a moment's thought he gave a slow nod. 'Oh, yes, a rather plump young woman, right?'

'Well, *then*, perhaps. Not now. She's shed a few pounds.'

He smiled. 'If my memory of her is correct, she needed to.'

'Oh, Charlie, don't.'

He shot a sideways glance at her. 'Why so sensitive?'

'Oh, I don't know. Well, she just came in for a good bit of teasing, I suppose. And I guess I did my share. But she was so nice, and willing, and good-natured, and — oh — ' her sentence went unfinished. 'Anyway, it was great to see her.'

Sitting in silence as they drove, she thought again of her meeting with Dolores. Of the three other girls in their little clique those eleven years ago, she had always liked Dolores the most. Warm-hearted, placid, well meaning, she had been the exact opposite of the self-absorbed Christie with her often outrageous behaviour and barbed wit. And equally different too, of course, from Ruby. Exquisitely beautiful Ruby who had hated her name, but which had seemed so appropriate. And what *she* was doing on a teacher-training course Addie had never been able to fathom. Never in a million years could Addie picture her as a teacher, see her standing in front of a class of unruly children. But there, her artistic talent had been insufficient to have enabled her to follow a career as a creative artist. To say the least, her ability had been limited. Addie had eventually come to the conclusion that Ruby had embarked on the course merely for something to do; lacking the necessary qualifications to study an academic subject, but having a flair for painting, she had turned to art as a last resort.

And she had got by, without ever appearing fazed by any sense of inadequacy. Addie recalled that on two or three occasions Ruby had been warned by her tutor that she was falling behind and risked failure when the time came for final exams and assessments. Ruby had taken it with equanimity, promising to make an effort. But nothing had changed.

And no one had expected it to. With all the assurance of the privileged and the supremely self-confident she had gone on doing more or less as she pleased. On one occasion Ambrose had performed some foolish act in duet with her, and whilst he had been severely reprimanded, she had suffered just a gentle ticking off. 'Some people get away with murder!' Ambrose had said afterwards, but he had laughed whilst saying it. The only times Addie had ever seen her in any way rattled was when she was unable to make an anticipated score with her dope-or coke-supplier, or when things didn't go as she had wished where one or other of her boyfriends was concerned. Other than that, she had just seemed to drift through the days, getting by on her extraordinary good looks and her charm — doing the minimum of work necessary for the moment, and more often than not considerably less.

But in the end Ruby had gone over the balcony. All her considerable charm had not been able to save her from that terrible death.

And now Christie, too, was dead.

Into the quiet in the car, Addie said, 'By the way, I'm going with Dolores to Christie's funeral next Thursday.'

Charlie was silent for a moment, as if

considering its possible ramifications. 'Well, fine — I guess,' he said, 'if that's what you feel you should do.'

'It's what I *want* to do,' Addie said.

6

Dolores telephoned that same evening with the information on Christie's cremation. It was to be on Thursday of the following week at twelve o'clock, the funeral to take place from the home of her sister Janice, in Northamptonshire.

Addie arranged to meet Dolores in London, and when the day came she drove the relatively short distance to Reading and there got the train into Paddington where Dolores, sipping a tonic water, was waiting for her in the station bar. They left at once, and not long afterwards were sitting in Dolores's seven-year-old Peugeot to which neither time nor its succession of owners had been kind.

The congested highway that took them out of London was to Addie made worse by the unremitting ugliness of the buildings that lined its way. At last, though, they turned off onto a comparatively quiet road winding through the Northamptonshire countryside. It was a fine day, with the sun striking warm from a clear sky. In the surrounding farmlands much of the harvest was in, and the ochre fields lay shorn, their surfaces dotted with neat bales of straw. Here and there around the fringes stood tall poppies, blood red against the gold of the corn stubble. Addie at last began to relax as she felt the tightness draining away.

The little town of Brackley was unknown to both women, and as they drove along its wide main street with its spacious, litter-free pavements and grassy verges, they were surprised by its attractiveness. Following the directions that Christie's sister had sent, they eventually found themselves at the crematorium, and with time to spare.

They chatted idly for a few minutes and then Dolores said, 'I looked up that poison they say Christie took — ricin.'

Addie nodded. 'I did too. My dictionary said it's from the castor-oil plant.'

'Right. And the poison comes from the seeds.' Dolores frowned. 'I can't imagine why on earth anyone would choose such means as a way out.'

When the time came they got out of the car and went to stand outside the chapel along with the other mourners. It wasn't long before a hearse drew up and Christie's coffin was taken from it and carried inside. Addie and Dolores followed the other mourners into the chapel and took seats at the back. During the service, conducted by a reverend with a speech impediment, an old male friend of Christie's got up and spoke a little about her life, after which a woman read an appropriate poem. There was recorded music — Verdi. Afterwards the flower-laden coffin gently glided away beyond the curtains, and the service was over. The whole thing had taken less than twenty-five minutes.

Outside, Addie was introduced to Christie's sister, Janice, who thanked them for coming, and soon afterwards Dolores and Addie set off to follow the other mourners back to Janice's house. It was set in a modern development at the far end of the town, one of a dozen dwellings with neat front gardens and newly planted trees and shrubs. Inside the house, Janice's husband and young daughter brought around drinks and platters of food. There were about thirty mourners gathered, and in between sips of sherry and bites of salmon sandwiches, Addie and Dolores were introduced to a number of them. Whereas they were asked how they had come to know Christie, no one mentioned Christie's death. But perhaps, Addie thought, that was only to be expected. There was an added cloud over this tragedy, and it was not to be spoken of.

After a time, while Dolores had gone off to the bathroom, Addie fell into conversation with a woman who introduced herself as Celia Lanford, a friend of Christie's. In her mid forties, she was small and slight, with little dress sense, and frizzy brown hair that she had tried, largely unsuccessfully, to control with a too-liberal application of lacquer. When Dolores returned, Addie introduced the two. Dolores made polite conversation for a minute or two, then said she thought perhaps they ought to be making tracks.

Celia said at once, 'I know it's a cheek, but if you're driving back to London, d'you think I could cadge a lift? I've got my train ticket, but I'd so much rather not go back on my own.'

Dolores agreed at once, and minutes later they had said their goodbyes and were getting into Dolores's car. With Celia sitting in the back, they set off.

As they left the town of Brackley behind them, Celia said regretfully, resignedly, 'Well, I don't know, I'm sure, but it seems to me that funerals are getting more and more regimented these days.'

Dolores murmured some words of agreement,

after which Celia said, 'Mind you, it's been such an awful business altogether. Not only her death, but the post-mortem — the inquest.'

'Did you attend the inquest?' Dolores asked.

'Yes.'

'As a witness?'

'Yes.' Celia's tone was contemptuous. 'But I didn't really get a chance to say anything.' She took out a handkerchief and dabbed at her eyes. 'I still can't get over that it had to end like that — and getting her name blasted all over the papers that way.'

'Yes,' Addie said, 'it's been terribly sad.'

'Christie had been feeling low, all right,' Celia said mournfully. 'But she'd been through rough times in the past and got through them. She was *strong*.'

'Oh, yes,' said Dolores. 'I thought if anybody was a survivor, then it was Christie.' She briefly focused on Celia's face in the driving mirror. 'Celia, tell me honestly: d'you think it's likely that Christie — well — committed suicide?'

Celia groaned. 'Oh, I don't know what to think. Such a thing was out of character for her, but some say it's the only thing that fits in with the facts.' She paused. 'I certainly don't think the problems with her career

86

would have made her do such a thing. In any case, she was starting to feel much more positive about that. I know she was very unhappy about her goddaughter, and I suppose some people might see that as being the last straw, in a sense, but I can't see it with Christie — not at all.'

Dolores lit a cigarette. As she opened the window an inch to let the smoke out she said, 'Her goddaughter? What was that about?'

'Oh, that was tragic,' Celia answered. 'She was a lovely little girl. Alice. Only nine. She lived in Derbyshire. She died just a short while before Christie herself was taken ill. I was with Christie when she got the news over the phone. She was very upset.'

They were on the motorway now, and the traffic was heavy. Dolores was taking her time, keeping to a steady sixty-five. 'Tell me,' she said after a while, 'what exactly happened with Christie? The papers told practically nothing.'

'When she was taken ill?'

'Yes.'

'Well, I hadn't seen her for two or three days, and I called round at her house. This was on the Tuesday — about a week or so after Alice had died. I went round about three that afternoon. I didn't get any answer when I rang the bell, but I knew she must be there because her car was outside. So I went back home and got the key to her place. We both had keys to each other's house — in case of an emergency, you know — or locking ourselves out or whatever — you know the kind of thing.'

'It's wise,' Dolores said.

'When I let myself in I could see at once that something was wrong. I mean, the washing-up hadn't been done — which was unlike Christie. And I called up the stairs, and she answered. Just about.'

'What d'you mean, just about?'

'Well, with a very weak voice. I went up and found her in bed. She looked just awful. She told me she thought she must have the flu, but it looked to be something more than that. For one thing she had a fever. I said I was going to call a doctor, but she said no, she'd be all right. So I got her some soup — that's all I could persuade her to have. She had no appetite. She took some of it, with a little bread and butter, and afterwards I helped her to the loo. When she was back in bed she said she'd be OK and that I should go on back home. I had a few other things to do, so when I'd made sure she was comfortable I told her I'd look in later to see how she was, and then left.'

'And did you?' Addie asked. 'Go back?'

'Yes. Four or five hours later. I let myself in and went straight upstairs, and I could see a difference in her at once. She was very weak, and she seemed to have difficulty in speaking. She'd got a bowl beside her bed, and I could see that she'd been sick. I said straight away I was going to call a doctor. She didn't object this time. So I looked up the number of her GP and phoned him, and he came round.'

Dolores said, 'Were you there when he came?'

'Oh, yes. Well, someone had to be there to let him in. It was about ten o'clock when he arrived. A very nice man. Scottish. And seemed to know what he was doing, thank God — which isn't always the case. He examined her. I was there in the room, and I could see at once that he was puzzled — and very concerned. I asked him what he thought was wrong, and he said he couldn't say at that point, but it was obvious he knew it was something a lot worse than flu, because the next thing he's saying he's going to have to get her into hospital.'

'And that's what happened?' Dolores asked.

'Yes, he phoned for an ambulance right away, and they were there not long afterwards. In the meantime I packed a few

89

things for her — her toothbrush and stuff, and a clean nightdress.'

'They took her to the Hampstead Royal, didn't they?'

'Yes. After they'd taken her off, the doctor asked if she had any family. I told him that she had a sister who lived in the country. I found Christie's address book and gave him Janice's phone number and address. Later, when he'd gone, I phoned up Janice and told her what had happened.'

'How was Christie when you saw her next?' Dolores asked.

A sharp little intake of breath, then Celia said, 'I never saw her again.'

'Ohhh, Celia . . .' Addie reached back and gently touched the other woman's hands as they lay clenched on her thigh.

As Addie withdrew her hand, Celia said, 'When I phoned the hospital next morning they asked if I was a relative. When I said no, they said they weren't at liberty to tell me anything. So I phoned Janice and asked her if she knew anything, and she said she'd just been on the phone herself, and they'd told her that Christie was seriously ill. Then she said she was coming to London to see Christie. With her husband away, she'd be coming on her own. She said she might come back to Christie's house to stay over afterwards, so I said I'd go in and get things ready for her. And I did that. A good while later she arrived at my place, having just been to the hospital.'

'And obviously with no good news,' Dolores said.

'No. She was terribly upset. She said Christie had just been moved into the Intensive Care Unit, and was lying there with all these tubes connected to her. The doctors told her that Christie had a fever, but they didn't know what was causing it, though it might have been due to an infection of one of the internal organs — like pneumonia or something. They'd taken blood samples and were testing them.'

'For bugs and stuff?' said Dolores.

'I suppose so.' Celia paused. 'Apparently he asked whether Christie might have taken something. Swallowed something.'

'You mean like — like poison?'

Celia nodded. 'Yes. I'm sure she didn't, though. Well, as I told you, when I asked Christie what she thought was the matter, she said she thought she had the flu. I'd told the doctor this.'

Dolores stubbed out her cigarette then said, 'And then what happened?'

'I gave Janice Christie's keys and she left. She didn't want to be away from the house in case the hospital phoned. She promised to let me know if she needed anything. It was a very difficult time for her.'

'Did you see her the next day?'

'Yes. She came round about one o'clock. She'd just been to the hospital. Apparently Christie was much worse. She'd stopped passing urine and was bringing up blood in her vomit. They'd also given her an electrocardiogram — I think that's the word — you know, to monitor the heart's action. Apparently there was some kind of blockage in the heart. As Janice wanted to be near the phone we went next door to Christie's. And we hadn't been there an hour when the hospital's on the phone, asking her to go in. She asked me to go with her. When we arrived we were met by a doctor who said Christie's condition had deteriorated even more. Janice went in with him to see Christie while I waited. She wasn't in there long, and she came out in floods of tears. Minutes afterwards there was panic — people rushing in with all this equipment. Turned out that Christie's heart had given out. We sat there while they tried to revive her. But it was no good. In the end they came and told Janice they'd done everything they could but that it — it was all over.'

Nobody spoke for a while. There was the

shine of tears in Dolores's eyes, and when she spoke her voice sounded careful, as if she was making a conscious effort to keep it steady. 'It must have been an awful time for you, Celia,' she said. 'But how fortunate for Janice that you were there. That's something you can be glad of.'

'I am,' Celia said. 'I wasn't able to do much, but as you say, just being there at that time did help her in a way.' She gave a sad little shrug. 'Besides, Christie was my friend and anything I could have done for her I would have done.'

Addie became aware that they had left behind the relative rural appearance of the landscape beside the motorway, and were now driving on the hideously unattractive A40. The White City and Shepherds Bush areas of London were not so far ahead.

Dolores, glancing at Celia's reflection in her driving mirror, said, 'Celia, how was it they found that Christie had taken poison? Do you know?'

'I only know what I learned at the inquest,' Celia said. 'Hearing the doctor's report on the post-mortem. There was a lot of medical jargon talked, and it wasn't always easy to keep up with it. But what I gathered was that it wasn't *absolutely* certain that she'd taken the poison, but that it was *very likely*.'

'How could they not be sure?'

'Don't ask me. You'd have to talk to an expert.'

They were driving on the flyover at White City now and Celia told Dolores that if possible she'd like to be dropped off at Shepherds Bush, from where she could get a tube to Belsize Park. After they had traversed the huge roundabout near the green, Dolores drew to a halt at the roadside. As Celia got out, Addie remarked to Dolores that she herself might as well get out also and catch a tube. Dolores, who was at this point so close to her home, didn't need any persuading, and when she and Celia had said their goodbyes she told Addie she'd call her soon, and set off again in the direction of Hammersmith.

Addie and Celia made their way to a pedestrian crossing and from there over to the far side of the green where the two tube stations were situated, one at either end. Addie would be catching a train on the Hammersmith and City Line at one station, and Celia on the Central Line from the other.

As they walked side by side, Celia said, 'There are other things about Christie's death that don't go along with the suicide idea at all.'

'What are they?' Addie asked.

'Well, for a start — why would she poison herself in that way when she had sleeping tablets available? She had a bottle full of them right next to her bed when she was lying there so ill. It seems to me that *that's* the way she'd have chosen. That would have made sense. Not the other. It's not only that, though.'

'Oh?'

'Well, if she actually *did* take the poison, then I must have been with her round about the time she took it. And I've racked my brains to try and remember some clue that would point to her being — well — suicidal, but there was nothing. In fact, she seemed to be feeling better on that day, the last day I saw her before her illness. I remember her saying something to the effect that things were looking up.'

'Really?'

'Yes — if I remember correctly she'd just been invited to some fashion thing. And she gave me to understand that there was the chance of a good job at the end of it. She was quite excited. I know because she got me to post her letter of acceptance. It was the second time they'd written to her, so they were obviously keen.'

They had reached the pavement and come to a halt facing the pedestrians' light. When it turned green they crossed over onto the other side. Standing there while the traffic roared past, Celia dipped into her bag and brought out a notebook and pen. Quickly she wrote on a page and handed it to Addie. 'My address and phone. If you're ever round my way it would be lovely to see you. I mean that.'

'Same here,' Addie said, and from her bag took out a card which she put into Celia's hand.

Celia glanced at it and put it into her bag. 'I suppose the thing to do now,' she said, 'is try to put all this sad business behind us.'

'Yes.'

Celia frowned. 'Why would a woman who's looking forward to getting a new job go and eat those berries? She wouldn't. I don't believe it for a moment.' She paused. 'And where would she get them from, anyway?'

7

The lingering melancholy of the funeral remained with Addie on her arrival at Reading, and rather than go straight home she decided to go and call on Charlie at Adanco's company offices which were situated not far away on the outskirts of the town. It wasn't yet six; there was no way he'd have finished work for the day.

She reached the small office block in a fairly short time, parked in the lot — there was no sign of Charlie's BMW — and went inside. The offices were not large, comprising, apart from the usual facilities, just three rooms. As Addie entered the foyer, its appearance took her by surprise; it was so much smarter and more elegant than when she had visited last, and she realized that it must have been over three years since she had set foot in the place. There was no one at the reception desk — the receptionist, Joanna, would have gone home by now — but the door to an office on the right opened and Marion, Charlie's personal assistant, appeared. A tall, motherly woman in her late forties, she greeted Addie with a warm smile, adding that Charlie had gone to see a printer in Slough, and would be back shortly. 'Why don't you wait for him in his office,' she said. 'I'll bring you a cup of tea.'

Addie thanked her, opened the door to Charlie's office, and went in. Like the foyer, its appearance surprised her. The last time she had been there it had had an almost seedy appearance — not improved on since the time of her father who had justified its lack of elegance on the grounds that no clients ever visited, all business meetings being held at other venues. Things were different now. It was elegantly furnished, the floor tastefully carpeted, and its pale coffee-coloured walls hung with pictures, two or three being her own paintings, and others being designs of the boards used in some of Adanco's games.

On the desk, apart from the usual office paraphernalia there were several photographs. One was of herself, in earlier, happier days. The others were of Robbie. One showed him as a baby in his crib; another showed him sitting in a tall-backed armchair, and a third showed him holding a brightly coloured ball, his head thrown back and laughing as if just having heard the greatest joke ever told.

'There you are, Addie.'

Marion had knocked and entered without Addie being really aware, and a cup and saucer were placed on the desk before her. Addie thanked her. Was there anything else she could get? Marion asked. Addie shook her head, no, thank you. 'I can't get over the look of this place,' she said. 'It's so different.'

Marion glanced around with an air of pride. 'A sign of progress, we hope.'

Addie nodded, aware with a little stab of guilt that she knew little of the details of such progress. She had chosen not to involve herself, leaving it all to Charlie.

There came the sound of a door opening, and Marion said, 'There's Charlie now. Excuse me,' and left the room. Seconds later Charlie was coming through the door. 'Well,' he said, 'this is a surprise.'

'I got back to the station and thought I'd come and check up on you.'

'There's thoughtful.' He looked at her with narrowed eyes, and his amused glance softened. Putting a couple of fingertips gently under her chin he said, 'No smile? Come on. You know what they say: smile and the world smiles with you.'

'Yes, sure.'

'Was the funeral distressing?'

'What you'd expect.' She shrugged. 'I don't know — I just wanted to see you.'

He gave a sympathetic nod. 'Listen, give me five minutes to clear up a few things and then we'll go. I'll follow you home. We'll go out to eat, shall we?'

★ ★ ★

99

Later, they set off from home in Charlie's car for a restaurant in Pangbourne. There, at a table next to a window, they ordered aperitifs and made their choices from the menu.

'So,' Charlie said when the drinks had been brought, 'tell me about your day.'

Over the course of the meal she told him of the funeral, of Christie's friend, Celia, and of what she had said during the journey back to London.

'And?' Charlie said. 'D'you think Christie did it — took her own life?'

She sighed. 'God, I don't know. On the one hand she was depressed over her goddaughter's death and the failure of her own career, but at the same time she left no note. What's more she told Celia she thought she had the flu. And I'm sure you don't say that if you've just intentionally swallowed poison. Also, Celia said Christie was going after a new job and was feeling quite positive.' She paused. 'But they brought in an open verdict . . .'

'Well, you'd have to do that if there's the slightest doubt. You wouldn't want to stigmatize somebody — which a verdict of suicide would have done. In my opinion all her behaviour points away from suicide.' He frowned. 'You said just now that at the

100

inquest it was said that she *probably* died of ricin poisoning.'

'That's what Celia said.'

'Well, it sounds to me as if nobody was very sure about anything.'

When they had finished eating, the waiter served the decaffinated coffee they had ordered.

As they drank, Addie said, 'Another thing — why would anybody choose such a means of suicide?'

'Yes,' Charlie said, 'it seems to have been a very unpleasant death. You say Christie lingered in great discomfort — not to say agony — for three or four days. You wouldn't choose to put yourself through that, would you?'

'But perhaps she wouldn't have known how it would affect her. She might never have guessed it would be that bad.'

'But you wouldn't take the chance, would you? Not when there are tried and tested means at hand. It seems to me that if you're so desperate that you decide to end it, then you'd take the handiest and surest means available.'

'Who's to say the ricin seeds *weren't* handy?'

'Maybe they were — but they weren't necessarily the *surest* means, were they?

You'd never heard of such a poison, had you? You had to look it up. How many people know about it? I should think not many. Surely you wouldn't go and take some relatively obscure poison. You'd take one you knew about. Or use some other means. Which is why people jump off buildings, and swallow huge doses of sleeping pills or breathe in the exhaust fumes from their cars.'

'You're right,' Addie said. 'You don't swallow poison if you don't know whether it'll kill you quickly and painlessly, or slowly and agonizingly. And according to Celia, Christie had more than enough sleeping tablets to do the job.'

'Well, there you are.' He reached out, touched her hand. 'Anyway, it's over.

She gave a melancholy little sigh. 'Yes, it's over.'

★ ★ ★

On Sunday, just after 12.15, they set off for Lydia's. The day was fine with barely a breeze to stir the foliage. Their journey taking them through attractive villages set in the Berkshire and Oxfordshire countryside, they eventually reached their destination, Heronbrook, a small village on a river near

102

the town of Wallingford and the eastern edge of the Chiltern hills.

Lydia's home was a spacious, sprawling dwelling set on the south side of the village. Charlie drove through the gateway onto the gravelled forecourt, circled the monkey-puzzle tree in its centre, and parked beside a black Fiat Uno that stood in the shade of the house's Virginia creeper-decked walls. As he turned off the motor, Addie saw the front door open and Lydia appear, one hand pushing back her black hair. Charlie took the keys from the ignition and murmured *sotto voce*, barely moving his lips, 'Just grin and bear it, that's all you can do. And keep her sweet.'

'Of course,' Addie replied. 'I'd be terrified to try anything else.' Unbuckling her seat belt she flashed Lydia a smile while Charlie opened the door and got out. Together they crunched over the gravel to where Lydia stood in the doorway.

'We expected you a little earlier,' Lydia said, directing her words to Charlie. 'But you're here at last.' She leaned forward and gave Addie a peck on the cheek. 'Good to see you, Addie. How *are* you?' Her tone was expansive, her eyebrows expressive. It was as if she was determined to make it clear that *she* cared and, more to the point, understood, where others might not. Looking to be somewhere in her late thirties, she was two or three inches taller than Addie and attractive in a no-nonsense kind of way: little or no make-up, and her hair in the very simplest style — parted in the centre and cut just above her collar, a fringe low over wide brown eyes and spectacles. She had on a white blouse and blue jeans, her feet in sandals, and wore no jewellery other than a wedding ring, and small diamond studs in her ears.

Walking behind her, Charlie and Addie stepped through onto the old flags. When Charlie had closed the front door behind them, he and Addie followed in Lydia's brisk steps. 'We're in the kitchen,' Lydia threw back over her shoulder, 'so come and get a drink. Adam's upstairs. He'll be down in a minute.' She laughed. 'Or he will be if he knows what's good for him.' Behind her back, Charlie and Addie exchanged glances, Charlie briefly pulling down the corners of his mouth.

Entering the kitchen they found Peter Lavell drying glasses. Lydia introduced him and Addie to one another. He wore a short-sleeved check shirt and jeans; he was in his early forties, tall, broad-shouldered and rangy, with thinning brown hair.

'You timed that well,' he said. 'I'm just opening up the bar. What'll it be?'

Addie said she'd have white wine, and Charlie that he'd have a Scotch and soda — though a weak one, as he was driving. Addie observed Peter as he poured the drinks. She had learned that he lived in the Oxfordshire village of Buscot, midway between Lydia's home and hers and Charlie's. He was principally a painter, working a good deal in the field of portraiture. His partnership with Lydia, according to Charlie, was little more than a sideline, his contribution being principally in the design concepts of Lydia's games. To Addie, his laid-back warmth seemed at odds with Lydia's keen, almost aggressive efficiency, and she wondered how well the new partnership was working. By all accounts, Lydia was not the easiest person to get on with.

Footsteps sounded in the hall, and the next moment Adam, Lydia's husband, entered the room. He was a grey-haired, hard-bodied, fit-looking man in his late forties. The very active director of a small computer production company, his work took him travelling over the country. Wearing crisp, washed-out jeans, a white shirt and trainers, he came forward, kissed Addie on the cheek and shook Charlie's hand. Asked by Peter what he'd like to drink he said he'd have a beer.

When Peter had finished pouring the drinks — along with gin and tonics for Lydia and himself — they took their glasses out onto the patio and settled on seats in the shade, looking over the lawn. In a nearby yew tree, missel-thrushes gorged on the red berries, while in a central flowerbed a blackbird searched for food, flicking aside the dead leaves that lay scattered about the stems of tall daisies.

Wasting no time, Lydia spoke of her new game. Called *Hurricane*, it was based on just that phenomenon. It was a game of luck and strategy, placing competing players in varying degrees of peril. With roads and bridges on the game board becoming blocked or collapsing, the object of the game was to escape to safety with the minimum material loss and the maximum safety. The game's putative excitement was added to by the use of moving parts, so that model trees and buildings fell under the force of the 'wind'. Enthusiastically Lydia suggested that they test the game under play once they had eaten.

Lunch was served soon afterwards, and as they ate, Addie began to relax. The food was good, and the conversation light and generally interesting. Charlie cracked a couple of rather risqué jokes, and Adam responded with one of his own. Peter was surprising, Addie found; in his quiet way he came over as a much stronger personality than she had previously guessed. He was certainly very different from Adam, who was more extrovert and vocal. By the time Lydia came to serve the dessert — a summer pudding and lemon sorbet — Addie had relaxed to a degree greater than she would lately have dreamed possible. Her only moment of relative uncertainty came when Lydia made reference to her recent visit to London.

'Charlie told me you're going to start painting again,' Lydia said to her. 'Said you'd gone up to London to take in a few galleries. Get a little inspiration.'

'Well, that was the general intention,' Addie said. 'Or something like that.'

'And did you get it?'

'Get what?'

'Your inspiration.'

It was amazing, Addie thought, how trivial and ludicrous Lydia could make the enterprise sound. But maybe it was. Addie didn't know how to answer. What was there to say? What should have been a relaxed, productive day, with her spending quiet hours looking at paintings, had turned into something quite different.

'I didn't know you painted,' Peter said, also seeming anxious to retrieve the previous calm.

'I don't,' Addie said. 'Not any more.'

'Oh, shame,' Peter said; then, 'Did you study?'

'At Chelsea for my diploma, then a year at Birmingham doing teacher-training.'

'*You* studied at Birmingham, Peter, didn't you?' Adam said.

Peter nodded. 'I did the whole thing there. My diploma *and* my teacher-training. When were you there, Addie?'

She didn't want to get into this, but she muttered an answer.

'I did my teacher-training the year after you,' Peter said, smiling. 'Though as you can see, I was obviously a late starter.'

'Listen,' Charlie said, 'why don't we get the game out? Give it a run. Then we can relax.'

Lydia said, 'Yes, let's do that,' and rose to her feet. 'Peter'll set it up while I make the coffee.'

'I'll give you a hand,' Adam said, getting up beside her.

He and Lydia collected the dishes and cutlery and left for the kitchen, while Peter went off to fetch the board game. He came back with it a few minutes later and unfolded the board and began to set out the various pieces. As he finished, Adam entered with a tray laden with cups and saucers, cream and sugar. Seeing the board laid out, he said to Peter, 'Did you bring your new design — the one you've been working on?'

'No, I'm afraid I forgot.'

'Ah, shame.' Adam set down the tray and turned to Charlie. 'You'd have found it very interesting.'

Lydia came in carrying the full cafetiere. Picking up on Adam's words, she said, 'Charlie would have found what interesting? What are you talking about?'

'My new rough design for the game,' Peter said.

'Didn't you bring it?' She set down the cafetiere. 'I expected you would.'

'I meant to.' He turned to Charlie, grinning. 'I'm in trouble now. I'll get it to you. I'll send you a laser copy. But don't expect too much; as I say, it's only rough.'

'Still,' Charlie said, 'I'd like to see it.'

'And so you shall,' Lydia said. She sat down and looked over the pieces of the game.

Addie asked of no one in particular, 'Do you need me for this? You don't, do you? You don't need more than four.'

Charlie frowned, disapproving. 'Do you want to do something else?'

'I thought I might go outside for a little walk,' she said. 'Get some air.'

'I think it would be nice if you stayed,' he said. 'Why don't you stay and join in?'

'Don't press her,' Lydia said, then added, smiling at Addie, 'I shan't take offence, believe me. And besides, it's a lovely day for a walk.' Turning her glance to the men, she added, 'We can manage — the four of us.'

Charlie nodded. 'Fine.' Then, to Addie, obviously regretting the pressure he had applied, 'Yes, you go on, darling. We'll manage all right.'

Addie got to her feet. 'Right, I'll see you in a while.'

'Don't you want coffee first?' Lydia asked.

'No, thank you. Maybe I'll have some when I come back.'

She left the room, went through the kitchen and let herself out onto the patio, hovered on the flags for a moment, then set off across the grass. Reaching the gate she passed through and started along the tree-shaded way of the narrow little public footpath that ran beside the garden.

Once, when she, Charlie and Robbie had come visiting, she and Robbie had walked along this same path. A memory that she could not avoid. But you couldn't do that anyway — go through life dodging the cues for painful recollections, like would-be attackers lying in wait. Sooner or later they were bound to get you.

She walked on, and suddenly, suddenly there was Robbie ahead, staring in at the trees on the right, at the same time putting a finger to his lips in a bid for care and silence. And as she draws level she sees that the focus of his attention is a little bird's nest, held in the fork of a hawthorn. She nods at him, one finger to her own lips in acknowledgement of his warning, and together, on tiptoe, they walk on . . .

After a time the path led to the end of the copse, and then along beside the river where, here and there, anglers sat over their rods and lines. It was so peaceful, and for some moments she stood on the high bank in the silence looking out over the steadily moving water. Then, turning, leaving the riverbank, she followed another path that led over a stile into a meadow where cows lay in the grass. And in her imagination

111

Robbie was still with her, never content to walk at a steady pace, but forever dashing away for some reason or other and often — so it seemed to her — for no reason at all. There was not a ditch that he did not feel compelled to jump, no fallen log that could be passed but must instead be climbed and walked upon. As she walked he was with her everywhere.

★ ★ ★

As she entered the house she could hear the murmur of voices. They were still in the dining-room. She paused, listening. They were discussing Adanco's games. She stood there for a few moments, then moved quietly away, not wanting to join them yet. From the sitting-room she opened a door and found herself in the conservatory. Turning in a full circle she saw growing all about her a great variety of exotic plants. Of all shapes and hues, some were short and dwarf-like, while others towered above her head. All of them looked quite unfamiliar. She didn't linger; the heat was so strong, and the strange mingled scents were over-poweringly unpleasant. Turning, she went out again. Back in the sitting-room she sat down on the sofa. Her feet felt hot and tight after the

112

walk, and she slipped off her shoes. Leaning back against the soft cushions, she closed her eyes.

She was awakened by Lydia's voice.

'Oh, you're *back*.'

Opening her eyes she saw Lydia standing in the doorway. She pulled herself up, trying to look alert.

'We didn't hear you come in,' Lydia added. 'What did you do — creep in quietly?'

'What? No, of course not.' Addie could hear the defensive note behind her words, and she thrust it away. 'I didn't want to disturb you,' she said.

'I'm just making some fresh coffee. You want to come and join us?'

'Yes.' Addie put her shoes back on. 'I'll give you a hand.' She got up and followed Lydia into the kitchen. 'How did the game go? All right?' She tried to sound relaxed.

'Oh, it went very well. I thought so, anyway. Now I've got to persuade Charlie that he needs it.' When the coffee was made Lydia led the way into the dining-room. 'Here she is,' she announced, glancing back at Addie. 'Crept in while we weren't looking.' Addie wanted to protest, *I didn't creep in; it wasn't like that*, but said nothing, only sat down, returning the smiles that Peter and Adam turned to her, and then asking as she looked about her, 'Where's Charlie?'

Lydia replied that he had gone to the bathroom, then went on, 'We've been discussing the finished artwork for some of the games, the artwork that will be based on Peter's designs. I was just saying that I think Charlie, should start using some different talent.'

'Like who?' Peter said.

Lydia shrugged. 'Well, if it were up to me I'd go for somebody like Harry Comrie.'

Hearing the name, Addie sat up straighter in her chair.

'Harry Comrie,' Peter said. 'One hell of a talent.'

'Yes,' Lydia said, 'I think Charlie should try getting somebody like him, if it's possible.'

'He must charge a fortune,' said Peter. 'Though it wouldn't hurt to find out if he's available.'

'What are you talking about?' said Lydia. 'I didn't say *try to get Harry Comrie*, I said try to get somebody *like* him. It's obvious you haven't read the papers.'

'Read the papers?' Peter said. 'Why?'

'Harry Comrie. The piece about him — in this morning's *Times*.' Lydia gave a nod in the direction of the sitting-room. 'A small article on him. The poor guy's dead.'

8

That night in bed, Addie sat propped up against the pillows, an open book before her. She had read the same paragraph three times without taking anything in. Looking at the bedside clock she saw that it was just on 11.25. Charlie was still downstairs. He would be in soon to say goodnight. She felt disorientated, unsure not only of herself but of everything around her.

A few moments after Lydia had delivered the blow about Harry, Addie had excused herself and gone into the sitting-room where that day's papers lay on the coffee table. It had taken some minutes, but eventually she had found the article she sought. The death of a children's book illustrator would not usually have rated a mention in a national newspaper; Harry, however, had been set a little apart as he had just been awarded a prestigious prize for his work.

As she had sat there over the newspaper, she had heard footsteps and, turning, had seen Adam approaching. He came around the coffee table and sat on the sofa facing her. His expression looked concerned. 'Are you all right, Addie?' he said.

She nodded. 'Yes, I'm fine.'

'I thought you looked a bit — shocked,' he said. 'Back there, when Lydia mentioned the death of that artist, Harry Comrie.' He put his head a little on one side, studying her. His eyes were pale blue; the uniform grey of his hair made him appear older than his years. 'You were, weren't you?' he added.

There was no point in denying it. 'Yes.' she said; and then, 'He was a good friend of mine. We were at university together.'

He gave a little shake of his head. 'Oh, I'm so sorry. And with Lydia blurting it out like that.'

'She wasn't to know.'

'No, but — oh, I am sorry.'

Addie shrugged, forced a smile and nodded down at the paper. 'I wanted to see what it said about him. There's a bit about his work, and that he died in hospital after a brief illness.'

'How old was he?'

'Thirty-five.'

Adam sighed. 'It's a bloody shame. A young guy, with all that talent.' He reached out and briefly laid a hand on her wrist. 'You sure you're all right?'

'What? Oh, yes, I'm fine. It was just — like

116

you said — something of a shock.'

'OK.' He got to his feet. 'Listen, I won't mention anything in there right now, otherwise they'll all start making a fuss. It'll keep till you've gone.'

He had left her then, going back into the dining-room. When she herself had gone in a minute or so later she found that Charlie had returned to the table. Soon afterwards, they had set off back for home.

Now into her thoughts came the sound of Charlie's soft foot-falls on the landing, bringing her gaze towards the doorway as he appeared there.

'Still awake,' he observed as he came in. 'I thought you might be asleep.'

'It's only just half-past eleven.'

'Still, you've had a long day.' He sat on the edge of the bed and took her hand. 'You've been quiet ever since we left. Is something the matter?'

She hesitated before answering. 'While you were out of the room at Lydia's, I found out that an old friend of mine had died.'

He frowned. 'Really? Who?'

'Harry Comrie.'

'The illustrator? He was a friend of yours?'

'Yes.'

'When I went back in, Lydia mentioned him — and that he'd died. But I had no idea you knew him.' He looked at her more closely. 'Are you saying that he — he was *that* Harry? One of your friends at Birmingham?'

'Yes.'

'When you spoke of *Harry* on the odd occasion I never knew he was that one — the illustrator. Not that you ever talk about that time, anyway. And when you do you only ever speak of your friends by their first names. They could be anybody.'

'Well,' she said, 'it was the Harry I knew.'

'How did he die?'

'The paper didn't say.' She paused. 'First Kieron, then Christie and now Harry. After Ruby's death there were seven of us — and now of those seven, three have died in the space of weeks.'

He frowned. 'What are you saying?'

'It's some coincidence, isn't it?'

'Addie, I don't know what you're getting at, but, well, Kieron died of natural causes, Christie died of eating poisoned berries — either intentionally or by accident — and Harry? Well, you just said you don't know what caused his death.'

'No, but . . . '

'Don't start tormenting yourself without reason. There's enough to think about

118

without looking for problems.'

She wanted to believe that he was right, that she was seeing phantoms where none existed. It wasn't so easy.

'Come on, Ads,' he said. 'Don't dwell on it. Please don't.'

She gave a little nod. 'No, I mustn't. I won't.' Abruptly changing the subject, she said, 'What did you think of Lydia's game?'

He gave a little groan.

'Like that, huh?'

'There's nothing new there, I'm afraid. It's just a variation on a hundred others.'

'So you won't be offering a licence on it?'

'I doubt it. I can't see it going anywhere. It wouldn't take off.'

'Does she know how you feel?'

'No, I told her it's something I'll have to consider. She wasn't that pleased, I could tell. Obviously she was hoping I'd leap at it.' He shook his head. 'She's come up with some brilliant things in the past, but not for a while, I'm afraid. Which is a shame, as I think she needs the money. They both do.'

'Oh?'

'Going by a couple of things that were said while you were out. I don't think Adam's business is doing that well lately. Too much competition.'

'Shame.'

'That's life.' He got up and leant down, bending his face to her. 'You sleep well now, you hear?'

'Yes.' And *On the mouth*, she wanted to say as his kiss came to her. But his lips only rested briefly on her cheek.

'Goodnight, Ads.' He moved towards the door, and a moment later he had gone and she was left looking at the space that he had so recently occupied, at the same time her fingertips touching her cheek where his lips had brushed.

If it was a matter of fault, she reasoned, then the fault was hers. All the way. He had had too much to cope with. After Robbie's death she had wanted nothing of any intimacy. Then, just when she had set about mending the situation, he had contracted mumps. With his illness he had moved into the guest room — and had remained there after his recovery, making the room his own. Lately she had dropped the odd hint that he might move back into the main bedroom, but he hadn't picked it up. Now she was beginning to fear that if they didn't get back together soon they never would.

She was beginning to feel sleepy now. She put aside her book, straightened her pillows, switched off the lamp, then lay down and closed her eyes.

When she slept she dreamed of Harry. He was there in the house, in her work-room painting a picture. But when she looked closer he was not holding a paintbrush but a little white porcelain bust of Tchaikovsky.

* * *

After Charlie had left for work the next morning she took the newspaper and opened it to the obituary page. There was nothing on Harry. Though it was probably too soon; if he *did* rate an obituary they were probably still gathering information for it.

And Charlie was right; she mustn't dwell on Harry's death — she must get on with her life. She had said she wanted to get back to her painting, and this she must do.

Leaving the breakfast dishes for Carole to deal with, she made herself a mug of coffee and carried it into her work-room.

Her easel, unused for so long, stood there still, just as she had left it at the time of Robbie's death.

And what should she paint? After so long it would be almost like starting from scratch. From a shelf she took down the sketchbook she had last used, and began to leaf through it, looking at the varied images — some the very roughest sketches and others more developed — searching for something she could take as a subject or at least a jumping-off point. She had to make a start. She must. For one thing there was the possibility of the baby — and if she was to be seriously considered as a potential adoptive mother then she must present the best possible front.

When she heard Carole arrive an hour later, she was still sitting there, the opened sketchbook before her. Putting it aside, she went into the kitchen where Carole was loading the dishwasher. A single mother in her late thirties, Carole lived in Pangbourne with her eight-year-old daughter Trudy. Deserted by her husband for a younger woman, she seemed to have resigned herself to a man-less future. Not, she had remarked to Addie, that she thought she was missing anything.

Addie stayed chatting to her for a few minutes then returned to her studio where once more she tried to make some headway. She got nowhere, though, and eventually she gave up, turned her back on the easel and went from the room. Carole was upstairs now, making the beds. 'Carole, I'm going out,' Addie called to her. 'Lock up if I'm not back.' Picking up her keys and a pair of secateurs, she left the house and moved to one of the herbaceous plots where she cut half-a-dozen perfect yellow roses. That done, she set off to drive the short distance to the cemetery.

At Robbie's grave she sat down on the cropped grass, her knees drawn up, held by her encircling arms. It came on to rain after a while, but she remained, numb and unseeing, while the raindrops darkened the soil and turned Robbie's stone a darker shade of grey. As it increased in strength it plastered her hair to her head and ran down beneath the collar of her blouse. There was no discomfort.

The rain continued as she drove back, but was lessening as she pulled into the drive. It was almost two o'clock. Carole would have long gone. As Addie turned the corner at the rear of the building she saw a black Fiat Uno parked on the gravel. It looked familiar, but she couldn't think of the setting in which she had seen it. Then as she pulled to a halt, a figure emerged around the corner of the kitchen wall, and she saw Peter Lavell coming towards her.

As she got out of the car she was aware

of how she must look with her wet hair and clothes. 'Well, hi,' she smiled, trying to sound at case. 'Charlie's not here. He'll be at the office.'

'It doesn't matter; I was passing so I thought I'd drop in the photocopies of my designs.' He held up a large brown envelope. 'Saved putting them in the post. When you arrived I was just trying to find a spot where I could leave them out of the rain.'

She took the envelope from him. She would see that Charlie got it on his return, she said. They stood facing one another on the wet gravel. 'Well — ' she added, smiling, self-conscious, 'come on in for a minute.' She unlocked the rear door. 'Would you like some tea?'

'That would be nice, but I don't want to hold you up.'

She shot him a glance, as if to ask, *what is there to hold up?* and led the way inside. As he closed the door behind them she caught her reflection in the mirror by the coat rack. She looked like a crazy woman. Her hair stuck out at all angles, while one wing of the collar of her blouse was folded inward. She gave a nervous little laugh that held a faint, distant ring of hysteria. 'I'm afraid I got caught in the rain.'

In the sitting-room he sat on the sofa. He

wore corduroy trousers and a coarse-weave shirt. He was not handsome; his nose was too large and his chin too small. Nevertheless, it wasn't an unattractive face. Laying the envelope on the coffee-table she went into the kitchen and put on the kettle. Then she hurried upstairs and changed her blouse and dried and brushed her hair. Back downstairs she made the tea, put biscuits on a plate and carried the loaded tray into the sitting-room. As she entered he looked at her over the top of the newspaper that she had left there.

'I was looking to see if there was an obituary on the artist, Harry Comrie.'

'It's a little early, I guess,' she said. She poured the tea and handed him a cup.

'They had a bit on him in my paper,' he said. 'Apparently he spent a year at Birmingham University. That would probably have been about the same time that we were there, you and I. He paused, then added, 'After you and Charlie left yesterday, Adam mentioned that you and Harry Comrie had been friends.'

'That's right,' she said, 'we were.'

'I wondered why you went out of the room as you did. It must have been quite a jolt for you — hearing that. Although, of course, there's no good way of getting bad news, is there? Whichever way you learn it, it's going to be a shock.'

'Yes.' She turned to the window and saw that the sky had grown darker. Low clouds were moving on the wind. Suddenly there came a flurry of raindrops against the window pane.

Peter said, 'You'd have been at Birmingham the same year that that girl died — were you? Ruby Burnham.'

' — Yes.'

He nodded. 'You were based in the department at Edgbaston, right?'

'That's right.' Her tone didn't encourage conversation on the subject.

'I was in the *town*, at the art school. But of course we heard all about it.'

'I should think everybody did.'

'You'd have known Christie Harding too — the fashion designer who died recently.'

' — That's right.'

He shook his head. 'That was very sad, wasn't it? And then the question over her death — whether it might have been suicide. It also seemed quite a — bizarre business. If she did do it, I mean. Poison herself like that.'

'Yes.'

Silence fell between them. the only sound that of the rain on the window. He put down

126

his cup and saucer and got to his feet. 'I'd better be off,' he said. 'I've already taken up enough of your time — without bringing up depressing matters.'

'It's all right.' She noticed that there was a paint stain on the cuff of his denim shirt. His eyes behind the metal-rimmed spectacles were grey.

He smiled at her. 'Well, I thank you for the tea.'

'Thank you for bringing the photocopies. Charlie'll appreciate it.'

He left then, and she watched through the rain-streaked window as his car turned out of sight on the short drive leading to the road.

★ ★ ★

When Charlie had left for the office next day, Addie went through the morning paper. It carried a brief obituary for Harry, giving the salient details of his career and listing his achievements. There was no mention of his having left a wife or children.

Later she went into her studio. Carole wasn't due in today so there would be no interruptions and no excuse for not working. In a search for ideas she once more sat going through her old sketchbooks, and afterwards through a folder of photographs she had built up over the years — not just pictures she had taken but also many that had come from other sources — newspapers and magazines. Nothing of it worked, however; nothing gave the slightest sense of excitement; produced the wish to begin a new picture. To add to her difficulties, she found it impossible to give the problem her full attention, for images of Kieron and Christie and Harry would appear in her brain, swimming in and out of focus, a barrier to concentration on anything else. After a while she turned from her easel and left the room.

* * *

The days that followed went by with an equal lack of productivity, each one passing with nothing to set it apart from the next — the only difference being on Wednesday when Carole was back and provided company of a kind for a few hours. As for Charlie, Addie saw little of him; he was off early in the mornings, and back late in the evenings. His trip to Hong Kong was only days away, and all his efforts were going into preparing for it. Left to her own devices, Addie found herself moving from one inconsequential diversion to the next, while always at the back of her mind were the deaths of her former friends. She was unable to see their deaths as nothing more than bizarre coincidences. She felt she needed someone who would understand. Charlie and Dolores were the obvious ones, but neither was available. With so many pressures already upon Charlie, Addie feared he would have neither the time nor the mental energy to give, and when she dialled Dolores's number she got no response but a recorded greeting on her answer-machine.

On Saturday morning, Addie visited the cemetery to lay fresh flowers on Robbie's grave, and back at the house once more made a half-hearted attempt to do something about her painting. But it was no more than lip-service to effort, and after a few minutes she left her work-room knowing she wouldn't return to it that day.

As she sat in the kitchen over a cup of tea, a thought took hold in her mind, and rising, she went up the stairs to the guest bedroom where she opened a tall, narrow cupboard and took from it a step-ladder. After positioning it, she climbed it to a hatch in the ceiling, pushed up the trap-door, and hoisted herself up through the aperture into the attic. There she tugged on the light-switch cord, and with the space lit by the single bulb that hung in the centre, stood up and looked around her.

It had been years since she had been up here. She was surrounded by small items of discarded furniture, and boxes holding accumulations of junk. Some of the things had been stored there since before she and Charlie had come to the house. So much of it was quite useless now. On a box of books to her right stood a glass dome containing two small, stuffed brown birds, still clinging to a petrified twig, their spread wings with their dry, dead feathers looking as if they had never been capable of flight. Nearby lay a box with a glass lid revealing a collection of butterflies. Everything lay under a coating of dust.

Her eyes roamed over the various items until they came to rest on a cardboard box, which she knew at once by the sticker that she had left on the side, a round disc with a black-and-white drawing of the Beatles. Picking it up, she placed it under the light on the seat of an old bentwood chair. After lifting out a collection of folders and other items from her student days, she came upon a photograph album. She took it up and turned the leaves, watching the images go past. It was what she had been searching for. Closing the album, she moved to the hatch and climbed back down.

After dusting the album and washing her grimy hands, she went into the sitting-room, sat on the sofa and opened the album again. And there they were, the familiar photographs: pictures of her standing beside her easel in a cavernous studio (how young she looked!), pictures of her sitting with other students, pictures from holidays and weekends; her whole life from those times was laid out before her.

She was still there half an hour later when the telephone rang. The sound, erupting into the silence of the room, made her start. As she took up the receiver she saw that it was just after four o'clock.

'Addie?' the woman's voice said, 'Is that you? It's Dolores.'

'*Dolores.*'

'Am I calling at a bad time? Are you in the middle of something?'

'No. Oh, I'm so glad to hear from you. I've been trying to call you.'

'I haven't been home for a few days. I'm at my sister's in Bristol.' A brief pause, then she said, 'Addie, I've just been reading about Harry Comrie. Did you know about him?'

'Yes. I saw it in the papers.'

'I didn't even know he'd died till I picked up a paper and saw a report on the inquest into his death.'

'There's been an inquest?'

'It was on Thursday, and I —'

Addie interrupted: 'Dolores, did they say what he died from?'

'No, they didn't. The inquest was adjourned — apparently for tests to be made.'

'Tests?'

'Yes.' A pause. 'What did you think? When you read about Harry's death?'

Addie gave a worried little shake of her head. 'It — oh, it's just so sad, Dolores. It's such a dreadful thing.'

'It's terrible, but I'm not phoning to commiserate and say how tragic it all is. I don't mind telling you that I'm *worried*. It was one thing with Christie going. But then you told me about Kieron. And now Harry's gone as well. I don't know what's happening, but three friends dying within weeks of each other can't be put down to coincidence. Even though one of them dies from supposed natural causes.'

She meant Kieron, of course. Though she knew nothing of the suspicion that had surrounded his death. And now Harry had died, and tests were to be carried out to determine the cause of his death.

'Are you saying that maybe there's something behind these deaths?' It was what Addie had been afraid to face.

'I don't know, but — oh, it's just too *weird*. Addie, we've got to meet.'

'Yes.' Addie's thoughts were spinning. 'Charlie'll be away next week so — '

'Next week?' Dolores cut in. 'Addie, I mean like *soon*. I mean like *tomorrow*.'

'Tomorrow?' That would be Charlie's last day before he left for Hong Kong.

'You think this is something that can wait?' Dolores said.

'What? No. Of course not.'

'I'll see you tomorrow, then,' Dolores said. 'I'll leave after lunch, so I should think I'll be with you around four.'

★ ★ ★

Dolores arrived just on 4.15 the next day. Hearing the sound of her car on the gravel, Addie went out to greet her.

'Is Charlie in?' Dolores asked, as she followed Addie inside. She wore her beige slacks and light jacket and blouse with the kind of careless air that Addie recognized from long ago. Now, though, the effect was very different.

'No, he's working right now. Last-minute stuff before he goes off tomorrow.'

Dolores smiled wryly. 'I'll bet he was thrilled to hear I was on the way.'

'He's fine about it.' Addie closed the front door, her averted face hiding the lie. When she had told Charlie of Dolores's planned visit he had groaned, saying, 'Does that mean she's going to be here for dinner?'

'Oh, Charlie,' she had protested, 'don't say it like that.'

'Have you forgotten I'm going off first thing Monday morning? I was expecting us to have the evening on our own.'

'I'm sorry, but this — this is really important.'

'What's so important that it couldn't wait a few days?'

When she didn't answer he added, 'Is this about what I think it is? Your friends who've died?' He gave a nod. 'Well, OK. Whatever'll put your mind at rest.'

Now, with Dolores following, Addie led the way to the kitchen where she filled the kettle. Dolores took out her cigarettes. 'Dare I ask whether Charlie smokes?'

'Sometimes. Go ahead.' She set down an ashtray and Dolores lit a cigarette. When the tea was poured the two women sat on stools, facing one another across the kitchen counter. 'Well,' Dolores said, 'what the hell do we do?'

'Are you sure there's something we *should* be doing?'

Dolores frowned. 'I don't get you.'

'Well,' Addie said hopefully, 'perhaps there's nothing to it all — this business.' It was what she hoped for, would keep on hoping for.

'Oh, Addie,' Dolores said, 'I know how you feel. And I wish I could believe there's no cause for alarm. But I can't. And neither can you. Whoever thinks there's no connection has to be out of their mind. It's not just two people any more, now it's Harry as well.'

'I know, but — but Christie's death was quite a different thing. She died from *ricin* poisoning which she might or might not have brought about herself.'

'Listen, I don't pretend to know what's happening, or how. I just know that something is. Haven't you thought about all this?'

'Yes. Of course I have.'

Dolores stubbed out her cigarette. 'Have you talked to Charlie about it?'

'A little. But he doesn't see anything sinister in it.'

'Well, in that case he doesn't know what happened, does he?'

'You mean? OK that. No. He knows about Ruby's death, but not what happened afterwards.'

'Don't you think it's about time he did?'

'This isn't the time. He's got enough on his plate. His work takes up every minute. He's leaving for Hong Kong in the morning.'

'What's he going there for?'

'The company has component parts made over there. He has to go to see the manufacturers. He'll be gone for days. I can't load this onto him as well.' She put her hands up to the sides of her face. 'Oh, Dolores, I — I just don't want to think about this. It was eleven years ago, and as far as I'm concerned, it's finished.'

'But it isn't, is it?'

Addie shook her head. 'This whole thing's getting like some awful nightmare.'

Dolores pressed Addie's hand. 'Come on, don't let it get to you.'

Addie lowered her eyes, for the moment not trusting herself to speak. Dolores watched her in silence for some moments, then said, 'If we're right — and I'm certain we are — then we know what this is all about.' She waited till Addie nodded in response, then went on, 'So we'd better try to decide what to do. For a start I think Charlie ought to know the full story. Then I think we should go to the police.'

9

When the telephone rang a few minutes later it was Charlie, saying he would be working late and would snatch a bite when he could. In the meantime, Addie and Dolores should have dinner without him. He'd be back as soon as he was able.

After Addie had hung up, she said to Dolores, 'You're right, of course. I've got to tell Charlie. I should have done it years ago.' She got up and left the room and came back carrying the photograph album which she opened and laid on the counter in front of Dolores. 'Remember this?'

'Oh, my *God* . . . ' Dolores stared down at the photograph. 'I'd forgotten all about it. I used to have a copy once.'

'I think we all did, didn't we?'

'God knows what happened to mine. Look at us, we were so young.'

Addie smiled. 'We were.'

Dolores groaned. 'And I was so *fat*. When I look at me there I can see why I haven't got the picture any more. I probably threw it away.'

They shared a light dinner of cold cuts and salad, followed by fresh fruit, and with it drank chardonnay. Charlie arrived back at 8.45, and came into the dining-room where the two women were just finishing their meal. After Addie had made the introductions he excused himself and went upstairs to shower and change.

As the sound of his shoes faded in the hall, Dolores murmured, 'God knows what he's expecting. That I'm some nutter from your past who's simply here to drive you to distraction.'

When Charlie came back down a while later they moved to the sitting-room where he poured more wine for the two women and a Scotch and soda for himself. That done, he sat in his favourite chair by the fireplace. 'Well, cheers.' After taking a drink he added, 'Dolores, you're the first of Addie's old friends I've had the pleasure of meeting.'

'This isn't the first time,' Dolores reminded him. 'We met a few years back.'

' — Ah, yes, so we did.'

'In Earls Court — and which meeting was obviously unforgettable.'

He smiled politely, and the conversation limped along, until eventually he said, 'Well, is somebody going to tell me what's up, or have I got to stay in suspense all night? You're fretting about the death of your friend Harry, aren't you? That's understandable, but I don't think you should read anything sinister into it.'

'But he was the third one, Charlie,' Addie said. 'You know that.'

'Besides,' said Dolores, 'according to what Addie tells me, you don't know the whole story — of what happened in Birmingham.'

'What? I don't know *any* story.' To Addie: 'All I know from the bits you've told me over the years is that there was a bunch of seven or eight of you who — '

'Eight,' said Dolores.

'Right, eight friends who went everywhere together — and that Christie Harding was one of them. And Kieron too, and the illustrator, Harry Comrie. Is that right?'

'Yes,' Addie said.

'And I know that one of the girls — Ruth — was killed during your time there.'

'Ruby,' Dolores said. 'Ruby Burnham. Yes, she died during our year there. Just a few weeks before the final term ended.'

'She went over the balcony, isn't that right?'

Addie winced. 'Yes.'

'But why are you raking this up now?'

139

Charlie said. 'That was years ago.'

'Eleven years,' Dolores said.

'It was a terrible tragedy, a young girl dying like that, but accidents happen.' He took a swallow from his glass. 'How did it come to happen, exactly?'

'We don't know,' Dolores said. 'As far as we know, nobody saw anything.'

'I don't get it,' Charlie said, then, focusing on Addie, 'For God's sake, you're going on as if someone's accused you of causing her death.' His laugh died as he took in the look on her face. 'I'm sorry — was that in bad taste?'

'It's not that,' Dolores said, 'it's just that you're pretty near the truth.'

'Look,' he said, 'I don't know what's going on, but one of you had better tell me or we shall be here all night — and I've got to make an early start.'

Addie got up, picked up the album and laid it open across his lap. As he looked at the photograph she watched his face for signs of recognition. The picture showed four young men and three young women in various casual attitudes in front of a rather battered Ford Escort. Their youthful, bright smiles beamed out. Behind the Escort was a Renault 5.

'There's you, Ads,' he said. 'God, you look so young.'

'I *was* young.'

'And there's Kieron.' He sighed. 'So this is your group from Birmingham.'

'Well, seven of us.' Addie pointed, her fingertip hovering over the figure of a young woman who stood leaning against the Escort's bonnet. She had a mop of red hair, and wore blue jeans and a white sweater. 'That's Christie.'

Charlie peered closer. 'Yes, I recognize her from her picture in the paper. Who's this next to her?' He raised his head and looked at Dolores.

'The pudding on the right?' Dolores said. 'Yes, you got it in one.'

Charlie's mouth moved in a smile. 'Well, I must say you've changed a bit.'

'I thank you for that,' she said.

He went back to the picture. 'And this big fellow with his hand on your shoulder?' This was to Addie.

'That's Ambrose.'

'Ambrose? Is he the one who had the bust of Tchaikovsky?'

'No, that was Harry.' She pointed to Harry with his plain features. 'Ambrose went in for old records. Music from the thirties, forties and fifties; that was his thing.'

'And the handsome guy on the left?'

'Matt,' Addie said shortly, and then, 'I

141

wanted you to see us — as we were.'

'You said there were eight of you. Who's missing?' A nod of realization and he said, 'Oh, yes, Ruth — Ruby — she's not here.'

'She was taking the photograph,' Addie said. 'Kieron gave us copies of that photograph — and others, on the evening Ruby died.'

He looked at the picture a moment longer, then closed the album. 'Go on.'

'It didn't start well,' Addie said, 'but no one could have imagined that anything so awful would happen. We weren't all getting on as brilliantly as we had been. Everybody knew that. I mean, for one thing, there was friction between Christie and Ruby over something or other.'

'Something or other?' Dolores said with a little snort. 'Matt and Christie had been having a fling. I was living in the same flat as Christie and you couldn't miss it. But then Matt dumped her for Ruby. That's why Christie was pissed off with her.' She looked at Addie for confirmation, but Addie said nothing. 'Anyway,' Dolores went on, 'as I say, Matt dumped Christie for Ruby, and then in turn got dumped. Much to Christie's pleasure, I'm sure — though I think he was quite affected by it.' She turned to Addie. 'Wouldn't you say so?'

Addie gave a shrug. 'I wouldn't know.'

'Oh, yes, he'd been so keen. Buying her ear-rings, perfume. Making a complete idiot of himself, you knew it was all going to end in tears. Ruby wasn't the type to get pinned down.' She frowned, thinking back. 'Usually at weekends most of us went home to our families after Friday's classes, but this particular Friday we were all going to be there, so somebody came up with the suggestion that we should get together. It would be about the last opportunity with the end of the year coming up. So, we agreed to meet, have a Chinese takeaway, a few bottles of wine and watch a couple of videos. Try to have a relaxing evening. Though one or two needed some persuading.'

She paused as she stubbed out her cigarette then went on, 'You could soon see it wasn't going to be any smash hit as far as social occasions went. But it didn't start too badly — on the surface, anyway. We all met in the flat shared by Christie and me. Well, it was a decent-sized pad and wasn't too difficult to get to. I had one bedroom — quite a small one — and Christie had the other. Hers was much larger — she got first choice, of course — as she usually did.'

'I had a room on the floor above,' Addie

said. 'Ruby had a nice place, but it wasn't that handy.'

'And what happened?' Charlie asked.

'Well,' Addie said, 'there was a good bit of coming and going between the eight of us. Ambrose went off to pick up our take-away and Matt and Harry went off to get the drink, and Kieron went to pick up the videos. For most of the time before they came back I was with Dolores in her room — doing her hair.'

'That's right,' Dolores said. 'Christie was having a bath — and taking three days over it, as usual. Ruby went out onto the balcony — in a bit of a sulk, or to get away from people. It was like Waterloo Station — everybody in and out of the place, and nobody knowing where anybody else was at any particular time.'

Addie said, 'Then when everybody was back and we were ready to eat somebody asked where Ruby was. Nobody knew, so we carried on without her.'

'Yes,' Dolores said, 'but that was after Matt had gone storming out in a rage, wasn't it? Over something Christie said.'

'Right,' Addie nodded. 'And after we'd eaten I went out onto the balcony to throw out some scraps, and I looked over and — and there she was.'

'It was you who found her,' Charlie said.

'Yes.'

'You never told me,' he said. 'That must have been the most terrible shock.'

'It was.'

Dolores said, 'One of the videos had just ended and we were clearing up the plates and things. And then, suddenly, we heard Addie screaming.'

With Dolores's words, Addie raised a hand to her mouth, as if even now she might cry out. Dolores went on, 'We all dashed out onto the balcony and — looked over the rail.'

'What happened then?'

Dolores gave a shake of her head. 'It was chaos. We were like headless chickens. I can remember Christie standing there shrieking, totally helpless. I think a couple of the boys — or maybe all of them — dashed down into the garden. I ran inside and called the ambulance. They said I should call the police too — so I did.'

'And Ruby — she was quite dead, was she?'

Dolores nodded. 'Ambrose came back upstairs as white as a sheet. I asked him, and he said yes, she was dead. Apparently two of the spikes had . . . ' Briefly she closed her eyes, as if the memory was too much to deal with. 'To think,' she added, 'that we were all sitting around eating and drinking and watching the film while all the time she was — was down there.'

'And then,' Charlie said, 'the police and the ambulance came.'

'Yes,' Dolores said. 'They made us stay in the flat. There were people in and out, and going round the garden. Neighbours gawking over. There was nothing to be done for Ruby, of course. The police were taking photographs, measurements, examining everything.'

'And taking statements.'

'I'll say. One after the other they took us into Christie's room and asked us questions. We were up all night. Later we went to the police station to make statements.'

Charlie looked in silence at Dolores for a few seconds longer, then turned to Addie. 'Why did you keep this to yourself all these years?'

'Oh, Charlie,' she said, 'I couldn't bear even to think about it, let alone get into a conversation about it.'

'I know how Addie feels,' Dolores said. 'I had nightmares for ages afterwards. I didn't want to talk about it either. It's not like telling a story and that being the end of it.

You tell something like this and then all the questions come.'

'You either said nothing,' Addie said, 'or you had to say everything.'

'But you're talking about it now,' Charlie said. 'What's changed things?'

There was a moment of silence, broken by the distant, ghostly hoot of an owl. Then Dolores said, 'The inquest was held a few days later, and then adjourned for the police to make more enquiries. They questioned us so much. You'd think, God, how many times can they ask the same questions?'

'Did they suspect that it mightn't have been an accident?'

'Well, they had to examine that possibility. But who knows what they thought? They certainly questioned Matt a lot. I mean, his fling with Ruby just having ended. I think they gave him quite a grilling.'

'But you all had alibis,' Charlie said. 'You were all there in the flat.'

'It's like we said,' Dolores replied, 'everybody was in and out of the place, and nobody could account for other people's movements a hundred per cent.'

Addie said, 'I can vouch for Dolores *for most of the time* — I told you, I was doing her hair. Christie was in the bath — but I couldn't swear to that — and the boys were

147

off out — as far as we knew. At one time I went to get some water from the kitchen, and I glanced out and saw Ruby on the balcony, sitting on the little chair that was kept there.' She shrugged. 'For that short time I didn't have an alibi, I guess.'

Dolores said, 'I was there just before the boys went off to get the wine. I remember Christie going into the bathroom and Ambrose going out onto the balcony to ask Ruby what she wanted from the takeaway. When he came back he got on the phone and a while later he went off. Kieron had already gone to get the videos.'

'I went up to my room when I'd finished Dolores's hair,' Addie said. 'To get a couple of glasses. But I was only gone a few minutes.'

'Could anybody else have come into the flat?' Charlie asked.

Dolores shrugged. 'The downstairs door wasn't locked — the lock wasn't working. And the door to the flat wasn't locked either. With everybody in and out it was just put on the latch. I guess anybody could have walked in.'

Charlie nodded. 'And nobody heard anything?'

'You mean like a cry or something?' said Addie. She shook her head. 'Well, I didn't.

And we had the video on.'

'And before that there was music,' Dolores said. 'Christie's choice. It was a permanent background. And sometimes quite loud. I mean so loud that on one or two occasions the neighbours asked us to turn it down.'

'And what was the outcome of it all?' Charlie asked. 'The inquest verdict. Accident, wasn't it?'

Addie nodded. 'Yes. There was no note, and nobody could think of any reason why Ruby would even consider taking her own life.'

'And no reason anybody would want to harm her.'

'Good God, no.'

Dolores said, 'The police found some cocaine when they searched her room. And for a while I suppose they wondered whether she might have been in some drugs-related disagreement or something. But there was no evidence of anything like that.'

'So,' Addie said, 'they brought in a verdict of accidental death. Which is what we all thought it was, anyway.'

'Did *you*?' Charlie addressed both women.

'Yes,' Addie said. 'Well, *I* certainly did.'

Dolores agreed. 'I had no doubt of it.' She paused. '*Then*.'

'*Then*?' Charlie said. 'You mean now

you think differently? D'you think now that perhaps her death wasn't an accident after all?'

Dolores flicked a glance at Addie, then said, 'It's something we're having to consider. After all this time, we're having to think that, after all, Ruby might have been murdered.'

★ ★ ★

A silence in the room, then Charlie said, looking from one to the other, 'What's led you to that conclusion? And what difference could it make now? Unless you've got some evidence that'll nail the one who was responsible.'

'No,' Addie said, 'it's not that. But certain things happened afterwards.'

'What sort of things?'

'Well, along with the inquest verdict, we assumed that Ruby's death was an accident. But then, just a week later, when the investigations seemed to be finished and we were beginning to relax and look forward to going home, we got some notes. Anonymous notes.'

'*Anonymous* notes? What did they say?'

'As far as I know, they were all identical,' Addie said. 'I didn't keep mine, but I can remember what it said; I read it so many times. It said, 'Ruby's death was not an accident. Nor did she commit suicide. I know who killed her, and in time I shall reveal the culprit's name'.' She glanced across at Dolores for confirmation. 'Yes?'

Dolores nodded. 'That's about it, word for word. I didn't keep mine either. I hung on to it for a few weeks, and then burnt it. I didn't want it around. I just wanted to put the whole thing behind me.'

'And you both got identical notes,' Charlie said.

'We *all* did,' said Dolores. 'All seven of us.'

'And you've no idea who wrote them?'

'No.' Dolores again. 'There was no way of knowing whether it was one of us seven, or somebody outside our little group.'

'Why would you think it might be one of the seven of you? You just said that each one of you got an identical note.'

'Well, if it *was* one of us seven who sent them, and the sender didn't get one himself — then that would be a bit of a giveaway, wouldn't it?'

'Yes, of course. How did you know the others had received identical notes?'

'Well, speaking for myself,' Dolores said, 'it was the first thing I wanted to find out — whether anyone else had got one. So, I

151

started asking questions.'

'Same with me,' Addie said.

'How did you receive the note?' Charlie asked her.

'Through the post,' she said. 'My name and address printed on a label. The label had been done on a computer printer. It was totally anonymous.'

'Like mine,' said Dolores. 'No clue at all as to who'd sent it. The postmark was central Birmingham — so it could have been anyone in the city, and the labels could have been printed on the other side of the world for all we knew.'

'When I got mine,' Addie said, 'I thought it was a direct attack on me, till I found that the others had also received them. Dolores and I got the bus in together that morning — I don't know where Christie was; I think she'd stayed out for the night. But as soon as I could I had to find out whether Dolores had also got a letter.'

Dolores nodded. 'We were both after the same thing. When I saw Addie I could see at once that something was up.' She turned to Addie. 'You were so edgy — which was just the way I felt. Then you said you'd received something in the post that morning and watched me, for my reaction, I guess. And I said yes, I had too. And we compared

152

the notes — and then set about finding out whether anybody else might have got one. It didn't take long to find that each one of us had.'

'And did you think there was any truth in what the notes said?'

'I don't know,' Dolores replied. 'I could never make up my mind. I used to look around, wondering, is there somebody watching me and having a damn good laugh? Everybody seemed totally innocent on the surface. Everybody professed to having got the note through the post that morning. And they probably had. Except maybe one of them had sent the note to himself.'

'Or herself,' Addie said.

'Or herself.'

'And you never,' Charlie said, 'had any suspicions as to who it might be?'

'No,' Dolores said, 'I could never place anyone in the role.'

'Could it have been someone from *outside* your group?'

'There were about forty of us on the course. It could have been any of them.'

'Or,' said Charlie, scepticism clear in his voice, 'it could have been anybody who'd got your addresses, right?'

'You don't sound impressed,' Dolores said. 'D'you perhaps think I'm here on

153

some scaremongering wild goose-chase? I can assure you that this is all very real.'

He nodded. 'Go on.' There was a challenging note in his words. 'OK, so you each got a note saying that Ruby had been murdered. What happened then?'

'Nothing,' Addie said. 'We all went our separate ways, and nothing more was heard about it.'

'So it was all finished with?'

'Well, I don't think you could say that,' Dolores said. 'There was still the fact of the note saying Ruby had been murdered. Though like Addie I wanted to believe it was somebody's idea of a joke. Though, of course, there were times when you had to wonder whether there was any truth in it.'

'And you too, Addie?' Charlie said.

'How could one not?' Addie replied. 'And if there was truth in it, then who was the killer? And if Ruby *was* killed, then it was likely that it was one of us who did it. I know it's possible that someone came in from the street, but it's hardly likely.'

He studied her for a moment. 'And all this had obviously got something to do with the death of your friend Christie, right?'

'Yes. And Kieron and Harry. It's Harry's death coming so soon after Christie's and Kieron's that makes us so unsure.'

'But Kieron died of natural causes,' Charlie said. 'Septicaemia. And Christie swallowed that poison — either accidentally or she committed suicide, and — '

'It was an open verdict,' Dolores broke in.

'All right, it was an open verdict, but some people think she was just given the benefit of the doubt. And now, sadly, your other old friend, Harry Comrie, has died.' He paused. 'But there's nothing suspicious about his death, is there?'

'The jury's still out,' Dolores said. 'Further tests are being made. But he's the third. As far as I'm concerned that's cause enough for suspicion whatever the final verdict. Look, I know how it must sound, but we're convinced that these deaths are connected with Ruby's. Just for the moment go along with us, will you?'

'OK.' He spoke the word on a sigh.

'Well, we believe that the deaths of Christie and Kieron and Harry had nothing to do with any accidents, or suicide, nor to natural causes.'

'You think they were killed.'

'Well, they were all three there on the evening Ruby died. And think about what the note said — that she was murdered, and that in time the killer's name would be revealed.

And suppose she *was* murdered — '

'I know what you're getting at,' Charlie said. 'Suppose Ruby was murdered, and the murderer was one of you other seven. But the inquest says accidental death, so the killer thinks he's got away with it. But then afterwards comes the note saying, Don't think you can relax, because one day I shall spill the beans. Well, the killer's going to be scared, right? He's not safe at all.'

'Right,' Dolores said. 'And?'

'Well, he'd want to shut up the witness who's threatening to tell.'

'But suppose he doesn't know who it was?'

Charlie nodded. 'Then his only answer is to get rid of *all* of you.'

Silence. Addie became aware that night had fallen and that the crescent moon had risen.

After a while Charlie said into the quiet, 'That means that if the killer was somebody outside your little clique then he's got to get all seven. And if the killer is one of your number, then the other six will be on his list.'

'And half of his work is already done,' Dolores said. 'Christie and Harry and Kieron are already dead. That leaves just Addie, Matthew, Ambrose and me.' She paused. 'I know the killer isn't me — and I'm sure it isn't Addie. So if the killer is indeed one of our seven, then either Matt or Ambrose is the one.'

'Never Ambrose,' Addie said emphatically. 'Never him.'

'Whoever,' Dolores said irritably. 'The thing is, we can't sit around and wait to find out which one is left at the end of it all, because by then it'll be too late.'

'Charlie,' Addie said, 'what do we do?'

'I don't think we've got a choice,' Dolores said. 'We go to the police.'

'With what?' said Charlie. 'A bunch of suppositions that won't convince anybody? You need proof.'

'We haven't got any proof,' said Dolores patiently. 'And we can't afford to wait for it to fall into our laps. Christ's sake, we could be dead before that happens.'

10

Dolores had already been shown the room where she would be sleeping, but Addie accompanied her now to see her settled in. It was almost one o'clock. She herself was tired. Stifling a yawn she asked, 'What time d'you want to get up?'

'Say seven-thirty? I must get back home as soon as I can.' Dolores hung her jacket in the wardrobe then turned. 'Christ, Addie, what a weird situation this is.'

Addie nodded. She and Dolores and Charlie had talked for hours, but how far it had got them, she didn't know.

'He's still not convinced,' Dolores said. 'He doesn't really go along with it.'

Addie sighed. 'Well, I must say I hadn't expected him to be quite so sceptical.'

'I think he sees the logic of it, but that's all. It's just too big a step from the idea that such a thing *could* happen, to the belief that it actually *is* happening. And if *he* doesn't believe us, then who will?' Dolores gave a wry smile. 'And it would help if he didn't feel quite so antipathetic towards me.'

'Oh, Dolores, don't.'

'Really, I think that's part of the problem. If he had at least *liked* me — well, I feel sure he'd be more sympathetic to what we've been saying. As it is, I think he regards me as some meddling busybody who's come to stir things up and get you all upset.'

'I'm sure that's not true,' Addie protested, though it was clear that Charlie hadn't gone out of his way to be pleasant to Dolores, and had frequently treated her words with open scepticism. Eventually he had risen, saying that he had to finish his packing and get to bed. Wishing Dolores goodbye, he had added, 'I'll be long gone by the time you get up.' His tone was merely polite.

In the kitchen, he had said to Addie, 'Is it just for tonight she's staying?'

'Of course,' Addie had replied; then, 'Charlie, please, she's my friend.'

'Yes,' he had said, 'and I'm delighted if you have a friend come to stay, but I'd like it to be someone who's not going to fill your head with a lot of nonsense. You've been doing so well lately. The last thing I want is to see you get hung up on some paranoid bloody nightmare.' He wrapped her in his arms. 'Oh, Ads, I don't mean to sound negative. I just can't stand to see you upset. And just think — if you go rushing to the police and get involved in some sensational kind of wild goose-chase — well, how will it look with any child adoption application? Think of that.'

His words left her with nothing to say. He was right, of course he was right.

'Anyway,' he said, 'I must get to bed. I've got to be up before six.'

'D'you have to leave so early?'

159

'I'm driving over to Lydia's before I go to the airport. She's been reworking a couple of components for one of the earlier games, and I've got to pick them up. They should have been ready yesterday, but she got delayed.'

'You'll wake me before you go, won't you?'

'Are you sure you want me to?'

'Of course.'

Now, with Dolores bemoaning Charlie's less than enthusiastic reception of their theory, Addie felt her loyalties torn. Lamely, without conviction, she said, 'He'll come round — in time.'

'Time is something we haven't got on our side.'

'But, don't you think he could be right? That we're reading something into this?'

'Well, you go ahead and think that if it gives you comfort,' Dolores said. 'I don't believe that's the case.' She sighed, turned and glanced at the bed. 'And, now, I'd better get some rest before I pass out.'

For Addie, later, lying in her own bed, some considerable time passed before she eventually drifted off into the oblivion of sleep that she so desperately wanted.

★ ★ ★

She was awakened by Charlie's voice, little more than a whisper, and opened her eyes to see him placing a cup and saucer on her bedside table.

'A cuppa,' he said. 'Though I think the sleep would do you more good.'

'No,' she said, 'I wanted you to wake me.' As she pulled herself up in the bed he adjusted her pillows. He looked very handsome in a light-grey suit, pale-blue shirt and darker blue tie. Addie put up a hand and touched his cufflinks. 'Are you taking your lucky links?' she said. She'd had a pair made for him, small gold replicas of the box designed for one of his first big-selling games.

'Of course,' he said. 'I wouldn't dream of going off without them.'

She took a sip from her cup. The clock radio showed 6.45. 'You've got such a long day ahead,' she said. With the eight hours' time difference he would be arriving in Hong Kong in time for breakfast. 'You're going to be exhausted.'

He shrugged. 'Can't be helped. I'll call you when I get a chance.'

'I wish you weren't going.'

'I did ask you to come with me.'

'Yes, I know.'

'But listen, if you need to get in touch

161

with me urgently, Marion's got a copy of my itinerary. She'll generally know where I'll be when I'm not at the hotel.' He gave her another kiss, this time on the mouth, and then he was straightening, moving away across the room. 'You want a little light?'

'Please.'

As he drew back the curtains the sun came in bright. It was going to be a fine day. In the doorway he stopped and gave her a last smile, and then he turned, closed the door and was gone from her sight.

She switched on the radio, low. Radio Four's *Today* programme was on, with the familiar, comforting voices of two of its regular presenters. She sipped at her tea. After some minutes she heard the sound of the garage door opening and closing, and then Charlie's car moving away until it faded to nothing.

Later, showered and dressed, she went downstairs and into the kitchen where she put on the kettle. As she did so she heard footsteps in the hall and Dolores came in. Addie wished her a good morning and asked how she had slept.

'OK — eventually,' Dolores replied. 'I had a lot going through my mind. Did Charlie leave?'

'A while ago.'

162

Dolores wanted little for breakfast, just coffee, juice and toast. Addie prepared the same for herself. Dolores was ready to leave soon afterwards, and Addie walked outside with her. Beside her car, Dolores turned to her.

'I don't know what to say. Let's just hope Charlie's right, and this has all come from our imaginations. But if he's wrong — well, I don't want to think about that. I still think we should go to the police, but maybe Charlie's right there too — maybe there isn't enough evidence to get them to take us seriously.'

Addie didn't know what to say, and said nothing.

'Anyway,' Dolores said, 'I must get going. You've got my number.' They embraced, then she got into the car and turned on the motor. Addie stepped back to allow the vehicle to reverse, then gave a wave as it moved off down the drive. Just before it vanished from her sight, the postman came into view, cycling up towards her. He came to a stop at her side and wished her a good morning. 'Thoughtful of you,' he said, grinning, handing her the mail, 'to save me getting off me bike.' He was a good-looking young man, not exceptionally bright, but pleasant of manner and anxious

163

to please. Addie thanked him, and he said, 'See you tomorrow,' and pedalled back down the drive.

Addie looked at the envelopes. One was addressed to her, the rest to Charlie. The envelope with her name on it was larger than would be used for an ordinary letter, and bore no sender's name and address. Inserting a fingernail under the flap, she tore it open and drew out a photograph. Measuring about eight by ten inches, it was a copy of the photograph that she had shown Charlie only the evening before.

Standing in the sunlight with the birds singing and the sweet scents rising from the garden, she began to shake. Inside, in the kitchen, she put the other envelopes aside and looked at the photograph. It looked like a laser-copy, and the paper had become creased through its passage in the post. She laid the picture on the counter and sat, mouth dry, looking at it. There they were, in front of the old Escort, all seven of them, just as Ruby had snapped them with Kieron's camera that day. Addie's fear, however, did not spring just from the fact that a copy of the photograph had been sent to her in the post; it stemmed from what had been done to it.

The images of Harry, Kieron and Christie

164

had been treated in the same way. Where there had been smiling faces there were now only round burns.

She got up. If Dolores had delayed her departure by only a minute she'd have been here when the photograph arrived. Now it might be another hour and a half before she reached home and could be contacted. After a brief deliberation she picked up the phone and dialled Lydia's number. A man's voice answered.

'Adam?' she said. 'Is that Adam?'

'No, Adam's not here,' said the man; then, 'Addie, is that you?'

'Peter . . .' she said, now recognizing his voice.

'Addie, hello!'

'Peter, is Charlie there?'

'No, I'm afraid you missed him. Lydia's out too. I believe Adam's off up north somewhere. There's only me. I've just got here.'

Addie made a sound that was half moan, half sob.

'Addie,' Peter said, 'what's the matter? What's wrong?'

She must get herself under control. 'I — I'm all right.' She sat with the telephone pressed to her ear, then Peter's voice came again. 'Addie? Are you still there?'

'What?'

'I'm coming over.'

'No, please — it's all right. Besides, you've got your work to do.'

'It'll keep. I'm leaving right now.'

Forty minutes later he was at the front door, dressed casually in a sweater and jeans. Carole would be coming in any minute. 'Can we go out somewhere?' she said.

'Of course. Let's go and get a cup of coffee.'

* * *

They drove the short distance into the town centre, parked and then walked to a department store with a cafeteria on one of its upper floors. While Peter went to the counter Addie sat at a table. At other tables people sat eating late breakfasts. There seemed to be a preponderance of the elderly. For so many with time on their hands this would be a part of their morning, she surmised; get the bus into town, do a little shopping and meet for coffee or late breakfast in the high street.

Peter appeared carrying a tray. He set down the cups of coffee and sat opposite her. 'So,' he said, 'tell me what's wrong.'

She stirred cream into her coffee. Then, raising her glance to his, she said, 'You

166

remember I told you I was at Birmingham when Ruby Burnham died.'

'Yes.'

'And you'd heard a good bit about it at the time, you said.'

'Well, we read all we could in the papers — naturally. And a lot of stories were going round that were not in the papers. As you know, the artschool building was in the town, miles away from your place, so all our news was secondhand. But there was plenty of it. For a time there was talk of nothing else.'

'There were a few things that I don't think you would have heard about.'

'Oh?'

Her decision was made. Trying to keep the events in chronological order, she told him of her year at Birmingham, of her friends there, and of the fateful evening when Ruby had died. She told of the investigations, and of the anonymous letter each had received saying that Ruby had been murdered and that the sender of the letter would one day reveal the murderer's name. 'Not even the police learned about the letters,' she added. 'We never told them. We'd had enough of it all.' The course had ended, she went on, and they had gone their separate ways. Then, earlier this year Kieron had died, his death attributed to septicaemia. She had never considered that his death might have some sinister significance, but then Christie had died also, her death due to eating poisonous seeds.

She also told of how, on the day she had learned of Christie's death, she had run into Dolores again, and that with Dolores she had gone to Christie's funeral.

'And soon after that,' Peter said, 'Harry Comrie died.'

And following Harry's death, Addie said, Dolores had telephoned to say that she was afraid, believing that all three had been murdered. 'Dolores believed that Kieron didn't die of natural causes, and that Christie didn't administer the poison to herself. She believes also that Harry's death was not a natural one.'

'And the reason,' Peter said, 'is to do with Ruby's death, yes?'

'Yes. Dolores and I, we believe that Ruby must have been murdered — as the letters said. And that the murderer is setting out to get rid of all of us — to make sure of eliminating the one who sent the letters.' A thought occurred to her. 'And there's something else: the murderer could also be afraid that the witness might have told one of the others. So that would be another reason to get us all out of the way.'

'Christ,' Peter said, 'it's bizarre, to say the least. But at the same time it makes sense.' He paused. 'So, what are you doing about it?'

'We don't know what to do. Dolores came over and we told Charlie what we thought was happening. But he's so sceptical. Mind you, we didn't catch him at the best time — not with him all keyed up for going off to Hong Kong this morning. And he didn't take to Dolores, so I think anything she came up with he was going to take with a pinch of salt. Anyway, he thinks the deaths are probably coincidences — *weird* ones, but coincidences nevertheless. He doesn't think it's a good idea going to the police. Thinks they'd laugh us out of the office.' She would say nothing of his comments about the hoped-for adoption. 'Naturally, Dolores wasn't too pleased. I can see her point but at the same time I tell myself that Charlie could be right too. I mean, we live in a real world, and this sort of thing doesn't happen.'

'But it does,' Peter said.

'Yes, I've had that proved to me.' She opened her bag and pulled out the envelope containing the picture. 'The postman came just seconds after Dolores went off this morning. They passed each other on the drive.' She extracted the picture and turned it towards him. 'The postman brought this. Those are my friends from Birmingham. Not Ruby — she was the one taking the photograph.'

He turned the picture further towards him. 'There's you.' He tapped Addie's image. 'Who are the others?'

She named the rest of the group. He nodded, then touched in turn the three of which the faces had been almost obliterated. 'And these are the three who've died?'

'Yes.'

'And you got this in the post this morning? No wonder you panicked. Was there anything with it? Any note or anything?'

'Nothing.'

He took up the envelope and peered at the franked stamp. 'Posted yesterday morning in central London. So it could have been posted by anybody. Though whoever posted it isn't going to give away their geographical position.'

'I guess not.' Addie took a drink from her cup. 'I've got a photo just like this. I only found it again a couple of days ago. Each of us had a print. We'd gone off on a picnic. There were others taken that day, including some with Ruby.'

Peter gazed at the picture in silence for some moments, then said, 'Have you any

170

idea at all as to who might have sent this?'

'No. I've been over and over it, and each one — Ambrose, Dolores, Matt — no, I can't see any of them doing such a thing. It's just inconceivable.'

'Mind you, it could be someone other than a member of your little group.'

'I can't think who.' She looked at his lowered face. 'Why would someone send this to me? You think it could be a — a warning of what's to come?'

'Who can say?' He paused. 'You said that Kieron died of septicaemia. Well, if that's the official medical verdict, who can argue with it?'

'That's what Charlie says.' She took up the picture, slipped it into the envelope and put the whole thing into her bag. She looked around; the place was filling up. 'Can we go? I want to get out of here.'

Peter drove her back to the house and brought the car to a stop near Carole's old Toyota that was parked near the back door. 'Are you going to be OK?' he said.

'Yes, I'll be fine. You've been so kind.'

'I haven't done anything.'

'You listened. And I must have sounded really hysterical.'

'Not without cause. Will you call Charlie later?'

She sighed. 'He'll be up to his eyes in his work. He won't be able to do anything except worry. I'll have to call Dolores, though — let her know about the photograph.' She paused. 'I'm scared, Peter. I'm really scared.'

'I don't think you've got any option but to go to the police.'

'But Charlie says we've got nothing to go on.'

'That was before the picture arrived. And that goes against the notion that Kieron died of blood poisoning and Christie committed suicide.'

She gave a deep sigh. 'Yes, it does. But how can one find out how the poison was administered? How did it get to them? Perhaps if I could find out more about the poison . . . '

'Listen,' Peter said, 'I've got an old friend who was in the Metropolitan Police. It's possible that he might be able to help in some way. At least point you in the right direction. It might be worth a try.'

★ ★ ★

Addie spent much of the rest of the day moving from one chore to another, first working with Carole, and then later on her own; she was anxious only to find a means

172

of passing the time. Just after six o'clock the telephone rang. It was Dolores.

'Addie,' Dolores sounded tense, 'I don't want to upset you, but — I had to let you know.' A brief pause. 'I received a photograph in the post today.'

The news should have come as no surprise. 'Yes,' Addie said, 'a photograph of all seven of us, right?'

'You mean, you got one as well?'

'Yes. With the faces of Christie and Kieron and Harry burnt out.'

'Oh, God. Well, that proves it if nothing else — we were right.'

Addie told then of her meeting with Peter, and of his offer to try to help.

'Great,' Dolores said, 'but what do we do in the meantime?'

'I don't know, except just — just be very careful.'

After Addie had hung up she went into the kitchen and poured a glass of white wine. Then, glass in hand, she went out onto the patio and sat on the bench. The shadows were lengthening on the lawn and a light breeze stirred the leaves of the cherry tree. If only she could forget the events of the day, but they were all too real. If there had been doubt before, then the photograph proved the threat — to herself, to Dolores, and probably

173

to Matt or Ambrose as well. Feeling a sudden chill, she looked up and saw that clouds had obscured the sun. After a few moments she got up and went back inside the house.

As the evening wore on she felt very much on her own. She had been alone in the house before, but tonight it seemed vast, and full of unexplainable and unidentifiable sounds. When the telephone rang close on eleven, she hesitated before picking up the receiver. When she did she heard the reassuring sound of Charlie's voice at the other end of the line.

'Charlie.'

'Addie, are you all right?' Beyond his weariness he sounded concerned.

'Yes. Yes, I'm fine.'

'You don't sound too sure.'

'I'm OK. How was your flight?'

'Tiring, but what you'd expect. I've just this minute arrived at the hotel.'

'What time is it there?'

'Nearly seven in the morning.'

'You must be exhausted.'

'I'm OK. What about you? You didn't sound too brilliant when you answered.'

She hesitated. She didn't want to load him down with her own fears and anxieties. On the other hand, they weren't born of her imagination. 'Something happened,' she

174

said, 'just after you went.'

'What d'you mean, something happened?'

She was committed now. 'In the post, soon after you left — there was something for me. A — a copy of that photograph I showed you. Of the seven of us.'

A little silence, then his voice said quietly, 'Go on.'

'The faces of three of the people,' she said, 'of Christie and Harry and Kieron, had been destroyed. Burnt out.'

'Good God,' he muttered. 'Have you any idea who might have sent it?'

'No.'

'I don't know what to say — except this means that I was absolutely wrong.'

'Dolores got one as well. She phoned and told me so this evening.'

'Listen,' he said, 'I can't get back any sooner than I'd planned, Addie. There are meetings fixed up.'

'Of course not. I know that.'

'I wish I could. I'd like to be with you right now.'

'I'll be fine.'

'I'll call you again when I can. And Addie — I love you, remember that.'

His words remained with her as she went around the house checking on the locks, and later, as she lay alone in bed.

11

'Jack Harrington. Ex-Detective Inspector Jack Harrington,' said Peter. 'He's only recently retired. Apart from being a friend, he's the husband of my sister-in-law.'

'The husband of your sister-in-law,' Addie said. 'I'm working that out.'

'My wife and his wife were sisters.'

'Ah, I see.' She had not heard him speak of his wife before.

It was just after twelve the following day. That morning Peter had telephoned to tell Addie that his ex-police officer friend would be happy to see her, and that he, Peter, would be happy to accompany her to the meeting. Now, in his Fiat, they were heading along the M4 towards London.

'Your wife,' Addie said, 'what was her name?'

'Rachel. She died. You probably already know that.'

'Charlie mentioned it, yes. I'm sorry.'

He gave the briefest nod of acknowledgement. 'Thank you.'

They turned off the main highway at

176

Hammersmith (Dolores came to Addie's mind as they did so) and headed for Putney. Once there, Peter searched around for a parking place and eventually found one in a narrow side street. They were heading for The Golden Cage, a pub situated nearby on the Lower Richmond Road.

When they arrived, Addie sat at a table near the window while Peter got in drinks, a gin and tonic for her and a beer for himself. The taped music with its thudding bass was anathema to Addie, but for now she had to put up with it.

Five minutes later, Jack Harrington walked in. Peter introduced Addie, and then returned to the bar for another beer. Jack sat down facing Addie. He was in his mid-fifties, tall, brown-haired and good-looking. Glancing over at Peter where he stood at the bar, he said, 'One beer and I must make it last. Though not for too long; I've got to be at work in half an hour.' His speech bore an unmistakable Welsh lilt.

'Peter told me you'd retired,' she said.

'I have — from the Force. But my wife runs a charity shop, and I've got roped in to help out. It's less interesting than catching villains, but you meet a better class of person.' He paused. 'Anyway, Pete says you want some information on poisons.'

'Well, yes, if possible.'

'Who are you planning to bump off?' He grinned. 'And let me caution you now.' As Addie laughed he added, 'Pete says you're writing a book.'

'I'm trying to,' she lied. 'A novel. My first.' She and Peter had come up with the idea of a book as they thought it best to make no mention of the deaths of her former friends, or her suspicions. 'I hate to lie to him,' Peter had said, 'but it's the only thing to do at this point. Later on you can tell him the truth.' With this in her mind, Addie now said that she had been considering various poisons. 'And the one I'm hoping to use,' she said, developing her lie, 'is ricin.'

'That'll be something new,' Jack said. 'Make a change from arsenic.'

At this juncture Peter arrived back at the table, set a glass of lager before Jack and sat down.

Jack said, 'Addie was just telling me about a poison she's interested in — ricin.' He turned back to Addie. 'There was a case of ricin poisoning recently. A woman in North London. A fashion designer.'

Addie was unprepared for this. ' — Yes, I read about her. Christie Harding.'

'That's the name.' He took a drink. 'I *might* be able to help you. I can't make any promises, but I happen to know the pathologist who carried out the autopsy.'

'On the woman — Christie Harding.'

'Yes. Dr Mukerjee his name is. Sajit Mukerjee. We worked together on a case just over a year ago. That pop star who died — Alan Midas.'

Peter nodded. 'Drugs overdose, right?'

'Yes. The autopsy found he'd died of a massive heroin overdose.' He shook his head. 'What a way to go. And that's the way they see of improving life. I worked with Dr Mukerjee on that case, trying to find evidence of foul play — there were rumours. Though we found nothing suspicious. Anyway, that's neither here nor there. As I say, he carried out the autopsy on the Harding woman.' He looked at his watch again. 'Look, I'll try and phone Dr Mukerjee and ask him if he'd mind talking to you. He's the one who can give you the information — if he's willing.' He took a small notebook from his pocket. 'I'll try his office. Once he's there he tends to stay all day.' He looked from one to the other. 'Has either of you got a mobile?'

When they replied that they had not, he looked towards the bar. 'They know me here. They'll probably let me use the phone. Cross your fingers.'

Addie watched as he crossed to the bar

179

and engaged the landlord in conversation. Next thing he was going behind the bar and picking up the telephone. Two minutes later he was back at the table. 'You're in luck,' he said. 'You've caught him at a good time. He says he'll be glad to help you as long as it doesn't take all day.'

★ ★ ★

The journey across London was prolonged by one hold-up after another. It was after 3.15 by the time they reached the Hampstead Royal Hospital, and Addie was beginning to fret in case the doctor became too busy to see them. After finding a parking spot they walked the hundred yards to the hospital where they were given directions to the mortuary. There they found the doctor's assistant, a young, white-coated woman, working at a desk. She greeted them with a smile, and when Peter gave their names at once said yes, the doctor was expecting them. She got up, knocked on a door and entered, and a moment later was back, asking them to go in.

Addie had somehow expected the pathologist's office to be a forbidding place, reflecting the unhappy business of examining the dead. It was not so; the room was light and pleasant, with plants at the window, photographs of two small children on the desk, and colourful pictures on the walls. Dr Mukerjee stood up behind his desk as she and Peter entered, shook their hands and urged them to sit. He was Indian, in his fifties, with thick, greying hair and a lean, upright frame. His smile was wide and his manner warm.

'So,' he said, sitting down and leaning back in his chair, 'my old partner in crime Jack Harrington sent you to see me. How's he enjoying his retirement?'

'I don't think he's had much time for it,' Peter said. 'His wife keeps him busy.'

The doctor laughed. 'It happens. He probably told you that we worked on a case together not too long ago.'

'Midas, the rock star,' Peter said. 'Yes, he told us.'

'High profile, but not so interesting; nothing out of the ordinary. Anyway' — and here he turned his attention to Addie, smiling at her — 'You've come here to get a little information. You're writing a book, Jack says.'

'That's right,' Addie replied, while from her bag she took a notepad and ball-point pen. 'D'you mind if I make some notes?'

'I'd expect you to,' he said. 'So, fire away.'

Before getting onto the subject of the

181

poison itself, she had a different matter to clear up. One concerning the question mark over Harry.

'Supposing,' she said, 'there was suspicion over a death, and the inquest was adjourned for further tests to be carried out.'

'It's not uncommon,' the doctor said.

'And what would happen,' Addie said, 'if the tests revealed that, after all, the person had died of natural causes?'

He shrugged. 'Well, the death certificate would be signed and the body released for burial. And unless the case was fairly high profile the general public would probably hear no more about it.'

'I see.'

'Is that it?' He smiled. 'Is that all you wanted to ask me?'

'Oh, no,' she said quickly. 'I wanted to ask you about a specific poison.'

'Ricin, yes? What made you choose that particular poison?'

' — I wanted something a little unusual.' She was lying so easily. 'Something that, as far as I know, hasn't been used to any great extent in fiction before.'

'It's an interesting poison,' the doctor said. 'And its use in Britain is very rare as far as we know — though a good deal of research has been done on it. Probably Jack told you that

I recently dealt with a case of ricin poisoning, did he?'

'Yes,' Addie said; 'the fashion designer, Christie Harding.'

'That *was* an interesting case. Though, as you probably know, unresolved.'

'Yes.'

'There was no verdict that could be brought in other than the one that was delivered. It was my firm belief that the poor woman died of ricin poisoning, but as to how she came to be poisoned I'm afraid we shall probably never know.' He opened his palms. 'There was just no evidence pointing to anything. I understand she'd been going through a bad period in her life, and had been depressed, but on the other hand that wasn't new. She'd been depressed before, and her reduced circumstances hadn't just recently come upon her. And she left no note either. Besides which, I can't imagine anyone taking ricin in an attempt at suicide. In this country it's unknown in that respect.'

'Could you,' said Addie, 'take it and not die?'

'Oh, no, it's a very virulent toxin — one of the most toxic of all natural poisons. For an adult a quarter of a milligram is enough to prove fatal.'

'A quarter of a milligram,' Addie said.

183

'That's such a minute amount.'

'The tiniest pinch. But the effects often don't show up for many hours, and then death doesn't usually occur for several days. It's a very unpleasant way to go. Take my word — there are far easier and less painful ways of ending it all. Which is one reason I couldn't accept that the woman took it intentionally. Besides which, if you do it by means of eating the seeds you'd need nine or ten; only a very small part of the seed is poisonous.'

'Would they be easy to swallow?' Addie said.

'There wouldn't be any point in swallowing them. They're impermeable. They'd just pass straight through you without doing any harm. No, you'd have to chew them — well.' He shook his head. 'That's no scenario for a suicide.'

'What, then,' Peter said, 'would be the alternative — to suicide?'

'Well, I hardly think she could have taken the poison by accident, so the only alternative is that it was given to her by somebody else. But as for that — murder — I understood the investigators could find no evidence. For one thing they could find nobody with a motive. As for the opportunity — well, I wouldn't know about that.' He sighed. 'All very mysterious — and it's left the detectives very unsatisfied. There they were, wanting to clear the whole thing up and they couldn't even make a start. But that's the way it is sometimes.'

Addie glanced at her notes and said, 'You said just now it was your firm belief that the woman died of ricin poisoning.' She paused, frowning. 'What did you mean — your *belief*? I didn't understand that.'

'It was simply that. Some things you just can't be a hundred per cent certain of. Though in this case I'm ninety-nine per cent sure.'

'I still don't understand,' Addie said.

'Are you saying,' Peter asked, 'that it's not that easy to spot?'

'It's very difficult.'

'But you diagnosed it all right.'

'I *believe* I did. But I had an advantage; I'd come across it before. I did my initial training in India, working at a hospital on the outskirts of Bombay. Which is where I first came across cases of poisoning with ricin. Sad to say, it's not so rarely used there. I'm afraid some of my poorer countrymen have used it to kill off their neighbours' cattle. And sometimes their mothers-in-law' — an ironic smile here — 'which some people might regard as more understandable.'

'So,' Addie said, 'having come across cases in India, you were able to spot it here in the case of — in this recent case.'

'That's right. But without my previous experience, I can't guarantee that I'd have diagnosed it. And if another doctor had performed the PM it might possibly have been missed. Not through negligence — I must make that perfectly clear — but simply through the fact that it's not in the experience of British-born doctors, and also, as I said, it's virtually undetectable.'

'Undetectable?' Addie said.

'Oh, yes, I thought I'd made that clear. You see, no traces of the poison remain in the body. The poison's a protein, which breaks down and then — well, there's no trace left. One can only detect it by the symptoms exhibited during the patient's illness, and by the effects that are apparent during an autopsy.'

'And what would they be?'

'The poison affects the walls of the blood vessels, breaking them down, so that haemorrhaging occurs — all over the body. Also the white blood cell count rises very rapidly and very high. The heartbeat increases too.'

'You said a very tiny amount of the poison will prove fatal,' Addie said.

'Yes. You know what it's from, don't you?'

'The castor-oil plant.'

'Right.'

'And would it be difficult to get hold of?'

'Oh, I wouldn't think so. Castor oil is produced in many parts of the world; India, Brazil, Thailand, many African countries. Even in Russia. I think you'd find the plant growing in just about any tropical and sub-tropical region, though it's probably native to Africa and Asia.'

'People take castor oil as a medicine, don't they?'

'Oh, yes, it's beneficial in some circumstances. Not so the cake.'

'The cake?'

'That's the term used for the solid part of the bean's interior once all the oil has been extracted. It's that, the cake, that's deadly.'

'So,' Addie said, 'in my book I'd need to grind it up, the seed, before feeding it to my poor victims.'

He smiled at her words. 'Yes, I should think that would be the way.'

'And there'd be nothing left of it in the body by the time death occurred?'

'Not in my experience. It takes a while before death occurs, so every part of it would have been excreted through the bowel and the bladder. Mind you, as I said, so little of it is needed for a fatal dose.' He spread his hands. 'Look at the Markov case.'

'Markov?' The name meant nothing to Addie.

'Georgi Markov. The poisoned umbrella.'

The Markov case. The poisoned umbrella. Addie had never heard of it. Peter, though, was nodding. He had recognized the name.

'I vaguely remember it,' he said. 'It was famous. A good while ago, though.'

Dr Mukerjee nodded. '1978. And as far as I'm aware it was the first *known* case of ricin poisoning in Britain. It caused quite a stir. And one of the remarkable things — apart from the means used to administer it — is that the poison was held in a tiny, hollow pellet no bigger than the head of a hatpin. That shows how virulent it is.'

'Waterloo Bridge,' Peter said. 'Wasn't he walking over Waterloo Bridge?'

'Waiting at a bus stop at the end of the bridge,' said the doctor. 'I know the case well. I read up some literature on it again the other week when that poor lady, Harding, was brought in. According to Mr Markov, he felt a sharp sting in the back of his thigh, and turned round to see a man bending to pick up an umbrella. The man apologized in a

188

foreign accent, then dashed off and jumped into a taxi.'

'And what had happened?' Addie said.

'The man had injected into Markov's leg this tiny pellet containing the poison. The umbrella had most probably been fitted with some gas-firing mechanism that was strong enough to propel the pellet through Mr Markov's trousers and into his leg.'

'But why would anyone want to hurt him?'

'He had defected from Bulgaria. A dissident. And obviously had powerful enemies. He was a clever man, a playwright, and apparently he'd written a play that caused something of a furore and made his government very angry — to put it mildly. Anyway, it seems that a friend of Markov gave him the tip to get out of the country without delay, and he left that same day, and came to England via Italy. Over here in London he got a job with the BBC World Service — and this job enabled him to continue with his work against the regime. He was a brave man. A very brave man. But then, eventually, it seems, they — whoever *they* were — decided that enough was enough, and they set out to put a stop to it.'

'And they did it with the poisoned pellet,' Addie said.

'Yes. He died four days later.'

'Oh, poor man. Poor man.'

'Indeed, He suffered greatly — as did Miss Harding, I'm sorry to say.'

'They managed to diagnose the poison in the case of Georgi Markov,' Peter said. 'But how was that, if no traces of the poison could be found in his body?'

'Well, you must bear in mind that he'd told the medics at the hospital that he thought an attempt had been made on his life. He told them that he was a dissident and that certain people were out to get him. So the medical team were more vigilant when it came to the autopsy. They actually *looked* for an *unnatural* cause. And they found it. They didn't find any poison, but they found the pellet in his thigh. It was in an experiment with a pig that they concluded that ricin had been the means.'

'They tried the poison out on a pig?' Peter said.

'Yes. Thinking that ricin was the most likely cause, they injected a pig with it and watched the results. The pig's symptoms convinced them that they were right. It died in two days.'

'Sad for the pig,' Peter said.

'Yes, sad for the pig.'

Frowning, Addie said, 'If they hadn't

thought of ricin, then — what do you think they might have concluded?'

'Well, looking just at the symptoms,' the doctor said, 'it might very well have been concluded that death had resulted from PUO. Poisoning of unknown origin. Septicaemia, that is — blood-poisoning.' He nodded. 'In this case, blood-poisoning of unknown origin.'

★ ★ ★

'So,' Addie said as they drove back along the M4, 'ricin poisoning can be diagnosed as septicaemia. I'm certain now that Kieron was murdered — just as Christie was. She didn't take her own life.'

'And what about Harry?'

She sighed. 'Who knows. It's almost two weeks since he died and I've no idea whether there have been any further developments. I rather think not.'

'No, I suppose not. If the further tests came up with a diagnosis of poison we'd probably have read about it by now.'

'Yes. Which makes one wonder what the tests did come up with.' She was silent for a moment, then, 'The thing is, if Christie and Kieron were murdered, then how did it happen? And who did it? The only ones left now are Matt and Ambrose — apart from Dolores and me. I didn't do it, and I'm sure Dolores didn't either. But by the same token I'm equally sure that Ambrose isn't guilty. Matt neither for that matter.' She sighed. 'I can't think of anyone it could be.'

'I wonder,' Peter said, 'if we could find out whether Kieron or Christie — and Harry too for that matter — had visits from anyone from your time at Birmingham.'

Addie considered this. 'I suppose I could ask Milla if Kieron had any particular meetings before he died. But I don't know how I'd find out about Harry. And Christie lived alone, so she could have had any number of visitors that nobody knew about. Though it's possible her neighbour Celia might have seen somebody.'

'There's also the problem posed by the action of the poison,' Peter said. 'Dr Mukerjee said the symptoms don't show until some time after it's been ingested.'

'Right — so a visit at a particular time isn't necessarily going to tell us anything.' She looked at Peter's profile as he gazed at the road ahead. 'After all that — chasing into London, meeting the doctor — are we any closer to finding answers?'

★ ★ ★

With traffic delays it was after six by the time they got back to Liddiston. Addie had invited Peter to stay for dinner, and he had accepted. Indoors, at his request, he was directed to Charlie's bathroom upstairs to take a shower. He could also have a fresh shirt, Addie said, and she took one of Charlie's and laid it on the bed. While Peter was occupied, she set a couple of steaks to defrost, then showered and put on a pair of cream cotton slacks and a pale lemon blouse. Back downstairs she found Peter in the sitting-room, standing at the window. He turned to her as she entered.

'You look nice,' he said. 'Very fresh, very sharp.'

A little self-conscious, she thanked him. 'You too.' It was odd seeing him in Charlie's shirt. And it didn't suit him. The colour blue was all wrong and the cut was unflattering to his long neck.

After drinks on the patio she served dinner in the small dining area just off the sitting-room. Neither wanted dessert after the main course, and she made coffee, which she served in the sitting-room. Darkness was falling now.

'The summer's on its last legs,' Addie

said, looking out at the cherry tree, dark against the sky. 'The nights are beginning to draw in.'

A silence fell. 'Are you all right?' Peter asked into the quiet.

'Since you ask,' she said, 'no, not really. Somebody's wanting to kill me — and I know I must be on the look-out — but I don't know where to look.'

'I don't think you should be alone,' he said. 'Would you like me to stay tonight?'

'I've got to be alone at some time,' she said. Suddenly she began to shake. In an effort to regain control she took up her coffee cup, but her hand shook so that she set the cup down again. 'My God,' she said, with a desperate little laugh, 'what's happening to me?' Peter got up from his chair and moved to her side. She felt his arm come across her back and his hand rest upon her shoulder.

'Tell me what I can do to help,' he said.

She willed herself to be calm. 'I'm sorry. And I was doing so well, I thought.'

'You are. You're doing brilliantly.'

His sympathy almost brought her to tears; she had to struggle to keep them at bay.

'Addie,' he said, 'I can understand what you're going through. Believe me. And God only knows how I'd cope in the same situation.'

'I can't give in,' she said. 'It won't get me anywhere, falling to pieces.' She was very much aware of his arm across her upper back.

'I think you should go to the police,' he said.

'But I still haven't got any evidence. They're just going to look at me as if I'm some mad woman. I can't afford that.'

'What d'you mean — you can't afford it?'

After a moment she said, 'There's a baby — coming up for adoption, and — oh, I so want it. It could be our last chance. So I can't take the risk of even a breath of — of scandal or sensationalism or anything like that — anything that might put them off considering us. Charlie and I could offer a good life to a child, but if I start screaming that I'm being pursued — and with nothing to go on — how's that going to appear? They'll look at me as if I'm demented. We won't even get a chance.'

The ringing of the telephone sounded shrill in the room. As she leaned across to pick up the receiver, Peter got up and moved away, giving her privacy.

'Addie,' came Dolores's voice, 'I've been wondering about you — how you are. I've been out all evening and only just got in.'

'I was going to call you,' said Addie. 'I've been up in London today and I met the doctor who carried out the autopsy on Christie.'

'*What?*' Although the word came as little more than a whisper, there was astonishment in Dolores's tone. 'How did that come about?'

Briefly, Addie told her about Peter introducing her to Jack Harrington, and through him of the meeting with the pathologist. 'And,' she said, 'we were told that the symptoms of ricin poisoning are practically indistinguishable from some kinds of septicaemia.'

There was a little silence at the other end of the line then Dolores said, 'Well, as far as I'm concerned that only leads to one conclusion — that Kieron was poisoned with ricin — just as Christie was.'

'That's what I think. I don't think there's any getting away from it.'

'So — what's the next step?'

'I wish I knew. But I can't sit around. I've got to do something.'

'I know the feeling.'

'Listen,' Addie said, 'I've got Peter here right now, but we can talk again tomorrow if you want.'

'Fine,' Dolores said, then added dryly, 'And if you get any good ideas in the meantime, let me know. I don't mind telling you, I'm getting very jumpy.'

They said their goodbyes. Addie replaced the receiver and turned to see that Peter was standing in front of a small picture beside the fireplace. It was an unfinished oil-painting of Robbie. She moved, came to a stop near his shoulder.

'This is lovely,' he said.

'I did it from a photograph — as you can probably tell. It was the last thing I did or tried to do. I didn't finish it.'

'It's just — beautiful.'

'He was beautiful.'

Peter stood in silence looking at the small boy in the snow. With deft and loving touches of her brush Addie had managed to write in paint the determination in the child's mouth, the slight frown, the winter-reddened cheeks framed by his woollen hat; had so surely caught the angle of his body as he pulled on his toboggan. For all the nature of the subject, however, there was no sentimentality in the picture.

'Why didn't you finish it?' Peter asked.

She shook her head, the gesture saying no, she would never finish it now. He nodded understanding.

'I never had the chance to paint him from life,' she said, adding, smiling, 'He was never still for more than three seconds at a time.'

'We wanted a child,' Peter said after a moment. 'But it just never happened.'

Suddenly, her need to tell was there. 'Well, we had Robbie,' she said. 'And he was all we could ever have wished for.'

Peter reached out, a hand hovering for a moment in the space between them, and then falling back to his side. 'Lydia told me there was an accident.'

She was glad to hear the implied question, the question that was never ever asked, the subject that was never touched upon. Talk about anything, but don't mention Robbie, don't speak of the child. In the end it was almost as if for other people he had never existed.

'Yes, there was an accident,' she said. 'I was driving on the M4, going up to London. Robbie was belted into the back seat. We were in the middle lane when a car pulled out from the inner lane, right in front of us.' All so far on a single breath, it was easier that way. 'I had to brake suddenly. And we were hit from behind. By a lorry. The back of the car was smashed right in. Robbie was killed outright.' With her words she could see him again, as she always could, would. She herself had been half stunned by the impact, but nevertheless she could still see him, belted

198

into his own little seat, but now with the seat at a strange angle, almost upside-down, and thrust forward, rammed up hard against the passenger seat in front. She could see the blood trickling from his mouth. Sometimes she wondered how much of it was real and how much imagined; perhaps now she would never know.

Moments of silence went by. 'I don't think Charlie has ever forgiven me for it,' she said. 'But then I've never forgiven myself either.'

Peter turned and wrapped her in his arms, and she was drawn up to his chest in a rush, smelling the smell of him, his clothes, his skin, the faint scent of sandalwood soap, and she let herself go against his strength. In what seemed to be a continuation of the same movement he was lifting her face and lowering his mouth to hers. She let it happen; it had been so long. And he was kissing her, his mouth pressing on hers, lips parting, tongue moving against her teeth, between them, onto her own tongue.

She let it happen, but then she was drawing back, one hand lifted, fingers over her mouth like a shield. 'Peter . . . ' Her head was turned away, eyes averted. He made no attempt to persist or pursue, but with his hands falling to his sides stood there in awkward silence. After a few moments he gave a sigh and said,

'I think maybe you're right, I guess I ought to get on home.'

12

Addie's sleep that night was troubled by strange dreams. Peter was there beside her in the car on some busy highway, only now she herself was driving. And turning she saw Robbie moving towards her, propelled violently forward from the rear seat. And throughout it Peter behaved as if nothing were happening, sitting calmly looking out through the windscreen. When after a while he turned to her she noticed on his cheek the bite of a small pink scar, and she saw that it was Matt.

Notwithstanding that she had slept badly, she was awake and dressed just after 6.30. Just after ten o'clock Charlie telephoned. It was early evening in Hong Kong, and he had returned to his hotel after visiting a factory in the suburbs. When he asked how Addie was she said she was fine. She mentioned nothing of the trip with Peter to London. When the call had come to an end, she dialled Milla's number at the solicitors' office in Swindon where she worked.

'I was wondering what your plans are for lunch today?' Addie asked when she got through. 'I was thinking of coming over.'

'Oh, that would be lovely!' The pleasure was clear in Milla's voice. 'As a matter of fact I've got the afternoon off. And I've nothing much planned other than to pick up Helen from school later on. Yes, let's have lunch. I get off at one.'

Later, Addie drove to Reading, parked her car and got a train into Swindon, from the station taking a taxi to Milla's office. There she waited in the reception area, and after a while Milla appeared and the two of them left the building.

They went to a restaurant near the Wyvern Theatre, and there were shown to a pleasant table near a window that looked out onto a small courtyard. As they sat down, Addie glanced around at the seemingly carefree patrons eating and drinking and chatting away and was suddenly overcome with doubt, thinking that a quiet meeting at Milla's house would have been more appropriate — but they were here now, and the waiter was handing them menus.

Deciding to pass on aperitifs and just

have wine with their food, they gave their orders. When the waiter had gone, Milla smiled at Addie across the table and said, 'What a good idea this was, and what a nice surprise.'

Addie felt a fraud. She hadn't called Milla out of affection but for an entirely different reason — one which she now realized she had no idea how to broach.

By the time the first course was finished she had still said nothing of her purpose in being there. Instead they had touched on other subjects — Helen's schooling, Charlie's current trip, Milla's work with the law firm. The entrees were served — a pasta dish and side salad for Milla, fish for Addie — and still they spoke of inconsequential things. Even when Milla spoke Kieron's name, Addie could not take her cue and bring up the subject that was foremost on her mind. The time was slipping away.

Then Milla said, 'I think I know what's on your mind, Addie.'

Before Addie, somewhat taken aback, could respond, Milla went on, 'It's the baby, isn't it? I'm afraid I've heard nothing. My friend's spoken of you and Charlie to Susan, and given a very strong recommendation. But she can't do any more right now, so I'm afraid you'll just have to be patient a while longer.'

Addie found herself voicing her thanks. She had frequently wondered about the situation, and while she felt great relief that she and Charlie were still in the running, she nevertheless had to speak of what was now the purpose of her being there. Leaning forward slightly in her chair, she said quietly: 'Milla — you know I love you.'

Milla frowned and smiled, as if to say, What on earth has brought this on? 'Well, yes,' she said, 'and I love you too, Ads.'

'What I mean,' Addie said, 'is that I don't need a reason to come and see you other than affection. You know that.'

'Of course . . . Addie, what are you trying to say?'

Addie took a breath. 'I had a special reason for coming to see you today. But it wasn't about the — the baby — as important as that is.'

At this moment the waiter appeared beside them with their coffee. They waited till he had gone away again, then Milla said to Addie, 'Go on.'

Now there was no going back. Picking up her large embroidered bag that lay propped against the table leg, Addie took from it an envelope, and from the envelope the original photograph of the seven friends. The mutilated copy that had come in the post Milla must never see. Addie glanced briefly at the photograph, then held it out.

Milla took it, looked at it. 'Oh, there's Kieron.' There was the glisten of sudden tears in her eyes, but she blinked it back. 'There's you as well, look.' She gave a little laugh. 'I've never seen this before.'

'I've had it for years. It was taken with Kieron's camera. He gave all of us copies. There were other photos too, taken that day. We were out on a picnic.'

'There must be a copy of it at home somewhere — ' Milla said, 'if I could find it; Kieron had hundreds and hundreds of photos.' She paused. 'Is this for me?'

'I — I'll get you a copy if you'd like one.'

'Oh, I would. Thank you.'

Addie hesitated, then said, 'Do you recognize anybody else in the picture?'

'Well, I met all your group that weekend, didn't I — when I came up to see you?' Milla pointed to the photograph. 'That heavy-set girl there — I remember her.'

'Dolores.'

'Yes. Nice girl. And the big guy with the curly hair. Ambrose. Oh, and here's that very handsome one. I've forgotten his name.'

'Matthew.'

'Yes. According to Kieron, a regular Casanova.' She pointed again. 'And here's the girl who became the designer — Christie Harding. She died recently, I believe.'

'That's right.'

Milla nodded. 'And the fellow with glasses. I remember him — vaguely.'

'Harry Comrie.'

'Uh huh. And where's the other girl? The one who died. Ruby.'

'She was taking the photograph.'

'Ah.'

'You know about her, of course.'

'Oh, yes. Kieron told me all about her death, and the inquest and everything and those anonymous letters you all received afterwards. What a horrible business.'

'Yes, it was.'

In a preoccupied fashion Milla added cream to her coffee, stirred it and took a sip. As she set the cup down again, she said, 'Addie, what's this all about?'

Addie paused, then: 'I was wondering if you knew whether Kieron might have seen any of those people? Over later years, I mean.'

'No. Once he left Birmingham that was it. That whole business was something he wanted to leave behind. He's never seen any of them. Apart from you, of course.'

'None of them ever visited you? Came to the house?'

'Why would they do that?' Milla held out the photograph across the table and Addie took it.

'I just wondered. You're quite sure of it?'

'Absolutely. Certainly not while I was at home, anyway. And if they'd called on him while I was out I'd have heard about it.'

'Did Kieron ever mention running into Ambrose or Matthew . . . ?'

'Not that I recall.'

Seeing Milla frown, Addie said hurriedly, 'Just — just bear with me, will you?' And then: 'Do you recall whether Kieron received any gift through the post just before he was taken ill? Any food or anything?'

'Food through the post? Like some kind of care package? Why in God's name should anyone send him food? Of course not.' Milla stared at her. 'Addie, why don't you get to the point? You said you had a special reason for coming to see me, so please, just tell me what this is all about.'

After a moment Addie said, keeping her voice low, 'I know this'll sound so melodramatic, but . . . ' She paused, dropping her voice even further. 'I think somebody is — is out to kill me.' The words were said; she studied Milla's expression, watching for signs of disbelief. She saw only deep concern.

After a moment or two Milla said, 'Let's pay the bill and go. We can't talk here.' Without waiting for a response, she raised her hand and signalled to the waiter. A few minutes later the two women were emerging onto the sunlit street.

'I've got a while before I pick up Helen,' Milla said. 'Let's go into the park.'

With Milla leading the way, they made their way into some nearby public gardens, and finding a vacant bench, sat down.

'Now,' Milla said, 'tell me what this is about.'

'The thing is,' Addie said, 'it doesn't only involve me.'

For a moment Milla looked back at her without comprehension, then she said, 'Are you saying that this involves Kieron?'

'I'm afraid so.'

While other people chatted on the nearby benches, and small boys sailed their boats on the margins of the pond, Addie told Milla of her conclusions in connection with the death of Christie — that she had been murdered — and then, hesitatingly, of her belief that Kieron also had been killed — and by the same means: poisoning with ricin. At the latter revelation Milla gasped and put a hand to her mouth. Then after a moment she gave a little nod. 'I'm all right. Go on.'

It was possible, Addie went on to say, that Harry might have died from the same cause; there was suspicion over his death, and the results of further investigations had yet to be learned.

The fact that Milla knew about Ruby's death was a help in her acceptance of what Addie had to tell; the knowledge to some degree already preparing her. For one thing she could see the rationale behind the suggested motive. She herself had seen the anonymous letter that Kieron had received.

And then Addie came to the photograph that had come through the post, and here she hesitated again. How could she tell of the mutilation of Kieron's image? She had gone too far to stop now, though, and as gently as she could she told of it. Soft words could not lessen the horror, however, and Milla moaned and closed her eyes. It was this, though, that finally convinced her that Addie was right.

When Addie had finished her story, Milla sat looking dully across the breeze-ruffled water of the pond. Then, with her grief glistening in her eyes, she said,

'Kieron was the best man I ever met. And to have him taken through an illness is bad enough, but to think that he's gone because someone wanted him dead — set out to kill him. How can there be such evil? Somebody took away his life, and that I could never forgive. And then to send you that mutilated photograph. It's as if they're boasting.' She looked down at the handkerchief held in her fingers. 'I suppose in time I'll get used to this — knowledge, but for now I can't take it in. I want to believe that Kieron died as the doctor said he did — of septicaemia.' She raised her head, and the flicker of the smile that touched her lips was bitter. '*That's* what I've been learning to deal with — a *natural* death. But this is something else again.'

Silence between them, and into their little oasis of quiet a small boy came running, another boy dashing in laughing pursuit. For a few moments the two dodged back and forth around the bench on which Addie and Milla sat, and then were off again, tearing away across the grass.

Milla said, 'I don't suppose there's any way that a doctor could confirm that Kieron died of natural causes or from this — this poison.'

Addie shook her head. 'The doctor we spoke to said the poison leaves no trace. We might never have it proved. But for me,

I don't need proof; I'm sure.'

Now, silently, Milla began to weep, the tears coursing down her cheeks. 'I can't take this in,' she said. 'Someone took from me my husband, and from Helen her father. And from Kieron — everything.'

After a while Milla's weeping subsided, and she raised her reddened eyes. 'You need help now for yourself,' she said, 'for your own protection.'

Addie gave a nod. 'Yes.'

'So what are you going to do?'

'I just don't know, but if you can think of anything at all that might give a clue, a hint as to how it all happened . . . '

'*If* it happened,' Milla said. 'The trouble is, I *can't see how* it happened. If Kieron was given that poison, then *how*? And when?'

Addie sighed. 'Apparently one of the things that makes it so difficult to deal with is that there can be quite a while before the really bad symptoms show up. At least ten hours. If it were a case of swallowing it and reacting immediately it would be easy to pinpoint when it was taken, but it doesn't work like that.'

'*If* it was swallowed,' Milla said.

'Well, how else would it be given?'

'You said the journalist was killed by the

poison being injected inside a pellet.'

'Yes. And later the doctors injected a pig with the stuff — not in a pellet, but with a hypodermic. It took a couple of days for the pig to die.'

'It's terrifying,' Milla said. 'It's absolutely frightening.'

'It is. And there's no way you can think of in which Kieron might have come by the stuff? — either by swallowing it, or by getting jabbed with something? Probably just a little jab with something that's coated with it would be enough.' She shook her head. 'I'm grabbing at straws here, Milla.'

'Well, as for being jabbed with something — I don't think for a moment that that happened. He would have mentioned it. Somebody sticks a needle or some other pointed object into you, you're going to notice it.'

'Well, yes, but supposing it's such a tiny little discomfort? You might just brush it aside and forget about it.'

'I suppose so. But it would leave a mark, surely.'

'But if the poison gets in by some other means — a little cut, or a graze — that's not going to cause much concern, is it? Particularly when the symptoms don't show for hours. By then you'd have forgotten about somebody scratching you as you got on a crowded train, or jabbing you with a sharp corner of a briefcase or whatever. I think the doctors only found that Markov had been poisoned because he insisted that it had happened. In normal circumstances you're not going to get a little knock and run to the police saying someone's made an assassination attempt on you.'

'No, of course not. So I suppose, really, there's no way of knowing whether it might have happened to Kieron. Of being absolutely sure.'

Addie said, 'What about his having eaten something?'

'He'd usually take sandwiches — though occasionally he'd go to a café.'

'There again, you can't be sure he didn't eat something that was poisoned.'

'No, but I just don't see how it could happen. If you've got sandwiches in your desk I suppose somebody could tamper with them without you knowing. Or I suppose they could put the stuff in your coffee. But in Kieron's office, with others around, somebody would have noticed a stranger hanging about, behaving suspiciously. In any case, he didn't take sandwiches to work that day — the day he came home feeling ill. I remember at breakfast he said he'd be lunching with a client.'

'Oh?' Addie was at once alert.

'It was a regular client of the company,' Milla said. 'Nobody to be suspicious about. When he got home he told me what he'd eaten. I remember that, because when he felt ill he wondered whether it might have been the food he'd had at lunch. But it was a restaurant he'd used often, and he had his usual dishes.' She gave a little groan. 'Addie, that day is imprinted on my mind. When he got home he was saying he thought he'd picked up a flu virus or stomach bug, or had eaten something that had disagreed with him.'

'And he couldn't account for it any other way?'

'Why would he try? As I said, we thought it was just some bug he'd picked up, and we assumed he'd be over it before long. He was a fit, healthy man, Addie. And he was only just thirty-six.' A pause and then: 'I remember his going into work that day. He was going to pick something up on the way, and he couldn't do it before a particular time, so he was able to have breakfast with Helen and me — and then take her to school, which was usually my job. She liked that. Being out of her usual routine, she saw it as something of a treat.

She adored her father. Of course, as you know, I wasn't working full time then. Anyway, that was the only difference in our day — that Kieron stayed late and took Helen to school. That breakfast was our last meal together; when he got home that evening he had no appetite.' She gave a sad shake of her head. 'It was really nice, our breakfast together that morning. He looked at the paper — which he never usually had time for — and also had a chance to look at the post — which was usually delivered after he'd gone. Yes, and I remember he was very pleased because he got an invitation for us to go to this photographic exhibition. Victorian photography. That was always a passion of his.'

Addie smiled. 'I can remember.'

'Anyway, he and Helen went off in the car, and the next time I saw him was when he came in just after six, saying he felt sick and thought he was running a temperature.' She gave a little shrug. 'The rest you know.'

And suddenly Milla was getting to her feet. 'I must go.' Her words were clipped, controlled. 'I have to pick up Helen from school. I'll drop you at the station on the way.' Even as she spoke she was turning, stepping away.

Addie rose and hurried to catch up with her. When they reached the car, Milla got in and opened the passenger door. Addie got in beside her and Milla drove off without speaking.

At the railway station Milla pulled up, turned and said, 'I don't thank you for what you did today, Addie.'

'No, I'm sure of that. I'm sorry.'

'Though of course I understand why you did it. Knowing your reasons, though, doesn't make it any easier to bear.' Her face was set. 'I thought I was beginning to find some kind of equilibrium. You've really thrown me, I don't mind telling you.'

'Milla, I'm sorry. Truly.'

Milla nodded, gave a sigh and glanced at her watch. 'I must go, or I'll be late.' She looked into Addie's eyes for a moment then raised her arms and wrapped them briefly about her. 'I don't thank you,' she said, 'but I forgive you.'

Addie got out onto the pavement and closed the door. As the car moved off, Addie raised a hand in a melancholy goodbye. She could see Milla's silhouette against the sun-drenched street, and was sure that Milla could see her in her driving mirror, but there came no answering wave.

13

Addie sat on the sofa drinking from a mug of tea. The trip to Swindon had left her feeling drained. It had caused grief to Milla and had yielded nothing in the way of information. She was no richer for the meeting, while Milla was infinitely the poorer.

Rising to her feet, she moved to the French windows that looked over the patio and the lawn. In the falling shadows she could see only shrubbery and tall trees beneath the overcast sky. To right and left her view afforded not even a glimpse of the nearest neighbour's house. She felt isolated and solitary in a way that she never had before. Someone was out there, somewhere, and it was only a matter of time before she was targeted — if she had not been already.

On an impulse she crossed to the telephone and called Dolores's number. It was answered after a few rings, and at once Addie detected a note of wariness in Dolores's voice. When Addie had told of her visit to Milla, and of what had passed between them, Dolores said,

'So where do we go from here? I don't know how to handle this, and I'm not hanging around waiting for somebody to hand me a box of laced chocolates.'

Addie said, 'Maybe I could make some enquiries about Christie. Her friend Celia might know something. She gave me her phone number after the funeral.'

'What about Harry? Has there been any news about the results of those tests?'

'I haven't seen anything. Perhaps we can find out. Though I don't know how. I know hardly anything about him, apart from his work. I know he came from somewhere in Sussex.'

'Yes, he did. Was he married at the time of his death?'

'His obituary made no mention of a wife. But let's take it a step at a time. First I'll call Celia and try to arrange to see her.'

'You don't plan on telling her the reason, do you?'

'No. I'll have to think of something.'

'When were you thinking of going?'

'Tomorrow if possible.'

'I'll come with you. I'm in this as much as you.'

It was not until the evening that Addie got through to Celia. 'Celia,' she said when she heard her voice, 'this is Addie Carmichael.

217

We met the other day after — '

'Addie,' Celia broke in, 'how nice to hear from you.'

'Dolores and I,' Addie said, 'we're going to be in London over the next couple of days and we thought we might drop in and see you.'

'That would be lovely. When were you thinking of?'

'Well — are you available tomorrow?'

'I'll be here from about half-past three onwards. Come any time after that. Come and have a cup of tea.'

Addie thanked her, said they'd be there about four, then hung up and called Dolores. 'Well done,' Dolores said. 'And I think we should try to find out what we can about Harry too. But where to start? I don't suppose it'd be any good asking his publisher where he lived.'

'No,' Addie said, 'they won't give out personal information on him. We could look in the newspapers. They might give some information.'

'How do we do that?'

'Try the British Newspaper Library in north London. I'm told they've got copies of papers going back to the year dot.'

'And what if we do find out where Harry lived — how's that going to help us?'

'He might have family who could tell us something. It won't hurt to try.'

'We can't just go barging in, asking questions.'

'Of course not. But — listen, let's try to find out where he lived, then we'll think of something.'

★ ★ ★

As before, Dolores was waiting in the station bar when Addie arrived at Paddington the next morning, and soon afterwards they were sitting in Dolores's old car heading for Colindale. The journey was tedious but eventually they reached their destination and pulled into a vacant parking space outside the library building.

On entering they were issued temporary passes and then directed up the stairs to the main reading room. There, at adjacent seats at one of the tables, they filled in requisition slips for some of the national tabloids and broadsheets, covering the periods in which Harry's winning of his award and death had taken place. There would be some little wait while the newspapers were located and delivered, so they went downstairs to a small cafeteria where they got coffee from a machine and joined other readers who sat

219

eating and drinking at small tables along the walls. A few younger members of the library staff were there as well, lounging in their chairs with their feet up on the tables in front of them.

Twenty minutes later when Addie and Dolores got back to the reading room, they found waiting for them the broadsheet newspapers they had asked for. A note on Addie's table gave the information that there was a six-month wait for recent tabloid newspapers to be available.

'Do they expect us to wait?' Dolores said dryly.

With the papers divided between them they set to work. It was generally quiet in the spacious room — a quiet broken only by the murmurs and whispers of the researchers and librarians, and, more noticeably, by the men who brought around the trolleys to deliver and collect the huge bound volumes of older newspapers. Addie found herself wincing at the way some of the men handled the volumes, dropping them onto the trolleys and the floor with such resounding, jarring thuds that she could only be surprised that any of the bindings remained intact. Right now, however, she had more important things to think about. Sitting with the unbound newspapers before her, she carefully and methodically began to scan them.

It was a long task, but by the time they finished they had found two references to Harry. In the arts section of one of the Sunday papers Dolores had found a piece in the form of an appreciation which spoke in glowing terms of Harry's work and of the loss that his death spelled to children's book illustration. And then, in one of the colour supplements, Addie found an article that had been published soon after he had won his award. Beside the text it showed a photograph of him and reproductions of two of his illustrations. With the article spread out before them, the two women sat reading it, shoulder to shoulder.

The piece revealed that Harry lived in East Sussex, in the small town of Hailsham. ('Of *course*,' Addie breathed.) His mother, the article said, lived close by. There was no mention of any wife or girl-friend. It stated that he had taught for a couple of years before turning full time to book illustration. The half-page photograph showed him in his studio, sitting beside his drawingboard and looking off at something with a faint, rather uncertain smile on his homely face, as if uncomfortable in the eye of the camera and not sure of what to do with his features. On the wall behind him hung several of his pictures, while a shelf held pots and ornaments — among the latter one or two small pieces of white porcelain which Addie recognized as Parian. On the work surfaces around him were pens and pencils and all the rest of the paraphernalia that went to make up the tools of his creativity.

'He hadn't changed an awful lot, had he?' Dolores observed.

'No, he hadn't,' Addie agreed. A moment, then she added, 'I believe I've got a drawing of him at home somewhere — amongst all my old sketches and things.'

'A drawing? Of Harry?'

'A little sketch I made of him one day when we were in the common room.'

Taking in Harry's half-smile as he looked off out of the picture, Dolores sighed, 'What a bloody tragedy. A lovely guy like that. There's no justice.'

Gathering up their belongings they went outside. In the little parking lot Dolores lit a cigarette and drew on it with obvious pleasure. 'So what's next?' she said. 'We know now where Harry lived, so we'll have to find a way to make contact with his mother. That might not be so easy.'

'We'll think of something,' Addie said. 'We must.'

'Fine.' Dolores nodded. 'Well, let's head

back somewhere more central, shall we? We can have some lunch and then go and see Celia.'

★ ★ ★

In Hampstead they found a small Italian restaurant where they ate pasta and salad and drank a little red wine. There was time to spare afterwards, and they spent it wandering around the shops in and around the High Street. Later, aided by Addie's *A to Z of London* they set off to walk the short distance to Celia's house.

She lived in a rather shabby Edwardian terrace in a dusty street that had seen better days. Standing at the gate of the house, Addie and Dolores looked to the left, to number 17, which once had been Christie's home. In the front garden a FOR SALE sign stood as a sad testament to her passing.

Addie's ring at the doorbell was answered at once, and there was Celia's familiar face before them.

'Hello! Come on in,' she beamed, and stood aside to allow them into the narrow hall. Closing the door she directed them into the sitting-room on their left, and they found themselves in a small room crowded with furniture and bric-a-brac.

'I've put the kettle on,' Celia said, following them in, 'so make yourselves comfortable.' As they sat down on an overstuffed sofa she went away. From a room along the hall they heard the sound of a television and then the faint murmur of Celia's voice. In a few minutes she was back, carrying a tray laden with tea and biscuits. She set it down on a coffee-table, saying, 'I'm childminding today. My neighbour's little girl, Shelley — she's watching a video in the other room. During the holidays she comes in a few afternoons a week while her mother's at work.'

The tea was poured and handed round, and Celia sat in an armchair, sipped from her cup and said: 'I'm so glad you phoned me. I don't get that many visitors.' She paused. 'I do miss Christie, you know.'

'I'm sure,' Addie said sympathetically, then, taking her cue, added, 'We wondered — while we're here . . . ' She dipped into her bag and pulled out an envelope. 'The thing is, we're trying to trace some old friends of Christie's and ours — and we wondered whether you might have seen them visiting at any time . . . ' The photograph she pulled from the envelope was the one she had taken from the album. She moved to Celia's side. 'This picture's eleven years old, and we don't know how much the people have changed — in addition to the fact that they must certainly have aged. Still, there's a chance that you might have seen some of them.'

'I doubt it,' Celia said. She took the photograph and studied it. Bending at her side, Addie said, pointing, 'That's one of the men we're trying to trace. He's named Matthew Dixon. And there's the other — Ambrose. Ambrose Morgenson.'

Celia shook her head. 'No, I can't say I've ever seen them. Though I recognize Christie there, of course.' She smiled at Addie. 'And you.' Her glance settled on the image of Dolores. 'Is this you?' She held up the photograph.

Dolores nodded. *'All of it.* And you *are* allowed to say I've changed.'

Celia laughed, then, more serious again, said, 'Well, it doesn't look as if I can be any help, does it?'

'You're quite sure,' Dolores said, 'that you don't recall seeing either of them here on a visit to Christie?'

'Quite sure.' Celia handed the photograph back to Addie. 'But that doesn't mean anything. We were good friends, but we didn't live in each other's pockets. I respected *her* privacy and she respected mine.'

'And their names mean nothing to you?'

'No, I'm afraid not.'

'Did Christie,' Addie said a trifle tentatively, 'mention going out to dinner or lunch or whatever with anybody just before she was taken ill?'

Celia shook her head, clearly somewhat puzzled at the question. 'No.'

Addie put the photograph back in the envelope and they chatted of other things. After a time there came a sound from the hall, then the door opened and a little girl appeared. She was slightly built, wearing a dark-blue skirt with a pale-blue blouse, and strawberry blonde hair tied back in a ponytail. She looked shyly at the two strangers, then at Celia who looked around at her and smiled. 'Shelley, dear, what's up? Anything wrong?'

'It's the video. It's going funny again.'

'Oh, dear.' Celia got up from her chair. 'We'd better have a look at it.' Murmuring an excuse me to Addie and Dolores she followed the little girl from the room. She was back a few minutes later, and settling in her chair again. 'It's OK now — until it goes again.' She nodded in the direction of the room from which she had just come. 'It was young Shelley who was round at Christie's with Alice that day.'

'Alice?' Addie said.

'Christie's goddaughter. From Derbyshire. Didn't I mention her to you?'

'Oh, yes. You told us she died, and that Christie was very depressed about it.'

'Oh, indeed. Particularly as Alice was taken ill just after she and her mother left.'

Dolores, frowning, said, 'I'm sorry, you've lost me here, Celia . . .'

'I thought I'd told you about her,' Celia said. 'Alice, Christie's goddaughter, was staying with her just before she — Alice, that is — was taken ill and died.'

'She was staying with Christie?'

'Yes, just for a couple of days. Her mother and Christie had been friends for years. I think the mother, Clare, had some business in London. A very nice woman. On the second day of their visit, while the mother was out, Christie invited Shelley round. Company for Alice, you see. They were the same age, and they got on like a house on fire. Oh, they had great fun. Shelley often used to go round to see Christie anyway. Well, Christie'd never married and had no children of her own, and she enjoyed Shelley's visits. I remember that particular day when Shelley was invited round for tea with Alice, and they were dressing up and everything.'

Smiling, Addie said, 'I used to do all that when I was small.'

'Christie had a room full of clothes,' Celia said. 'Well, that was her business, wasn't it? Shelley used to love going round there and dressing up in all the gear. And that's what they did that afternoon.' She gave a little chuckle. 'I saw the two of them. I was in my front room when they came along to the post box on the corner. You should have seen them. They were a real sight! Both of them made up with lipstick and mascara, and in these long frocks and feather boas, and big hats and ear-rings. I went out and got them to pose for a photograph. They looked wonderful, and they really fancied themselves! Then, later that afternoon Alice and her mother set off back for Derbyshire.' She sighed. 'And that's where Alice was taken ill.'

'And . . . she died,' said Dolores.

Celia nodded. 'She became ill later that same day, I believe, and died in hospital two or three days later. Her parents — well, they were destroyed.'

A question was framed on Addie's lips, but before she could ask it, the door opened, and Shelley was there again.

'What is it?' Celia asked. 'Is it flickering again?'

'Yes, it won't stop.'

Celia got up. 'It might be the tape. Let's have a look.' She went out. Shelley looked from Addie to Dolores and said, 'Celia told me you were coming. She said you were friends of Christie's.'

'That's right,' Addie said.

'I knew Christie,' Shelley said. 'She was a friend of mine, too.'

'So I understand.' Addie nodded. 'Celia said you used to visit her.'

'Yes. Sometimes when I came back from school I'd go and stay with her till my mum came to collect me. She used to let me dress up in all her clothes.'

'That must have been a lot of fun,' Dolores said.

'Yes, it was. Alice was there too, one day. She died as well, did you know?'

'Yes,' Addie said. 'That's very sad.'

'Christie had millions of dresses and hats and — oh — everything. She let us put it all on. And her lipsticks and all that, too. And her ear-rings and necklaces. It was terrific. Some of her things were very old.'

'It sounds as if you had a nice time,' Addie said.

'Oh, we did! And when we were dressed up we had some tea and cakes, and then helped Christie do some work.' Chuckling

229

at the memory, she said, 'When we went outside Celia took our photographs. Later on, of course, we took off all the clothes, and I went home, and Alice went off with her mum.' She moved to the piano, reached up and took down a photograph wallet. 'These are the photos Celia took.' From the wallet she took some colour photographs, sorted through them and held two of them out to Addie. 'This is me and Alice.'

Addie looked at the photographs that showed the two small girls standing side by side in Celia's tiny front garden. They were done up to the nines in long dresses, feather boas and large, wide-brimmed, straw hats, Shelley's trimmed with ribbons and artificial fruit, and Alice's with roses and forget-me-nots. They stood with their backs to the fence, a dustbin half in the picture, both smiling at the camera, slightly self-conscious, their heads a little on one side, arms linked.

Addie said, 'They're lovely pictures, Shelley,' and handed them to Dolores. As Dolores looked at them Celia came back into the room. 'I think it's all right now,' she said to Shelley. 'If not we'll just have to try another tape. I've also poured you a Coke,' she added.

Shelley needed no further words, and with a last shy smile, she went from the room. Celia watched her go. Addie and Dolores, exchanging glances to signal that it was time they went, prepared to make their final moves and got up, offering their thanks. As Dolores put the photographs on the coffee-table Celia saw them and said, 'Oh, Shelley's been showing you the photos, has she? She's very proud of them.' She gave a little sigh. 'I had copies sent to Alice's mother. Poor woman. For a little child to die like that, so suddenly and so completely unexpectedly — it's just awful.'

'Yes,' Dolores said. A pause, then she added, 'What did she die of?'

'I was with Christie when she got the news over the phone,' Celia said. 'It was blood-poisoning — or septicaemia as they called it. She was terribly upset.'

★ ★ ★

'I keep thinking of Christie's goddaughter,' Addie said as they walked back to the car, 'dying of blood-poisoning.' It seemed to her that with Celia's news about the death of the little girl, they were further than ever from an answer — for she couldn't escape the belief that in some way the child too was involved. She turned to Dolores. 'Isn't it weird? About that little girl?'

Dolores said a little sharply, not looking at her, 'I don't want to think about it.'

Her tone silenced Addie for a while, and they didn't speak again until they reached the car. There, Addie asked Dolores what her immediate plans were.

Dolores shrugged. 'Drop you at the station so that you can get your train, and then go on back home, I suppose. There's not much choice.'

Addie eyed her closely. 'Are you all right?'

'Yes, I'm fine.' Dolores gave a weary sigh. 'I'm sorry for snapping your head off just now. I'm just getting so jumpy.' A little laugh. 'I've got to get a grip.'

'We'll be all right,' Addie said, with less than certainty in her voice. Then she added: 'Have you got anything arranged for tomorrow?'

'No, not really.'

'Well, why not come back home with me? I could do with company.'

Dolores considered this. 'And Charlie won't be there?'

'No,' Addie smiled. 'Charlie won't be there.'

Dolores gave a sheepish grin. 'I'm sorry, I don't mean to sound like that, but — yes, thank you, I'd like that.'

Once they were out of London, Dolores headed for Reading so that Addie could pick up her car. That accomplished, and with Dolores following, Addie led the way to Liddiston. It was after eight when they got to the house. Inside, Addie ushered Dolores into the sitting-room where she flopped down in a chair and kicked off her shoes. They'd have a drink, Addie said, and then get freshened up.

Over drinks they discussed the situation.

'If we could get to talk to Harry's mother,' Dolores said. 'We might be able to find out something from her.'

Addie agreed. 'Finding her shouldn't be a problem. We know the name of the town, and the name of Comrie is very unusual.'

'Yes, but how do we make contact?'

They sat in silence for a few moments, then Addie straightened in her chair and got up. 'I have an idea.'

She went to her little workroom where, after a minute of rooting in a cupboard, she brought out a large stiff-covered folder. Opened up, it revealed a number of drawings and water-colour sketches. Most were from her student days. A swift sort through them and she stood looking down at her drawing of Harry Comrie. It showed him, full figure, lounging in a chair, reading a book, his left leg hooked over the chair-arm. Behind the round rims of his spectacles his eyes were intent.

Returning to the sitting-room, she opened the folder and laid it on the sofa at Dolores's side. 'I think this could be our answer.'

Dolores looked at the drawing and gave a nod. 'It *is*.'

Addie moved to the chair beside the telephone and called Directory Enquiries. When the operator came on the line, she asked if they had a listing for Comrie in Hailsham, East Sussex. The operator came back saying that there were two listed. Addie noted both numbers.

'There's an H. Comrie and an R. Comrie,' Addie said when she had hung up. 'The H. Comrie is probably Harry's number. No good calling that one. We'll try the other.' Forcing her nerve to the fore, she pressed out the number. It was answered quickly, the voice that of an elderly woman.

'Is this Mrs Comrie?' Addie asked.

'Yes, it is.' The woman's tone was circumspect.

'Oh, Mrs Comrie,' Addie said, 'I hope this isn't an intrusion — and I hope it isn't too late in the evening — but I just wanted to tell you how very sorry I was to read about Harry. I only learned about him a couple of days ago.'

The briefest pause, then, 'Well, thank you very much. That's very kind of you.' Another pause. 'May I ask who's calling?'

'My name is Addie Carmichael. Harry and I were very good friends years ago. We were at Birmingham University together. I was very fond of him, so it was a great shock to read about him in the papers. I do hope you don't mind my phoning you. I got your number from the operator.'

'Not at all. I'm glad to hear from anyone who was a friend of Harry's.' The woman's tone was changing, growing warmer by the word.

'One reason I chose to call you this evening, Mrs Comrie,' Addie said, 'is because I'm hoping to be in your area tomorrow, and I wondered whether, if it's convenient, I might call on you.' She added quickly, 'The thing is, I did a drawing of Harry while we were at university. I've still got it, and I'd like you to have it — if you'd care for it, that is.'

She could hear a little intake of breath, and then the woman said, 'Oh, that is so *kind* of you. So very kind. I'd love to have it — indeed, yes. I'm sorry, what did you say your name was?'

'Carmichael. Addie — that's Adelaide — Carmichael. Though Harry knew me when I was Addie Haroldson.'

'I see. And you say you're going to be in this area tomorrow?'

'Yes, I plan to be. And I was thinking — well, perhaps I could call sometime in the afternoon.'

'That would be fine.' A pause. 'D'you think you might make it fairly *late* in the afternoon?'

'Whatever time suits you.'

'It's just that if you could wait till a little after five, Gerald can be here.'

'Gerald . . . ?'

'Gerald Fraser, Harry's friend. Oh, but you wouldn't have met him, would you? You were before his time.'

Not knowing what to say to this, Addie said, 'Anyway, we can be there after five if you like.'

'That would be lovely,' Mrs Comrie said, then: 'Did you say 'we'?'

'My friend Dolores McCaffrey will be with me. She was on the same course, and was a friend of Harry's as well. Will it be OK if she comes along?'

'Oh, of course. I'll phone Gerald now, and we'll look forward to seeing you and your

236

friend — say between five and half-past, if that suits you.'

'That'll be fine.'

It was just a matter then of getting the address and some directions and the arrangements were complete.

When Addie had hung up, Dolores said, 'You mentioned someone called Gerald. Who's Gerald?'

'That's what *I* was wondering,' Addie smiled. 'I think our Harry was a bit of a dark horse.'

'You mean — ?' Dolores looked at her in surprise, then smiled and gave a slow nod. 'Yes, I think he was.'

14

From the materials in her workroom the next morning Addie selected a piece of cream-coloured mounting card, and then spent some time making a mount for the drawing of Harry. She was pleased with the results, and wrapped the finished product — along with a stout piece of cardboard for support — in crisp brown paper.

Just after twelve, in Addie's car with

Dolores driving, the two set off. They stopped for a leisurely lunch on the way, and reached Hailsham still with plenty of time to spare. After wandering around the town centre for a while they made their way to the address that Mrs Comrie had given.

Mrs Comrie, it turned out, lived in an Edwardian house in an attractive, tree-lined street on the outskirts of the town. It was just after five when Dolores pulled up outside. With Addie carrying the wrapped drawing, they walked up the path to the front door and rang the bell. The door was opened almost at once.

Mrs Comrie was in her late sixties, a small woman with hair that was almost white. She wore a pale-grey woollen trouser suit with a gold chain at her throat and gold ear-rings. As she smiled her wide smile, Addie could see Harry in her features.

When the introductions had been made — with Mrs Comrie insisting that they call her Ruth — they stepped into the wide hall, from where they were shown into a spacious sitting room. There was unostentatious evidence of wealth there, Addie thought as she took in her surroundings, the tasteful furniture, the brocade curtains. The walls of the room were hung with oils and water-colours — some of them, she saw at once, the work of Harry. There were framed photographs of Harry too, some of him alone, others showing him with a dark-haired man. The man himself, in person, had risen from an armchair as they entered, and stepped smiling towards them. This, Ruth Comrie said, was Gerald Fraser, Harry's friend. After the introductions, Addie and Dolores sat side by side on a sofa against which Addie leant the package holding the drawing. Saying that she would go and get some tea, Ruth left the room.

When she had gone, Gerald turned to Addie and Dolores and asked after their journey. He was in his early forties, Addie reckoned. Quite tall, and strongly built, he was good-looking with a lean face and brown eyes. The three chatted for a while about the difficulties of driving on today's roads and then Ruth came in carrying a laden tray which she set down on the coffee-table. She poured tea and cut slices of fruit cake and handed it around.

'So, Addie,' she said as she sat down, 'you and Dolores were at Birmingham with Harry. He used to tell me about you all.' Setting down her cup and saucer, she got up and took from a bureau an envelope. From it she drew three or four photographs. 'Harry had these,' she said. 'Gerald and I looked them out after you phoned.'

Without needing to look closely at them Addie recognized the pictures as having been taken on the day of the picnic.

'Harry wrote on the back who you all were,' Ruth said, turning over one of the photographs. 'So after your call Gerald and I were able to see what you looked like. She turned the picture around again. 'You haven't changed very much,' she said to Addie. Then to Dolores, 'Though I think you've changed somewhat, Dolores, if I may say so.'

Dolores chuckled, 'You may. I'm pleased to hear it.'

Focusing on one particular photograph, Ruth Comrie said, 'The girl in the check shirt — she's the one who died, isn't she?'

'That's right,' Addie said. She didn't need to look.

'Harry told me about it at the time. How tragic.' She put the photographs in their envelope back on the bureau. 'And you say,' she said, looking at the flat package at Addie's side, her voice brightening, 'that you've got a drawing of Harry . . . '

'Yes.' Addie unwrapped the mounted drawing. 'I did it one afternoon in the common room while he was sitting reading.'

240

She got up and put the picture into Ruth's hands.

While Addie sat down, Gerald moved to the woman's side, and together they studied the drawing. 'It's lovely,' Ruth said. 'You really captured him.' She turned to Gerald. 'Don't you think so?'

'Oh, yes, that's him exactly.' He gave a little laugh, and the woman chuckled and laid a hand on his arm. Then to Addie she said, 'And we may keep this?'

'Of course,' Addie said. 'It's for you.'

'We'll get it framed right away,' Ruth said. 'Gerald'll choose something really nice for it.' She handed the picture to him and he put it on the bureau, propping it against the wall. When he had resumed his seat the talk moved on to the subject of Harry's work. Not once did it come anywhere near his death, however, and Addie began to doubt that she would get an opportunity to enquire about it. So be it; it had always been a long shot, even had she known exactly what she was searching for. Now, to begin asking this vulnerable, elderly woman questions that could only bring further grief was something she couldn't bring herself to do.

The chat went on, and the teacups were emptied, and soon it was after six. Addie turned and looked at Dolores, raising her eyebrows in a little questioning signal to which Dolores responded with the hint of a nod. 'Well,' Addie said, taking in both Ruth and Gerald, 'we'd better think about getting back.'

As they got to their feet, Gerald said, 'I'll walk out with you,' then to Ruth, 'I wondered whether Addie and Dolores might like to see some of Harry's work before they go. See his home too.' He turned to them. 'Would you care to? It's not very far. Just in the next street.'

They would, they said at once, and thanked him. The goodbyes between the women over, he opened the front door and Addie and Dolores stepped past him into the porch. Just as the three of them started down the path, Ruth called Addie's name and Addie turned back to her. Ruth held out her hand as Addie came up the porch steps, and Addie took it.

'I just wanted to thank you again.' Ruth squeezed Addie's hand and released it. 'I shall treasure that drawing, always.'

'Oh, I'm so pleased to have been able to bring it,' Addie said.

Ruth Comrie looked past her to where Dolores and Gerald were moving through the gate onto the pavement. 'We cope as well as we can,' she said. 'I'm just so glad he had

Gerald. And I suppose Gerald's all I've got in the way of family now that Harry's gone.' She half turned, her moving hand taking in the house behind her and added, lowering her voice, 'I'd like him to come and stay here with me if he would. This place is far too big for one person. But I doubt that he will. Not with them having got their place the way they wanted it. Still, he's close by, so that's comfort.' She gave a little sigh. 'Anyway, you go on — they're waiting for you. But if you're ever in the area again, do come and see me, will you?'

Addie pressed her hand and leaned forward and kissed her on the cheek. 'I will. I'd be happy to.'

Reaching the gate she found Dolores sitting in the car, Gerald standing beside it. He opened the front passenger door for Addie and they set off. Following his directions, Dolores turned to the right at the first corner and then pulled up outside an attractive Victorian detached house with evergreen shrubs on either side of the gate. Gerald led them inside and into a large sitting-room. As they took seats on the sofa he said, 'Maybe you'd like something a little stronger to drink, would you? Now that the sun is over the yard-arm, or whatever the saying is.'

Addie looked at Dolores who gave a nod and said, 'Well, I'm driving, but I can allow myself just *one*. Thanks. A very small gin and tonic would be great.'

Addie said she would have the same. When he had gone out of the room they took in their surroundings with glances of approval. The tasteful furnishings had an eclectic appearance, though it was mainly a mixture of Victorian and colonial, the sofa and armchairs covered with velvet or an elegant print fabric. On the surfaces of bureaux and small tables stood several busts and statuettes which Addie recognized at once as Parian, some of the pieces quite large and striking. On the walls hung a variety of pictures: original water-colours, oils and acrylics, as well as other items, such as prints of newspaper front pages and other curiosities. Again, some of the framed pictures were works by Harry. And again there were photographs — some with unfamiliar faces, others showing Harry and Gerald together.

Gerald came back carrying a tray with their drinks which he handed out — for himself he'd poured a whisky and soda — and then sat in an armchair. 'That was such a nice gesture,' he said to Addie, 'bringing that drawing.'

244

'It was a pleasure,' she replied. 'When I read about Harry I remembered the drawing and looked it out.'

'It'll mean a lot to Ruth — and to me too.' He took a drink; the glass looked small in his large hands. 'The main reason I asked you back was so that we might have a little chat. I'm so glad to have the chance to meet old friends of Harry's.' Getting up, he moved to a chest, opened a drawer and brought out a folder, which he placed on the coffee-table. 'Look at all these.' He opened it and revealed a collection of papers. 'Letters of condolence. Not only from his friends, but also from people he'd never met, but who'd appreciated his work. They're all here.' He picked up a couple of the letters and looked at them, then put them back, replaced the folder in the drawer and pushed it shut. 'We were together just five years, and we thought we were only starting.' He took a swallow from his glass. 'It's helped having Ruth around. Harry was her only child, and with no other family I was the only one she could turn to. We couldn't both go to pieces. Particularly with the inquest and everything.'

Addie said nothing, waiting for him to continue.

After a moment he added, 'You know

about that, I suppose.'

She nodded. 'Yes. I read about it.'

He curled his lip in an expression of disgust. 'As if we didn't go through enough with his death there had to be all the questions, and then the inquest adjourned for more tests.' He gave a deep sigh. 'Thank God it's over at last, though, and we can go ahead with the funeral.'

Addie could sense Dolores's eyes touch upon her; she must be thinking the same thing. 'That must be a great relief,' she said. 'When is it to take place?'

'In a week. Next Wednesday. A simple cremation. It'll be a private affair. No flowers. We'll just be family and one or two of his closest friends.' As if afraid of giving offence, he added, 'We just don't want any fuss. There's been so much already. We only got word two days ago that we could go ahead and arrange it. We haven't known where we were. All those questions from the police and the suspicions.' He shook his head. 'It was a terrible business. I tried to shield Ruth from it as much as possible, but she couldn't avoid being affected.'

'Still,' Addie said, 'you say it's all over now.'

'Yes. In the end they signed the death certificate and . . . ' He let the rest of the sentence trail off. A moment of silence, then he went on, 'When it started there was no indication that it was anything remotely — momentous. I mean there was no warning. A bit of a fever first of all, and you think, oh, it's flu or something. And then — three days later he's dead. I've played it over and over in my mind, as if it's a scenario that could somehow be rewritten. You can't accept it; you're not prepared.'

Addie said, 'What did they say it was?'

'Septicaemia. That's what they concluded after they'd carried out more tests. But even then they couldn't find the *cause* of the blood-poisoning. 'Of unknown origin' was the way they put it.'

Dolores said, 'You sound a bit sceptical.'

He turned to her. 'Well, how can they come up with an answer like that, with all the advances in medicine? I wondered whether it could have been food-poisoning or something, but apparently not. Besides, he didn't eat anything unusual. I know that because he was monitoring his food. He was having some tests for allergies, and several common foods were off his menu. He was eating very simply.'

'So there was nothing out of the ordinary at all in his diet,' Addie said.

'Nothing. And he hadn't long been out

of hospital after a hernia operation, so he was taking things easy. A little gentle exercise, but generally, just relaxing. He was recovering well and looking forward to getting completely fit again — at which time we were going away for a few days. We've got a cottage in Buckinghamshire, and we planned to go there for a while. His only disappointment was that he wasn't fit enough to go and look at some Parian that was being offered for sale at auction.'

'Oh, the Parian,' Dolores said. 'I was admiring the pieces here. They're really beautiful.'

'I can remember,' Addie said, 'his buying a piece when we were at Birmingham. A little bust of Tchaikovsky. It had suffered a bit of damage, I seem to remember, which is why he didn't pay much for it.'

Gerald smiled at her. 'Turn around.'

'What?'

'Turn around.'

She turned in her seat and found herself facing a shelf with more ornaments on it. And there in the centre was the little bust of Tchaikovsky.

'That must be the one,' Gerald said.

'Oh, yes!' She stood up. 'May I?'

'Help yourself.'

She picked up the piece, feeling the silky

smoothness of its finish. Looking at it more closely she could see the areas where Harry had restored it. As she ran a finger over the repairs, Gerald said, 'He got really expert at the restoration in time.'

She handed the piece to Dolores who looked at it for a moment and handed it back. Addie replaced it on the shelf and sat down again.

Gerald said, 'It's ironic that the one particular piece he was seeking was in the auction. That would have been such a thrill — to go there and see it, and then bid for it — and get it.'

'It was a rare piece, was it?' Dolores said.

'Apparently there were fewer than two hundred made. Called *The Veiled Bride*. A lovely piece — by Copeland — and much sought after. Harry had only ever seen it in photographs, so he was thrilled when this one came on the market and he was invited to send in a bid. That was only days before he died. I think he was already . . . already gone by the time the auction took place. I guess somebody else got it, the porcelain — we didn't hear anything else about it.'

A little silence fell, and into the quiet Dolores said, 'I've got very fond memories of Harry. That lovely dry humour. He could be so funny in that subtle way of his.'

'Yes, he got on with everybody,' Addie said, and then, asking one of the questions that were uppermost in her mind: 'Have you ever met any of his other friends from that time?'

'From his year at Birmingham, you mean? No, none of them.'

'It's so often the way,' Dolores said. 'People are brought together for some purpose or other, and become friends. And when they leave they vow to keep in touch. And maybe they do for a while, but usually it ends. The friendships fade out.'

'Yes,' Gerald said, 'it's so easy to lose touch. I remember Harry reading about the death of that designer, Christie Harding. He spoke a little about her, but he didn't really like to talk about that time. Mainly, I think, because of the association with what happened to that other student, Ruby. He told me about her, of course, but he didn't dwell on it. I think that might have been one of the reasons he never kept up with anyone from the group. I can't say I blame him.'

'I suppose,' Dolores said, 'If any of his old Birmingham friends had called while he was recuperating you'd have known about it, wouldn't you?'

He looked surprised at her words. 'Well, I might not have been here if they'd called; I do have a job. I work for a local estate agent. But if any visitors had come, Harry would certainly have mentioned it. Why do you ask?'

Dolores gave an awkward shrug. 'Oh, just that we'd quite like to get in touch with some of them again, if it's possible.'

'I see.' He nodded. 'Well, the only one I knew anything about was Ambrose.'

'Ambrose?' Addie said. 'You knew Ambrose Morgenson?'

He paused. 'Well, I didn't *know* him, I just knew *of* him.' He looked from Addie to Dolores. 'I mentioned showing you some of Harry's work,' he said. 'Would you like to see it?'

A little surprised at the abrupt switch of subject, they said they would, and got to their feet. Glass in hand, he led the way into the hall, past a partly open door revealing a small cloakroom, and up the stairs into a large room on the first floor. Harry's studio. The walls here were hung with sketches and finished artwork, some of it framed, other items just fixed with Bluetack or pins. Near a window with a north light stood Harry's drawing-table and drawing-board along with all the artist's implements that went along with it, the pencils, brushes, paints and crayons.

Moving around the room, Gerald pointed out pictures and sketches that he thought might be of particular interest. And as he did so his pride was clear in his tone and his manner. His favourite work, he said, and which he pointed out, was a large painting in gouache, illustrating a scene from *The Arabian Nights*. In it a magnificently patterned carpet was sweeping across a star-studded sky, carrying upon it a young man and woman. He stood before it for a minute or so, speaking of Harry's work; then, abruptly breaking off, he said, 'I don't know why I'm being so unforthcoming, for God's sake. And I must say Ambrose wrote a very nice letter when he heard about Harry.'

'You heard from Ambrose?' Addie said.

'Yes. When Harry died.'

'How did he get your address?' said Dolores.

'He and Harry ran into one another in Eastbourne about a year ago.'

'And they'd kept touch since then?'

'Well, I think Ambrose would have liked to, but Harry didn't want to take it any further. That was all water under the bridge.'

Addie looked at him uncomprehendingly, and glancing at Dolores saw the same look in her expression. Gerald caught it too. 'Didn't you know about them at Birmingham?' he said.

'You mean,' Dolores said. 'Harry and Ambrose?'

'They were lovers for a time.' He smiled. 'Didn't you know that?'

'No,' Addie said, and Dolores added, 'I had no idea.'

Gerald gave a little smile. 'And there was Harry convinced that every single person on campus must have been aware of it. Well, it just goes to show.'

He turned away, moving towards some other pictures. As he did so Dolores caught Addie's eye and signalled with swift gestures and silently mouthed words that Addie should follow up the questioning while she herself made things easier by getting out of the way for a minute.

'Gerald,' Dolores said, 'd'you mind if I use your bathroom?' She was already starting back across the room.

'What?' he said, turning to her. 'Of course.'

'It's OK.' She pointed off. 'I know where it is.'

When Dolores had gone, Addie moved to Gerald's side as he stood before another of Harry's framed illustrations.

'What you told us just now about Harry

and Ambrose,' she said. 'I never guessed there was anything special between them. I did wonder once or twice about Ambrose, but never about Harry. Though I guess I should have done.'

'Oh?' Gerald's exclamation, though soft, sounded slightly defensive, as if he would brook no criticism of his dead friend.

'Oh, not in any critical way,' Addie said quickly. 'I meant I might have wondered about him simply because he never showed interest in any of the girls on the course — in a sexual way, that is. And there were a few who were quite stunning.' She smiled. 'And you must remember what it's like among some students, Gerald. The amount of bed-hopping that goes on is sometimes astonishing.'

'Yes,' he said, 'and it was ever thus.'

'But as for him and Ambrose — well, they managed to keep that well hidden.'

'So it seems.' He nodded. 'Though not from everybody. She knew about it. Ruby, the girl who died.'

'She did?'

'Oh, yes. This was all long before I came on the scene, you understand. According to Harry, she made a couple of cracks about how Ambrose's father would feel about it — their relationship — if he knew. And

254

jokingly she talked about phoning him and having a quiet chat.' He pursed his lips. 'I rather think that although Ruby was undoubtedly a bit of a charmer, there was another side to her. And I'm sure her words would have touched a spot where Ambrose was concerned. Apparently Ambrose's father was something of a tyrant in his quiet way. A puritanical bigot, to be more accurate. But that's the way some people seem to be affected once they've been 'saved'.'

'Yes.' Addie thought back to those earlier times. 'I do recall Ambrose hinting at a few problems with his father. Certainly, when he came back after spending a weekend at home he sometimes seemed rather subdued. Perhaps his father had something to do with that.'

'Possibly. Also, the more I think about it, the more I think it might have been fear of his father that had something to do with him breaking off his relationship with Harry. Guilt and fear — they're a potent combination. Not that in the long run I'm complaining. I mean, if they'd stayed together Harry and I wouldn't have met. But I believe Harry was quite upset when it happened, the split between them.'

'This was in Birmingham?'

'Yes. Then, as I say, a year ago they just

happened to run into one another.'

'In Eastbourne, you said.'

'Yes. I think Ambrose was teaching. Of course, by that time Harry was well established. Plenty of commissions coming in. More than he could handle, in fact.'

'Not surprising,' Addie said. 'With a talent like his it was only a matter of time. I never did see him ending up as a teacher. His talent was just too great to spend in a classroom, trying to keep order among a bunch of unruly kids.'

Gerald said, 'You got to know him quite well, didn't you?'

'Well, obviously not as well as I thought — not now you tell me about him and Ambrose.'

Gerald smiled. 'I guess he was pretty good at putting up a front. Sometimes it's something you have to learn to do.'

'What happened after he and Ambrose met again?'

'As I said, Ambrose phoned, but nothing came of it.'

'So you think they never met after that?'

'I'd be extremely surprised if they had.'

'D'you know where he was living at that time? Was it in Eastbourne?'

'I — I don't know.'

'But if he wrote to you, perhaps you'd

have his address, would you? With the other letters . . . ?'

'Yes, I might well do. I'll have a look, and if I find it I'll send it to you.'

'Thank you. I'd appreciate it. I'll write down my address and phone number.'

She took the pencil and paper he handed her. As she finished writing there came the sound of steps on the stairs and Dolores came back into the room. 'Addie,' she said after a moment, 'I think we ought to think about starting back, don't you?'

Addie murmured agreement and said to Gerald, 'And we've taken up enough of your time, too.'

'It's been my pleasure,' he said, 'believe me.'

He asked if he could get them more drinks before they left, but with thanks they declined his offer, and moments later were starting down the stairs. He accompanied them to the front gate where he shook their hands. 'Thanks so much,' he said, 'for coming to see us, and bringing the drawing. We shall treasure it.'

'I'm glad you like it,' Addie said. 'And thank you for showing us Harry's work.' She looked past his shoulder. 'You two made a lovely home. It's beautiful.'

He turned and looked at the house. 'Yes.

Though for me it's not the same. It never will be.'

* * *

The two women were well clear of the town before any reference was made to Gerald's revelation. 'Septicaemia,' Dolores said. 'So poor Harry was another victim. And another instance of ricin poisoning being put down to natural causes.'

Addie gave a nod. Although Gerald's news had come as no great surprise, nevertheless it was not something she wanted to deal with. For a while they drove on without speaking, until again Dolores broke the silence.

'And Harry and Ambrose,' she said. 'They kept that quiet, didn't they? It's amazing what can be going on under your nose without your being aware of it.'

'Yes,' Addie replied, 'though apparently Ruby knew. And even hinted — jokingly, Gerald said — that she might let Ambrose's dad in on it.'

'Are you *serious*? Ruby? She said she'd do that?'

'That's what Gerald was told by Harry.'

'She can't have meant it.'

Addie shrugged.

'Harry was doing well, wasn't he?' Dolores

said. 'He must have been earning really good money. So Gerald's not going to be short of a bob or two now, is he?'

'No, I suppose not.'

They drove on in silence for a while, then Dolores said, 'What else did you find out — while I was out of the room?'

Addie gave a look of quiet triumph. 'I think Gerald's got Ambrose's address.'

'He has? Did you get it?'

'He's going to send it to me.'

'So he *says*.' Dolores's tone was sceptical.

'Oh, I don't think he'll forget. If he does I'll phone him. I think Ambrose lives in Eastbourne, though — so in any case we can try to find his number.'

★ ★ ★

Back in Liddiston, Addie got on the telephone and enquired after Ambrose's number. It was ex-directory. 'At least, though,' she said to Dolores, 'we know he's there.' Remarking then that it was too late for Dolores to return to London, she suggested that she stay over. Dolores, however, said she had an appointment in the morning and had no choice but to go back. A while later, after a cup of coffee and a sandwich, she was ready to go. Standing beside Dolores's car, Addie said, 'Once we get Ambrose's address we can decide on our next move.'

'Can we?' Dolores's tone was decidedly jaundiced. 'Whatever that might be.'

'I'm doing my best, Dolores,' Addie said.

'I know, and I appreciate it.' Dolores gave a deep sigh. 'I won't let this get to me — I won't.'

Addie watched Dolores's departure, then went back into the house.

★ ★ ★

In the morning of the next day, Saturday, Addie went to visit Robbie's grave. On her return she saw that there was a message on the answer-machine. Her hope was that it was from Gerald, calling with Ambrose's address. It was not. 'Hi, Addie,' came an immediately recognizable voice, 'it's Lydia. We were hoping to take you to lunch. Another time, maybe. 'Bye now.' Addie was glad she'd been out; Lydia's high-voltage persona was something she could do without.

Not that she was to escape it for much longer. She was at the back of the house later, pulling a few weeds from one of the herbaceous borders, when she heard the sound of a car and turned to see a shining black Volvo coming to a halt. Another moment and Lydia and Adam were coming towards her.

'Addie, hi there!' Lydia embraced her and gave her a peck on the cheek. 'We caught up with you at last.'

'Hello, Addie.' Adam tightly pressed Addie's shoulder. She returned his greeting, then Lydia said, 'We were going into Newbury on business for Adam and thought we might take you to lunch — but you were off gallivanting.'

'I was at the cemetery,' Addie said. 'But it was a nice idea.' She took off her gardening gloves. 'Would you like some tea or coffee or something?'

'I thought you'd never ask,' Lydia said. 'We'd love some.'

With Addie leading, they trooped into the house, and to the kitchen where Addie put on the kettle and Lydia and Adam sat on stools at the breakfast bar. 'Did you have a nice lunch?' Addie asked, for something to say. 'It was OK,' Lydia replied. She put her head a little on one side. 'We just felt it wasn't healthy for you being on your own all the time while Charlie's away.'

'I'm fine,' Addie said. 'Really, I'm used to it.'

'You can get *too* used to some things,' Lydia said. 'And in the end it becomes a habit that's hard to break.'

When the tea was made, Adam carried the tray into the sitting-room. There Addie poured it and handed the cups around. Lydia sipped from hers and gave a sigh of pleasure. 'Oh, I need this.' As she put down her cup and saucer she added, 'You had a day out in London the other day, I understand — with Peter.'

Addie smiled. 'You make it sound like a pleasure trip. It was just — business.'

Lydia gave a little nod, as if waiting for Addie to elaborate, Addie said nothing more; the last thing she needed was Lydia's involvement.

'By the way,' Lydia said, 'how's Charlie getting on?'

'As far as I know everything's going all right,' Addie replied. 'He's busy. Seeing different manufacturers here and there.'

Lydia nodded. 'It's a lot to do. And he'll soon have to make up his mind on his plans for next year. I don't suppose he's mentioned anything to you about it — what he's thinking of . . . ?'

'No, not so far.'

'No.' Lydia nodded. 'But you don't involve yourself much in the business, do you.' It was more statement than question.

Addie felt the little surge of defensiveness rising. 'Well, I haven't for a while, but that can all change.'

'Yes, of course.' Lydia smiled. 'I hope you will. You'd be such an asset with your artistic ability.' She paused. 'I was just wondering whether Charlie might have said anything to you about *Hurricane*.'

'Oh, your game — the one you were trying out the other day.' Is this her reason for dropping by? Addie thought, to get me as an ally in order to help secure a licence for her game?

'I've been working on a few adjustments to it,' Lydia said. 'When they're done it's going to be better than ever.'

'Tell you the truth, darling,' Adam said, 'I don't think Addie's that interested.' Lydia shot him a disapproving glance. 'Perhaps not,' she said, 'but like Addie said: that can all change.'

Adam gave a nod then glanced at his watch, 'Anyway, I think we should get on our way, don't you? Let Addie get back to work.'

'Of course.' Lydia got to her feet. 'I wouldn't want to hold anybody up.'

As Addie rose from the sofa Lydia smiled at her. 'I'm sure *you* don't misunderstand me, Addie,' she said, 'even if other people are intent on doing so.'

At the front door Adam lingered while Lydia strode on towards the car. Turning to Addie he gave a little shrug, then turned and followed Lydia across the gravel.

Moments later the car — with Lydia waving and smiling an overbright smile — was moving back down the drive. Addie watched it with a sigh of relief.

★ ★ ★

Close on seven she took a long, leisurely bath, and afterwards put on a tracksuit and made herself a light supper which she ate in front of the television. It was tuned to a hospital drama which, for all its pretensions of gritty accuracy, appeared totally unconnected with reality. After a time she switched it off.

By 10.30 she had heard nothing from Gerald Fraser and when she tried telephoning Dolores there was no answer.

With the house securely locked up for the night, she was just starting up the stairs, preparing to go to bed, when she heard the sound of a car moving past the front of the house and coming to a halt. She stood quite still. Seconds later there came a ring at the doorbell. She waited. The ring came again, more insistent. Her heart pounding, she crept down the stairs and along the hall to the front door. Peering through the spy-hole she saw Dolores standing in the porch, a small overnight bag in her hand. Quickly Addie pulled the bolts, unhooked the chain and opened the door.

'Dolores!'

Dolores looked distraught, her eyes wide and wild. 'Oh, Addie . . . '

The next minute she was pushing past Addie and into the hall.

'What's up?' Addie said. 'I've been trying to phone you.'

'I'm sorry,' Dolores said, 'but I couldn't stay at home. I had to get away.'

'Why? What's happened?'

'I saw him. Matt.'

'What?'

'Matt. Matthew Dixon. I saw him tonight.'

15

Addie poured drinks and handed one to Dolores where she sat on the sofa. 'Right,' she said, 'tell me what happened.'

'He was outside the house,' Dolores

said. 'Outside my flat.'

'You're certain it was him?'

'Yes.' Then, with a little less conviction, 'I — I'm sure it was.'

Addie nodded. 'What was he doing?'

'Just . . . just walking there.'

'And you got a good look at him?'

'Well, fairly good. He's gone very grey.'

Yes, Addie could imagine that would be the case. Even in Birmingham, as young as he was, he had begun to go grey. 'Tell me what happened,' she said.

Dolores drank from her glass. 'I'd just started preparing dinner,' she said, 'when I realized I needed a couple of things. So I popped out. I only had to go fifty yards along the street. I got what I wanted and crossed back over the road, unlocked the door and stepped through into the hall. And it was then that I saw him — as I was closing the door. He was walking along, slowly, on the other side. I couldn't see his face but there was something about his figure that took my attention. I looked at him, and in the same moment he turned and looked at me.'

'What did you do then?'

'I closed the door and went upstairs and looked out the window. He was still there.'

'Doing what?'

'Just standing there — but why would he

be there if it wasn't because of me?' She took a cigarette from her bag. As she lit it, Addie could see that her hand was shaking slightly.

Dolores deeply inhaled on her cigarette then said, 'I dodge back behind the curtain and just stayed there — for ages. The light began to go, but I was afraid to switch on a lamp. Eventually, I peered round the curtain, but there was no sign of him. The light from the launderette shines on the pavement there — and it was empty. He might have been gone for ages; I don't know. I couldn't rest, though, not after that. So, I threw a few things into a bag and got out.'

Addie could see in Dolores's eyes the shine of unshed tears. In an effort to bring a sense of practicality to the moment, she said, 'You didn't get to eat, is that right?'

'What? Eat? No, I couldn't hang around to eat.'

Addie picked up her glass and started for the kitchen. 'Come on, let's get you something. Bring your drink with you.'

In the kitchen she prepared scrambled eggs and toast and set a place at the counter. Just when the food was ready and Dolores was sitting down to eat, the telephone rang. It would have to be Charlie. Addie lifted the receiver. 'Hello?'

'Addie — ' Charlie's voice came to her across the miles.

'Charlie . . .'

'I've just had breakfast. It's already tomorrow here. You weren't in bed, were you?'

'No. Oh, I'm so glad to hear from you.'

'What's the matter? Something's wrong — what is it?' He had picked up the tension in her voice, and now she could hear anxiety in his own.

'Dolores is here,' she said. 'She's just this minute arrived.'

'At this hour?'

'It — it's a long story.' Turning, she saw that Dolores was not eating, but was sitting with her head lowered, one hand up to her forehead. 'Charlie,' she said, 'I have to go. Let me talk to you tomorrow, OK?'

'What's happening there?' he said.

She took a breath, quickly deliberating. 'Dolores thinks she saw Matt — Matthew Dixon — hanging around outside her flat this evening.'

'I don't *think* I saw him,' Dolores said. 'I *did* see him.'

'I heard that,' Charlie said to Addie. 'She's in a bit of a state, is she?'

'You could say that.'

He paused. 'How are *you*? Are you OK?'

'I'm fine.'

'You don't sound fine.'

'Well, this whole thing is — oh, I don't know what to do.' She sighed. 'Look, I have to go now. I'll talk to you tomorrow.'

'He'll think I'm crazy,' Dolores said when Addie had hung up. 'I shouldn't have come.'

'Of course you should,' Addie said. She sat facing Dolores across the counter. 'Now, please, try to eat something. You'll feel better. And later on, whenever you want, you can go up and sleep.'

'I guess,' Dolores said, picking at her food, 'I'm not so capable as I thought.'

'You can stay here for a few days if you want. Have you got commitments?'

'None I can't get out of.' A pause. 'I've got to go back home at some time, but I don't want to go back while he might be there.'

Addie frowned. 'I don't understand what he could be doing — hanging around your flat.'

'No. Unless he was — you know — getting the lay of the land, as they say. It might not make sense to you, but it does to me.' Dolores set down her knife and fork and pushed her plate to the side. 'Addie, I'm sorry, but I can't eat any more.'

With refilled glasses they returned to the

sitting-room. As they sat down, Dolores said, 'Where's the sense in my coming here to see you? If he knows where I live he probably knows where *you* live as well. He found out how to get to Christie and Kieron and Harry, didn't he? And he wasn't standing outside my flat by chance.' As she took a swallow from her glass Addie could see the tension in her hand. In the past Dolores had always seemed so in control. Not now.

The telephone rang, loud in the quiet. The two women looked at one another. Addie glanced at her watch, hesitated a moment, then picked up the receiver.

'Hello . . . ?'

'Addie?' It was Peter Lavell. 'Charlie's just been on the phone to me. He's very concerned about you and your friend being on your own. So I told him I'd come over if you'd like me to.' When she said nothing, he added quickly, 'No strings, Addie, but just say the word and I'll pack my toothbrush and get in the car.'

Another brief moment of hesitation, and she said, 'Yes,' the relief sweeping over her. 'Thank you. I'd be very glad. We both would.'

★ ★ ★

Peter arrived not long afterwards. Addie introduced him to Dolores then poured him a whisky. As he drank it, he listened while Dolores told of her sighting of Matthew.

'But even seeing him there doesn't mean he's the one who's been doing these things,' he said.

'You think he was just passing her home by chance?' Addie said.

'Well,' he said, 'if he really *was* there — I mean if Dolores wasn't mistaken — I suppose you'd be hard pressed to come to any other conclusion.'

'Yes,' Dolores said, 'and I think we should go to the police. Once they hear our story I don't see how they could doubt it.'

'Or would they,' Addie said, 'put it down to a woman having a bad case of hysterics?'

'Well, we can't just do nothing,' Dolores said.

'But you haven't,' Peter said. 'You've been making enquiries.'

'True,' Addie said. 'Traipsing around all over the place. And we still haven't found out a damn thing.' She went on to tell him of their visit to Harry's mother and friend. 'And if we can trace Ambrose through Gerald, that means that one way or another we'll have traced everyone. Everyone, that is, except Matt.'

'Yes,' Dolores echoed, 'except Matt.'

'And what will you do,' Peter said, 'when you find out Ambrose's address?'

'Well, go and see him. Maybe he'll be able to tell us something. In any case, we'll be able to warn him. Trouble is, we don't know what to look out for.'

Soon afterwards Dolores remarked that she was tired and would like to go to bed. As she got to her feet, Peter rose too. 'Believe me,' Dolores told him, 'I shall sleep a lot easier tonight knowing you're in the house.'

He smiled. 'I'm glad to be of service.'

When Dolores had wished him goodnight she picked up her bag and followed Addie into the hall and up the stairs. At the door of the guest room they stopped.

'You'll be all right, won't you?' Addie said.

'I shall now, yes.' Dolores sighed. 'Oh, I'm sorry for being such a wet week. You need somebody strong and I'm running around like a headless chicken.'

Addie smiled. 'Listen, if I'd seen Matt hanging around outside my door I'd be ten times worse than you.' A pause. 'If I don't hear from Gerald by tomorrow evening, I shall call him.'

'Yes. I guess we've got to go and see Ambrose, haven't we? If we can.'

'Yes, of course.' Addie frowned. 'Why do you say that?'

'Oh, it's just that I'm so tired of all the pressure. There's no let-up.'

'I know what you mean.' Addie nodded. 'But we'll get through it.'

'Yes, we will.' Dolores sounded unconvinced. 'I probably seem like an awful coward, but right now — well, I just feel I want to put my head under my wing and hide.' She put her bag down on the carpet and wrapped Addie in her arms. 'But just give me a chance to get my breath and I'll be OK, I promise.'

'Sure you will.'

'We've got to stick together through this, right?'

'We've got to.'

'You're a good friend, Addie.' Dolores released her, picked up her bag and opened the bedroom door. 'Goodnight.'

'Goodnight.'

Returning to the sitting-room Addie sat down on the sofa. Peter, in the chair facing her, gestured to the floor above. 'I like your friend.'

'Yes, she's a terrific person.' She added with a smile, 'Usually she's in control. But that business — seeing Matt — that really gave her a jolt.'

'How could it not?' He paused. 'If it *was he.*'

'You think she could've been mistaken?'

'Well, she didn't sound a hundred per cent certain. And after all, it's been — what? — eleven years since they last met? Some people can change a lot in that time. And for *what reason* would he be outside her flat?'

Addie drew down the corners of her mouth and gave a shrug. 'To check up on her? Make sure of where she was living?'

'But why would he do it so obviously? I'd have thought that'd be the last thing he'd want — to be *seen watching* her. Stalking her, you might say.'

She nodded. 'I hadn't thought of that.'

'I mean, if it really *was* Matthew, then that truly would be something to go to the police with. It's a slim chance, but it's possible there could be other witnesses to his being there. Then they might be able to locate him and ask him a few questions.'

'But if Dolores was mistaken, then we're still in the dark.'

His silence gave her his answer. After a moment she began to tell him of their visit to Celia in London. There was a child, she said, a little girl, who also died of septicaemia; she had been with Christie only hours before being taken ill.

He gazed at her in silence for a moment, then said, 'Are you saying you believe her death was somehow connected with the others?'

'Yes. I am.'

'My God,' he said, 'this gets more bewildering by the hour.'

'It does.' With a sigh of weariness she got to her feet. 'I'm just so tired. I'm going to make some tea, and take a cup up to bed. You can have Charlie's room. You'll be comfortable there. The bedding's all been changed.' He nodded acknowledgement and she went out to the kitchen where she put on the kettle. Hearing his steps behind her, she turned to see him leaning against the doorjamb.

'I want this to be over,' she said. 'I want it to end. You tell yourself it'll all work out in time, but you know it doesn't happen like that for everybody. You only have to read the papers to see that there are lots of unfortunate people for whom things don't turn out right. And who's to say that I shouldn't be one of them?'

'Don't think that way,' he said.

'That's easier said than done. And Dolores is so edgy. I don't think she's keen on going to see Ambrose.'

'So will you go on your own?'

'I don't know. I don't know anything any more.' She felt so tired, she was almost past caring. Then, 'Yes,' she said, 'I'd have to see him. I don't have any choice. If I didn't and something happened to him I'd never forgive myself.'

★ ★ ★

Dolores came downstairs the following morning heavy-eyed. She had slept badly, she said. Peter offered to remain after breakfast, but in the bright light of day Addie's fears seemed less real and she insisted that she and Dolores would be all right. He had just left when Charlie telephoned. Addie took the call in her bedroom. He asked whether Peter had come over, and she told him that he had and had now gone back home. Shifting the focus, she asked him about himself. He had just come in from visiting a factory on the outskirts of the city, he told her; he sounded weary.

'It's Sunday,' she said. 'You have to work every day?'

'This is Hong Kong, Addie,' he reminded her. 'People like to get things done. Besides, I've only got one more full day before I start home. I've got to make the most of the time available.'

Afterwards, with Dolores lending a hand, Addie worked about the house, taking refuge in mundane chores. Later they drove to the supermarket. Addie rarely shopped on a Sunday, but nothing lately was as it usually was. Pushing the trolley up and down the aisles, Addie had the strange feeling that they were being watched — though her brain told her it was extremely unlikely. Back at the house she checked the answering machine — there were no messages — and then set about packing the groceries away. Just after five o'clock Gerald Fraser telephoned.

As Addie spoke his name she saw Dolores, in the nearby armchair, look over with interest. Addie gave her a triumphant little nod of affirmation.

'Addie,' Gerald was saying, 'I've got the address and phone number of Ambrose Morgenson. It was with all the others, as I thought it would be.'

Addie wrote down the information. They chatted for a little while longer, and then the conversation came to an end.

'So you got Ambrose's address,' Dolores said as Addie replaced the receiver.

Addie nodded. 'Yes, and he *is* living in Eastbourne.'

At intervals, both before and after dinner, Addie tried without success to get Ambrose on the telephone. At 10.15 Dolores, feeling the effects of her lack of sleep the previous night, said that if Addie would excuse her she would like to go to bed. Not long after she had gone upstairs Addie tried Ambrose's number again. It was answered on the fourth ring.

'Hello,' said the man's voice, and even after all this time she knew it. 'Hello — Ambrose?'

'Yes.' There was a questioning note in his tone, as if somehow, just from the two words Addie had spoken, he was beginning to recognize her voice. 'Who's this?'

'Ambrose, it's Addie Haroldson — as I was at Birmingham. Do you — ?'

She didn't have a chance to continue. He burst in at once: 'Addie! How great to hear you. Your voice sounded familiar, and I was just trying to place it.' He gave his familiar laugh. 'My God, what a surprise.'

'I've been trying to get you all evening.'

'I've been in the country. I've only just walked in.' He chuckled. 'Boy, this is something — hearing from you after all this time. How did you get my number?'

She hesitated before she answered, then said, 'From Harry Comrie's friend Gerald.

He mentioned that you'd written when Harry died.'

'Yes, I did.' His sigh came sharply over the line. 'Poor Harry. That was a sad business. And Christie too. You know about her, of course.'

'Yes.'

'Did you keep up contact with anyone?' he said.

'Well, Kieron married my cousin, but as for the others, no, I'm afraid not. Though Dolores and I met up again recently.'

'And how's she getting on?'

'Fine, fine. She's staying with me right now. You just missed her; she's just gone up to bed.'

'Give her my best wishes, please.'

'I will.'

'How are you, Addie?'

'I'm fine. I'm very well.'

'Are you married?'

'Yes, I'm Addie Carmichael now.'

'Carmichael, huh? And have you got children?'

' — No. No children.'

'I'm on my own,' Ambrose said, 'and it looks likely to remain that way. But that's life, as they say.'

'As they say.' She paused, trying to assess whether they'd done enough small talk and catching up, then said, 'Ambrose, you'll be wondering why I'm phoning you after all this time.'

He chuckled. 'It crossed my mind, I must admit.'

'Yes — well — ' Her tone was graver now. 'We want to come and see you, talk to you — Dolores and I.'

'Oh?' he said, and she heard the note of puzzlement in his tone. Calling him out of the blue after eleven years, she'd need a good reason. 'Talk? What about?'

'Can it wait till we see you?' she said. 'Our reason?'

'Boy, this sounds pretty mysterious. Can't you even give me a clue?'

'Oh, Ambrose, I'd rather wait till we meet, if that's all right with you. Will you indulge me?'

'It's the first favour you've asked in eleven years. How can I refuse. So, when do you want to come to sunny Eastbourne?'

'As soon as possible. What about tomorrow?'

'Tomorrow? No, tomorrow's not good. Can we make it Tuesday?'

Tuesday was the day Charlie was due home. But she had no choice but to work things around his return. 'All right, Tuesday.' She trusted to luck that it would be OK with Dolores. 'In the morning sometime?'

'No, I've got the dentist. It would have to be the afternoon. Is that difficult?'

'No, that's fine.'

'Good. Have you got my address?'

She read out the address that Gerald had given her.

'That's right,' Ambrose said. 'Will you be driving?'

'Yes — either Dolores or me.'

He proceeded then to give her directions from the point where they would enter the town. 'So,' he added, 'I'll expect you around three or so, yes? Come for tea. I'm not the most domesticated animal, but I can manage a cuppa.' His tone more serious, he added, 'It'll be great to see you both again.'

'It'll be great to see *you*.'

'You said just now that Kieron married your cousin . . . '

'Yes, Milla — Camilla.'

'Oh, right. I remember when she visited you that weekend and we all went out together. She and Kieron clicked right off.' She could hear the smile in his voice. 'That's really nice they ended up together. I always liked him so much.'

She paused and then said, 'He's dead, Ambrose. I'm so sorry to tell you.'

'*What?*' The word was little more than

a breath. 'Kieron? Dead? Oh, God, Addie, when was this?'

'In June.'

'Had he been ill? What was it?'

'They said he died of blood-poisoning.'

He gave a low groan. 'Oh, poor Kieron. I can hardly believe it. His wife must be devastated.'

'Yes.'

'Did they have children?'

'A little girl, Helen.'

'It's tragic,' he said. 'It's absolutely tragic.'

'Yes.'

There was a longish silence between them, and then Ambrose said, 'Our little group's had pretty bad luck, wouldn't you say?'

'You could say that.'

'First Ruby, and now Christie and Harry, and Kieron as well. Of our group of eight, four are gone. And not one of them, I should think, over the age of thirty-six or thirty-seven. If this were some detective novel I'd be starting to get suspicious.'

'I know what you mean.' She was anxious now to bring the conversation to an end before they got embarked on things she didn't want to discuss over the phone. 'Anyway, we can talk on Tuesday,' she said. 'We'll try to be there about three. We can catch up then. If there's any problem I'll give you a call.'

Later, sitting in bed with a mug of tea at her side, she thought again of Ambrose's words: *Our little group's had pretty bad luck, wouldn't you say?*

16

Over breakfast Addie told Dolores of her conversation with Ambrose, and of the arrangements for their meeting. Dolores responded with a lack of enthusiasm that did not bode well. Soon after they had eaten, Carole arrived and, keeping occupied, Addie and Dolores helped her with some of the chores. From her bedroom after lunch, when Carole had gone, Addie called Charlie at his hotel. He had just come in from dinner, and was starting to pack in preparation for his return the following day. She wanted to know, she said, what time he would be back. He said he expected to be home sometime in the late afternoon. In that case, she said, unfortunately she wouldn't be there when he arrived. 'I have to go off,' she added. 'Dolores and I — we're going to Eastbourne.'

'*Eastbourne*? What's at Eastbourne?'

'We're going to see somebody. Ambrose Morgenson.'

'Ambrose? Wasn't he at Birmingham with you?' It came out almost like an accusation. 'What on earth are you going to see him about?'

'Oh, Charlie, I can't go into it now. I'll tell you about it later.'

'Listen, Addie, I don't know this character. You obviously do — or think you do — but just — well, be careful, all right?'

'Yes, I'll be careful.' He was right, he didn't know Ambrose; if he did he wouldn't give such advice. 'Anyway,' she said, 'I'll see you sometime tomorrow.'

★ ★ ★

When Dolores came downstairs the next morning Addie at once noted the quiet preoccupation in her manner. 'What is it?' she asked, already sure of the answer.

'Addie,' Dolores said, 'would you hate me if I didn't come with you?'

'You really don't want to, do you?'

'I just want to get away from it all.'

'I know how you feel. What will you do? Go on back home to Hammersmith?'

'I don't know. I suppose I could go to my sister in Bristol. Stay with her till I get on her nerves. That won't take too long. Anyway, whatever I decide, I'll phone and let you know.'

Within half an hour Dolores had gone, and soon afterwards, leaving a note with Ambrose's telephone number, Addie, at the wheel of the Citroën, set off. With Dolores no longer being available to undertake the driving she had considered going by train, but eventually had decided against it. She took the route that she and Dolores had taken when going to see Ruth Comrie and Gerald. Sellotaped to the dashboard was a sheet bearing in large felt-tip words and symbols the directions for her journey.

She approached the M4 with considerable trepidation, but once committed there was no turning back. She reached Eastbourne in good time, and eventually found a parking lot. That done she went into a newsagent's and bought a map of the town. It being not yet two o'clock, she decided to get some lunch and stopped at a pub where, for the sake of convenience, she put up with the thudding noise of the taped music and ate a few bites of a mediocre cottage pie. It was as palatable as the music, and leaving it on the plate she was soon out again on the street. After spending a little time browsing in a bookshop she set off once more.

Ambrose's flat was in a three-storey terrace house in a narrow street in an older part of the town. Addie pressed his doorbell then ran a smoothing hand over her hair. She had still not decided on the tack she should take in her conversation with him — whether she should voice her suspicions about the deaths of their former friends, or try to find out what she could without revealing anything more. With luck, circumstances would dictate her course. She waited, rang the bell again, and then checked her watch. Two fifty-five. She rang once more. Then, just when she was considering going to find a telephone and calling him, the little metal speaker above the bells panel crackled with static and Ambrose's voice was heard.

'Addie? Is that you?'

'Yes, it is.'

'Push the door and come up to the first floor.' A buzzer sounded as the lock was released, and she pushed open the door and stepped through.

The entrance hall was functional rather than prepossessing. A strip of carpet led past a small, scratched table bearing pieces of mail and copies of a local paper. She went up the stairs — only linoleum here, and its painted walls bare of decoration — and on the first-floor landing came to a door with the number 2 fixed to it. She heard a sound at the catch and then the door was opening.

'Ambrose . . . '

His appearance took her by surprise. Not because of what the intervening years had done — he had changed physically very little — but because of the fact that he looked sick. There was a strange waxy look about his skin; he was pale and she could see that he was perspiring.

He grasped her hand, but as she moved to kiss his cheek he stepped back. 'Don't come too close — you might catch it. I think I've got a touch of the dreaded lurgy.' He gestured for her to enter. 'Sorry I took so long answering the bell; I was in the bathroom.' As she went in he looked past her. 'Where's Dolores?'

'She couldn't come.'

He closed the door and led the way into a good-sized sitting-room overlooking the street. 'Please — sit down.' He gestured to an armchair beside a gas fire which burned with a low flame. A fire? she thought — in August? He wore sandals, jeans, and a sweater over his shirt. 'I've been in bed most of the morning,' he said, 'so I'm a little behind. I'll put the kettle on. Sorry I haven't got any cake. I meant to do some shopping on the way back from the dentist, but I didn't make my dental appointment.'

She took off her jacket and sat down and he went out of the room. She looked around her. The carpet and furnishings were in soft earth colours. On the cream walls hung framed prints and photographs — some of the latter of pop singers from bygone eras: young women in glamorous evening frocks and strange hairstyles stood before microphones the size of tea plates. A white-painted unit of shelves supported a hi-fi stereo system and rows of records.

Ambrose returned and sat down facing her. 'It won't be long.'

'I see you're still collecting your old records,' she said.

He smiled. 'I've just written off for some more. Some things about us don't change.' He looked her up and down. 'What about you, Addie? Have you changed?'

'No,' she said with a little chuckle, 'I haven't changed either.'

He gave her a wide, warm smile, a little wan, but nevertheless very much his own. 'It's really good to see you.'

'It's good to see *you*, Ambrose.'

As if a little short of breath, he said, 'Though I know what you're thinking; you're thinking I look a real bugger, right? Well, I feel it, I don't mind telling you.'

'I have seen you look better, I must admit,' she said. 'What's wrong with you? You sounded all right on the phone on Sunday.'

'It came on last night. I felt great during the day, but then as the evening wore on I began to feel so weak. I was at dinner with friends and came home early. I had no energy. I felt lousy this morning — which is why I stayed in bed and cancelled the dentist. I had a temperature, and then about eleven I was throwing up. Right now I seem to be feeling worse by the minute. I don't know what it is.' He smiled and at the same time gave a little groan. 'I'm sorry, Addie, I was so looking forward to seeing you. As a matter of fact I tried to phone you, to put off our meeting till I felt better, but you'd obviously already left.'

'I left pretty early.' She got up, moved to him and placed the back of her hand on his forehead. Over the heat she could feel the moistness of his perspiration.

'I've got a temperature, right?' he said.

'You certainly have.'

'My pulse rate is up, too. I took it not long ago. It's way up.'

'Have you eaten anything today?'

'I couldn't face breakfast. I feel as if I've got the flu or something.'

'You haven't called a doctor, I suppose.'

'No.' He dismissed the suggestion with a wave of his hand. 'I'll be all right soon. It's probably one of those twenty-four hour bugs that do the rounds.'

'Have you got some aspirin? That might bring your temperature down.'

'I took the last one this morning.'

She stepped away, picked up her bag and dipped into it for her purse. 'Give me your keys and I'll go out and get you something.'

'No, really,' he protested, 'I shall be OK.'

'Ambrose,' she smiled, 'don't be brave. Come on, give me your keys.'

He pointed. 'On the table there, next to the door.'

She picked them up. 'Anything else you need?' She took up a couple of letters. 'You want these posted?'

'Oh, please. I had them ready to post yesterday and forgot. It's my brother David's birthday tomorrow. He'll expect a card. The other's for some records.'

'You want anything else?'

'Maybe you could get me a loaf of bread? White, medium sliced.'

'OK.'

He directed her. 'Turn to the left outside.

290

The shops are just along the street.'

In ten minutes, her errands completed, she was back. He was sitting in the chair as she had left him. She took the bread into the kitchen. It was clean but a little untidy. On the draining board were a few items of used china and cutlery, in the sink a bowl almost full of breakfast cereal and milk. The kettle had boiled and switched off again. She switched it back on then took a glass from a cupboard and filled it at the tap. Returning to the sitting-room she found Ambrose leaning back in his chair, the sweat sticking his hair to his forehead. She handed him the glass along with a couple of aspirin tablets. She watched as he swallowed them, then took the glass from him and set it down. 'This is ridiculous.' he said. 'I'm never ill.'

Back in the kitchen she made tea, then carried it into the sitting-room, setting the tray on the coffee-table. 'Could you eat something?' she asked.

'No. No, thanks.' Then, with an uncertain smile, and clearly making an effort, he said, 'So how's life been treating you, Addie?'

'I'm fine. It's you I'm concerned about right now.'

'I'll be all right. I'll be fine by tomorrow. Anyway, what was it you wanted to see me about? You made it sound so mysterious.'

She had questions she wanted to ask, but this wasn't the time, not when he was like this. On the other hand, time was of the essence — and not only for herself and Dolores, but perhaps for his own sake as well.

'We . . . we wanted to talk to you about the others,' she said after a moment. 'Christie and Harry and Kieron.'

'Ah, yes.' He sighed. 'Who would have believed it? All three of them.'

'Exactly. In so short a time, all three of them.'

He looked at her more closely, narrowing his eyes slightly, as if trying to read something written behind her expression. 'Addie, what are you here for? After eleven years you haven't tracked me down just to chat about old times.'

'No, I haven't.'

'Three of our old friends have died,' he said. 'That's why you're here, right? I've been thinking about it. You think it's not just a coincidence that they've died.'

'Right.' She'd come all this way; there was no point in prevaricating.

He frowned, was silent for some moments, then said, 'What you're saying, Addie — my God, this is really shocking. You're suggesting something . . . sinister. I think, no, that kind of thing doesn't happen outside the movies. But on the other hand I have to wonder how come three young and supposedly healthy friends all die within a few weeks of each other. And how strange that nobody sees anything odd in it.'

'Not so strange. The authorities probably aren't aware that there's any connection between them — the three people, I mean.' She poured the tea and set a cup before him.

He thanked her then said, 'I learned about Christie and Harry, and it was tragic. But I could accept it as a coincidence. Though I don't know what Harry's supposed to have died of. But then when you told me about Kieron too — no. I don't know the facts about all the deaths. But hearing about Kieron — that was one death too many.'

'That's what *we* felt, Dolores and I. And when you look more closely you see that in each case the symptoms were identical.'

He frowned. 'You'd better tell me what's been going on. I've got time. I'm not going anywhere. Tell me everything.'

Moving backwards and forwards in her narrative, Addie spoke of the supposed causes of the deaths of Kieron and Harry and listed some of the symptoms they had manifested. She spoke too of Christie, whose symptoms had been identical; the only difference in outcome being that a pathologist familiar with ricin poisoning had performed the autopsy on her body. She told him also of the death of little Alice Marshall who, shortly before her death, had been visiting Christie.

'So, you believe they all might have been poisoned.' He spoke rather haltingly, as if he had some difficulty in forming the words and was having to concentrate. 'The child too? You think she was also a victim?'

'Yes. I don't know for what reason *she* might have been poisoned, but I can think of a reason with the others.'

'What is that?'

'Think,' she said. 'What did they all have in common?'

He shrugged. 'Well, the fact that they were all together in Birmingham.'

'And can you think of any incident that stood out in any way?'

'Oh, come on, we're talking about Ruby here, aren't we?'

'I think so, yes.'

His nod was barely perceptible. 'That — that was the strangest, most awful business. Not only her death, but what happened afterwards. Those letters, and all the suspicion they engendered.'

'It was never the same afterwards, was it?

I doubt it could have been anyway, after Ruby's death, but as soon as the letters arrived things were changed even more.'

'How could they not? And was there truth in those letters?'

'What else is there to think?'

'And Ruby was killed, then. It wasn't suicide or an accident. She was killed.'

'Is there any other conclusion to be drawn?'

'But why would anyone kill her? She managed to rub a few people up the wrong way, but I can't think of anything that could lead to such a drastic step.'

'No, I can't either.'

A pause, then Ambrose said, 'She got me really pissed off at one time.'

'Oh?'

'Yes.' He paused. 'Did you know about Harry and me?'

'I did hear a little about it. Gerald, Harry's friend, mentioned it.'

'Did he, now.' He shrugged. 'Well, we had a little fling. I guess you could call it that. We both thought everybody'd guessed.'

'I don't know about the others, but I had no idea.'

'It didn't last that long. For one thing I had so many hangups. Kindness of my father, I have to say. Anyway, it all came to an end. But not before Ruby found out.'

'How did that happen?'

He hesitated briefly. 'Well, it's all water under the bridge now. I was kissing him. It just happened. In the kitchen at Christie's flat when we were all there one evening. And Ruby walked in on us. Boy, was that embarrassing.'

'I'll bet. She never mentioned it.'

'She did to me. In a joking way. She said she wondered how my father would react. I thought she was serious. It would have given him a seizure. He always said he'd disown any son of his who was that way. He couldn't understand how some parents were so *forgiving*, as he put it.'

'She didn't tell him, did she?'

'No. She got enough from the threat. We all get our kicks in different ways, and that was one of hers.' He paused. 'Did Gerald Fraser tell you anything else?'

'What? No, just that you'd written when Harry died. That's how he was able to tell me where you lived.'

'He already knew where I lived. He even came round here to see me.'

'What?'

'Not long after Harry and I met up again.'

'But . . . why did he do that?'

'To warn me off.'

'Are you serious?'

'Of course. Harry and I met again by chance, and as we lived so close — comparatively — I thought it would be nice to renew our friendship. Gerald, though, had different ideas. I think he was afraid I'd try to start it all up again with Harry — try to kindle old fires. Though that wasn't my intention. Anyway, imagine my surprise to have Gerald call round to see me. He made it quite clear that he wouldn't welcome any renewal of our friendship.'

'He never hinted at anything like that.'

'Well, he wouldn't, would he? It isn't something you'd talk about. I don't think Harry knew about his visit.'

Addie sat in silence for a moment, taking this in, then Ambrose said, 'Anyway, all that business with Ruby — didn't you yourself have cause to be less than enamoured of her . . . ?' He let the question hang in the air.

After a moment she said, 'It wasn't serious between Matt and me.'

'No?'

'Well, not for him, anyway.'

'Oh, Ads, what a shame.'

She shrugged. 'In any case it only lasted a matter of days.'

'Sometimes just a few days can be everything.'

'Well, where he was concerned it never amounted to anything.'

'Probably not, once he'd set his sights on Christie.' He put his head a little on one side. 'Isn't that what happened?'

'Yes.'

'And then in turn old Rubes set her sights on him, and he ended up getting a taste of his own medicine. Did you ever see him again? Afterwards, I mean?'

'Never.' Her tone didn't encourage continuation of the subject.

'I did,' he said. 'I ran into him when I was in London for the day. Ages ago. We swapped addresses and exchanged Christmas cards for a couple of years. But then I never heard again.'

She was alert at this. 'Was he living in London?'

'No, in Leicestershire. A place called Syston, as I recall. I had his address around here, but this is going back a bit.' He paused. 'He wasn't the kind of man you could really make a friend of. He never really allowed you to get close.'

Addie said nothing.

'Anyway,' Ambrose said, 'it's all in the past, isn't it?'

'Not all of it, I'm afraid.'

'No, I suppose not.' He nodded slowly. 'So after all this time we find out that Ruby was *indeed* killed and that somebody — either one of the remaining seven, or somebody from outside — knew something, and wrote those letters.'

'Threatening exposure.'

'Threatening exposure, right. And now, you think, the murderer — whoever that is — is out to prevent that exposure.'

She nodded.

'But why wait eleven years? Why wait till now?'

'I've wondered about that, but I've no idea. Does it matter?'

'Who knows. The fact is, it's happening.' He frowned. 'Whoever that was, who wrote the letters — you realize what they did? They made each of us a target.'

'Yes.'

'I always thought it was a wind-up, that probably nobody actually saw or knew anything. But the effect's the same whether they did or not, isn't it? Somebody took the letter seriously and decided that something had to be done.'

'And is doing it.'

'Yes.' He picked up his cup and abstractedly drank from it. 'There are two people to identify. The one who did the killing, and the one who sent the letters.'

'The one who sent the letters could have been any one of us seven.'

'Yes. I know about myself, but as for the others — for all I know, it could have been any one of them — Harry, Kieron, Christie, Matthew, Dolores — even you.'

'It wasn't me,' Addie said. 'But just suppose it was Kieron — I can't imagine it, but just suppose it was. He was the first one to be killed. In which case the killer's already got rid of the threat.'

'But he wouldn't know that. So he won't be satisfied till the rest of us are out of the way. Who was it, Addie? Who sent those letters?'

'I don't know. Perhaps it doesn't matter now. The damage is done.'

She watched as he wiped again at his forehead. His head drooped and he lifted it again as if with effort. Throughout their conversation he had been growing more and more lacklustre, and she suddenly realized that all the while a fear had been stirring inside her. She had not acknowledged it even to herself, but it was there. She watched again as his head tipped forward, then as he recovered and sat upright.

'I'm sorry,' he said, 'I'm not usually such bad company. It's this bloody bug.' He leaned forward to reach for his cup. But then abruptly the action changed, and he was rising to his feet, clapping a hand over his mouth and hurrying across the room and into the hall. She heard a door close and then a moment later the muffled sound of retching. She sat clutching the arms of the chair, listening as he vomited, and with every second that passed her fear grew.

After a while the sound of his vomiting ceased. She heard taps running, and then he was coming back into the room, holding a hand towel to his face. She got up and went to him. It was astonishing how his condition had deteriorated just in the time she had been there.

'Come and sit down.' One arm around his broad back, she walked with him to his chair and saw him settled into it. He was gasping.

'Sorry about that,' he said. 'I haven't eaten anything so there's nothing for me to bring up.'

He closed his eyes and she laid the back of her hand on his forehead again. He was burning up. Turning, she went into the bathroom where she put his washcloth under the cold tap and wrung it out. Beside him again, she gently laid the folded cloth on his brow. At the touch he gave a little sigh. 'Oh, that's so good.' She sat facing him. The only sounds in the room were those of his increasingly laboured breathing and the traffic from the street below.

After a while, into the quiet, he said, still with his eyes closed, 'According to — to what you discovered, Addie . . . ' His speech was more laboured than ever. 'According to what you discovered, all three of the deaths — Christie's and Harry's and Kieron's — had — certain things in common.'

'Ambrose, don't talk. Rest, please.'

'Listen.' He waved a weak, impatient hand. 'You said — you said — all three had feelings of weakness at the start, later accompanied by high temperature and — increasing pulse rate. Right?'

'Right, yes.'

'And later — later there had been — vomiting.'

'Yes.' She knew what he was going to say.

He gave a little laugh, brief, weak, and without humour. 'Well, Addie, in case you — in case you hadn't noticed, they're — they're my symptoms too.'

302

17

Ambrose's words, voicing Addie's own thoughts, brought a rush of apprehension to her heart. She stared at him, the tears springing to her eyes. 'Oh, Ambrose.'

The look in his drooping, heavy eyes was touched with irony. 'Well, Addie, this isn't what we expected, is it?'

She crouched before him, hands catching at his wrists. 'Ambrose . . . '

'Now,' he said, 'we can't have you panicking. I'm relying on you to help me.'

'Of course.' She straightened, started towards the telephone. 'We must call your doctor, so he can get you to a hospital. Where's his number?'

He gestured. 'In my address book. Barwick is his name.'

Addie looked up the number and dialled it. It was answered by a woman. When Addie said that the doctor was needed as soon as possible the woman replied that Dr Barwick was busy, and that the doctor making house calls was Dr Lumsden.

'Well, whoever,' Addie said, 'but somebody's got to come and see Mr Morgenson immediately. He's very ill.'

'Give me the name and address,' the woman said coolly — she didn't care to have demands made of her, emergency or not, 'and I'll pass the message on to the doctor. She'll get there as soon as she can.'

Addie gave the information, then the woman asked, 'And what d'you think is wrong with the patient? The doctor'll want to know. What are his symptoms?'

'Tell her . . . tell her that Mr Morgenson might have swallowed something — perhaps poison.'

'*Poison*?'

'Yes. Please, get the doctor here as quickly as possible.'

Addie hung up and turned to Ambrose. 'It won't be your Dr Barwick but a woman — Dr Lumsden.' She glanced at her watch, marking the time. It was close on six. Now when she looked at Ambrose she could see fear in his face. The brief show of bravado had gone. 'The doctor will know what to do,' she said.

'Oh, yeah?' Ambrose said. 'Doctors didn't help the others.'

'Well, no, but if it *is* what we fear, then you've got an advantage over them.'

304

'Which is?'

'Well, no one knew it was poison they were dealing with in the other cases, did they?'

He gave a distracted shake of his head. The act of speaking seemed to be getting more and more arduous. And suddenly he was thrusting himself out of the chair and hurrying to the bathroom again. Seconds later she heard once more the violent sounds of his retching. As she stood there, feeling totally helpless, there came the ringing of the telephone. She took up the receiver.

'Addie? Is that you?'

'Charlie!' Relief welled up like a tapped spring. 'Oh, thank God you've called.'

'I've just got in from the airport and seen your note. What's up?'

'Oh, Charlie, I'm so glad to hear your voice.' It took all her control not to burst into tears.

'What's the matter? Tell me what's the matter?'

'It's Ambrose — he's so sick. I've just rung for a doctor.' From the bathroom she could still hear the sound of Ambrose's retching. 'I'm so afraid for him. They'll have to get him into hospital, I know.'

'As bad as that?'

'Yes.'

'And is this connected with all that — that other business?'

'Yes, it is.'

'I see.' He paused, then said, 'Give me the address. I'm coming down.'

It was what she wanted to hear. She gave him the address, then added, 'Charlie, listen, if Ambrose is taken to the hospital I'll have to hang around. I can't leave.'

'No, of course not. I understand that. So you'll need some things, right?'

'Yes.' She silently blessed him for being so understanding. 'I'll need a nightdress and some toilet things. I shall want — '

'Leave it to me,' he cut in. 'I think I know you well enough now. I'll throw some things into a case and leave right away. I'll be with you just as soon as I can. In the meantime, hang in there. And if you find you have to leave or anything, you've got my mobile number, so you can let me know.'

As she replaced the receiver Ambrose reappeared, walking unsteadily to his chair. As he sat down he said, 'Addie, there's a — a bowl in the kitchen. Would you get it for me, please?'

She went into the kitchen, found a red plastic bowl and brought it into the sitting-room. He mumbled thanks as she set it down beside him. 'I'm sorry you have to go through this,' he said. 'You'll be w-wanting to get away, get back home.'

She sat down facing him. 'I'm not leaving you, Ambrose. Not like this. In any case, my husband's coming here. He phoned while you were in the bathroom.'

'He's coming here?'

'He's on his way right now.'

He tried a smile that didn't quite work. 'You've g-got somebody s-special there, Addie. I'd hang on to him if it w-were me.'

'I intend to.' She paused, then said, 'Ambrose, just supposing you *have* swallowed some of that — that poison, how d'you think you came to take it?'

'I don't — know. I've been — trying to — to w-work it out . . . ' His head drooped forward on his chest, and with obvious effort he raised it again. His eyes were half closed. 'I didn't s-see anybody till I went out to see my f-friends. We were meeting at a p-pub for a — a — a drink and then — going on to a — a restaurant.'

'What time was that? That you met them.'

He frowned, thinking back. 'About s-six-thirty. Before I got dressed I did a — a couple of little chores and odd jobs. I wrote away for m-my old records, and wrote my brother's card, and m-made out

307

a list of things that I — needed from the supermarket the n-next day. Oh, yes, I also m-made a couple of phone calls. Then I went out. And — as I told you — I began to feel a bit — unwell — when I was in the — the restaurant. So I — I came home early.'

'Did you meet anyone unusual or . . . ?'

'I just met my — friends, that's all.'

'Ambrose, try and think, was there anything in the least out of the ordinary about the evening?'

'No. If you're asking did I run into — into M-Matt, the answer is no. I just left here and — went straight to the pub. I didn't talk to anybody except some guy who stopped me — and asked me for d-directions to the — t-town hall.'

'Oh? Was there anything about him?'

'What? No, nothing.'

'Can you remember what you ate at the restaurant?'

'We ate Thai food. And several of us ate the s-same dishes. It was nothing s-special. It was — ' His words came to an abrupt halt and he reached down and snatched up the bowl. He vomited into it, bringing up some dark liquid. Afterwards, still with the bowl on his lap he lay back gasping. 'I — I'm sorry.'

'Please, there's nothing to apologize for.'

Wearily he said, 'I think I — I'd like to try and s-sleep for f-five minutes.'

'Yes,' she said, 'it'll do you good.' She placed the bowl on the carpet beside his chair then took a cushion, gently lifted his head and placed the cushion beneath it. He gave her a faint smile of thanks and closed his eyes. On the back of the sofa lay a tartan rug, and she laid it over his knees. For a few moments she stood looking down at him, then quietly stepped to the window. Down on the street the lights of the motor traffic were coming on; the shop windows further along were lit up. She felt as if she were in limbo. And the thought went through her mind: supposing Ambrose didn't recover? Christie and Kieron and Harry had all been victims, as possibly also had been the child — and if Ambrose was another, then the chances were that he would die.

And what about his family? She had no idea whether his parents were still living, but he obviously had a brother; she had posted a birthday card to him only that afternoon. She moved over to the telephone and took up Ambrose's address book. There was just one Morgenson listed, and seeing the first name, David, she recognized it at once. If Ambrose's condition deteriorated much further, or if the doctor decided to admit him to hospital then she must call him. She looked at her watch. It had been almost fifty minutes since she had rung for the doctor. Going into the kitchen she got on the telephone extension and called the practice's number again. The same woman answered.

'I telephoned almost an hour ago,' Addie said, 'to ask for a doctor to come and visit Mr Ambrose Morgenson, and there's been no sign of anybody. Can you tell me what's happening, please?'

In stiff, defensive tones, the woman replied that she had passed the message on, adding that there had been a great many calls for the doctor's services.

'This is an emergency,' Addie said. 'There is a man here who may be dying.'

★ ★ ★

A further forty-five minutes went by before the doctor arrived, and in the meantime Ambrose's condition had clearly worsened. Not only had he vomited several times, but he seemed to be having even greater difficulty in speaking.

Dr Lumsden was a woman of medium height, dark-haired, and with a slightly officious air that belied any surface warmth

310

engendered by the wide smile she flashed as she entered the hall. Addie led the way into the sitting-room where Ambrose sat in the armchair, eyes closed and breathing heavily. He opened his eyes, and the doctor beamed a smile of greeting at him and said, 'Right, let's see what we can do for you, Mr Morgenson.' As she put down her bag, she turned to Addie. 'Are you his wife?'

'I'm a friend who's visiting from out of town. He has no wife. I think his only family is a brother who lives in Lewes.'

The doctor nodded and efficiently began her examination. As she did so, Ambrose said, the words bursting out of him,

'Doctor, I — I think I know what's — wrong with me. I've been p-poisoned.'

The woman betrayed no emotion. 'That was the message I was given,' she said. 'Are you saying you've taken something?'

'Ricin,' Ambrose murmured, but indistinctly, and the doctor turned to Addie for elucidation.

'Ricin,' Addie repeated, and seeing the blank expression in the doctor's eyes, added, 'It's a poison that comes from the castor-oil plant.'

The merest flicker in the doctor's glance said this did not happen every day. As she resumed her examination, checking pulse, temperature and heart, she asked her questions, and in response Addie told of their fears that Ambrose had in some way had the poison administered to him. She tried to keep her voice calm and make her revelations sound reasoned for she was aware of how fantastical they must appear. When the doctor asked why would anyone want to poison Mr Morgenson, Addie replied that it was a long story. The doctor then asked Ambrose about the onset of his symptoms, but as the act of speech cost him so much effort, she turned once more to Addie. Addie repeated what Ambrose had told her, of how the night before he had returned home early from an evening with friends, of how she had found him on her arrival today, and of his deterioration in the hours since then.

Having completed her examination, the doctor's perplexity was obvious. She asked Ambrose whether he had taken any medication, and Addie said that he had taken two aspirin tablets a couple of hours earlier. 'Though I doubt that he kept them down,' she added.

'Well,' the doctor said, 'disregarding for the moment your own beliefs, I have to say that I don't know what's causing the problem. Your pulse is very rapid, Mr Morgenson, and you've got a high temperature. But all kinds of things can bring on such symptoms. However, you tell

312

me they've been brought on by *poison*.'
She followed her words with a little half
smile; clearly she was not accepting what
she had been told. And who, Addie asked
herself, could blame her? She doubted that
she herself would believe it if faced with such
a situation.

'What I'm going to do,' Dr Lumsden
said after a moment or two, 'is give you
something to bring your temperature down.
And I'll come back and see you again in a
couple of hours. In the meantime I'm going
to look into this — this ricin poison you
speak of.' To Addie she said, 'Can you stay
with him for the time being?'

'Of course. D'you think he should go
to bed?'

The doctor looked at him. 'Would you feel
better in bed, Mr Morgenson?'

'N-no.' Ambrose shook his head decisively.

'Leave him where he is for the time being.'
From a small phial the doctor took two
tablets and placed them on the table at
Ambrose's side. 'Take these and I'll look
in again.' She snapped her bag shut and
glanced down at the red plastic bowl into
which Ambrose had vomited. 'Don't throw
that away,' she said. 'It might be needed for
examination later.'

Down in the main hall the doctor opened

the door and turned to Addie. 'Phone me at once if his condition should worsen. I'll be back later. And hopefully we'll get this all sorted out.' With a last judicious and sceptical look at Addie, she stepped out onto the pavement and started away along the street.

Half an hour later the doorbell rang again, and Charlie was there.

In the downstairs hall, Addie clung to him, fighting back the tears. He held her, arms wrapped around her.

'It's all right,' he soothed her. 'It's going to be all right.'

She shook her head. 'No, it isn't. I know it isn't.'

Too much had taken place in his absence for her to relate then and there, but she told him a little of what had happened, and what she felt he needed to know.

Upstairs she introduced him to Ambrose, and then, while Charlie sat near him, went into the kitchen and put the kettle on for some tea. As she was setting out cups, Charlie came in. 'We must decide what to do,' he said. His voice was low. 'Suppose this *is* that poison — ricin . . . ' He let his question hang in the air.

'I'm sure it is. He has all the symptoms.' She studied Charlie's face. 'You don't have any doubts now about what's going on, do you?'

'No, not at all. And now the police are bound to become involved; it'll be out of our hands. The hospital will bring the police in. There was nothing in the way of proof before, but — well, if poor Ambrose has been poisoned they'll have to start making investigations.'

'Yes.' She was silent for a moment, then she said, 'I've been thinking about what Dr Mukerjee told me. If he's right, then there's no real way of diagnosing such a poisoning while a person is still alive.'

He frowned. 'Really?'

'The way I understand it, it's only after death that the signs of it can be found.'

He gave a slow nod. 'I see. They won't know whether Ambrose has been given the poison until he dies from it.'

* * *

When Dr Lumsden returned less than an hour later she found that Ambrose's pulse rate had risen further. Taking Addie aside in the kitchen, she said, 'I'm going to have him admitted to hospital. I'll be quite frank — I don't know what's wrong with him. But if he has ingested some kind of poison, then it's essential they treat it as soon as possible. I'll phone now and try to find a bed.' She moved to the telephone and lifted the receiver. 'I believe you said he has a brother, did you?'

'Yes, in Lewes — going by his address book.'

The doctor nodded. 'When I've arranged for his admittance to hospital, perhaps you could give his brother a call and put him in the picture.'

'Yes, of course.'

After numerous phone calls a bed was found at a hospital not far away, and less than half an hour later an ambulance was there and Ambrose was being carried out on a stretcher. Addie was in tears as she watched him go, following him down the stairs and onto the street where she pressed his hand and said she'd see him soon. He gave a shadow of his old smile, and mumbled, with difficulty, 'Yes — see you soon.'

In the flat she looked up the number of his brother. Her call was answered by a woman, his wife, Emily. David was out at present, she said, but would he back soon. Addie gave her name and said that Ambrose had just been taken by ambulance to the Eastbourne Park Hospital. She had to be honest, she said, and not play down the seriousness of his condition, for it could prove to be quite grave. Therefore, if Ambrose had other close relatives, perhaps they should be informed. No, the woman said, Ambrose had no close relatives apart from his brother. She was clearly shocked. She asked Addie where she could be contacted, and Addie replied, 'My husband and I will find a hotel nearby. I'll phone and let you know.'

When the call was over she turned to Charlie where he sat on the sofa. Answering her unspoken question, he said: 'I packed a bag for you and for me. It's in the car. We'll go find a hotel whenever you want.'

There was no shortage of vacancies in the numerous hotels in the area, and after a while they found a pleasant, spacious room in a hotel looking over the promenade.

As soon as they were installed, Addie telephoned Emily Morgenson and gave her the hotel's number, adding that she had a set of keys to Ambrose's flat. Emily told her that she had called David, that he was returning home at once and would leave for Eastbourne as soon as possible.

Less than an hour later, close on eleven, David arrived. Four years older than Ambrose, he was very like him in facial features, but not as tall, and of slimmer build. He was on the way to the hospital, but wanted to talk to Addie first. He suggested that if she wanted to see Ambrose they could travel together and talk on the way. At this Charlie proposed that if Addie rode with David, he would follow in his own car.

Minutes afterwards, sitting beside David in his Astra, Addie was faced with his questions. When he asked what she thought was the nature of Ambrose's illness, she didn't know how best to reply, and merely spoke of his fever and high pulse rate. There would come a time when she would have to speak about her suspicions, she knew, but for now she shied away from it.

They reached the hospital in good time, and while David went off to enquire after Ambrose, Addie and Charlie sat alone in a waiting-room, an unattractive place furnished with a tea-and-coffee machine, and several pieces of ugly, much-abused furniture around its scratched and stained walls. After some twenty minutes they heard footsteps, and the door opened and David appeared. He looked pale and shaken.

'I had no idea he was so sick,' he said. Then, to Addie, 'He says he's been poisoned. That somebody's out to kill him.'

Addie said nothing.

'You knew about this,' he said.

'Yes, but I couldn't tell you, not right

at the start. I didn't know what to do for the best.'

He frowned. 'I don't know what to make of it all. This is a nightmare that's getting worse by the minute. The police have been called.'

Afraid of the answer, Addie asked, 'How is he? Do they think he's any better?'

'Better?' He spread his hands before him in a gesture of helplessness. 'I don't know what he was like before. But according to what he himself says, he's dying.'

18

Addie stood at the French windows in the sitting-room, looking out at the rain falling on the patio, the heavy drops darkening the flags and the weathered wood of the furniture. She felt as if she were living in a dream. And nothing seemed able to alleviate the fear and distress in which she seemed to be steeped.

After the conversation with David in the hospital waiting-room she had briefly been allowed to see Ambrose. She had sat at his bedside and he had smiled at her and said, stumbling over his words, 'Well, Addie, I t-told D-Dave.'

'Yes, so I gather.'

'The cat's — out of the b-bag now.'

'And no mistake, right?'

'And no m-mistake. The cat's out of the b-bag and the b-beans are s-spilled.' He had paused, gulping at the air. 'He didn't — believe me at — first. I'm n-not sure that he does even now. I t-told him that y-you know all about it.'

She had pressed his hand. 'Tell me what I can do for you, Ambrose.'

'G-get the bastard who d-did this to me.'

Fighting back tears she said, consciously brightening her expression, 'Damn it, Ambrose, we'll do it together. You'll be out of that bed soon, and we'll nail him.'

He had smiled at this, humouring her. 'Is th-that wh-what we'll do, Addie?'

'Yes.' And as she had lied her little lie she had felt the pain of grief in her throat and the sharp pricking of tears in her eyes.

'Sure we — w-will,' he said, and faintly she had felt the pressure of his fingers in hers.

★ ★ ★

That night at the hotel she and Charlie shared a room, shared a bed, for the first time in what seemed ages.

Wearing the nightdress he had brought for her, she got into bed and lay with eyes closed as he climbed in beside her. He put the light out and she felt his pyjama-clad arm come around her and draw her to him. They lay in silence, she cupped into his body, feeling him warm against her back. After a while he shifted his position so that he was raised slightly above her and she felt his breath, toothpaste-scented, against her nostrils, and then his mouth coming down onto her cheek. It was what she needed — the contact — and the closer the better. Anything that even for a little while could shut out reality; it was too much to cope with cold. A little moonlight filtered into the room, and in its dim glow she could see his shape as he bent to her. She turned her head and met his lips in a tentative kiss, like a nervous swimmer testing the water. At the first touch she expected that he would retreat, but his mouth lingered, his tongue on hers. She matched the sound that came on his breath with a little moan of her own. It had been so, so long. And then his hands were at her waist, pulling up her nightdress, and she lifted her body and felt the fabric slide up to her breasts. She saw his hands fumble at his pyjamas and moments later felt his hardness against her. Yes, she wanted to whisper, yes, yes, it would all be all right. They would come through it all. His lips were on hers again, and she felt his hands moving over her abdomen, touching lower, and she opened herself to him. She saw the shape of his torso as he loomed above her. She could feel his eyes burning into hers. The seconds passed, and then she realized that there were too many seconds, and he had come no closer. Reaching out, she touched him, his thigh, his flaccid member.

In silence he moved away from her, and in the gloom she watched as he sat at her side, his head bent, one hand lifted to his face. She sensed despair, agony, and sat up and wrapped her arms around his chest. A tremor passed through his body, and she held on tighter. 'Oh, Charlie,' she murmured against his shoulder, 'it'll be all right.' He said nothing. In the faint light she could see that he was staring ahead into the shadows. 'It's my fault,' she said. 'Oh, my darling, I'm so sorry.'

'No.' The word came out a broken sound, and she felt him struggling to hold on to his composure. 'You mustn't blame yourself,' he said. 'It was beyond your control.' He lifted a hand and tapped at his forehead. 'In any case, it's all up here. The problem's up here.' He paused. 'Give it time, Addie. Just give it time. I promise you it'll be all right.'

'Yes. Yes, it will. All the time you want Charlie. I'm here. I shall always be here.' And she raised her hand to his face and felt on his cheek the wet of his tears.

★ ★ ★

She and Charlie spent two nights at the hotel, keeping in touch with the hospital at regular intervals. On Addie's first return visit she had seen two men come from Ambrose's room, and had learned from David that they were police officers.

On this occasion she had met David's wife, a pleasant woman in her early thirties. Leaving their two young children in the care of a neighbour, Emily had snatched a few hours to come to Eastbourne to see Ambrose and lend support to her husband. Later, reluctantly and tearfully, she had set off back again to Lewes.

Addie had seen Ambrose at the hospital three times in all. On the first two occasions she had briefly sat at his bedside, stroking and holding his hand, her heart ready to break at the sight of him lying there with the tubes attached to his body. The third occasion had been following a telephone call from David, saying that although Ambrose was considerably worse he had nevertheless expressed a desire to see her. Charlie had at once driven her to the hospital. Entering Ambrose's room, she and David were met by a nurse who had asked them not to stay long.

As the door softly clicked shut, Addie turned to the bed. She had learned from David that earlier there had been a dramatic collapse of Ambrose's blood pressure, and while his temperature had fallen, his pulse had risen still further. The difference in him now was so obvious. She looked at him as he lay there, shivering and sweating, no more than a shell of the robust and handsome young man she had known, and the tears sprang to her eyes and ran down her cheeks.

'Ambrose,' David said softly, 'Addie's here.'

Ambrose's heavy-lidded eyes swivelled in their sockets then settled upon her. 'A-Addie . . . ?' He spoke with difficulty.

'Yes, Ambrose.' She moved closer, sat in the chair next to the bed and softly laid her fingers on his cold, clammy hand.

'Addie . . . ' There was a worried, fretful look on his face.

'Yes? What is it?' She wanted to urge him to rest, not to tire himself, but he seemed intent on trying to talk. His words, though, came mumbled, stuttering and stammering from his tortured mouth. She had the greatest difficulty in making out what he was saying, and when she did the words didn't make sense. He spoke names to her, names that were unfamiliar, and then lapsed into silence again. David, standing at Addie's side, whispered, 'He keeps on like that. He's just wandering now. Going in and out of consciousness.'

Then, seconds later, eyes rolling in his head, Ambrose's hands came up and feverishly began to pluck at the intravenous lines, trembling fingers yanking on the tubes and the needles, ripping them out of his flesh, sending blood spraying. 'Get the nurse in here!' David said sharply, and while she hurried out of the room he stepped to his brother's side, reaching out to stay his hands.

Addie never saw Ambrose again.

As she and Charlie sat in the waiting-room, David came in and said that Ambrose had gone into cardiac arrest, and that they were trying to resuscitate him. With nowhere else to go, he remained there, sometimes sitting, at other times pacing the room. He was still there forty-five minutes later when a doctor came in and said that all efforts to revive

Ambrose had failed. He was dead.

A few minutes later, two members of the local police force had come to her, the senior officer asking to speak to her privately. When Charlie asked if he might be present there was no objection. The room they were shown into was someone's office. There was a desk and three chairs. Addie and Charlie were invited to sit facing the desk behind which the detective inspector seated himself. The sergeant stood to one side.

Detective Inspector Alan Davis was in his mid-forties, a tall, dark, good-looking man with spectacles and a navy-blue, pin-striped suit. Sergeant Williamson, his assistant, was in his late thirties, a large man with reddish hair and a Scottish accent. The charcoal grey suit he wore hung uneasily on his burly figure.

'Apart from the *tragedy* of Mr Morgenson's death,' Davis said, 'we're very concerned about the manner of it. I'm sure you realize that.'

Addie said yes, she did.

'You're aware that Mr Morgenson claimed that he'd been poisoned, is that correct?' He held a pen and notepad and was already making notes.

'Yes.'

Davis nodded. 'There'll be a post-mortem

examination of the body, you understand. Not only because of Mr Morgenson's statement, but also because the doctors aren't willing to commit themselves on the cause of death. And without a death certificate there has to be an examination of the remains.'

'I understand,' Addie said.

'The matter will be in the hands of a coroner very shortly, and then the post-mortem will be carried out. You don't live in Eastbourne, do you?'

'No, we live in Berkshire. Near Newbury.'

Davis nodded. 'And you'll be returning home today?'

'Yes.'

'Right. Sergeant Williamson will take your address. You may be called as a witness at the inquest. In any case, if the post-mortem reveals that Mr Morgenson did indeed die of poisoning, then we shall most certainly want to speak to you again.'

'I understand.'

She was free to go. As she and Charlie stood up, Charlie said, 'Mr Davis, I don't know how much you know about all this.'

'I know as much as I've been told,' Davis said. 'Which is what Mr Morgenson told us — that he believes he's been the victim of — well, not to mince words — an assassination. With poison. And Mrs Carmichael here is of the same opinion. I'm correct there, is that so?'

'Yes,' Addie said, 'I've no doubt of it whatsoever.'

Davis turned back to Charlie, 'Mr Morgenson wasn't able to tell us very much partly because of his weakened condition — but according to what he had told his brother, he's not the first victim.'

'That's what I believe,' said Charlie. 'I didn't at the beginning, but I feel now that such a conclusion's inescapable.'

'I see.' And then to Addie, 'According to Mr Morgenson, his illness — if it was caused by poisoning — is connected with an incident that happened a number of years ago. Is that correct, Mrs Carmichael?'

'We believe so.'

Davis glanced at his sergeant, then back to Addie and Charlie. 'We won't go into it any further now, and if the results of the post-mortem show that Mr Morgenson died of natural causes then you won't be hearing from us. If not, we'll almost certainly be in touch with you.'

And that had been it. After further words of condolence to David, Addie and Charlie had set off back to the hotel where they had checked out to head back for Berkshire,

328

Addie following Charlie on the road.

That had been yesterday, and since their return Addie had tried on several occasions to telephone Dolores. All she had got, however, was Dolores's recorded voice on her answering machine.

Later, Addie decided that Gerald Fraser ought to be told, and during the evening she rang his number. As soon as he was on the line she told him of Ambrose's death.

'He's dead?' he said. 'Ambrose is dead?'

'Yes. The night before last.'

'My God.' A pause. 'Addie, what did he die of?'

She paused. 'No one's sure. There's going to be a post-mortem.'

She told Gerald of her visit to Ambrose and of his sickness and admittance to hospital. 'This is strange,' he said. 'His symptoms sound just like Harry's.' In spite of his further questions she proffered little else. She was reluctant to go any deeper into the matter, and was relieved when at last the call came to an end.

And today, she supposed, the post-mortem would be conducted — if it had not happened already — and she had no doubt what the result would be. And she welcomed it; it was the uncertainty that was difficult to deal with. Besides, if the post-mortem did show poisoning as the most likely cause of Ambrose's death, then she herself would begin to feel safer. Whereas before there had been no solid evidence to set before the police, they would now gather it for themselves.

As she stood there, she heard the sound of Charlie's car on the drive, and minutes later he was coming into the room. He had gone off earlier to a factory where some of Adanco's games were assembled, the purpose of his visit to inspect a shipment of components that had arrived from Hong Kong. Now as Addie looked at his face she could see that his errand had not pleased him. 'As bad as that?' she said.

'As bad as that.' His expression grim, he went on to tell her that the plastic components, ordered weeks earlier, had not been made to the correct specifications. 'Can you believe it?' he said. 'This is the second time they've fucked it up. I wrote, I phoned, and I got assurances, and in the end it all meant nothing. Their quality control is bloody useless. Why is it you can never depend on anything going right? There's always something to screw it up. This means I've got to go back out there.'

She groaned. 'Oh, no. Really?'

'I've already had Marion book the flight

and the hotel. I'm going on Tuesday.'

'Oh, Charlie, *no*.'

'It can't be helped. I've got to be there and make sure it's done properly. Time's getting on, and we can't afford another cockup. And at least I can make good use of my time there; I didn't manage to get all my business finished last week, so it'll give me a chance to do that.' He paused. 'I've got Marion to book for you as well.'

'But Charlie,' she said, 'I never go with you these days, you know that.'

'Well, isn't it time you did? A change of scene would do you good. And I'd feel at ease if you're with me, instead of being here on your own. Get you away from all this for a while. You've been through so much lately.' He stood, waiting. When she said nothing, he sighed. 'I guess I'll have to take that as a no.'

'I'm sorry.'

'Well, it's up to you.' He shrugged. 'All in all this hasn't been the best of days so far. I also seem to have lost two or three items during my trip.'

'Oh? What have you lost?'

'I can't find my spare set of house keys, or my cufflinks, or my pen. The pen and the keys I can replace, but the cufflinks are the ones you gave me.'

'Oh, that's a shame,' she said. 'Where did you have them?'

'I think they were in my flight bag, but I can't be sure. I got Marion to phone the hotel to see if they've been handed in. No luck, I'm afraid.'

'Could you have lost them here in England — on your return? Could they have been stolen?'

'No — ' He frowned. 'They're probably just mislaid.'

'I hope so. I don't like the thought of a set of keys in someone else's pocket.'

'They'll turn up. Besides, I hardly think that's the worst of our problems.' He came to her, put his hands on her shoulders. 'How are you feeling now?'

'Oh — OK.'

He looked into her eyes. 'You can't lie to me; I can always see through you.' He drew her to him. 'I know how this whole thing's got to you. But it'll all be over soon. They'll catch whoever it is and we can rest easy again.'

'Yes.' A pause. 'I can't stop thinking about Ambrose.' She closed her eyes, sighing, wincing at the memory. 'The way he was ripping those tubes out of his body. I can't get the pictures out of my mind.'

'Try not to think about it.'

'How could anybody do that to him? He never hurt anyone in his life. And it's when you see it first hand that you realize what Kieron went through as well. And Christie, and Harry.'

As she finished speaking, the telephone rang. Charlie moved to it and lifted the receiver. Listening to his side of the brief conversation, Addie realized that he was talking to Detective Inspector Davis. Yes, he was saying, they would be at home for the rest of the day. When the call was finished he said, 'Your detective wants to come and talk to you. He'll be here later this afternoon, between three and four.'

'Does that mean that the post-mortem on Ambrose is finished? It must do. And they know that he was poisoned.'

'He didn't say. But it's a reasonable assumption. They're not coming all this way for nothing.'

'Will you be here?'

'Of course. I know at the start I was sceptical — and who wouldn't have been? but that's all changed now.'

* * *

Detective Inspector Davis and Sergeant Williamson arrived just after three o'clock.

Charlie showed them into the sitting-room where they sat in armchairs. Addie made tea. When it was poured and handed round she sat next to Charlie on the sofa. Davis took a sip from his cup, set it on a small side table and took a notebook and pen from his pocket.

'You know why we're here, Mrs Carmichael,' he said. 'We've had the results of the post-mortem on Mr Morgenson.'

'We guessed as much,' Addie said.

'Yes,' Davis went on, 'and the pathologist's report indicates that Mr Morgenson was right. It can't be proved, unfortunately, as that particular poison leaves no residue in the body. But apparently all the signs of it were there. The pathologist says that ricin poisoning was almost certainly the cause of death. The inquest is set for Wednesday in Eastbourne. You might well be called as a witness. You don't plan on going away anywhere, do you?'

'No,' Addie said, 'I have no plans.'

Charlie said to Davis, 'I've got to fly back out to Hong Kong on Tuesday, and I was hoping to persuade Addie to come with me.'

Davis frowned. 'I'm afraid Mrs Carmichael might be needed here.' He turned to Addie. 'In any case we shall need to interview you again soon. I wouldn't want you to be away at such a vital time.' To Charlie he said, 'How long will you be gone?'

'Just a week. I thought the break and the change of scene would do her good.'

'Don't worry about me,' Addie said. 'I'll be here, Inspector, you can depend on it.'

'That'll help enormously. We've got to find out how Mr Morgenson was poisoned. It should be easy to verify that he left his friends on Monday evening complaining of not feeling well, but we also need to ask you certain questions.'

And so it began, right then. Addie told them everything, going right back to Ruby's death and the letters they had received. With luck, Davis remarked, some of the officers who had looked into the case might still be on the force; he would get in touch with the Birmingham police. Addie then told what she had discovered about the deaths of Kieron and Christie and Harry, and then brought out the mutilated photograph. Davis studied it, then requested that she indicate on a separate sheet the names of the individuals portrayed. She told them also of the death of the little girl, Alice Marshall. Eventually it came to Dolores and what she had told of seeing Matthew standing on the pavement opposite her flat.

Davis said, 'We shall need to trace Mr Dixon, and also talk to Mrs McCaffrey.'

Addie gave him Dolores's address and telephone number, adding, 'Though I don't know whether she's there right now, I got no answer when I tried to phone her. As for Matt Dixon, I haven't seen him since we all split up, though I understand that Ambrose had been in touch with him not too long ago. I believe he said Matt was living near Leicester. He mentioned a place called Syston — I think that was it. Though whether he still had his address he didn't seem to know.'

Davis made notes on his pad then said, 'Your experience with Mr Morgenson at the time of his death — that must have been very distressing.'

Addie shook her head at the memory. 'I'll never forget it. His suffering. And not only what it did to his body, but to his mind. The way he was rambling and raving.'

'What exactly did he say?'

'Well, it didn't make any sense. Which surprised me because he'd said he wanted to talk to me. I didn't understand him. It was just . . . meaningless.'

'Can you remember anything?'

'Not word for word. As far as I remember he mentioned a list.'

'A list?'

'That's what I understood. With certain names.'

'Names? What names?'

She shrugged. 'Men I'd never heard of.'

'But can you remember any of the names?'

'Well — Boswell — that was one. He mentioned him a couple of times.'

'Boswell. And it didn't mean anything to you?'

'No. He spoke of two other men. One named Wiley. Lee, I think. Lee Wiley. And Sullivan. I'm not sure, but I believe the first name was Max.'

Davis said hopefully, 'And these names didn't ring any bells?'

'No, I'm afraid not.'

'Could they have been students you were at university with?'

'No, definitely not. I remembered the names Ambrose mentioned because I felt they might turn out to be important, and that I *ought* to remember them. But I don't know anybody with those particular names.'

Davis made a final note, put away his notebook and the photograph and got to his feet. Almost two hours had gone by, and for now the questions were over. He shook Addie's hand and, with the sergeant behind him, followed Charlie from the room.

337

When Charlie did not return, Addie went into the hall and found that he had gone with them to their car. Through the open door she could hear their voices.

'So,' she heard Charlie say, 'what's going to happen now?'

'Sir?' said Davis. 'I'm not with you.'

'Well, what about my wife?' Charlie was keeping his voice low. 'I didn't say anything in front of her, but you realize what's going on as well as I do. This isn't going to stop here, is it? There are seven people in that photograph. And of those seven, four have already died.'

'I'm aware of that,' Davis said.

'Quite,' said Charlie. 'And we know they were poisoned. All four of them.'

'I don't think we can be sure of anything just yet, sir.' Davis's tone was slightly defensive. Charlie was taking the wrong tack, Addie thought; no man likes to feel he's being taught his own job.

'Of course they were,' Charlie said. 'And the one who killed the Burnham girl is the one who's killed them. And for obvious reasons.'

'Well,' Davis said, 'we must hope that our investigations will enlighten us there.'

'Inspector, I'm not trying to tell you what to do.' Charlie's tone was more conciliatory.

'I'm just concerned about my wife.' He lowered his voice still further and Addie had to make an effort to hear. 'Whoever's done this,' he said, 'is out to get them all — and something's got to be done.'

'What is it you want us to do?' Davis said.

'Oh, Christ.' Charlie sounded weary. 'I don't know. If we were dealing with some madman wielding an axe or a gun it would be easier. There'd be a way to deal with it. But for what's been happening here — well, I don't know what the answer is. How the hell is he doing this?'

'On the assumption that that's what's happening,' Davis said, 'that's what we aim to find out.'

'Yes,' said Charlie, 'and when you find that out we can find out how to protect my wife. Or, just as good, find the guy who's doing it.'

'Well, we're trying to trace this Matthew Dixon. If we find him that might well be the end of it.'

'And it might not. We don't know it's him, do we?'

'No, we don't. But until we find who it is we can only advise you to see that your wife takes every possible precaution.'

'Great,' Charlie came back, 'I really need

to be told that. I'm due to go halfway across the world and how do I know she'll be safe while I'm gone?'

There was a brief silence, then Davis said, 'I'm sorry, but we've got to get back. You'll hear from us soon. In the meantime, you've got our number, so if anything should crop up get in touch with us at once.'

Addie heard the car doors close and then the vehicle start away on the gravel. She was still standing in the hall when Charlie entered a few moments later.

'You heard,' he said, seeing her there.

'Yes.'

'I just wanted to get them moving. Get some results.'

'But you do believe it — that I'm in danger?'

'Well, they've got the matter in hand now, so things will start to happen.' He put his arms around her. 'Listen to me: regardless of what the police want, I think you should come with me. Let them get on with it. If you're here alone I'll be worrying all the time. But if you're out of the country with me we'll *both* know you're safe.'

'You heard him,' she said. 'I might be needed at the inquest. And they're going to want to talk to me. I've got to stay around. I haven't got an option.'

'Then I won't go.'

'Charlie, you must. After all the work you've put in — you can't jeopardize it all.'

'But I need to be sure you're OK.'

'I'll be fine. The police won't let anything happen to me.' She forced a smile. 'They wouldn't dare — I'm going to be their star witness.'

★ ★ ★

Later, Addie dialled Dolores's number again, and this time, to her great relief, the ringing was answered.

'I was beginning to think I'd never reach you,' Addie said. 'I've rung and rung.'

'I've been in Bristol for a few days,' Dolores said. 'Staying with my sister.'

'Are you all night?'

'Yes, I'm fine. I just had to get away.'

'Dolores,' Addie said, 'I've got some bad news.'

'Oh, no.' A pause. 'Go on.'

'It's Ambrose. Dolores, he's dead.'

'*What?*' Dolores groaned. 'Oh, no. Addie — *no.*'

Addie told her of how she had found Ambrose sick and he had been admitted to hospital. He had died two days later, she said, and a post-mortem had shown that the most likely cause of death was ricin poisoning. 'The police have been here this afternoon,' she added, 'asking all kinds of questions.'

'So the police are now looking into it all?'

'Yes.'

Dolores's deep sigh came over the line. 'Well, thank God for that. I feel as if you and I were the only ones who were aware of what was happening — or who were interested. So, what d'you think will happen next?'

'Well, I think they'll look into Ruby's death, and also try to track down Matt.'

'Do they know where to start looking for him?'

'It's possible that Ambrose had an address. They'll find out, though, I'm sure. They wanted your address and phone number, so I had to give it to them.'

'Of course. Though I don't know what I can tell them. I don't know anything that you don't. Anyway, I'm not sure I'm staying here much longer.'

'But you only just got back.'

'I know that. But I'm just — so damned jumpy all the time. I just feel like packing up and going off again.'

'Where will you go? Back to your sister's?'

'I don't know. We don't get on that well so — oh, Addie, I don't know what to do. I feel like going to ground somewhere, hiding away until this whole thing is over. But if I do go away I'll let you know, don't worry.'

When the conversation ended, Addie turned to Charlie who sat nearby. 'Dolores,' she said, 'she's only just got back home, and now she's going to pack up and run, I know it.'

'So?' There was contempt in the word. 'Why are you sounding so surprised? That's just the kind of thing she'd do. You can't depend on her, Addie. As I told you before, if you need to rely on somebody you must first turn to yourself.'

* * *

That night in bed Addie lay with Charlie beside her. With his body close her fears were less consuming. She sighed with the comfort of his nearness. Hearing the sigh, he murmured, 'What is it? You mustn't worry.'

She said, 'I'm sighing because I'm glad you're here with me.'

With a gentle pressure from his hand he urged her to turn to him. She did so; she could feel his breath on her forehead. They did no more than embrace, but she was glad of it, glad of his nearness, his touch. Held in the warmth of his encircling arm, she fell asleep.

19

'All ready?' Addie asked as Charlie came into the sitting-room. He had finished his packing and his bags stood in the hall.

'I hope so. I shan't have time to waste in the morning.' Sitting in his chair he took up the Scotch and soda that Addie had poured for him. 'I wish you'd think again about coming with me. There's still time.'

'Come on, we've been through all this,' she said. 'Your arrangements have been made with the manufacturers, and we've also fixed up with Carole. It's all settled.'

'OK, but any time you want, just pack a bag and come over and join me.'

'Don't worry about me.' She took a sip from her gin and tonic. 'By the way, does Carole know precisely why she's been asked to come and stay?'

'I said you were a little nervous at being left alone and would be glad of her company.

She doesn't need to know any more. She's not going to be in any danger. That's not the way this character operates. She'll be here for company, that's all. And with her little girl going off to stay with her ex it'll work out fine.'

'I guess so.' She must stop looking for problems, Addie told herself. The last thing she wanted was to make Charlie uneasy just when he was about to depart.

'Anyway,' Charlie said, 'you've got the open invitation from Lydia and Adam.'

'Yeah,' she said dryly, 'let's not forget that, right?'

Lydia and Adam had come visiting just that afternoon. Lydia had telephoned earlier to say that she had finished the modifications to her board game, *Hurricane*, and was anxious for Charlie to look at the revised version. Charlie had thrown out hints that he was busy preparing for his trip, but Lydia had avoided picking up on them. It wouldn't take more than an hour, she had said, and in the end Charlie had given way. Having been told of her visit during his previous absence, he was not unprepared for her new approach. So, today, close on 3.30, Lydia and Adam had rolled up, Lydia bringing the components of her board game. Observing her arrival, Addie found herself unusually impressed with her appearance. Lydia's pale-grey suit and blue blouse were surprisingly elegant; and perfectly complemented by her dark hair, so black that in some lights it shone almost blue. Also, she was wearing contact lenses in place of her usual spectacles. It only went to show, Addie thought, what could be accomplished.

'So what did you think about Lydia's game?' Addie asked now. 'Did it make you change your mind?'

He shook his head. 'The changes are superficial. It's basically the same game.'

'She'll be disappointed.'

'It can't be helped.'

While Lydia had been showing Charlie the game's modifications Addie and Adam stayed out on the patio. Glancing back over his shoulder while they sat there, Adam said, his voice low, 'She's put so much into this game; it means so much to her.' And Addie had thought, don't do it, Adam, don't try to involve me; it's not fair. But she had merely nodded and said, 'Yes, I'm sure she has.'

'She's got so much faith in it, herself,' he went on. 'And she's generally a very good judge of what will work and what won't. She's so experienced.'

'Yes,' Addie had dutifully agreed, 'there's no doubt of that.'

'She's got such imagination,' he said.

'Oh, indeed; that comes through all the time.' She paused then added, choosing her words, 'Adam, I should tell you that — well, I don't get involved in the company work any more. Everything's left to Charlie.' She left the words hanging there. Adam coloured up, realizing he had gone too far in soliciting her aid, and an awkward silence fell, dispelled, to Addie's relief, by the reappearance of Lydia and Charlie.

It was soon after Lydia had resumed her seat that she had invited Addie to go and stay with them during Charlie's absence. Charlie had made a reference to Carole coming over, and Lydia had asked why, for what purpose.

'Oh — ' Addie brushed it aside. 'It's just Charlie being over-protective.'

'Over-protective?' Adam had said with a chuckle. 'Protecting you from what? From whom?'

'Nothing — no one,' Addie had said. 'He worries unnecessarily.' Charlie had assured her that Lydia and Adam knew nothing of their current difficulties, and she wanted to keep it that way.

'Are you sure?' Lydia's eyes had searched her face. 'Because if you're at all uneasy about staying here on your own, then come and stay with Adam and me.'

'Oh, no, really,' Addie said. 'That's very kind of you, but Carole will be here and I shall be fine.'

Lydia shrugged. 'OK, but if you change your mind, just get on the phone.'

Now, thinking back to the words she had exchanged with Adam, Addie said, 'Charlie, when you come back I mean to start taking a greater interest in the company.'

'Well, if you *want* to,' he said, 'but don't do it just to please me.'

'No, I want to. I've left everything for you to get on with. Adanco would have gone under years ago if it hadn't been for you.'

'I've loved doing it, Addie. You know that.'

'Even so, I haven't been pulling my weight. But as I said, when you get back, and all this other business is behind us — things are going to be different.'

★ ★ ★

The next morning Charlie was carrying his bags out to the car when the telephone rang. Addie took the call in the hall. She was replacing the receiver when Charlie came back into the house. 'Who was that?' he asked.

'Carole.'

348

'I thought she'd have been here by now.'

'She's not coming.'

'What? Why not?'

'Her little girl's not well, and she's keeping her at home.'

'Oh, for Christ's sake.'

'These things happen, Charlie. There's nothing to be done about it.'

He stepped towards the phone. 'I'm going to call Lydia and Adam.'

She held up a hand. 'Don't even think of it.'

'But at least I'll know that you — '

'Charlie, no. Please, that's final.'

'Then I'll postpone my trip.'

'Don't be foolish. You've got all kinds of appointments made.'

'Then come with me. It isn't too late.'

'Of course it is. Now please — go. You've got the rush-hour traffic in front of you, and you don't want to be delayed.' She stretched up and kissed him. 'Now go — and have a good trip.'

Moments later she stood watching as his car moved off down the drive.

In the house she busied herself making the beds, sorting laundry and running the washing-machine. Just after three o'clock, Detective Inspector Davis telephoned to say that she wouldn't be called as a witness at the inquest next day, so there'd be no need for her to attend. She felt great relief at his words. She had dreaded not only making an appearance on the witness stand, but also making the journey there again.

'The pathologist will give his report,' Davis said, 'and I shall request an adjournment. That will enable us to get on with our enquiries. You might well be called when the inquest is resumed; I don't know yet. But just so long as I know where I can reach you when I need to.'

'I'll be here, Mr Davis.'

'By the way,' he added, 'we've talked to your friend Mrs McCaffrey.'

'She was at her home in London?'

'Yes, one of my men spoke to her on the phone for a few minutes. She wasn't able to tell him much. She seemed rather nervous.'

'She is. She's been talking about going away somewhere — until the whole thing's over.'

'Well, as long as she keeps us informed as to where she'll be. We've almost certainly got a murder on our hands — possibly the victim of a serial killer — and we can do without one of the witnesses doing a vanishing act.'

★ ★ ★

350

That night when Addie was preparing for bed, Charlie called from his hotel in Hong Kong where he had just checked in. He asked her how she was, and she replied that she was fine. 'I do what you tell me to do,' she said.

'Oh, what's that?'

'I keep smiling.'

It was a brief call, and when it was over she went around the house checking on the locks.

* * *

Davis was on the telephone again the next afternoon. The inquest had been relatively short, he said, and as expected the main witness had been the pathologist who had reported that the signs of ricin poisoning had been present in the body. The inquest had then been adjourned to allow for further investigations. 'Which is where you'll come in,' Davis had said.

* * *

Time passed in the achingly slow manner to which Addie was becoming accustomed. She used up the hours by going to the supermarket and doing chores around the house, tasks that required little mental effort. In the evenings she prepared simple meals for which she had no real appetite, and watched television programmes that went through her head without registering. Each day she talked to Charlie, and on several occasions tried to phone Dolores — but without success. (Had she done as she had hinted she might, and gone to ground somewhere?) Somehow, however, Addie, got through the time, and as each day passed she began to feel a little more secure.

On the Friday morning, with the delivery of the second post, her growing sanguinity came to an end.

She was in the kitchen cleaning the oven when she heard the sound of the letter box flap. In the hall she picked up from the mat a largish envelope and three smaller ones. Two of the envelopes were addressed to Charlie, the third bore the logo of a well-known charity. As she looked at the last and largest envelope, she could feel her heart begin to pound, she knew the look of this envelope with its little white label bearing her name and address so neatly and anonymously printed.

She pulled off her rubber gloves, tore open the envelope, then extracted a single piece of paper. It was what she had feared, and seeing it she gave a little cry and, as if she had been burned, opened her fingers and let it fall.

The copy of the familiar photograph of the seven of them was a little different from the one she had received previously. As before, the faces of Christie, Harry and Kieron had been burnt out, but now that of Ambrose also had been destroyed. Only three faces were now untouched: those of herself, Dolores and Matt.

After some minutes she took up the telephone and dialled Dolores's number, only to be greeted once again by the recorded message on her answering machine.

She was still sitting there by the telephone when Charlie called. He asked how she was, and quickly discerned the fear and disquiet in her voice. 'Addie,' he said, 'what's the matter?'

She was loath to tell him; he was too far away to be able to help her, and the knowledge would only cause him to worry. But in pausing in her deliberations she left it too long.

'I got another photograph in the post,' she said.

'You mean — with you and your friends on it?'

'Yes. It was like the other one — except that Ambrose's face also has been burnt

353

out.' Her words were followed by silence. 'Charlie,' she said, 'are you still there?'

'Yes, I'm trying to think what to do. Why don't you give Lydia a call?'

'No, thanks.'

'Well,' he said, 'I'm not leaving you there on your own.'

★ ★ ★

An hour later there came a ring at the doorbell. When she looked through the hole in the front door she saw Peter Lavell standing on the step.

'Charlie called me,' he said as she opened the door, 'and asked me if I'd come and see if there was anything I could do for you.'

She sighed. 'This is getting to be a habit of Charlie's — and I can't say I approve. On the other hand, I'm very glad to see you.'

★ ★ ★

With a mug of coffee beside him, Peter sat in the kitchen looking at the mutilated photograph. In the time since his arrival Addie had told him of what had happened since they had last met, relating the details of the visit to Harry's friend and mother, and then of Ambrose's death.

'I'm wondering,' Addie said, 'whether Dolores has received a photograph as well. I've tried phoning her but I only get her machine.'

He took up the envelope again. The postmark showed that it had been posted in London's W1 district the previous day. 'Which tells us nothing,' he said. He looked at the label bearing Addie's name and address. 'And that's been done on a computer printer so it won't give any clues either. But I still don't understand why someone would send this photo? It's so . . . melodramatic. I couldn't see the point of it before, and I can't see the point of it now. What purpose does it serve? The scenario that someone has set out to eliminate your little group of friends in order to silence them is a horrific one — but it makes sense. A clean sweep — it's pragmatic. If you know it's *one* of them, then get rid of them *all* and you'll be sure you've got the right one. But why this?' He tapped the photograph. 'Is it just some joke?'

She watched him as he put the picture back in the envelope. 'Whatever it is,' she said, 'I don't know what to do.'

He took a swallow of his almost-cold coffee. 'Well, I think you should pack an overnight case and come back to my place.'

When she said nothing he gave a sigh and added, 'Addie, this isn't the time to be over-sensitive. If you come back with me I can get on with my work and also make sure you're safe. It's what Charlie'd want. It's why he called me in the first place.' He paused. 'Have you got a better idea?'

She shook her head.

'Fine,' he said, 'then that's what we'll do. And once we're there you can call your detective and tell him about this,' — he tapped the envelope — 'and let him know where he can reach you. Call Charlie too. We can pop back here any time you want, and pick up any mail and make sure everything's all right. Yes?'

Half an hour later the house was locked up behind them and they were moving down the drive in Peter's car.

As they neared the outskirts of the village Addie asked if they could stop by the cemetery. He pulled up near the gates. 'Take as long as you want,' he said as she got out. 'We're not in a hurry.'

Inside the grounds she made her way to the newer section. Beside the stone wall the narrow fringe of uncut grass had turned yellow and sere, and the tall thistles had gone to seed. Stopping before Robbie's grave, she said, 'I didn't bring you any flowers today,

Robs. Everything's at sixes and sevens. I'll bring you some next time.'

She plucked a dying blossom from the pot, gathered up two or three dead leaves, and stood with the leaves and the flower in her hand. Here beside Robbie's grave was the one place where she felt safe. After a while she turned and moved to the little headstone and with her fingertips gently touched its cool surface. 'I'll come again soon.'

★ ★ ★

Peter's home turned out to be a long, low building that had once formed two farm-workers' cottages, knocked into one in the 1970s with the addition of the necessary mod cons. It had a wide, shallow front garden, at the side of which an outhouse had been converted into a garage. Peter pulled up in front of it, they got out, and he took her overnight case from the boot.

In the house he led her up the stairs into a west-facing bedroom opening off a soft-carpeted landing. He set down her case and, gesturing to the bare mattress, said, 'I'll come up in a minute and make up the bed. The bathroom's right next door.'

Back downstairs, Addie helped with the preparations for a lunch of soup and sandwiches. Afterwards, she rang Dolores's number but was once again met by the familiar recorded message. Ringing Detective Inspector Davis, she found him in his office. After telling him that she had come to stay with a friend she told him of the photograph that had arrived that morning. He asked her whether she had kept the envelope. 'Of course,' she said, adding that it had been posted in central London, and that the label bearing her name and address had been printed on a computer printer.

'Well,' he said dryly, 'we could hardly expect them to put a sender's name and address on the back. Still, we must have a look at it — and in the meantime try not to handle it, OK? Are you going to be around tomorrow morning?'

She would, she said, and gave him the address.

He said he would aim to get there just after eleven, then went on, 'Right now we're trying to trace Mr Dixon. I've got some men working on it, and I hope it won't be long before they come up with something.'

When she had hung up, Peter made tea. As she drank it she sat looking out onto the untidy rear garden which for the most part had been allowed to grow wild. A cherry-tree had already lost many of its leaves, and they lay yellowing on the unkempt grass. At the same time, as if to deny the season's incipient end, a greenfinch was busily feeding a chick among the weeds and the straggling shrubs. It made a scene of peace that was so at odds with the turmoil she felt inside.

Later, at Peter's suggestion, they drove out into the countryside, stopping for tea in a small village teashop that seemed to belong to another age, and afterwards took a stroll along the village street, occasionally pausing to look in at the shop windows. At a small jeweller's shop Addie surveyed a tray of gold and silver items of jewellery. Was there something she was interested in? Peter asked. She replied that she was looking at the cufflinks, as Charlie had recently lost a pair. 'Not only his cufflinks,' she added. 'He lost a set of house keys as well.'

Further along they came upon an interesting-looking junk-*cum*-antique shop, and inside walked among the assorted pieces of furniture and looked over the array of items on the tables and shelves. Among them was a box of old 78 r.p.m. records, and seeing them, Addie at once thought of Ambrose.

Even here, away from everything, she could not be free of reminders of the threat.

Turning, she saw Peter's eyes upon her. 'What's up?' he asked.

'Ambrose used to collect these old records,' she said.

'I believe some of them can be quite valuable.'

'Oh, he didn't collect them for their monetary value. He just liked them. When we were at Birmingham he had some on cassettes that he used to play. Scratchy old things, they were — sounding as if the singers were frying hamburgers at the same time.' She smiled indulgently. 'They did the trick for him, though. When I was in his flat the other day I saw that he had shelves of them.'

Peter nodded. 'There's no accounting for the different passions that people have. Railway memorabilia, model cars, old bus tickets, jigsaw puzzles — you name it and there'll be somebody collecting it.' He smiled. 'What about you, Addie? What's your particular passion?'

She looked at him for a moment, then smiled and shook her head. 'I don't have one.' She turned from the box of records. 'Shall we go?'

20

Addie insisted on preparing dinner that evening, and after the dishes had been cleared away they drank tea in the sitting-room. The warmth of the day had gone, and now in the grate an apple log crackled and snapped and gave out its sweet-smelling scent and relieved the unusual chill of the late August night. The rather self-conscious silence that descended they covered with a mediocre made-for-TV movie whose stars were the usual second-rung performers who had found their niche. Addie didn't care; the sounds and images served to fill the void.

Close on eleven she called Charlie at his hotel where he was about to go down for breakfast. 'I'm so glad you're with Peter,' he said. 'That's a load off my mind.'

Peter had gone out of the room while she made the call. 'Maybe,' she said, 'but I feel it's a terrible imposition on him.'

'I'm sure it's not,' Charlie said. 'Have you spoken to the inspector yet?'

'About the picture? Yes. He's coming

361

round tomorrow. They're trying to trace Matt, he says.'

'Well, let's hope it isn't long before they find him.'

After they had spoken for a couple more minutes, during which Addie elicited that his work was going satisfactorily, the conversation drew to a close. 'I'm making an early start tomorrow,' he said just before hanging up, 'but I'll call you when I can, and I'll be home on Wednesday. Less than five days now. Then we'll see the end of all this business.'

It was not late when Addie went to bed. She said goodnight citing a tiredness to a degree that she did not feel. Later, lying in the comfortable bed with its sweet smell of fresh linen, she heard Peter coming up the stairs and moving to his room across the landing. She lay awake until at last the only sounds were those of the house's timbers settling in the dark.

★ ★ ★

Detective Inspector Davis, accompanied by Sergeant Williamson, arrived just after 10.30 next morning. Peter was introduced to the two men, then made coffee for them all, after which he returned to his studio, leaving them to talk. Addie showed Davis the photograph. He studied it, asked her a few questions regarding her receipt of it, then put envelope and photograph into his briefcase.

He told her that since their last meeting he had been liaising with the Force in Birmingham over the matter of Ruby Burnham's death, had been studying the file on the case and talking to a couple of the officers who had been involved in the investigation. Unfortunately, he added, the senior investigating officer had died less than a year ago, so all they had from him were his written reports. Going by what he had read so far, though, Davis said, he could find nothing that might cause any finger of suspicion to be directed at anyone. They were still, however, studying the papers. With regard to the other supposed victims, he added — Christie Harding, Kieron Walderson, Harry Comrie and the little girl Alice Marshall — he would be arranging with the relevant police forces to look into the circumstances of the deaths.

'And we're hoping,' he went on, 'that we might soon make progress in tracing Matthew Dixon. You told us that Mr Morgenson had heard from him some time ago — and in searching his rooms we found an address. We're checking it out.' He sighed. 'If only we could find out how the victims came to be poisoned. The pathologist made a minute examination of Mr Morgenson's body, and found no unexplained needle wound or anything like that.' He paused. 'Those names that Mr Morgenson mentioned shortly before his death — have they come to mean anything?'

Addie shook her head. 'No, I'm sorry.'

The men left with the inspector telling Addie he'd be in touch again soon, and requesting that she continue to keep him informed of her whereabouts. She promised she would, adding that she expected to be going back home on Tuesday ready for her husband's return.

★ ★ ★

On the following day, Sunday, soon after lunch, she asked Peter if they might drive over to Liddiston. She wanted to pick up a couple of things and check the house.

It was a pleasant day. There was a fresh wind blowing, but the sky was clear and bright. Arriving at the house, Addie was relieved to see that everything appeared to be all right. The morning paper, too bulky to go through the letter-box, lay on the step. She picked it up and, followed by Peter, unlocked the door, gathered up the previous day's paper and mail from the mat, and went into the hall.

There was just one message on the answering machine — from Carole to the effect that she would have to stay at home for a day or two longer, but hoped to see Addie very soon.

Addie asked Peter if he'd care for some tea while she was getting her things together, but he was content to sit and look at the morning paper. From her bedroom she got a sweater and a couple of toilet articles and then, back downstairs in the sitting-room, went through the post. Apart from some junk mail there was a bill, two letters for Charlie, and an envelope addressed to both of them. She tore it open and took out a few folded papers, among them a letter. When she had read it she looked across at Peter where he sat in an armchair reading the paper.

'You asked me what my passions were,' she said after a moment.

He looked up. 'What?'

'All these people with their passions, you said to me. And *what* consumes me? you asked.' She looked down at the letter. 'Here it is.'

Her sudden happiness was infectious, and he smiled, though frowning slightly in puzzlement at the same time. 'Well, don't leave me in suspense.'

'I already told you,' she said. 'A baby. Don't you remember?' She looked back at the letter. 'I mustn't start counting my chickens, but — we might have found a baby.' She laid the letter on the coffee-table before her. She could hardly believe it. The young woman, Susan, Milla's contact, had not forgotten her.

'We're in touch with several adoption agencies, but it's so difficult,' she said. 'There was a time when so many babies born to single mothers were given up for adoption. Not any more. Today's single mothers keep their babies, whether they're able to give them a decent upbringing or not. Nowadays there are comparatively few babies available for adoption — about one for every six couples wanting to adopt. Not only that, though, Charlie and I are regarded as on the mature side for prospective adoptive parents.'

Peter said, with a nod towards the letter, 'But this is good news, is it?'

'Well, it's nothing definite, but at least we'll be considered. My cousin knows of a young woman who's pregnant and doesn't want to keep her baby. And she's given our names to the adoption agency, asking that we be given first consideration.' She gave a breathless little laugh. 'Who knows, perhaps this time it'll be different.'

'Well, let's hope so. That'll be good news for Charlie when he phones.'

When she said nothing to this, Peter said, 'Will it? Be good news for him?'

She hesitated. 'To be honest, I don't really know. I think at times he goes along with it merely to make me happy — but he doesn't truly think anything's going to come of it.' Reading questions in Peter's gaze, she said, 'You're wondering *why* we're trying to adopt, aren't you?'

He didn't answer. After a moment she went on:

'After Robbie died I felt that no child could ever take his place. And of course no child ever could. But as time went by I realized I wasn't being realistic. A child has his own place. Another child wouldn't be a replacement. He'd be there for his own sake. And — oh, I wanted another child. But . . . by then it was too late.'

'Too late?'

She gave the saddest smile. 'I caught mumps, and passed it on to Charlie. As you probably know, mumps in an adult male can be fairly catastrophic.'

Peter groaned. 'Sometimes life's so bloody unfair.'

'God,' she said, 'he'd hate it if he knew I'd told you this.'

'It won't go any further.'

She looked at the letter, and then unfolded a paper that was with it. 'They've sent an acceptance form for an interview. They want to see us.' She looked at the date of the proposed interview. 'Monday, a week tomorrow. It doesn't allow much time.' She frowned. 'If I wait for Charlie to get back it might cause delays, the chance might be gone. I'll tell him about it when he calls.' She stood up and looked about her, checking that she had what she came for. 'You go on out to the car,' she said, 'and I'll lock up.'

She watched him go. Yes, she'd tell Charlie about the letter if he called tonight — though she wasn't happy at the prospect; it would put him on the spot, and he would hate that. The big question, though, was whether he truly wanted another child. Or, rather, did he want *another's* child? The way she saw it, he'd had all he wanted in Robbie, and with Robbie's death and the advent of his own infertility, the reality of fatherhood was something that he had pushed out of his mind.

And also, she reminded herself, their relationship was improving of late; they were growing closer again. Was it smart of her, now, at this critical juncture, to introduce what could turn out to be a wedge between them? Yet at the same time, if she waited they might have lost their last opportunity.

She picked up a pen from beside the telephone and completed the form. Then, going into the study, she took an envelope and wrote out the address, stuck on a stamp, and put the form inside. That done, she dropped it into her canvas shoulder bag, locked the house behind her and joined Peter in the car. At least the application would be ready to post when she and Charlie had had a chance to discuss it.

★ ★ ★

Not long after they got back, she and Peter were in the sitting-room when she turned and found him looking at her with his eyes narrowed, studying her.

'What is it?' she asked.

'You know what?' he said. 'I'd like to paint you.'

'Are you serious? A painting?'

'Or maybe a couple of sketches.'

'You mean — now?'

'Why not? Unless you have other plans.'

She thought perhaps he was making the proposal merely to keep her occupied. But she had nothing against the notion. She gave a shrug. 'OK.'

They made tea and carried their mugs into his studio. She hadn't been there before, and she looked around her with interest. The walls were covered with his paintings — many of the canvases unframed. They were nearly all figurative; some were straight portraits, others were studies of figures caught in the midst of various actions. There were several of children playing, adults standing, sitting. It was likely, she thought, that he worked a good deal from photographs.

After a little deliberation he had her sit in an old grandfather chair that was raised on a dais. She sat, hands in her lap, with her face partly towards the north-facing light. Taking up his sketch-book he sat on a tall stool beside his paint-stained work table, studied her for some moments, and began to draw.

All she heard for a time was the whisper of the conté crayon on the paper, the distant sound of birdsong from the garden, and his occasional remark. 'Lift your head slightly . . . A little to the left . . . A little lower . . .'

With a few short breaks, she sat for almost two hours, at the end of which he set his pad and crayons aside and told her, 'Enough — we'll continue tomorrow.'

★ ★ ★

When Charlie didn't ring that night she wasn't surprised, as he'd prepared her for the eventuality. She was, however, disappointed; she'd wanted to tell him about the adoption application. As soon as she awoke the following morning she began to think about the letter. Perhaps, she said to herself, she should go ahead and respond without any further delay. After all, it wouldn't commit either of them, though it *would* ensure that they'd registered a positive interest. And Charlie would understand; he wouldn't expect her to keep waiting and possibly jeopardize what might be their only remaining chance.

Her mind was made up, and as soon as she was dressed she went outside to the postbox along the lane and mailed the envelope.

'Where did you vanish to?' Peter asked her when she came into the kitchen.

'To the post box.' She was slightly out of breath from running. 'I decided not to wait for Charlie's return.'

'You've sent off the form — about the interview?'

'Yes. I can always cancel it if Charlie's set against it.'

* * *

Detective Inspector Davis telephoned a little later. He was calling, he said, to tell her that there had been certain developments. 'I told you,' he went on, 'that I had a couple of officers trying to find Matthew Dixon — well, they traced him to an address in Syston but couldn't get any reply at his flat. It turns out that none of his neighbours have seen him in a while. So, we got a search warrant and went in. His mail's piling up on the mat. The man hasn't been there in weeks.'

'What about his work?' Addie said. 'Did he have a job?'

'Apparently he's had a whole succession — and the last one was working as a freelance copy-editor, doing work for a small publishing house.'

'What about his family? Perhaps they know where he is.'

'As far as we can gather, he's only got a mother, and she's in a retirement home with Alzheimer's. Our men have checked and I'm afraid the poor lady doesn't even know what day of the week it is, so there's no help coming from that direction. When she was asked about her son she couldn't say when she'd last seen him. The staff say it's been

372

some while since he visited.'

After lunch she and Peter got back to the drawing, with Addie taking up a new position on the dais. As she sat gazing out at the wilderness of the garden, she pictured Matt, hiding away somewhere, yet still managing somehow to get access to those who were to die. She thought also of the baby that was soon to be born and which, if her prayers were answered, might one day soon be hers and Charlie's. Before that could be, however, this other business, this nightmare, had to be ended.

As the thoughts and images revolved in her brain it seemed as if from the whole kaleidoscopic morass there was something that was becoming distilled, taking shape. But it was not close enough to touch, not near enough or clear enough to see. Like some sought-for word on the tip of the tongue, the more she strove to name it and grasp it, the more it stayed out of her reach.

The telephone rang after she had been sitting for almost an hour, and Peter said, 'You've been reprieved for a while,' crossed the room and took up the receiver. 'Hello? . . . Oh, hi, Charlie, yes, she's here.' Addie got down from her perch and took the receiver from him. 'I'll go into the kitchen and make some tea,' Peter said, and with his words went from the room.

'I just got in from dinner,' Charlie said to Addie, 'and I'm going to get an early night. But I thought I'd give you a quick call first. How are you?'

'I'm OK. I'm fine.' She paused. 'Charlie, a letter came on Saturday . . . '

'A letter? What about?'

'From an adoption company.'

A pause. 'And?'

'You remember that young woman who's pregnant — the friend of Milla's friend?'

'I remember.'

'Well, the letter's inviting us for an interview — with the prospect of giving us first consideration when the baby's born.'

'Good. When I get back we'll have to talk about it.'

She said quickly, 'Charlie, they wanted an answer. They have to know whether we'll be available for the interview.'

'When is it?'

'Next Monday. Just a week. There isn't much time, is there?'

'A couple of days won't make any difference. I don't even know what I'm doing then. Listen, I'll be home the day after tomorrow; we can talk about it then.'

'Oh, but — ' And then, in a rush:

'Charlie, it's too late. I've already sent off the application form. I posted it this morning.'

A moment of silence. 'Oh, well, if it's done, it's done. And if it turns out not to be convenient — the date, that is — I've no doubt we can make other arrangements.'

'Yes,' she said, grateful for his words. 'That's what I thought.'

When he spoke again, his voice was softer, kinder. 'Oh, Addie, I'm sorry to sound so — so negative. I know how much this means to you.'

'It does,' she whispered. 'Oh, it does — so much.'

'I just don't want you to be hurt again. You've had enough disappointments.'

'I know, but that's a chance we've got to take. There isn't any choice.' She paused. 'If you'll go along with it.'

'If it's what you really want, then it's what I want too.'

After she had hung up she stood and stretched, relieving in her limbs the lingering stiffness from the sitting. Idly, she began to move around the room, looking at the examples of Peter's work. Taking in the sureness of his touch, the delicacy and subtlety of his sense of colour, she was touched again by the extent of his talent. There were a number of paintings that were not on open display. They stood leaning inward against the walls. She bent and pulled one back and saw a half-finished study of a middle-aged woman. The next was a life study — a woman in her thirties. She glanced at other pictures, some of which appeared to be older works. And then, in her browsing, she came to a sudden halt. She was looking at a nude study of a young woman in her early twenties. The woman reclined on a bed, on her side, one elbow raised, the hand behind her head.

Addie was still crouching before the painting when Peter's voice came to her. She started slightly at the sound and looked up to see him coming towards her with a tray on which were two mugs. 'Found something of interest?' he said as he set the tray on his work table.

She leaned the painting back in position along with the others. Then, straightening, she said, 'I didn't know you knew Ruby.'

'What?' He was covering self-consciousness.

'Ruby Burnham.' She gestured with a wave of her hand. 'The painting of her there. I didn't know you knew her.'

'Ah,' he said, 'Ruby . . . ' as if tasting some strange fruit. 'Well, no, I can't say that I did know her. Come to that, I don't know that anybody knew her — or really got to know her. I certainly don't claim to.'

'But you painted her.'

'Yes, I did. So did a few other students at the art school. Didn't you know she posed for life classes from time to time? And for classes in photography, too. No?'

'Models are paid peanuts. She didn't need that kind of money.'

'What makes you think she was doing it for the money?'

He crossed the room, bent and flipped through the canvases, lifted out the painting of Ruby and turned it towards Addie. 'There's your answer. Because she looked like that. You know it gives some women great pleasure to show off their bodies — and they don't all have bodies worth showing off. It's the exhibiting that's the important thing. Perhaps to some women it's all that matters.'

'But you never mentioned that you'd met her, or that you were in any way acquainted with her.' Addie gestured to the canvas. 'And that wasn't painted in one of the college studios. That was done in a private room.'

'Yes — *my* room.' He paused, looking at Addie with slightly narrowed eyes. 'What's on your mind, Addie?'

She shook her head. She had no answer.

'I met her when she posed for the evening

class I was at,' Peter said. 'During the break she came round in her dressing-gown looking at the different drawings of her. She liked mine and we chatted for a bit, I said I'd like to paint her, and she agreed. I remember how she picked up one of my pencils and wrote her phone number on the corner of my drawing board. And that's how I came to paint her.' He lowered the canvas, resting its base on the toe of one paint-spattered sandal. 'Do you,' he said, turning back to her, 'want to know any more?'

'It's not my business.'

He smiled. 'That's not what I asked you.'

When she said nothing, he said, 'Yes, I slept with her too. As did quite a few other students, I believe. And some of them probably a good many more times than I did. Which was twice, in case you're interested. A first time and a last time, and I was well aware of which was which, believe me.'

With a little laugh she said, 'I don't know why you're telling me all this. As I said, it's none of my business.'

He looked at her for a moment longer then put the canvas back in its place. As he straightened, she said, summoning her courage, 'Listen, Peter . . . '

'Yes?'

'Charlie — on the phone there — he's on his way home.'

'Now? I thought he wasn't due for a couple of days yet.'

She added to the lie. 'No, he's coming home now. So, I'll have to get back.'

He gazed at her for a moment then gave a nod. 'OK, I'll drive you home.'

'Oh, don't go to any trouble. I can phone for a cab.'

He dismissed the suggestion with a contemptuous wave of his hand. 'All that distance? Of course you won't. Go on — go and get your things together.'

There was silence between them for most of the journey. Addie could think of nothing to say. When they arrived at the house she thanked him, took her overnight bag from the rear seat and got out. Feeling his eyes upon her as she unlocked the front door, she turned and gave a small, self-conscious wave. He just looked at her for a second, then turned the car and started away down the drive.

In the house she checked the answering-machine. There were three messages. The first was from Dolores, asking Addie to phone her back. The second was from Carole, who said she'd call again later. The third was again from Dolores. Sounding increasingly distressed, she said she couldn't wait but was about to leave; she'd contact Addie later. 'I've got to see you,' she said. When Addie tried phoning Dolores's number she got her recorded message.

She had no sooner replaced the receiver when Carole rang. She was calling to say that Trudy was now OK — 'it was one of those forty-eight-hour bugs' — and had gone off with her father. 'So if you want,' she said, 'I can come over and stay till Charlie gets home. He's still away, is he?'

'Yes, he's due back on Wednesday.'

'Would you still like me to come over?'

Addie hesitated, then said, 'Yes, I would.'

Ten minutes later Addie heard the sound of a car on the gravel. It was too soon to be Carole. Moving to the window she saw Dolores's old Peugeot pulling to a halt. Moments later she was outside and Dolores was stepping towards her.

'Dolores — ' Addie could see the distress in her face, 'I just got in and got your messages.'

'I'm just so glad you're here,' Dolores said. 'I prayed you would be.'

Addie could guess what it was. 'You got a copy of the photograph,' she said.

'Yes. I went away for a few days — just to get away. And I got back this morning

380

and found it waiting for me — the photo. Once I saw that I had to get out again. I tried calling you and in the end I just got in the car and took off.'

Indoors in the sitting-room, Dolores sat on the sofa, Addie beside her.

'What are we going to do, Addie?' Dolores said. 'This thing goes on and on. It's not going to end until we're all dead.'

'Don't,' Addie said. 'Don't talk like that. The police are making progress. They've found out where Matt's living.'

'They've talked to him?'

'No, he wasn't there. They'll find him, though. It won't be long.'

'But what if it's not him?'

Addie had no answer to this. 'Well,' she said, 'whoever it is they'll find him.' She got up. 'Come on — I'm going to make us some tea.'

In the kitchen she put on the kettle. Dolores, sitting on a stool, put a hand to her head. 'Have you got an aspirin or something?' she said. 'My head is pounding.'

'Sure. Is it that bad?'

Dolores massaged her temple. 'Hardly surprising, is it? I'm so stressed out I wonder I can function at all. I don't think the drive helped much either.'

'I thought driving never fazed you normally.'

From a cupboard Addie took a packet of Nurofen.

'No, well, these aren't normal times.' Dolores held out her hand and Addie dropped a couple of tablets into her palm. Dolores swallowed them with water.

'Are you feeling all right?' Addie said, watching her closely. 'Apart from the head-ache, I mean.'

'I don't feel that brilliant, actually.' Dolores took another swallow from the glass then set it down. 'I'll be all right soon. Get this sorted out and I'll be as right as rain.'

When the tea was made Addie carried the tray into the sitting-room where she and Dolores sat on the sofa again. As Addie poured the tea she said, 'So what are you going to do? You want to stay here for a few days? Why don't you? Believe me, I'd be glad of your company.'

Dolores sighed and gave a shake of her head. 'I can't, Addie. I'm grateful, really, but I can't. Honestly, I don't feel any safer here than in Hammersmith.'

'Well, what will you do?'

'I'm going back to my sister's place. She drives me nuts, but at least I'll feel reasonably safe there. Or at least *safer*.'

'What if the police want to talk to you?'

'Listen, I've got to look after myself.

Anyway, I've got the number of that detective — Davis — so I can phone him and let him know where I am.'

Addie nodded, then frowned as Dolores put her hand to her head again. 'Is your headache no better?' she said.

'If anything it's worse.'

'Would you like to lie down for a little while?'

'No, I'll be fine. I'm not going to stay that long. I shan't feel able to relax until I get to Kate's.' She picked up her cup and drank from it. As she set it down again on the coffee table she moved aside the items of the Saturday post that Addie had left there. The envelope from the adoption agency was amongst it, along with a couple of printed leaflets about adoption procedure.

Addie leaned over, picked up one of the leaflets, and said, 'Charlie and I — we've got a date with an adoption agency next Monday.'

'Oh, really? That's a good sign, right?'

'It could be. I don't want to get my hopes up too much, though.'

'When was all this fixed up?'

'Today. I sent off the form today. I decided I couldn't wait till Charlie got back.'

Dolores nodded, frowning at the same

time. 'Well, I hope it all works out.' She drew in her breath with a little grimace and put a hand to her stomach.

'What's up now?' Addie asked. 'You have stomach ache?'

'I feel a bit sick.' Briefly, Dolores closed her eyes then put the back of her hand up to her forehead. 'I think I've got a temperature. Probably getting a chill or something.' She sighed. 'Addie, if you'll forgive me, I think I'll get going.' She gave a little laugh that sounded forced and hollow. 'While I've still got the strength.'

Addie felt a coldness come over her. 'Dolores,' she said, 'why don't you stay for a while? At least until you feel a little better.'

'No, I must go. I don't know why I came in the first place. Just looking for comfort, I guess — after getting that photograph.' She got to her feet, picked up her bag and started for the door. 'Don't worry about me.'

Feeling totally ineffectual, Addie followed her out to the car. 'I haven't got your sister's number,' she said as Dolores climbed in.

'That's OK — I'll call you when I get there.' Dolores shut the door, wound down the window, then put a hand to her temple. Addie watched her with concern. 'Are you well enough to drive?' she asked.

'Yes, I'll be all right.' Dolores turned on the engine, then reached a hand through the window and briefly pressed Addie's arm. 'Thanks, Addie — for everything.'

★ ★ ★

As Addie collected the tea things onto the tray a while later she saw lying there the letter from the adoption agency. She picked it up and read it over again.

It would be unbearable if Charlie couldn't make the stipulated date, she thought. The idea began to prey on her mind, and after a couple of minutes she decided to telephone the agency and see whether alternative dates might be available — just in case. She looked at her watch: 4.45. If she called now, she might be in time to catch them before they left for the day. She leaned across and lifted the telephone. And then, looking again at the letter, she saw that no telephone number was given. Her eyes searched the letter. No, there was none. But why? Had it been omitted to prevent the possibility of anxious putative adoptive parents plaguing the office with phone calls? Hardly likely, but she could think of no other explanation. Then she saw that neither was any fax number listed.

She sat pondering the unusual situation,

then dialled Directory Enquiries and gave the name and address of the agency. A few moments and the operator came back to say that she could find no listing of such a body. She asked Addie to repeat the name and address, then after a further check confirmed that no number for any such organization was listed. When Addie asked whether the number was perhaps ex-directory, the operator replied no, there simply was no number.

Puzzled, Addie thanked her and replaced the receiver. *It couldn't be that such an organization wouldn't have both a telephone and a fax machine.* And then suddenly there it was again, flashing through her brain, that elusive little fact — a picture? — an image? — some act performed? It hovered unseen and just beyond her grasp, while into her mind came Peter's voice, like an echo: 'It's strange the different passions people have'.

He had been speaking of the various hobbies owned by her friends who had died. Each one had had some particular interest or passion. She thought about Harry and his search for a rare and sought-after piece of Parian. What was it Gerald had called it? Yes, *The Veiled Bride* — that was it. For Ambrose, it had been old records, the pop singers of the thirties, forties and fifties. For

Kieron, it had been Victorian photography. For Christie? Ah, that was different. But no, Christie, too, had had her passion. Her all-consuming preoccupation had been her career and the remaking of it. And for Addie herself? For herself it had been a baby.

Ambrose, Harry, Christie, Kieron . . .

What had Milla said that day in the park? She had spoken of Kieron being invited to some photographic exhibition. And Harry? Yes, according to Gerald, hours before Harry had been taken ill he had sent off a bid for the Parian statuette that he was seeking. And Christie? Yes, Christie too. Celia had said that Christie had been so cheered on that last day, just before she was taken ill, for there had come an offer for an important interview. And Ambrose, with his passion for pop music of the past? She recalled his shelves stacked with old records, the pictures of past singers on his walls. And she thought again of the words he had spoken when she had seen him on that final visit just before his death. He had talked of a list, and he had mentioned names, names that had meant nothing to her whatsoever. *Now* though . . .

With another call to Directory Enquiries it took only a minute to get the telephone numbers of two of the top record stores in London. She dialled the first and was greeted by a young woman who asked which department she required. When Addie said she wanted to enquire after pop music of the thirties, forties and fifties, the young woman said she would connect her to the Nostalgia department. Moments later a young man came on the line. Did he know, Addie asked him after brief preliminaries, of any pop singer from the past by the name of Wiley? — 'I think his first name could be Lee,' she said; 'and also one named Max Sullivan. There's also a Boswell — though I don't have a first name there.'

'Well, for a start,' said the young man, not without a note of pride in that he knew his stuff, they're not men; they're all women. And they were all American vocalists who recorded a good deal in the thirties. Lee Wiley, yes. But Max Sullivan, no. You probably mean Max*ine* Sullivan. And there were three sisters named Boswell — a singing trio. Very highly regarded. One of the sisters, Connie, had a successful recording career as a solo artist.' He added that there were CDs available featuring each of them.

Addie thanked him and hung up. She was almost sure now that she knew what Ambrose had been trying to say. He had come up with the answer and had been trying to tell her. And now with the realization, the little elusive image came into view and into focus, and she saw herself in the street near his flat, posting his mail.

Her fingers were close to trembling now as she picked up the items of mail from the coffee-table. She sorted through them until she found the envelope in which had come the letter and leaflets concerning the adoption. She looked inside, saw what was there and then sat back, her heart pounding.

She remained there for some moments, and then, after consulting her address book, called the number of Gerald Fraser. There was no answer. She looked up another number and dialled again.

'Celia?' she said, when the receiver was lifted at the other end of the line, 'it's Addie Carmichael.'

'Addie, how are you?'

They exchanged greetings and then Addie, anxious to get to the point, said, 'Celia, I need some information — and please — don't ask me at this moment the purpose of it, but I promise you that you'll know very soon.'

'Right,' Celia said hesitantly, puzzled, 'tell me what you want to know.'

'I want to know something about Christie's goddaughter and your neighbour's daughter whom we met — Shelley — about what happened when they were with Christie that day, and dressing up in all her fancy clothes.'

Celia, more puzzled than ever, said, 'Well, perhaps Shelley herself is the best person to ask. She's here right this minute with me. You can ask her yourself.'

Moments later Shelley's piping little voice came on the line. She was perfectly happy to answer Addie's questions.

After Addie had hung up she dialled Milla's number. No answer; she was probably not yet home from work.

It was at this point that Carole appeared. They chatted for a few moments, then Carole took her bag up to the guest room, then came back down and set about preparing dinner for the two of them. Meanwhile, in the sitting-room, at ten-minute intervals, Addie dialled alternately the numbers of Gerald Fraser and Milla.

It was just on 6.30 when she got through to Gerald. Without wasting time, Addie put her questions to him, and not without some ill-hidden puzzlement he gave her his answers.

Half an hour later she managed to contact Milla. Hearing Addie's voice, Milla at once sounded wary. The hurt of their last meeting was clearly lingering still.

'Milla, can you talk for a minute?' Addie said. 'Please — it's absolutely vital.'

Milla's sigh was a sound of resignation. 'OK, Addie, just for a couple of minutes. We've only just got in, and I've got to get Helen her tea.'

Without wasting time, Addie said, 'Milla, when we talked in the park you told me about Kieron's last day at work, the time before he was taken ill.'

'That's right.'

Five minutes later Addie had the information she needed. She thanked Milla, said she'd be in touch soon, and said goodbye. As to *how* it had all happened, she was sure now that she had the answer.

When she dialled the number of Detective Inspector Davis her call was taken by a female officer who said that he had left for the day and wouldn't be in till the morning. Addie asked whether there was any way he could be reached. Not at that moment, she was told, but if Addie would like to leave a message . . .

'As soon as he comes in tomorrow morning,' Addie said, 'or if he should call this evening, will you tell him that Mrs Carmichael phoned. And tell him I know now how the ricin was administered.'

The woman repeated the last words as she wrote them down. 'Is that it?'

'No. Tell him that in each case it was on the flap of the envelope.'

21

Over dinner Addie tried to pay attention as Carole spoke about her daughter and her relationship with her ex-husband, but her own preoccupations got in the way. For the same reasons, the food that Carole had prepared passed Addie by as if tasteless, and in the end she pushed aside her plate, apologizing, saying that she had no appetite. When Carole asked whether she was feeling all right, she pleaded tiredness and a headache. Just after 9.30 using the same excuse, she got up from the sofa where she had been watching television and, leaving Carole to the banal English sitcom unfolding on the screen, said goodnight. She'd be glad, she added, if Carole would answer the phone and take any messages. 'Unless Charlie calls and I'm still awake.' In the doorway she turned back. 'And I'm hoping for a call from a friend of mine — Dolores McCaffrey. If she calls, whatever you do, get her phone number.'

Upstairs in her room she unplugged the telephone extension. Her claim of tiredness had been no lie; so much had happened that day, and she felt exhausted. Even so, the fretful thoughts continued to go round and round in her mind, and at last, desperate to get a good night's sleep, she took a sleeping pill. Only then, after a while, did she drift off to sleep.

* * *

She awoke just after 6.30, got up, put on her dressing-gown and slippers and crept downstairs into the kitchen. There she made some tea and sat sipping it at the counter while she looked out at the grey, early September morning.

She wondered whether there had been any word from Dolores — and how was she now? Surely she would have called.

Her thoughts moved to the form she had posted. If the postal service was doing its stuff it would be delivered this morning. And then suddenly she realized — and how had it not occurred to her before? — that this very day the sender might be calling at the address to see if it had been delivered. He certainly wouldn't want it hanging about.

And if no one was there to see him, or intercept him, the chance of catching him might be lost for good. She didn't know what to do. The kitchen clock showed 7.20. Detective Inspector Davis wouldn't be in his office yet.

There came the sound of a door closing upstairs, and then soft feet on the staircarpet. Moments later Carole entered, clad in her dressing-gown. 'You're up early,' she said. 'How d'you feel today?'

'Not bad,' Addie replied.

Carole unplugged the kettle and took it to fill at the tap. 'You had two calls last night after you went to bed. The first one was from a Mr Lavell. I said you weren't feeling so good and were having an early night. Then Charlie called — about half-past eleven — I was just about to go to bed. He said he'd tried to get you at Mr Lavell's but had been told you'd come back home. When I said you had a headache and were having an early night he said he'd try and get in touch with you some time today.'

'Was there no call from my friend Dolores?'

'No, nobody else called.'

Addie gave a nod. It was worrying. All during yesterday evening she had expected Dolores to call, as she had said she would — and there had still been no word. And she had no way of getting in touch with her. She felt useless. Tomorrow morning Charlie would be leaving Hong Kong to come home — and then what? He would be able to help, she had no doubt, but — and all at once she knew it — she couldn't afford to wait for his return; his return could be too late.

Her decision made, she set down her cup and got up.

'Would you like some breakfast?' Carole asked her.

Addie was halfway across the room. 'No, thanks. I've got to go out.'

'You're going out?'

'Yes, and I must hurry.'

Upstairs she dressed, gathered up a few items then hurried back down to the kitchen. 'Carole, I don't know what time I'll be back. If Charlie calls tell him I'll talk to him tonight. And if Dolores phones, get her number.' She added a goodbye and then, pausing only to pick up her house-and car-keys from the bowl by the front door, hurried out.

In a journey lasting some twenty-five minutes on the minor country roads she eventually got to the M4 on which the east-and west-bound traffic roared by. On the slip road leading onto it she slowed until a blaring horn from a car behind drove her on, and in another moment she found herself among the throng heading in the direction of London.

She drove leaning forward, hands gripping the steering wheel, and with an effort tried to relax and slow her breathing. The dashboard clock said 8.45. Time was passing too quickly. She had visions of the letter being collected; she could see it happening. Looking at the fuel gauge she saw that the needle was low. She'd have to pull in and fill up — but that would also give her a chance to contact Detective Inspector Davis. A service station came into view ten minutes later, and she turned off, followed the curving way into the car-park and braked. In the complex she found a bank of telephones and called Davis's number. Moments later he was on the line.

'Mrs Carmichael, where are you? I got your message when I came in, and phoned your home. The lady there told me you'd left.'

'I'm on the way to London,' Addie said. 'Have you got a pencil handy?'

'Fire away.'

She read off the address to which she had sent the adoption form. Davis said, 'Got it,' and then: 'What's this about the envelope having the poison on the flap?'

Hurriedly, Addie gabbled out, 'In each case the person who died had received a letter that needed a reply. And each time the reply was sent back in a stamped, addressed envelope.'

'And the poison was on the envelope's flap. Neat, eh? So the victim licks the flap to seal the envelope and takes in the poison — and then posts off the evidence.'

'Yes — and each time to the same address. The address I've just given you — probably an accommodation address.'

'How do you know this?'

'Because I sent off an envelope yesterday to that same place.'

'*What?*'

'Don't worry, I'm fine. I didn't use the envelope I was meant to. Mr Davis, we're wasting time. Please, get there as soon as you can. I'm on my way there now.'

'What are you driving?'

'A silver Citroën. I'll try to reach you again later.'

'Right, call this same number and they'll contact me.'

She ran back to the car, got in and drove to the petrol station. Thankfully there was no queue, even so she fretted impatiently while she stood filling the tank. At last it was done, then a hurried dash to pay for it with her credit card and she was back in the car and moving towards the highway again.

* * *

Caught up in the rush-hour traffic leading into the capital, it took well over an hour and a half to get to her destination. But at last she was there and in the area she sought, and then in the actual street — Carshalton Street — that was named on the letterhead. Slowing her speed — to the irritation of other drivers — while she peered out at the numbers above the shops, she at last came to the one she wanted, number 34. It turned out to be a newsagent-*cum*-confectioner-*cum*-tobacconist, called *Target News*.

She drove on for some yards, then took a turning on the left, after which she drove around until she found a space to park. It was now after eleven. Making her way back to the main street on foot, she stopped on the corner and looked along to her right at the newsagent's. For all she knew, her letter had already been collected. She stood for some moments wondering what to do for the best, and then saw a café situated across the street, obliquely opposite number 34.

At a different newsagent's shop a little further along, she bought a couple of newspapers, and then headed for the café. Inside, near the window, she found a vacant table. It was the worse for wear with its chipped Formica top and uneven balance, but she accepted it as a godsend and thankfully sat down.

It being between breakfast and lunch there were only a few others in the place. A smiling, rather slovenly young waitress came over, and Addie said she'd start with a coffee and afterwards have something to eat. She might be there for some time, she thought, and she didn't want to do all the necessary eating and drinking in the first half-hour and then have to sit with an empty plate and cup.

With the coffee served, Addie sat with one of the newspapers open before her, her face to the window. At this distance it was unlikely that anyone glancing over from the opposite pavement would notice her. However, she must let Davis know where she was. There was a telephone kiosk a few yards from the café, and she got up and turned to the girl who stood making sandwiches behind the counter. 'Don't take my coffee away, please,' she said, and added, gesturing to the telephone box, 'I'm just going out to make a phone call.'

Addie went to the door, opened it, glanced right and left, then hurried across the pavement. In the phone box she rang the detective's office. The WPC who answered said the inspector was at that moment on his way to London; he'd left right after Addie's earlier call. Addie asked if a message could be conveyed to him, to tell him that she was sitting in the Victory Café, which was almost opposite the address he was heading for. She would wait for him there. Turning, she looked out at the badly painted sign over the café. 'It's number 47. And tell him that the place I'm watching — number 34 — is a newsagent's, called *Target News*. I'm watching the entrance.'

Back in the café she resumed her seat, took up her newspaper and sat looking over it at the shop front. When the coffee in her cup grew cold she signalled to the girl for a fresh cup. Throughout it all, never for more than a few seconds at a time, did she take her eyes from the view across the street. Later she ordered a ham sandwich. When she had finished it — eating slowly and without enthusiasm — she glanced at her watch and saw that she had been there for almost an hour and a half. The skies had darkened in the meantime, and now all at once rain began to fall, gently at first, then more heavily, sending the pedestrians scurrying for cover.

A further twenty minutes passed, and then just as the rain stopped Addie saw three men walking along the opposite pavement towards the newsagent's. One of them was Detective Inspector Davis; the man on his right was Sergeant Williamson; the third was unfamiliar. All were in plain clothes; Davis and Williamson wore raincoats, the third man a short, all-weather jacket. She watched as they went to the shop and disappeared inside.

Long minutes passed, and then she saw Williamson's tall form appear in the shop doorway. The next moment he was at the kerb and, dodging the traffic, was coming across the road in her direction. Entering the café, he came straight to her side.

'Mrs Carmichael,' he said, 'we got your message, and we're stationed in a back room of the shop. Inspector Davis asks that you come over right away. He wants to talk to you while we're waiting.'

Addie was up from her seat before he'd finished speaking and, moments later, her bill paid and a tip left for the waitress, was following the sergeant to the door.

'This could be the tricky part,' he said as they stood in the doorway. 'It would be ironic if you crossed the street just as our man chooses to go and pick up his mail.' He looked at Addie. 'Have you got something you can put over your hair — so that you're not immediately recognizable?'

She wore a silk square around her neck, and she lifted it over her hair, and pulled it close and low around her face. The sergeant nodded. 'Can't say it does a lot for you, but there you are.' Taking off his raincoat he draped it around her shoulders. 'This'll help.' Then, with a look to left and right, he wrapped an arm around her shoulders and they stepped out and across to the opposite pavement. There Addie was taken up a side street and then along a narrow alley that ran along behind the row of shops. At a gate, Williamson stopped and led the way into a back yard cluttered with empty cartons. Seconds later they were entering the shop by its rear door and Addie was being ushered into a room where the detective inspector stood talking in a low voice into a walkie-talkie. The other man, whom she did not know, sat nearby. He looked at her curiously and murmured a good morning. Addie returned his greeting, handed the raincoat back to Williamson and removed her headscarf. At Williamson's urging, she sat down on a sofa.

The room was small and overcrowded with furniture, and the items that decorated the walls and the surfaces — gaudy religious icons and framed photographs — indicated that it was probably the main sitting-room for the proprietor and his family. Evidently, though, for the time being the family had given it up to the needs of the police. The sounds coming from beyond a door indicated that on the other side was the shop proper; from it Addie could hear intermittently the sound of a bell as the outer door was opened by a customer. She could hear too the faint murmur of voices of the customers and the proprietor.

Davis spoke a little longer into his walkie-talkie, then rang off and turned to Addie. 'Well,' he said, keeping his voice low, and giving her a smile of approval, 'the lady done good.'

'Did she?' Addie smiled back, a brief rising of pride within her. 'I couldn't think what else to do.'

'Well, it was the right thing.' He nodded towards the shop. 'I've talked to the proprietor, Mr Patel, and the envelope arrived this morning — your envelope, addressed to the Apex Adoption Agency.

And already a man has phoned to ask whether anything's arrived in the post. So hopefully he'll be along later to pick it up.' He paused. 'The proprietor referred to him as Mr Dixon.'

Addie stared at him. So it was Matt after all.

'And apparently,' Davis said, 'there's a Mrs Dixon as well. Sometimes they come in together to pick up the mail, and at other times individually. According to Mr Patel, she's in her thirties, has dark hair.'

Addie nodded. So Matt had married, and his wife was in it with him.

'Anyway,' Davis, said, 'for the moment we can only wait.' He turned, gesturing to the other police officer, the stranger. 'By the way, this is Constable Waring. He's with the Metropolitan Police — come to help us out. We're on *their* patch now.' Addie and the man shook hands. 'And for your information,' Davis added, 'there are three other officers stationed close by, watching the shop, so when our man does get here we can make sure he won't get away.' He enquired then as to where Addie had parked her car, and she gestured, naming one of the side streets. Sergeant Waring nodded; he knew it, he said. Davis asked her then if she'd like some tea or coffee, but she replied that she'd had enough to last a while.

'There is one thing, though,' she said. 'I'd like to phone and find out whether Dolores McCaffrey has telephoned. I've been worried about her.' She told him of Dolores's brief visit the previous day, adding, 'And she wasn't feeling at all well. She was complaining of a headache and feeling sick. She seemed very much under-the-weather.'

'What are you thinking?' Davis said.

'I'm afraid for her,' she said with a little catching of her breath; and then, putting into words what she had previously feared even to think, she added, 'I couldn't tell her, but her symptoms seemed very like — like Ambrose's.'

'Can we get in touch with her? Is she in Hammersmith?'

'No. She went to Bristol. She'd also received a photograph like the one that was sent to me, and as a result she was afraid to stay in London. She's gone to her sister's. Kate her name is. That's all I know. I haven't got her number. Dolores said she'd phone me but there's been no word from her.'

At Davis's suggestion, she used his mobile to call home and speak to Carole who said, as Addie had feared, that there had been no word from Dolores. After giving Carole the officer's number in case Dolores should call, she hung up.

'Let's not worry unduly,' Davis said. 'We might hear from her yet.' He took a seat at the other end of the sofa. 'In the meantime, why don't you tell me more about what you've come up with. Then you'll be free to go on back home. We could be here for hours yet. Our man mightn't even come today — or tomorrow. We've got to be ready, though, just in case.' He turned and gave a nod to Williamson who, sitting on a nearby chair, had taken out his notepad and pen. 'So,' he turned back to Addie, 'let's hear how you came up with your scenario.'

22

'And it's in there.' With her words, Addie held out the envelope in which had arrived the papers from the supposed adoption agency

Some time had passed since she had entered the room and in that time she had told how she had come to realize what was happening. Throughout, the commerce of the shop had been going on as usual on the other side of the partition wall, creating a constant background of sound: the bell that rang with the opening of the shop door, the voices of the proprietor and the customers, and the ringing of the till. Each time the shop bell rang, the room's occupants fell silent, listening for a signal. Now and again the proprietor or his wife would come in from the shop, and go through to a storeroom nearby. They were Asian, in their early thirties, and each time one or other passed through the room they did so with self-conscious smiles and lowered gaze.

Now, while Sergeant Williamson and Constable Waring looked on, the Inspector put on plastic gloves, took the envelope from Addie's hand and drew out the neatly folded, smaller envelope. He straightened it out, exposing the attached first class stamp and the label headed with *Apex Adoption Agency* followed by the address of the premises in which they were now sitting.

'I just didn't notice the envelope at first when I got the letter,' Addie said, pointing at it. 'I was in such a hurry to get the form back to them that I wrote out another one. It was only later I realized what was happening. And I knew then that I'd find that envelope.'

Davis lifted the envelope's flap. 'And here,' he said, a fingertip hovering over the strip of gum on the flap's inside, 'is where you think the poison is?'

'I'm sure of it. And if I'd licked the flap I would have taken the poison into me, and then, as you said, I would have posted it and so got rid of the evidence. I'm sure that's what happened in each case.'

Davis placed the envelope in a transparent plastic bag, which he passed to Constable Waring. 'Mr Waring,' he said, 'I'd like you to take this and find some place where they can print out a label exactly like the one here, in this style. And get an envelope to match as well.'

'Where shall I go?' Waring said, getting to his feet.

'For God's sake, it's your area,' Davis said. 'Find an office or something. There must be five hundred computers within a hundred yards of here. And be quick, please, and don't take that envelope' — he jabbed a pointing finger — 'out of that bag, or let it out of your hands for a single moment. If you lose it, don't bother coming back or counting on your pension.'

When the constable had gone, Davis said, 'It won't do for our man to see a different label on the envelope. He'd take fright straight away.'

Addie said, 'But I wrote out the new one in

all innocence anyway. So the envelope that's waiting for him will have my writing on it.'

'That's all right, we don't want to give him any doubts.'

'Will it take long — to get the gum on the flap analysed?'

'Well, as the lab men will know what they're looking for it shouldn't be too demanding.' He pulled off the plastic gloves and dropped them into his case. 'And you've also done a bit of checking,' he said, 'on the other deaths.'

'Yes,' Addie said. 'Each person did the same thing. Each one sent off a letter — or prepared one — a few hours before being taken ill. Once I'd realized this, I got the idea that their deaths were somehow connected with the letters themselves. But I couldn't think how that could be. And then I realized that it wasn't the letters, but the envelopes that the letters went off in.' She paused. 'It came to me after I'd posted the form back to the adoption agency. Something rang a bell. At first I couldn't think what it was, and then all at once I knew that the address I'd written on the envelope was the same as on a letter I'd posted for Ambrose — when he was ill on the day I visited him. I posted some mail for him. Two envelopes.'

'And you're pretty sure that one of them

was a part of this whole scheme.'

'I'm certain. As I was going out and taking his post he said that one item was a birthday card to his brother, and the other was for some records. He said he'd had it ready to post the day before but had forgotten. I suppose as I went to the post-box I must have glimpsed the address on the envelope and it registered in the back of my mind. Then, later, as I say, it rang a bell.'

Davis glanced at Sergeant Williamson, as if checking that he was taking notes, then added, 'And the others? Harry Comrie — what about him?'

'The same thing. I learned from his friend Gerald Fraser that Harry was intent on getting a special piece of porcelain, and that he'd received a letter that morning — some hours before he was taken ill — saying that the piece was available in an auction. It was a rare piece and much sought after, so he had to move pretty smartly. I talked to Mr Fraser again last night, and he told me that the letter about the auction had a stamped, addressed envelope with it. He remembers going out to post the letter. Harry was very insistent, he said.'

'And Mr Walderson? Kieron Walderson? What's the story there?'

'As you know,' Addie said, 'he was the first

one to die. His widow, Camilla, told me that he'd received an invitation to the opening of an exhibition of Victorian photographs. She remembers him getting it that morning. He was later than usual going in to work, so he was still there when the post was delivered. She said he was so pleased to have been invited, and he posted his acceptance on the way to taking their small daughter to school. You know the rest. He came home from his office complaining of feeling ill — and that was it.'

'And Christie Harding, the designer?'

'Yes, she was next on the list. According to her friend and neighbour, there was a chance of Christie being offered some position or other in a fashion house. Christie's situation was pretty bad by that time, and she was ready to jump at any chance to get back on track, so to speak.'

'And she did the same thing.'

'I've no doubt at all. She didn't take her own life. She was too much of a fighter. No, she got a letter, just like the others, and as with the others there'd been a stamped, addressed envelope along with. it. Celia, her friend, told me that she herself posted Christie's letter of acceptance. And she said the people who'd approached her were obviously keen, because it was the second time they'd written to her.'

'They wrote two letters to her? What happened to the first one? The first envelope — didn't it — ?' Davis broke off as the realization struck him. 'Oh, yes,' he said sadly, 'of course.'

Addie nodded. 'Yes, it reached her all right.'

'Yes,' — the word was like a sigh in the room — 'when the little girl was visiting from Derbyshire. Her goddaughter, Alice Marshall.'

'Right,' said Addie. 'Alice's death was an accident. She happened to be in the wrong place at the wrong time. The poison was meant for Christie, but little Alice got it instead.' She sighed. 'I've had the story from both Celia Lanford and from the little girl, Shelley, who was with Alice on that last day. Shelley used to go round to Christie's and dress up in all her finery and stuff, and when Alice and her mother stayed with Christie, Shelley was invited round for tea. She and Alice got all dolled up in Christie's clothes, and then, apparently, they helped Christie with a few little things. I spoke to Celia on the phone yesterday, and Shelley was there with her. Shelley confirmed that Christie had a letter to post and that Alice licked the envelope to seal it. Poor little kid. Shelley even remembered how Alice remarked on the taste of the glue and said that Christie gave her a sweet to take the taste away. Then the two girls went out to post Christie's letter — and Celia saw them as they came along the pavement in all their finery, and got them to pose while she took their photographs. I've seen the photos. There they are, side by side in their long dresses and picture hats. And there in Alice's hand is Christie's letter. The rest you know. Alice got home and was taken ill and died, her death attributed to natural causes.'

'So,' said Davis, 'having got the letter back, our Mr Dixon would then have been expecting to read about Christie Harding's death. But it didn't happen, so he had to try again.'

'Right, and the second time it worked as it was meant to. Christie dealt with the envelope and that was it. In her case, though, her death was investigated by a pathologist who was familiar with ricin poisoning — otherwise it might also have been put down to septicaemia like the others.'

'Very likely,' Davis said. 'As it was eventually with the next one, Harry Comrie, yes? And then it was the turn of Ambrose Morgenson.'

'Poor Ambrose. And there he was, in his hospital bed, when he was having moments of lucidity, trying to tell me. But he could hardly speak by that time, and I couldn't make head or tail of what he was saying. He was coming up with these names, and they didn't mean anything to me. It was only later that I suspected and then had confirmed the fact that they were the names of past pop singers, and that in the letter I'd posted for him he'd been sending away for some of their old records.'

At this juncture the back door opened and Constable Waring appeared. Davis looked at him questioningly and Waring handed him the original envelope in the plastic bag and two others exactly like it, both bearing identical labels. 'No trouble at all,' Waring said. 'I went to an estate agent's along the road. They took one look at the printing on the label and recognized the font straight away.'

Davis transferred the contents of Addie's envelope to one of the newly labelled ones and, flicking an ironic glance at her, licked the flap. When the envelope was sealed he laid it on top of the bureau.

Addie said, 'I discovered another interesting thing, Inspector. Not one of the people I spoke to was aware of there being any follow-up to the letters sent. When I asked Gerald Fraser about the porcelain that Harry had written off about, he said there'd never been any further word about it. The same with the exhibition of Victorian photographs. Kieron's widow never heard another word. Nor with Christie's job offer, nor, probably, will there be with Ambrose's records.'

Davis nodded. 'Further evidence that the letters were not what they seemed.'

'Yes. There was no rare piece of porcelain for Harry, there was no job available for Christie, there were no old gramophone records for Ambrose, and for Kieron there was no photographic exhibition.'

Davis waited for her to go on, then said, a note of sympathy in his voice, 'And for you no baby up for adoption.'

She gave a sad little smile. 'There might have been a baby, but the chance of getting it wasn't being offered to Charlie and me.'

'If you're right about all this,' he said after a moment, 'and I do believe you are — then Dixon would have known about these particular weaknesses or obsessions or whatever you want to call them. He'd have known about Ambrose Morgenson's fondness for those old records, would he?'

'Oh, yes. Ambrose was collecting them while we were at University. The same with

415

Kieron's photography, and Harry's Parian pieces.'

'And of course, Christie Harding's situation was fairly well known. It had been written about in the papers.'

'Yes.'

'But what about you? How would he have known about your wanting to adopt a child?'

'Well, it wasn't a secret. Everyone we knew was aware of it. It would have been very easy to find out.' She frowned. 'What I can't work out, is how in each case the murderer's been able to find the address of each of the victims.'

'That,' Davis said, 'is something we hope to discover.' He patted his thighs with his broad hands. 'Well, as I said, we'll get that envelope tested, but I'm pretty sure your assumption will prove to be right. I'll also do some checking through the different constabularies on the other victims. We can check out the scenarios you've given us. I know it's going to be a hard thing for the bereaved relatives to have to deal with the notion that their loved ones might have been . . . murdered, but I'm afraid there's nothing to be done about that.' He nodded to endorse his words. 'Your husband's due back from abroad soon, isn't he, Mrs Carmichael?'

'Tomorrow. He'll be leaving first thing in the morning.'

'Good. And you've no qualms about going back home alone today?'

'Not now.' She forced a smile. 'If everything works out, this whole thing will soon be over and done with.'

'Yes.' His sigh was loaded with relief. 'And assuming that your supposition is correct then you've been extremely lucky — you're not in any danger at present.'

There was a knock on the door, it opened and the young shop proprietor came in. Murmuring, 'Excuse me, please,' he went to a drawer, got a couple of things from it and went out again.

'He's very accommodating,' Addie observed.

Davis smiled. 'No pun intended?'

'I beg your pardon?'

'Well, this being used as an accommodation address,' Davis said. 'All accommodation addresses have to be registered with the police. It's required by law.'

'Why is that?'

He spread his hands. 'It stands to reason when you consider that many of them are used as cover-ups for shady deals of one kind or another.' He nodded towards the door. 'That young man does well to co-operate with the police.'

'Why, was he not registered?'

Davis just looked at her. 'Let's just say that he was probably ignorant of the law — and he obviously wouldn't want to impede us now that he's become aware of the situation.' He looked at his watch. 'You know, I don't think we need to keep you any longer, Mrs Carmichael, so when you're ready we'll get Constable Waring to see you to your car. He'll take you round the back way again so you won't be seen. Will you be all right then?'

'Yes.' She got to her feet and picked up her bag. 'I'll be fine.'

'And rest assured, as soon as I've got any news I'll be in touch.'

Almost before he had finished speaking there came again the sound of the bell of the outer shop door, and a moment later another bell rang softly just above the closed door a yard from Davis's head. The three men froze. Davis turned swiftly to Addie, lifted a forefinger to his lips and then jabbed the same finger towards the shop. 'He's here,' he mouthed.

Quickly and silently, Addie, the sergeant and the constable moved to stand out of sight of the door while Davis himself stepped to a small, curtained inner window and peered through into the shop. Then, moving aside, he made contact over his walkie-talkie. 'He's in the shop now,' he whispered. 'He's wearing a fawn raincoat, and soft hat. Grey hair. Stand by.'

The next moment the door was opening and the young Asian man was coming into the room. As he passed through he looked at Davis and gave a nod. Obviously having been briefed, he hovered for a moment then returned to the half-open door. 'I'm sorry, Mr Dixon,' he said. 'I put it here, I know. Just a minute, please.'

'Well, hurry up, will you?' came the man's voice. 'I haven't got all day.'

'Ah, yes, here it is.' The young shopkeeper took the envelope from the top of the bureau and went back out, closing the door behind him. When the door had clicked shut, Davis spoke softly and urgently into the walkie-talkie again: 'OK, let's go. He's just about to leave. Follow him to his car and apprehend him there. We'll be right behind you.' He shut off the walkie-talkie and a moment later there came the sound of the outer shop door closing, followed by a ring on the alarm bell. 'OK,' Davis said, 'he's gone. Let's go.'

As the two other men stepped to the door, Davis turned to Addie. 'Just wait here for a minute and I'll be back, and then — ' He came to a stop, peering at her. 'Mrs

Carmichael, are you all right?'

Addie didn't speak.

'Did you hear him clearly?' Davis asked. 'Would you recognize the voice of Matthew Dixon?'

'Yes, I would.' She paused. 'But that wasn't Matthew Dixon; that was my husband.'

23

In a spartanly furnished room at the police station Addie sat in an armchair that had seen better days and better scenery, her hands over the ends of the worn arms. A policewoman, three or four years younger, sat on a nearby chair. Addie had been there well over an hour now.

Charlie. It had been Charlie's voice she had heard. It had been Charlie the police had arrested, pouncing on him as he opened the door of his BMW. There had been a dark-haired woman with him, but who she was no one yet knew — or if they knew, Addie had not been told.

'Can I get you another cup of tea? That must be cold.'

'Mmm?' As if coming out of a dream,

Addie turned to the WPC, a pretty, dark-skinned girl with straightened black hair and an accent that bore the faintest trace of her Caribbean origins. The tentative, encouraging smile the young woman gave showed the whitest teeth. Addie looked abstractedly at the mug of cold tea on the table at her side, a thin film on its undisturbed surface. 'Thank you,' she said dully.

She watched the WPC go out. She could hear doors closing and opening, the distant ringing of telephones. Footsteps sounded in the corridor outside and then the door opened and Inspector Davis came into the room. 'I just came to see how you are.' He moved as if in a hurry, anxious to get in and get out again.

'I'm fine,' she said. Fine? She was numb. Nothing of it made sense. That it was Charlie who had come into the shop was beyond her comprehension. She looked questioningly at Davis as he stood there, trying to read in his eyes an answer to her unasked question.

He, seeing the question there, said, 'We're talking to him, what else can I tell you?' He spread his hands. 'But he's not being very forthcoming. It could prove a long business. Right now we're as much in the dark as you are.'

'I suppose the wig, the grey hair, was all

421

a part of his disguise.'

'No doubt of that.'

'What about *her*? Who is she?'

'We're trying to find that out too.'

He went away then, and a couple of minutes later the WPC was back, carrying a mug of fresh tea which she placed at Addie's side.

'Have you seen her?' Addie asked. 'What does she look like?'

The WPC pursed her lips and nodded to the mug. 'Drink your tea.'

What, Addie asked herself for the hundredth time, could Charlie have had to do with Ruby's death? The question kept going through her mind, but she could think of no answer. And it was just one question among so many. And it wasn't only as if the answers were not forthcoming — the questions themselves didn't make sense.

And then, all at once, something flashed into her mind, and she turned so suddenly with the thought that her hand caught the rim of the mug and rocked it, spilling tea onto the table top. 'I want to see Inspector Davis,' she said, getting to her feet. 'I've got to talk to him.'

'Oh, well, now,' said the WPC, tutting while she pulled a couple of Kleenex from a box and began to mop up the spilt liquid, 'he's in the interview room and — '

'Please,' Addie insisted. 'I've got to see him. It's very important.'

The younger woman looked at her, dropped the sodden tissues into a waste basket, then turned and stepped away. 'I'll see what he says.' She went out of the room. After a little while the inspector entered, the WPC behind him.

Moving to meet him, Addie said at once, 'Will you let me talk to him?'

He frowned, lips open, breathing in over his teeth, studying her.

'Please,' she said.

'Are you sure this is what you want?'

'Yes.'

'You think it's going to accomplish anything?'

'Yes.' She waited. 'Will you let me?'

He remained silent, still considering the request. Then he nodded. 'Well, I can't see that it'll do any harm. But think carefully — when all's said and done, this isn't the man you thought you knew, is it?'

'I'm aware of that,' she said dryly. She paused, and then, 'You see, I think I know.'

'You know what?'

'*Why*.'

Her studied her for a second longer, then

nodded. 'OK, come with me.'

He led the way out into the corridor. As they moved along he turned to her and said quietly, 'You won't be left alone with him, you realize that?'

'It doesn't matter.'

He stopped at a closed door, opened it, stepped inside and beckoned to Addie to follow. The room had the cold anonymous look that she had registered from a dozen TV cop series. She went in and he closed the door behind her.

A uniformed constable stood just to the right of the doorway through which she and the inspector had entered. Another man, also uniformed, stood with his back to the wall on the left. Sergeant Williamson sat at a table that was bare but for a couple of empty polystyrene cups and an overflowing ashtray. On the other side of the table, the standing police officer stationed behind him, sat Charlie.

He took in her entrance on the periphery of his vision, not turning his head, only registering her appearance with a slight stiffening of his body. In some ways she knew him so well.

'Mrs Carmichael's going to have a word with her husband,' Davis said. He turned to the uniformed man at the door. 'You stay here, Constable. The rest of us'll go outside.' Williamson and the other man made their way to the door, and Davis followed. In the open doorway he turned to Addie. 'Twenty minutes. Is that OK?'

'Yes,' — not taking her eyes from Charlie's face — 'that should be long enough.'

When the door had closed behind the men, leaving just the one beside the door, she sat down. Now Charlie raised his eyes to meet her glance.

'What do you want?' he said. His lips barely moved as he spoke.

'To be sure,' she said.

'What?'

'Yes. You see, I've worked it out.'

'Oh?' A corner of his mouth moved in a semblance of a smile. 'Smart girl.'

She gave a little shrug. 'Well, I've worked out some of it. The rest of it I'll get in time.'

'I'm really thrilled to hear this,' he said. 'Like I'm hanging on your lips, you notice?'

She observed the curl of his mouth. 'Did you hate me so much, Charlie?'

He said nothing to this.

'Did you?' she said. 'I suppose you must have to do what you did.'

'Does it matter now?'

'My God — to kill five people — five

425

people who had done you no harm whatsoever — just so that you could kill *me*, and get away with it.'

'What?' He frowned, irritably, like someone trying to understand a foreigner with a poor grasp of English.

'You want me to refresh your memory?' she said. 'Kieron, Harry, Christie and Ambrose — and that little girl, Alice.'

The shake of his head was barely discernible. His voice dismissive with contempt, he said, 'You're fucking loopy, you know that?'

She smiled. 'You'd like to think that, wouldn't you? Five people, Charlie. Four intentional killings and one accidental. And Dolores, too, for all I know. The inspector was right. I don't know you at all.'

He gave a short laugh. 'Of course you don't know me. You're so self-absorbed, you're not aware of anything that's going on outside your head. I told you, you're crazy — coming up with these insane speculations.'

'Oh, no, I've just had time to think, that's all. Sitting out there, I've been able to work things out.'

'You haven't worked anything out. You're as crazy as your father.'

Now she smiled. 'My father, crazy? So crazy he could see right through you. Right from the start. And *I was* crazy — crazy in

426

love with you. Not now, though, now that I've come to my senses. I can see clearly now — as that old song has it. You remember it?' She sang a few words of the song: '*I can see clearly now, the rain is gone.* No? She shook her head. 'No. Too trivial for you, right?' She leaned back slightly in her chair, studying him, as if seeing him in a different light, as if seeing some new and interesting phenomenon before her. Notwithstanding the shock she had sustained, she felt stronger than she had dreamed possible, stronger than she had felt for months.

Straightening in her chair again, she said, 'You see, once I heard your voice and knew it was you — what I couldn't understand, what I couldn't see, was what you could possibly have had to do with Ruby's death. And I've been sitting out there' — she jabbed a thumb — 'going over and over it and I still couldn't come up with an answer. And then I realized — you *didn't*. You didn't have anything to do with Ruby's death.'

'Of course I didn't have anything to do with her death,' he said. 'I haven't had anything to do with anybody's death.'

Ignoring this, she said, 'You had nothing at all to do with Ruby's death, but you knew enough about it to be able to use it, didn't you? And that's what you did. You learned about the anonymous letter we each of us got, and the seeming mystery about her death — if there was a mystery at all. And you decided it was just what you wanted.' She gave a little nod of appreciation. 'You know, Charlie, it's no wonder you made such a success of the company. All those games. This one was right up your street, wasn't it? You with your imaginative mind. Oh, so imaginative — like no other, I used to think. And I was right, wasn't I? So, what did you do?'

'What did I do?' He smiled. 'You tell me. I'm listening.' Half turning, also taking in the police constable who stood beside the door, he added, 'Actually, this is marginally more amusing than the repetitive questions I've been getting up till now from England's finest.'

She looked at him in silence for a second, then said, choosing her words, 'It was a godsend, wasn't it — learning about Ruby's death? There you were — married to me and wishing you weren't — and wondering how in hell you could get out of the situation. And not only get out of it, but at the same time take out of it all that you'd put in. And *more*.' Now it was her turn to smile, though like his own it was a smile without humour. 'I thought my father was so hard on you,

Charlie. He never cared for you, did he? And no matter how hard I tried, how often I put in the good word for you, he never budged. He admired your abilities — oh, yes — but he never trusted you, did he? Which was why he left the company in my name, and insisted that it remain in my name.'

'Don't remind me,' Charlie said. 'After all I did.'

'Indeed, you worked so hard at it, and made it the success it is — which must have proved particularly galling.' She wasn't surprised to see the unmasked bitterness in his face. After a moment she said, 'Did you *ever* love me, Charlie?'

He didn't speak.

'Did you?' She waited. 'Ah, well, I guess I've got my answer there.' She paused. 'When was it you started to hate me?'

He turned away with a theatrical sigh as if she were some troublesome child.

'It was with Robbie's death, wasn't it?' she said.

He turned to her at this, sharply, his voice curt. 'Don't talk about him. I don't want to talk about him.'

'It wasn't my fault, Charlie, you know that. But you still blamed me.'

'He was with you when it happened. You took him out.'

'It could have happened when he was with you.'

'But it didn't. He was with *you*.'

'Yes, he was with me. And that's something I must live with every day of my life. And do.' And as she spoke the words all her control went, was swept away, and the tears sprang to her eyes, flooded them and ran down her cheeks. Wiping at her eyes with the knuckles of her right forefinger she saw in his gaze contempt for her display of emotion, for the ugliness that her grief had created. She didn't care. She had not wept for herself. Her tears were for Robbie, and they were not the last she would shed for him.

After a few moments the flood of her tears had been stemmed. Charlie had turned away, ostentatiously disregarding her. When she was calmer again, she said:

'But it wasn't only Robbie, was it? It was that . . . other thing.'

He turned his face to her at this. 'That *other thing*?' His tone was quietly withering. 'What *other thing* is that?'

'You know what I'm talking about. Mumps.'

'Mumps?' His face gave nothing away. 'Oh, you mean the sterility thing.'

'How could I help that? People don't have control over such things.'

His face went into shadow as he lowered his head. When he raised it a moment later she could see that he was laughing, but silently. She stared at him, and after a few moments the truth dawned. 'There wasn't any sterility, was there?' she said. 'You made it up.' She shook her head, profoundly shocked. This was yet another new side to him. There was no limit to his cruelty. 'Oh, Charlie, you made it up. All of that. That and the whole impotence thing. It was just another game. Why?'

He just looked at her, directly in the eyes, his gaze unwavering.

After a moment she gave a slow nod. 'I see. I think I see. To punish me still further, right? And to give you a reason not to sleep with me.' The discoveries were stunning. 'Yes, that would do it. It did.'

He turned from her again, sitting sideways on, his back to the door, so that now she saw him in profile.

She went on, 'You obviously had reasons for wanting me out of your life, didn't you? Hatred? Let's not mince words. Also the fact that you'd met somebody else. But divorce would have left you with nothing, wouldn't it? And that wouldn't do, not after all you'd done to make the company what it is. When was it you decided to kill me?

Not that it matters. You had to find the right way, though, didn't you? You couldn't just kill me — or take a contract out on me, could you? Of course not. The husband's always the first to come under suspicion, and particularly if he stands to inherit. You knew that if I'd died from unnatural causes and you'd inherited everything you wouldn't have lasted five minutes. So, that was your answer — make it look as if there was a serial killer at work. But not just some madman, who was killing at random; they'd have seen through that too. Good Lord, no, this had to be a serial killer *with a purpose*. This was someone who was setting out to eliminate a whole bunch of people — of which group I was just one. Yes, the police would think there was a reason behind these killings. Which is why I was left till near the end, right? You had to leave me till then, so that the pattern would be established.'

He looked at her with his head on one side. 'You've had that little brain of yours going, haven't you?'

She nodded. 'You could say that. Why did you choose that particular poison, Charlie?' And then, even as she finished speaking, the answer came to her. 'Oh, yes, I see. It was because the time of death was fairly arbitrary, was that it?' She gave a vehement nod as the

432

realization came. 'It wouldn't have done at all for your victim to lick the envelope and drop dead within seconds, would it? The police would soon have cottoned on. But ricin takes a good while to act — by which time the evidence would be well out of the way — and soon back in your own hands. Very clever, Charlie. But that's you, isn't it? — always the clever one.'

She paused, waiting for him to speak, giving him the chance to deny or affirm her speculations. He said nothing. She narrowed her eyes slightly, considering, deliberating. 'But after all that,' she said, 'ricin turned out to be less than perfect, didn't it? The first death — Kieron's — in spite of initial suspicions, got passed off as due to natural causes, but then the second — Christie's — was correctly diagnosed. I'll bet you didn't know where you were, did you? Who was to say what would happen when you got around to me?' She nodded. 'I have to admit that I've only just worked that one out, Charlie. Things are coming to me all the time. Even as I sit here I'm discovering new things. But that was it, wasn't it? — you had to make sure that the police believed that there was a serial killer at work and that the killings were connected with Ruby's death — were carried out by her murderer. That's why you sent the copies of that photograph to Dolores and me, wasn't it? My God, Charlie, so melodramatic — but you thought that once we'd got them the police would have to take notice and would see the pattern. Am I right?' She waited. 'Yes, I am. It wasn't until the police accepted the concept of a serial killer that it was safe to get the poison to me too, right? Yes?'

He turned to her now and raised an eyebrow.

'And of course,' she said, 'you were out of the country when the letter came for me, weren't you? And it wasn't you who posted it, was it? Who was it, Charlie?' She paused. 'I know who it was. You don't need to tell me.'

He spoke now, curling his lip again and looking at her with ill-disguised contempt. 'You think you know so much, don't you? You think you know it all.' With a shake of his head, he turned away again.

'Yes,' she said, 'lucky for me I *did* know so much. I found out so much. And just in time, too. The thing was, I didn't use the envelope I was supposed to use. I was in such a hurry to get that application off that I missed it and wrote out another one. But had it been otherwise we wouldn't be sitting here now, would we?' With each second that passed more truths were taking shape in her mind and making her more certain. 'You thought it had worked, though, didn't you? With me, I mean. I told you over the phone that I'd sent the letter off, and then later when you called and Carole told you that I'd gone to bed with a headache you must have thought the poison was beginning to work. Am I right?'

Charlie turned completely in his chair and looked at the police constable who stood beside the door. 'Do I have to listen to this shit?' he said. The man didn't answer. 'No,' Charlie said witheringly, 'I should have known — you can't expect a mere dogsbody to make a decision.'

'I've got another question for you, Charlie,' Addie said. A thought had occurred to her. 'Why did you blame it all on Matthew? Did you choose him because he'd fallen out with Ruby?'

'Only with Ruby?' Charlie's words came out fast, sharp, as if he had spoken without thinking.

She gave a slow nod. 'You know more than I gave you credit for. OK, with Christie as well. She'd been dumped by him too.'

'Go on,' he said. 'Tell the rest.'

A moment of silence. '*Me*?' she said. 'Yes, Matt had dropped me too. One week I had with him, right at the start of the year — which he probably doesn't even remember — but which meant a lot to me, and for which I hadn't forgiven him. Which is probably why I was more than half ready to believe that he was the one. But you took a chance, didn't you, putting it all onto him. Suppose the police had had suspicions right at the start and questioned him? He might well have had an alibi. Where would you have been then?'

Silence hung between them thick as a fog, while Charlie looked at her with his lips slightly parted. After a moment she gave a little groan and briefly pressed her hands to her mouth. 'Oh, Charlie,' she said, the realization taking hold, 'there was no chance of Matt's being picked up by the police, was there? There never is. He's never going to be picked up by anybody, is he?'

Charlie made no sound.

'He's not, is he?' she said. A pause. 'Was he the first one, Charlie?'

He continued to look at her for a moment and then turned away once more.

'Yes,' she said. 'That would make sure. You had to be sure that although the police would suspect him they could never find him to 'eliminate him from their enquiries'. Isn't that the phrase? The police said they found

Matt's flat in an abandoned state — as if he'd just gone off. What did you do to him, Charlie? What did you do *with* him? Oh, poor Matt. Him too.'

Lifting his head, Charlie spoke once more to the constable who stood beside the door. 'Can you get this neurotic woman out of here? I've listened to enough.'

Addie looked at the young constable. He didn't move a muscle. 'Yes,' she said softly, turning back to Charlie, 'I'm sure you have. Smart Charlie, clever Charlie. But too clever for your own good. You should have kept it simple. Didn't you ever learn — the more working parts a component has, the greater chance it has of going wrong? With all the games you've produced I should have thought you'd have kept that lesson in mind. No? Ah, well.' She gazed at him for a second longer, then got up. As she approached the door, the constable stepped forward and opened it for her.

It was just seconds later as she stepped through the doorway that another piece of the puzzle fell into place.

A man and a woman were coming along the corridor, the woman's arm held in the police officer's grasp. Addie, coming to a stop, momentarily blocked their way so that they were brought to a halt. She stared, taking in the wig of jet-black hair, and gave a little nod. 'Well, Dolores,' she said, 'I guess you weren't so scared after all. And congratulations on your miraculous recovery.'

Dolores merely twisted her mouth and glowered. Then Addie stepped aside and the pair moved on past. Addie watched them go, then whirled back to the door, flung it open and stepped through. As she appeared in the room, the police constable stepped forward as if to stop her. She waved a hand like a shield. 'I've still got a couple of minutes, and it won't take that long.'

Moving back to the table she stood facing Charlie across it. The new shock had effectively silenced her for a moment, but she quickly found her voice again.

'Neat, Charlie,' she said. 'Very neat. And there was I thinking it was Lydia.' The truths, the realities came one upon the other now as she examined the changed scenario. 'So that meeting between Dolores and me in the teashop was no accident, was it? It was all set up between you. And then the act you both put up — of you disliking her and disapproving of her. The two of you must have had a really good laugh, the way you manipulated me. How did you two come to get together like that?' She paused. 'Come on, Charlie, you can tell me that; that's not going to compromise you.'

'We met by accident,' he said. 'After that chance meeting in Earls Court.'

'I see, and your affair started then.' She nodded. 'So it was Dolores who sent me the photocopy of that photograph — and sent one to herself at the same time. Well, she'd have to, wouldn't she? Yes, it makes more sense now; it was through Dolores that you learned so much about all of us at Birmingham, wasn't it? And was it through her that you got to Matt? She told me she'd met him in London one day.' Other memories came back to her and, frowning with distaste and bitterness, she added, 'You know, she asked me about Robbie, and all the time she knew he was dead.' She would not cry again. She wouldn't allow him that cruel and final triumph. She would never cry in front of him again.

She stepped back to the door, as she did so giving a short nod to the policeman. She was in control now. The man opened the door for her. In the doorway she turned and looked back at Charlie.

'Goodbye, Charlie,' she said. 'I doubt that we'll meet again.'

He smiled at her, a smile of bravado; it was not the smile of a winner.

'That's it,' she said. 'You keep smiling,

Charlie. Smile and the world smiles with you, right?'

The door clicked shut behind her. A moment later as she moved along the corridor, she saw Detective Inspector Davis appear around the corner. He came forward, stopped before her. 'I was just coming to get you. Are you all right?'

'Yes.'

'We know who the woman is now,' he said. 'She's your missing friend, Dolores McCaffrey.'

Addie nodded. 'I know. I just had the pleasure of renewing our acquaintance.'

'We haven't found out much about her — but one thing we've discovered is that she doesn't have a sister. Though I'm sure that won't come as a surprise.'

* * *

In a private office she sat down with the inspector facing her across a desk. Sergeant Williamson sat nearby. She was there to tell Davis of her suspicions and beliefs and to make a statement.

'Did you know,' Davis said, 'that Mrs McCaffrey and your husband knew one another?'

'We met her once, Charlie and I. Quite

by accident, in London. That was the start of it between them. Obviously, later, I guess, she fed him all the information he needed, and what she didn't know they found out between them.' Memory touched her. 'You know, I think Dolores was really shocked when she learned that the little girl Alice had got the poison meant for Christie. I remember how she reacted when we were told how she died. She wasn't prepared for that. Not that it stopped her in the long run. How coolly she set about getting Ambrose's address. I've just realized how she did that. Harry's friend said he'd heard from Ambrose and had kept his letter. While he and I were talking, Dolores went out of the room — supposedly to the bathroom, but obviously it was to go and look through Gerald's file of condolence correspondence. Having got Ambrose's address, she sent his *special letter* off to him at the first opportunity.' She paused. 'And I've found out something else too: I'm quite sure that Matthew Dixon was their first victim.'

Davis thought about this, nodded and sighed. 'He's been clever, your husband. There's not one of those bodies that's going to show up the minutest trace of poison. I'm sure he's banking on that. So unless he makes a confession . . . ' He shrugged.

Addie closed her eyes and shook her head. It was out of her hands.

Later, when she had completed and signed her statement, Davis took her to the door. 'We'll arrange to have your car taken back home for you,' he said.

'What? I don't understand.'

'Well, you don't want to drive all that way, do you?'

'Do I have a choice?'

'Well, yes, you do.'

They were moving towards the lobby and the front desk, and as they turned the corner she saw Peter Lavell's tall rangy frame rise up from a chair. He came towards her while she looked at him open-mouthed. 'You ready to go home now?'

Behind her Davis said, 'I took the liberty of contacting Mr Lavell. I thought you needed a little support at such a time.'

She felt that she could weep again, this time from relief, but she kept the tears back and leant forward, briefly leaning her head against Peter's shoulder.

'Come on,' he said, 'the inspector knows where to reach you if you're needed.' With his hand under her elbow, she stepped out onto the street.

★ ★ ★

The police were thorough in carrying out their searches, and ricin was found both in Charlie's office and in Dolores's flat. Further, the computer-related paraphernalia that Dolores had hoarded turned up an old floppy disc that still, after all these years, held the document with the 'anonymous' letter that she had sent to herself and the other six in the group in Birmingham. Hearing of the discovery, Addie wondered at the reason behind Dolores's act. Later, she would learn that it had come simply from revenge. Ruby, Dolores had once remarked to Addie, had never really fitted in. But in truth it was Dolores who had been the odd one out. Overweight and unattractive, she had been a part of the group merely by dint of sharing Christie's flat. And anxious to please and be accepted she had made herself useful, always the dependable one, ready to help out — good old reliable Dolores — which even then had not stopped the jokes about her weight problems and her appearance. So, when the chance had come, she had sown the seeds of a little mischief. All of this, though to Addie of interest — and also satisfaction, in that a part of an old mystery was at last solved — was of mere passing interest to those investigating the poisonings, for they were only bent on finding sufficient evidence to secure convictions.

As Detective Inspector Davis had feared, however, the nature of the poison and the lack of evidence promised to make those desired convictions unattainable. But, as it transpired, when Charlie and Dolores eventually went for trial the murder charge against them was based on the killing of Matthew. Fortunately for Davis, but unfortunately for Charlie and Dolores, Matt's body was discovered by an angler soon after their arrest. With the strong current of the river, the wire that had bound Matt's body had gradually unwound, allowing his corpse to float to the surface. So, he had been brought to the bank where his dead right hand had been found to be clutching one of Charlie's lucky cufflinks.

Following this, and the discovery in her flat of Matt's wallet, Dolores's undignified struggles to save her own skin — with all erstwhile love going out of the courtroom window while she heaped the blame on Charlie — did nothing to save her but helped the prosecution's case immeasurably.

With Peter beside her, Addie attended the trial when required to give evidence, but was not in court to see the Crown's success. She was content to learn of that through the media and reports from Inspector Davis.

Even so, she couldn't begin to relax until the whole thing was over; then, and only then, along with Peter, could she begin to get on with her life again. It was necessary to have the trial behind her, to add punctuation to that concluded chapter of her past.

That was when she could begin to give her full attention to her future and deal with new demands — so willingly embraced — upon her time and her emotions. And there was plenty to think about, for both of them, not least by reason of the fact that a baby needs so much attention.

Epilogue

On the outskirts of Birmingham, children play on a patch of rough ground behind a tall, narrow block of flats. The area had once been a garden, and although never exactly well kept, it certainly looked tidier then than it does now.

As they play, a little girl gives a whoop and brings up from between two crumbling bricks set in the soil near the spiked railing a small shining object. It is a little peardrop ear-ring, of no value, but pretty nonetheless.

She and her friends search around for its mate, but without success. It must have been dropped by someone, they conclude — perhaps a woman who long ago had stood on the balcony up above. Perhaps she hadn't known that it had fallen. On the other hand, perhaps she had. Perhaps she had felt it drop and had stretched out her hands, reaching out, reaching down, to catch it as it fell.

We do hope that you have enjoyed reading this large print book.

Did you know that all of our titles are available for purchase?

We publish a wide range of high quality large print books including:
Romances, Mysteries, Classics
General Fiction
Non Fiction and Westerns

Special interest titles available in large print are:
The Little Oxford Dictionary
Music Book
Song Book
Hymn Book
Service Book

Also available from us courtesy of Oxford University Press:
Young Readers' Dictionary
(large print edition)
Young Readers' Thesaurus
(large print edition)

For further information or a free brochure, please contact us at:
Ulverscroft Large Print Books Ltd.,
The Green, Bradgate Road, Anstey,
Leicester, LE7 7FU, England.
Tel: (00 44) 0116 236 4325
Fax: (00 44) 0116 234 0205

Other books in the
Ulverscroft Large Print Series:

RETURN TO CARNECRANE

Mary Williams

Sequel to CARNECRANE. Carnecrane, the mansion on the Cornish cliffs, is once again the scene of the turbulent fortunes of the Cremyllas family in the mid-Victorian era. To Carnecrane comes Olwen, daughter of the vivacious Carmella Cremyllas, who had married a Welsh artist and left her native Cornwall for the stage. The arrival of Olwen, with her pale ethereal beauty, is the catalyst that sets in motion a dramatic series of events in which the dominant figure is the adventurer Leon Barbary — the stranger who came out of the blue to mine iron at Carnecrane.